THE MEMORY OF LOVE

THE MEMORY OF LOVE

Aminatta Forna

Atlantic Monthly Press
New York

First published in Great Britain in 2010 by Bloomsbury Publishing Plc, London

'The Harder They Come' words and music by Jimmy Cliff © Copyright 1972
Island Music Limited. Universal/Island Music Limited.
Used by permission of Music Sales Limited.

This edition is published by special arrangement with Bloomsbury Publishing Plc.

Printed in the United States of America
Published simultaneously in Canada

ISBN-13: 978-0-8021-1965-0

Atlantic Monthly Press
an imprint of Grove/Atlantic, Inc.
841 Broadway
New York, NY 10003

Distributed by Publishers Group West

www.groveatlantic.com

11 12 13 14   10 9 8 7 6 5 4 3 2 1

For Simon, with love

THE MEMORY OF LOVE

CHAPTER I

On the iron-framed bed a single, scant sheet has moulded itself into the form of the human beneath. On top of the bedside cabinet, a small pile of spiral-bound notebooks sits alongside a vase of flowers, bright-coloured and plastic. The notebooks are worn from handling, the leaves rippled with damp. In the atmosphere of the room the memories of a man float and form. The man in the bed is telling a story. His name is Elias Cole.

Adrian listens. He is new here.

Elias Cole says:

★

I heard a song, a morning as I walked to college. It came to me across the radio playing on a stall I passed. A song from far away, about a lost love. At least so I imagined, I didn't understand the words, only the melody. But in the low notes I could hear the loss this man had suffered. And in the high notes I understood too that it was a song about something that could never be. I had not wept in years. But I did, there and then, on the side of a dusty street, surrounded by strangers. The melody stayed with me for years.

This is how it is when you glimpse a woman for the first time, a woman you know you could love. People are wrong when they talk of love at first sight. It is neither love nor lust. No. As she walks away from you, what you feel is loss. A premonition of loss.

I never thought I would hear that tune again. Then a month, or perhaps it was two months ago, as I sat alone in the room in my house that serves as a study, the window was open, and through it faintly, I heard somebody whistling the tune and singing pieces from the refrain. A woman's voice. The very same tune from those years ago. I shouted for Babagaleh, who for once came on the first call. I sent him down into the street to find whoever was whistling. He seemed to be gone for ever. And all the time I waited what could I do but sit and listen to my heart keeping time with my impatience.

The person Babagaleh brought to me was a builder, a Fula, dressed in torn trousers, bare of chest and covered in cement dust, which reminded me of funeral ashes. Babagaleh ushered him off the carpets, but I called him close again. I asked him to sing and he did, some other tune. I wouldn't have put it past Babagaleh to have called the first person he saw from the gate. I hummed a few of the notes, as I remembered them.

And then the man in front of me sang, and there was the tune and his voice, girlish and high. After he had sung for me, I asked him to tell me the meaning of the words. The song was indeed about loss, but not of a woman. In the song a young man longed for a time past, a time he had only heard about in the words of those who'd lived it, a time of hope and dreams. He was singing of the life lost to him, because it had been his misfortune to be born much later, when the world was already a different place.

I had woken later than usual that morning. Babagaleh had been up for hours. A Muslim, a northerner, he's up with the call to prayer by five every morning, which is one good thing about him. Also, he doesn't drink and is an honest man, which is more than you can say of many. Quick to temper, though, those northerners. I called him to take a bucket of hot water to the bathroom, so I could shave. These days there is no hot water, we're lucky if there is water at all. The taps run dry, as had been the case for the last few days. We kept a barrel at the back of the house for such contingencies.

'I want to finish the study today,' I told him. 'When you come back from market come and find me there.'

'Today is Friday,' he replied as he filled the sink and prepared to withdraw. I was still in my pyjamas, sitting on the edge of the bath, summoning the energy to lift myself up and reach the sink. Of course, Friday. Babagaleh would be at the mosque. No one to help me all day.

'Very well,' I said. 'Mind you come straight back. No wasting time with all that *congosa* afterwards.'

No reply, which meant he intended to do just as he pleased. He poured the water into the sink and set down the bucket, came and hovered over me like a bluebottle. I waved him away. When he had gone, I took a breath, as deep as my lungs would allow, and levered myself up with the aid of the towel rail. Four steps to the sink. I rested my hands on the edge of the porcelain, steadied myself on my feet and stared into the mirror. The pale hairs on my chin gave my face an ashen cast. I leaned forward and pulled down each eyelid. My eyeballs were yellow, streaked with red. Admirable colours in a sunset, perhaps.

The night before, as on other nights, Babagaleh arranged the pillows behind me. By then I was forced to sleep virtually upright. I had lain gazing into the black listening to the creaking of my stiffened lungs, the air whistling through the tubes, like a piece of rusted machinery.

I picked up my shaving brush, wet the bristles and lathered my face with soap. The razor was less than sharp and pulled at the hairs, dragging them out of the loose folds of skin. Where the furrows were deepest the razor slid over the wet hairs. I stuck my tongue into the side of my cheek and with my left hand pulled the skin taut. When I had finished, I splashed the water in the basin over my face. It was still hot; I luxuriated in the feel of it. Afterwards I looked again in the mirror. The blood welled up in a number of nicks in my skin. Over the years my skin had grown thinner. It hung down, beneath my eyes, under my jaw, sliding off the bones of my face. I squeezed toothpaste on to my toothbrush and attacked my teeth. Blood on the bristles. My gums had shrivelled away, like slugs in the midday sun. When I was through, I rinsed my mouth and spat into the basin. Then I pulled the plug and watched the toothpaste, bloodstained suds, hairs and water swirl away down the hole, like so many lost years.

When Babagaleh returned from the market I was sitting on the unmade bed, struggling into my clothes. The effort of getting dressed had provoked in me a coughing fit, the sound of which must have brought him to the door of my room. Wordlessly he set down the tray containing my medicine, a jug of water and a glass, poured a little of the water and helped me to take a few sips. Gradually the coughing subsided. Then I sat still, submitting to his ministrations like a child or a halfwit. He freed my left arm from where it was trapped in the shirtsleeve, then he buttoned the cuffs. I pushed away his hands, insisted on buttoning the front myself. He bent and rolled a sock over each foot, pushed them into my shoes and tied the laces.

Starched white shirt. Black trousers. Proper footwear. I could shamble around, unshaven, wearing stained pyjamas, like my

3

neighbour opposite. All over town, you see them. Slumped on the balconies of their homes, amid the traffic fumes, staring into space, gradually being covered in a layer of dust from the street. The living dead.

As I left the room I caught a glimpse of my own reflection in the dresser mirror. A straw man in the half-light. The shirt and trousers billowed out above and below my belt. Every week I pulled the belt a notch tighter. A smear of blood on the collar of the shirt. What to do? I could not go through the effort of changing my clothes again. I expected no visitors.

Babagaleh came to tell me he was leaving. He was dressed for the mosque, wearing a long djellaba of pure white, leather sandals and an embroidered round hat of deep blue. It occurred to me, not for the first time, how easy it would make life to be able to dress like that. Each day Babagaleh performed his simple duties; on Fridays he took his place in the second row in the mosque. A day off every other week. Once a month he went to visit his wife. Though they had long since gone their separate ways, only last year he'd paid for a new roof and window frames. Together they drank coffee and spoke of their grandchildren.

Before he left Babagaleh returned carrying another tray, this time holding a Thermos of tea, a loaf of Fula bread, margarine, a pair of hard-boiled eggs. He poured me a cup of tea and loaded it with sugar. Like all his kinsmen he holds to the belief that sugar is heartening.

He walked the length of the room partially drawing the curtains against the coming heat, left without speaking again. I sat for a moment or two sipping the tea, aware of my sudden solitude. Thoughts like weevils burrowed into my brain. Nothing I did could shake them out; at night they forced me awake just as often as my bouts of breathlessness. There is nothing new in this, I'm sure. A condition of age. A consequence of insufficient occupation.

White-painted walls. Dark-wood floor. Parquet. It had cost money to have that laid. Over by the window, visible beneath the coat of wax, a parallelogram of bleached wood where the sun entered. A fringed, dark-red rug, with its own matching diamonds of sun-lightened wool. A pair of planter's chairs bought from the Forestry Commission thirty years before. Tooled red-leather pouffes, cracked and mildew-stained.

Increasingly I found it hard not to look around the place and do the sums in my head of what it might all fetch in a sale. One day I watched Babagaleh shaking out the curtains, wiping down the arms of the chairs with a damp cloth – I wondered if he was thinking the same. The thought got me going and as the day wore on I became preoccupied with the matter of my library. The volumes on the shelves amounted to hundreds. I decided to set myself the task of deciding which ones were worth keeping. The rest could go to the university library. A *donation*. That was the way to do it. This new angle on the idea invigorated my project with purpose.

We are like caged pets, we elderly. Like mice or hamsters, constantly reordering our small spaces, taking turns going round and round on the wheel to stop ourselves from going mad.

A year ago I'd ordered the whole interior of the house redecorated. Two painters arrived with dust sheets and set up their ladders. From time to time I'd mount the stairs to check their progress, make sure that they didn't spill paint on the parquet floor, but also to watch the pair of them balanced perfectly on a single board suspended between stepladders while they painted the ceiling. They talked between themselves, all manner of subjects, proletariat wisdom prompted more often than not by the words issued from their wireless. They did not mind me, it was not their place to do so and besides they knew I had little enough with which to occupy myself.

It was at this time I began to suffer problems with my breathing; the fumes of the paint, you understand. Before then, a dry cough that bothered me occasionally. I put it down to the harmattan wind, pollen from the garden, the smog of traffic fumes that lay across the city. I hadn't been to see a doctor. For what? So the man could tap my chest, write a prescription for some antibiotics and then chase me for an outrageous sum?

A spider had spun a web in one corner of the ceiling, silken trapeze wires. And over on the carpet, flecks of white powder, missed by Babagaleh. Cement dust.

I saw a woman once, the loss of whom I mourned, even before I had spoken a single word to her.

20 January 1969. The faculty wives dinner. We, the bachelors, gathered together at the bottom of the lawn, a patch of untended weeds. On the other side of the grass was the reception line. I was listening, or at least making the appearance of it, to my companion

complain about the reallocation of space in the faculty building. He had lost out, which was a shame, no doubt. I looked away, towards the arriving guests. She wore a blue gown and, as she descended the stone steps to the lawn, her fingers plucked lightly at the fabric, which clung to her in the heat. I watched her and felt a surge of feeling, that then nameless emotion.

The first conscious thought I had came moments later – and it struck me like a blow – the man coming down the stairs a pace behind was her husband.

Within a few yards of the receiving line, I saw him move away. Not her husband. Relief, a cold breath down my spine. Then I saw her reach out her hand and touch him lightly on the sleeve. And with that light touch, made with just the ends of her fingers, she may as well have had the strength of ten men, so quickly did he yield and alter his course back towards the long line of people. I saw how he submitted his will to hers. I saw her smile, an upward curving of her lips, faint and sweet. A smile he returned, gracious in defeat. Seconds had passed since I first laid eyes on her and I'd already lost her twice over.

I excused myself, placed my glass on the tray of a passing waiter, moved across the lawn and stood at the end of the receiving line next to the last man, a fellow I recognised vaguely from the faculty hierarchy. I nodded and he nodded back, barely registering me, having lapsed long before into the sort of stupor such social obligations are inclined to induce.

I shook one or two hands, muttered greetings. Nobody knew or cared, their minds were already turned to thoughts of alcohol and food. And then there she was, standing before me, her hand held out, smiling. I took her hand. I spoke my name. Saw her smile, a poor man's version of the smile she had given to her husband. She moved on and hovered a few yards away while I shook her husband's hand. Together they walked across the lawn, his hand once more at her elbow.

My eyes followed them. I realised I had no idea of her name, for it had been obliterated in the moment of our meeting, by the drumming in my ears.

The tea had cooled by the time I got around to drinking it. I have a dislike of lukewarm liquids. I carried the cup across the room and set it down on a low table while I heaved open the glass door to the verandah. Outside I poured the liquid over the railing into the flowerbed and watched with satisfaction as it bored a hole in the dry earth. The garden had suffered during the drought; bare patches of rough earth had appeared in the lawn, the beds looked more like neglected graves.

By the time I returned to the chair, the effort had brought me out in a sweat. I poured myself a fresh cup of tea, and drank it carefully. I cracked one of the eggs on the side of the tray, and picked at the shell with my fingernails. Then I poured a little salt on to the plate and dipped the egg into it. Babagaleh never had subscribed to the view that an egg could be overcooked. It was as much as I could do to swallow. I returned the rest to the tray. Still no appetite. It is a mockery. It should be liberating, the absence of a desire. Instead you feel another kind of longing, for the desire that is lost. I yearned to want food again, to feel hunger and then to indulge the pleasure of sating it. I felt a sudden, whimsical urge for a cigarette. What could be more pleasurable than casually inhaling toxins, deep into the lungs?

In time I levered myself back to my feet and went to sit behind the desk, swivelled the chair around to face the bookshelves. I selected a volume and brought it down. Banton's *West African City*, published under the auspices of the International African Institute. The book was cloth-bound with stitched seams, the paper yellow and grainy beneath my fingertips. I searched the front pages for the publication date. 1957.

I began to read where the book fell open, about the growth of this city: *The third stratum comprised the tribal immigrants, who were regarded by the Creoles as hewers of wood and drawers of water, and who were for a time content with their station.*

I turned back a page: *They called them 'unto whom', quoting from Psalm 95: 'Unto whom I sware in my wrath: that they should not enter into my rest.'*

In the margin were scribbled some words. Had I not been as familiar as I was with the hand, I would have struggled to decipher the words: *Give me a full belly and a hammock and I shall enter my own rest.* Julius. It had been a habit of his, typical of the man, to enter marginalia into a borrowed book. I closed the page, took a few minutes to bring control to my breathing. I leaned over the desk and let the book drop into the cardboard box by the side of the desk.

The next volume I picked up was Lethbridge Banbury's book on these parts. Now this one was actually worth something. A handsome deep-red volume. On the cover a gold-engraved image of an elephant and a palm tree. Hand-cut leaves. Black-and-white illustrated plates, each one protected by a leaf of tracing paper.

I can quote the first lines by heart, still: *Why I went to S is neither here nor there: perhaps I took that step from that insatiable wish to 'see the world', which so ardently possesses many Englishmen; or perhaps I was actuated by an ambitious desire of obtaining promotion in a service in which success is popularly supposed to come specially to those who depart from the beaten track in search of it.*

A tutor who knew my love of books gave it to me, a visiting fellow from a Scottish university. A first edition, published in 1888. It arrived in the post some months after he completed his research and sailed out. I remember that when he drank he liked to recite a rhyme, one about the last colonial Governor.

> *Beresford Stuke makes me puke,*
> *But in the Protectorate*
> *they expectorate.*

I laughed to humour him. And later again because he would urge me into drinking, behaving as though sobriety on the part of either of us was an insult.

That January evening I watched her, she and her husband. They moved through the party with ease, never alone for more than a few moments. Once I stood on the fringes of a group, beyond the edges of the circle, out of the light but so close I could have reached out and touched her. Her husband was recounting some incident, there was laughter – from everyone, except me. I hadn't been following his words. Instead I'd been watching her. Watching her as she in turn watched him. Our eyes met once. She smiled and looked away.

I remembered later where I'd seen him before. One lunchtime in the lecture theatre, a meeting convened by the students. To discuss the expulsion of one of their number, as I recall. I had been sent by my dean and took a seat in the back. My presence went unremarked, which suited me. A couple of paragraphs typed up and placed in the Dean's pigeonhole. Duty done.

In the minutes before the meeting was officially convened I noticed how they gathered around him, the students, breathless and eager. Some way into the meeting the speaker called him to the stage. At first he was reluctant, smiling and waving a piece of paper as if to dismiss the notion out of hand. At the murmured insistence of the room he rose to his feet, suddenly energised, jumped on the stage and delivered a few words. He stood with his elbow on the lectern, leaning forward, gazing directly into the faces of the audience members. The air trembled with the sound of his voice. A flurry of excitement. Clapping, like birds taking off.

What was it he had said to them? It's gone.

I spent the rest of the morning and the best part of the afternoon searching. My search was, by necessity, both slow and painstaking. When Babagaleh arrived back from the mosque, I asked him.

'Where are my notebooks?'

In answer he gazed at me, as was his way, his first instinct to conceal all knowledge, all evidence of intellectual process, to turn his expression into a smooth rock face upon which no accusation could gain purchase until he knew exactly where my question was heading. He left the room and returned with a cardboard box marked *Milo Milk*.

'Where were they? Why did you move them?'

'Storeroom, Master.' He gazed at me, a look of blank innocence.

'On the desk, please.' I could no longer afford to become overheated. I knew it. Babagaleh knew it too.

That night I sat up late, going through my notebooks. There was no power; Babagaleh lit a pair of candles, and though it strained my eyes and the fumes from the wax hurt my chest, I continued reading. The notebooks had survived, though the rubber bands that held them together fell to pieces in my hands. A few pages were missing, others latticed by the work of silverfish and termites, the occasional sac of desiccated eggs, filaments and threads of unknown insects. The ink of my fountain pen had faded to a muted grey on the pages. But yes, intact. More or less.

They were not diaries. Just notes I made for my own benefit. A relevant date. Thoughts on an upcoming lecture. The title of a book or paper. Lists of things to be done.

25 November 1968. Two months before the faculty wives' dinner. In my own hand, the events of that day. Brief minutes of the meeting, his address to the students. No record of his words.

I recalled I had included mention of his address in my report for the Dean.

9

Julius Kamara. An afternoon as I worked on my lecture notes I spotted him from my window. A distinctive walk: easy strides, one hand in his trouser pocket. I laid down my pen, the better to follow his progress. I watched him cut the corner of the grass, turn right and push with both hands through the double doors into the engineering department.

The next time I saw him I was on my way home. A Thursday, walking through the campus, I saw him ahead of me. For a minute or two I kept pace behind him. A couple of students sitting on the steps of the lecture theatre called out to him and stood up, brushing the seats of their trousers, gathering their books. He paused, waited for them to reach him. I passed by unnoticed.

Just outside the gates of the university, a white Volkswagen Variant was parked up, the engine idling. She was sitting in the driver's seat, her elbow resting on the ledge of the open window. She wore a sleeveless dress of pale cotton, her hair wrapped in a large orange scarf. From where she sat she might have seen me in the mirrors, but she didn't. I slowed my pace. I approached the car.

'Good evening.'

She started, pulled from her thoughts.

'Hello,' she replied, applying a sufficiency of good manners, accompanied by the barest of smiles. Something women do when faced with a man they don't recognise, hoping neither to encourage nor to offend.

'The faculty wives' dinner,' I said. 'Elias Cole.'

'Of course,' and she gave me a faint smile.

'Julius told me to tell you he's been delayed, but he'll be along in a moment.'

'Thank you.' And she smiled again, more generously this time.

'I'm afraid I've forgotten . . .'

'Oh,' she said as she caught my meaning and tapped her chest. 'Saffia.'

I moved away.

'Thank you,' she called again after me. I gave a modest wave of acknowledgement.

Minutes later they passed me, Julius at the wheel. The sun was low. I don't know if they even noticed me. Either way the car drove on without slowing.

I walked down the long road in the growing darkness. The

shadows of the trees that lined the way crept steadily outwards, the colours around me dissolved into grey. The white-painted bases of the tree trunks, illuminated by the fading sun, stood out like sentries. I watched the tail lights of the car until they were fireflies in the distance. I stopped and took out my notebook, pressed it against the smooth bark of a tree and wrote down the registration number of the car, while it was still in my head. And another, single word.

Saffia.

Friday. A few days after our encounter on campus I had an appointment in town. Afterwards I cut through one of the side streets to the main road, where I might catch a bus back to the campus. It was a quiet, once affluent residential street. There was a kiosk supplying soft drinks and cigarettes; further up a tailor's dummy displaying an embroidered gown stood outside a shop. Parked on the street in front, a white Volkswagen Variant.

The heat of the car's boot beneath the palm of my hand told me it had been sitting in the sun for some time. I took a moment to look around. Either Saffia was visiting a friend or she was inside the tailor's shop. I took the only option available. It occurred to me briefly, as I stepped out of the sun and into the shop, that perhaps Julius was using the car. But by then I had ascertained he spent long hours on campus. And in that matter I was correct. For there she was, at the back of the shop, wearing a simple print dress, standing together with one of the tailors. A magazine lay open on the table and they stood with their heads bent over it as she thumbed through the pages. I watched. It gave me pleasure, knowing she had not seen me. The line of her neck, the way she licked her thumb to turn a page, her solemn expression as she considered the merits of various styles, the indulgent smile she gave the tailor.

'Sir?' The tailor closest to me had paused his treadle and was looking up at me. I gave a wave of my hand in Saffia's direction. He nodded and bent back to his work. Presently she concluded her business and turned to leave. Saying goodbye, gathering up her magazines, looking for her car keys, she was distracted. Only when she nearly collided with me did she look up.

'I'm sorry. Please excuse me.' I stepped aside, as if I had been at fault.

'Hello there,' she said.

'Hello,' I returned. 'Mrs Kamara, isn't it?'

'Yes, yes.' She put out her right hand, and for the second time I took it in mine.

'Cole. Elias Cole.'

'Mr Cole. Of course. How are you keeping?'

'As you see. Perfectly well.' I made no move to cross the threshold, and this caused her to hesitate.

'Well, are you?' She tilted her head in the direction of the shop. 'Let me not keep you.'

I shook my head.

'A suit. It's not quite finished. Never mind.' Of course it was not exactly the truth, but neither did it count as a lie. Not when a man is talking to a woman. It is in the nature of things, wouldn't you say? And I added, 'No. I'm on my way back to work.'

At that she smiled.

'To the campus? Well, that's the way I'm going too. I'll give you a lift if you like. Or maybe you have your own car?'

'No, no,' I said. 'Let me help you with those.' And I lifted the pile of magazines from her arms. Saffia unlocked the car and I eased myself into the passenger seat, twisting to place the magazines on the seat behind. I saw it was folded down, the boot scattered with old newspapers and earth. So I sat with the magazines on my lap.

We travelled through the city. The schools had broken for lunch, the children chased each other down the sides of the streets. It was the middle of the windy season, the air heavy with a cindery dust. Saffia concentrated as she drove, her attention fixed on the road. While she drove I watched her hands. She gripped the steering wheel on either side, the way women do. No jewellery, save a gold wedding band. The nails were short and well shaped, unvarnished. Under one or two of the nails of her right hand I noticed a dark rim. Occasionally I allowed myself a glance at her face, her profile silhouetted against the glare of the window. The upward sweep of her eyelashes matched the curve of her top lip. As she slowed around a fellow pushing a barrow she bit faintly at her lower lip. And glancing left and right at a busy junction she ran her tongue fleetingly across the upper lip. Traces of light outlined the arcs of her cheekbones, her forehead, the bridge of her nose. The neck of her dress exposed her throat, below the collarbone the swell of her breasts. Across her thighs her dress lay faintly wrinkled, the muscles beneath tensing as she worked the pedals.

To the right of the road lay an area of wetlands, a nature reserve. They are there still. Too wet for construction. Back then you had a view over the wetlands from the road, all the way to the sea. I turned to look.

'I'm told there are some remarkable orchids growing there,' I said.

'You like flowers?'

'I'm no expert,' I answered. 'I live in an apartment and the garden doesn't belong to me. I enjoy them, though, who doesn't?'

'Swamp orchids. *Lissochilus*. That's what you're thinking of. They grow there. And you're right, they are remarkable. They grow to the height of you and me.'

'You've seen them?'

'Not recently. But a few years ago, yes. A group of us from the horticultural society made a visit. Once you know where they grow it's easy to find them again. Not so easy at first.' She stopped talking as she sped up to overtake a taxi cruising for customers.

'I must contact the horticultural society and see whether they have any more trips planned. Perhaps you can help me?'

Possibly she might offer to take me there. I felt her hesitation, considering whether such a thing would be appropriate.

Presently she said, 'I'm trying to grow some orchids at home. Not the *Lissochilus*. I'm not sure that would be possible. I haven't had much luck. But I do have some beautiful lilies, though – amaryllis – Harmattan lilies. They're in flower during the windy season. Perhaps you could come with Julius one evening.'

'Thank you,' I said. Though her words hadn't quite amounted to an invitation.

Minutes later we pulled up outside the faculty buildings. I stepped out of the car and leaned into the open window to thank her. She inclined her head and gave a slight smile of acknowledgement, which suddenly and without warning transformed into an expression of pure joy. In the instant of responding, I realised she was no longer looking at me. I straightened and turned. Julius.

In a way I'm lucky. For a long time I didn't believe it. I yearned to be remarkable, when in fact I was anything but. I have one of those faces, a face that looks like any other. With age you might say I have acquired a little distinction. The hair. But most of my life I had the kind of face – frankly speaking – the kind of face people forgot.

When I shook Julius's hand I could tell he was struggling to place me. Just as I once considered it my misfortune to be unworthy of being remembered, so it is the misfortune of more charismatic types to be rarely forgotten. With others around them to do the work they naturally become poor at retaining names and faces. It was evident that this situation was common to Julius and didn't disturb him in the least. Saffia explained we had met in town. He patted me on the shoulder; his expression was one of agreeable interest. Not the jealous kind, or perhaps he simply felt unthreatened. When Saffia mentioned flowers, I saw my opportunity and took it. I stood and watched while Julius opened the back door of the car, dropped his briefcase on top of the newspapers and walked around to the driver's seat, while Saffia shifted over on to the passenger side. He climbed in, released the lever and pushed the seat back.

They waved at me as they drove away. I stood there and my thoughts followed them. For a moment I felt strangely abandoned. But the feeling passed, because by then I was in possession of an invitation – to visit their house Monday coming. The address and the time were carefully noted in my book.

Saturday morning. I was sitting on the verandah after breakfast, looking through the newspapers and smoking a cigarette when Vanessa showed up. She wore a sullen expression, her lips pressed so tightly together that when she opened her mouth to speak I could see a line in her lipstick, like a tidemark. In the last few days I had completely omitted to call her. Clearly she had come to do battle.

Before she could get the words out I said, 'Just the person I was thinking about.' True, more or less. I'd woken filled with early-morning desire. Vaguely, before I got up to use the bathroom, I had wanted her there with me. Even now, despite her sour expression, I felt the returning urge.

She pushed her lips into a pout. She wore a narrow skirt and a tight-fitting *tamule* with puffed sleeves. Her hair had been straightened and tonged into outsize curls. It was not a style I particularly admired. Still, it spoke of the effort she had invested in her appearance that day. Certainly she wasn't on her way to church.

'Where have you been?' She stood, hands on hips.

'I've been here,' I said. 'Where else would I be? Coffee?'

In the kitchen I spooned some instant coffee into a cup, poured hot water on to it and filled the cup to the brim with Carnation Milk. Any less and she would act as if I was a miser. Vanessa was the kind of girl who deplored meanness, especially in a man. When I went back outside she had sat herself down at the table. I set the cup carefully on the table along with a box of sugar cubes.

'Help yourself,' I said. Sugar was still a small luxury to a woman like Vanessa.

After a moment's pause she reached out and took two cubes from the carton, dropped one into the cup, placed the other on a teaspoon and began to lower it in and out of the hot liquid, watching the cube crumble and start to dissolve. Still ignoring me she raised the spoon to her lips.

'I'm sorry,' I said. 'Things have been so busy. The exams are coming up and I have to prepare my students. Late home every night. Up early. I didn't want to trouble you.'

'I could have come and cooked for you.' She kept her eyes lowered.

'It would be too much.'

'I don't mind.' A pause; she pushed her lips into a more exaggerated pout, glancing at me upwards through her eyelashes. 'I could have sent something for you.'

'You're too good to me.' I stood up and went to stand behind her. I leaned over and pressed my lips into her neck. She made as if to squirm away. I bit the flesh lightly. She giggled and protested, but with no real conviction. I pulled her up, turned her to face me and kissed her. I tasted the sweetness of the sugar on her tongue, the wax of her lipstick.

We lay in bed together until mid-morning. Later I watched Vanessa as she moved around my apartment, tidying papers, clearing the table, putting my shoes away in the cupboard. In those moments I found myself already comparing her to Saffia. Vanessa was the younger and yet that did not make her any fresher or more innocent. Naive, yes. She tried for a greater sophistication than she possessed. I was happy enough to have her around, she barely had the power to irritate me. Each time the door closed behind her, the space was filled immediately, there was no vacuum where she'd been. My thoughts, in her absence, were not of her. Yet Saffia had already stepped into my dreams.

Vanessa wanted to be the wife of a university professor, the ambition she had set herself. And maybe one day she would be, though she gave herself too easily. I wished her well. I lay propped up against the pillows and watched her trying to create a place for herself in my life. It seemed a shame really, I told myself, but a time was coming when I would have to stop seeing her.

CHAPTER 2

The woman sat skewed in the chair opposite Adrian, knees together, arms pressed to her sides, shoulders forward, feet tucked in. A zigzag on the metal chair. The flesh was sparse on her bones. Around her waist she wore a cloth of yellow-and-black faded geometric shapes. Her breasts were covered by a loose blouse. Adrian could not guess her age. The people here seemed ageless to him. She called him 'Doctor,' proffered answers to his questions in a toneless voice, so low he strained to hear. Not once did she meet his eye, but studied her hands folded in her lap. She complained of headaches and asked for medicine for the pain, but the doctors had found nothing wrong with her. So they sent her to him.

Adrian talked about what he could do for her, searched for words he thought she might understand. On the paper in front of him was written her name. He spoke it out loud. For the first time she looked at him. She pointed at a bottle of vitamins on his desk and so he gave it to her. It was an easy thing to do.

That night Adrian Lockheart dreamed. One of the few times he had done so since arriving in the country. He was on the edge of a waterfall, leaning forward, hovering over the rush of water. Down below, he could see nothing beyond the torrent of water. In the dream he was a child again. He stretched out his arms and swallow-dived, waking just as he would have been engulfed by the falling water. The dream was not of death, because he woke softly laughing.

An echo of the feeling returns to him as he sits and gazes out of the window, his thoughts carried adrift on the tide of the voice of the old man lying in the bed. A child's face appeared over the top of the wall, a child's grinning face. The eyes met Adrian's own. A moment later the face disappeared. Then came the sound of laughter and a memory of the dream rose up. The feeling of falling, a surge in his stomach, the glee that comes from an innocent physical pleasure. He turns to where the old man lies, his arms above the cotton sheet, pressed against the length of his body. The old man has stopped speaking and is watching

17

him. His eyes, surrounded by curtains of ashy skin, are small, dark and liquid bright.

Adrian is silent a few seconds longer; he hopes his lapse will appear deliberate, a moment of contemplation.

'Shall I come by tomorrow?'

The old man inclines his head and continues to watch him.

Adrian, who might be used to such things, feels discomfited. Reflexively he continues, 'Is there anything you want? Books? Newspapers? I'll arrange it for you.'

'Thank you. I have everything.' The voice is hoarse. The words accompanied by a slight smile, a tightening of the facial muscles, a stretching of the lips, the impression more of pain than pleasure.

'Very well, then.'

Midday. Adrian rises, gathers his briefcase and jacket and steps into the shaded corridor, where the air is cooler by a degree or two. He leans against the wall. The building has no air conditioning except in the ICU ward, and even there it seems to battle unequally against the burning outside air, which seeps through every fissure in the brickwork. He breathes deeply, counts to three, and walks down the corridor into the daylight.

He crosses the quadrangle towards his office, sun beating squarely down upon the crown of his head. The quadrangle is no more than a patch of yellowed grass, divided into triangles by a pair of crossing paths. Each triangle is hemmed with concrete and contains a single concrete bench. Never has Adrian seen anybody sitting there. Whoever designed the place must have imagined the occupants of the building relaxing or eating their lunch here. But the sun makes it impossible.

Behind the door of his office he sets the briefcase squarely upon the desk, turns on the fan, removes his jacket and stands with his sweat-soaked back to the wind. He pours himself a glass of water from a plastic bottle, opens the briefcase and removes his fountain pen and papers.

When he was first shown to the room, his office, he recognised it for what it was, though neither he nor the woman hospital administrator made comment. Towering walls that reached up to a square of unpainted ceiling. A metal door fitted with a bolt and padlock. A solitary narrow window with six steel bars that reached across the outside sill. An oversized desk covered in scarred, orange-coloured varnish and faced by three chairs of different heights and ages. On a brittle wire a single forty-watt light bulb rotated and cast troubled shadows into the corners of the room. Adrian had knocked his head on it as he crossed the room and now was left with a burn, shiny and taut, on his forehead. Twice he has put through a request for the window to be enlarged.

In his converted box room he sits apart from the sounds outside: the creak of the gurney, the clatter of metal upon metal, names being called, footsteps: smart and fast; the shuffle and bump of a person on crutches.

The piece of paper in front of him he has already headed with his patient's name. Next to the words *Reason for Referral*, Adrian has written *Self.* For several minutes he writes down everything he has been told in the last two hours, as he remembers it. He writes swiftly, unhesitatingly. The smooth nib of the pen moves across the paper inaudibly, tracing in black lines the story of the man in the private room.

A fly is trapped, one moment frenziedly hitting the window, the next hurtling across the room above Adrian's head. He swats at it and misses. Now his concentration is broken and so he sets down his pen, crosses to the window and prises it open. Beyond the high walls he hears water running, the hollow knock of empty buckets, women's voices arguing, he thinks. He is not sure. He thinks how quiet affluence is: people living in private spaces, arguments in the shape of silences and closed doors. Compares it to the rowdy unselfconsciousness of poverty. The swooping laughter of children, though, is the same anywhere in the world.

That morning, after he woke from the dream, he pushed the sheets back and lay staring at the blank ceiling and listening to the noises of the morning. Perhaps because of the dream, he thought of his father and his mother.

Of his father, sitting opposite him in the parlour. Outside the trees gradually turning black against a silver sky, each possessed of its own lucent aura. Adrian watching his father's hands: the black hairs against the pale skin, the bony wrists, grey-veined, emerging from the cuff of his checked weekend shirt. His father's fingers fumbling with pieces of an Airfix plane.

For years Adrian assumed the idea for the afternoon's project must have belonged to one of his parents, most likely his mother. For

Adrian had no interest in model aircraft, could never see the point in gluing together pieces of moulded plastic. But now when he turns the notion around, he considers the possibility the idea may have been his: the trip to the shop to choose the aircraft, the drive home clutching the paper-wrapped box, spreading the pieces out upon the polished rosewood table all hint at a child's lack of imagination and eagerness to please. His mother seated at her desk answering correspondence, watching them both through averted eyes.

The model, though, is a Lancaster BIII. Adrian's own choice would have been more predictable. A Spitfire, say. His father tells him these planes raided German dams two years before the end of the war. Adrian watches his father fumble, knowing he must not help. There are occasions when an intervention might be disguised as filial duty: clearing his father's breakfast plates, fastening a tricky cufflink. But times when his father was bent over his shoelaces, Adrian saw no choice but to watch the knot slip over and over through his fingers. Sometimes Adrian's mother went to help. Adrian noticed how, as soon as she was through, his father levered himself up from the chair in stiff silence and left the room.

And so he sits silently, watching his father's hands. While his father in turn appears to have forgotten the presence of his son, fights to hold on to the pieces in fingers that tremble and flutter like a moth's wings. Another memory superimposes itself on the first. Of walking through woods with his father searching for ley lines, or was it underground streams? Each holding on to a forked stick. His delight when the stick in his father's hands began to tremble.

Since the first days of his arrival in the new country, without the order of his previous life, time had taken on a kind of shapelessness. In the early days he had risen, full of interest in his new surroundings. Every action, however small, held its own place in the day. Showering beneath the thin trickle of water that barely wet his shoulders. The sound of his own footsteps echoing in the corridors. The time he spent rearranging the shabby furnishings of his office. Each activity had its own purpose, pitch and resonance, like the notes from a tuning fork. But as the days passed the resonance had faded.

Breakfast in the canteen and he watched his colleagues come and go, each with a nod of the head. He knew their names, faces, their occupations. Some he had shared a beer with after work in a nearby bar, invariably marked by a late arrival or a drink left unfinished as someone hurried back to deal with another emergency. At mealtimes he sat over a cup of instant coffee, watching the tendrils of steam grow thin and fade, as around him others went about their business.

At other times he walked the long wards. Saw the occupants of a crowded minibus driven by a young man high on marijuana at the end of a sixteen-hour shift, encountered the unseeing gaze of a man beneath whom bamboo scaffolding had collapsed, watched listless mothers fanning inert babies.

Three weeks following his arrival, Adrian saw his first patients. This after he had obtained the consent of the hospital administrator for a system of referrals. The people his colleagues sent to him were outpatients mostly, the ones with whom the doctors could find nothing wrong. They sat with rounded shoulders and lowered eyes, hands curled in their laps like docile pets. What brings you here? The doctors sent me to you. Urged on by Adrian's gentle encouragement they described headaches, pains in their arms, legs, abdomens. Here, here, here. Touching body parts. When did the pains begin? Sometime after the trouble. Yes, I was healthy before then.

At Adrian's insistence they described in dampened voices what they had endured, as though the events described belonged to somebody else. Adrian had read the press accounts, the post-conflict reports. He knew how the war had begun – the barely remarked border crossing of a small contingent of foreign-trained rebel soldiers, who soon declared their presence by taking over a series of towns and vowed to march on the capital and overturn the bloated autocracy, which had ruled for twenty years. And he knew how it ended – how the civilians had borne the brunt of the rebels' fury from the outset and endured their agonies for a decade until the war was brought to a halt by the army of a nearby state with an ambitious despot of its own.

Adrian's empathy sounded slight, unconvincing in his own ears. So he nudged his patients along with questions, aware of the energy it cost him to obtain a sliver of trust. Later, in his apartment, he splashed water on his face. Once he filled the basin and plunged his face into the water, held his breath until his lungs ached. Alone he waited for his thoughts to be restored, for his jarred soul to settle.

And afterwards each of his new patients made the same request for medicines, to which Adrian explained he was not that sort of doctor.

A nod, of acceptance rather than understanding. They thanked him and left. None of them ever returned.

Late afternoon on a Saturday Adrian was walking past a row of stalls on the streets behind the hospital. A woman called out to him – he turned, recognising her by the yellow-and-black print of her wrap. Automatically Adrian smiled and raised his hand to wave. The woman was walking towards him with an unsteady puppet gait. A damp stain ran down the front of her blouse, the top few buttons of which were undone, partially revealing an arc of dark nipple.

'Doctor!' she'd called, grasping him by the arm. Her breath was hot. He couldn't understand what she was saying, wished he could remember her name. She lost her grip on his arm momentarily, stumbled and fell against him. A passer-by, a man in his fifties, intervened on Adrian's behalf and grasped the woman by the arm. The woman shrieked and in trying to pull herself free fell backwards, landing heavily on the ground before scuttling away through the legs of the onlookers. The man brushed at Adrian's arm, as if to remove the woman's touch.

'Sorry, sorry! That woman is a crazy woman. No family.' And touched his finger lightly to his temple, a butterfly taking to the wing.

Adrian shook his head, flustered, disappointed at the failure of his own response, but when he looked about for the woman she had gone.

He thinks about her sometimes, thinks of her now, at the open window. For days he had waited for her. But she never came.

It is nearly one o' clock. Lunchtime. These days he is acutely aware of the hours of breakfast, lunch and dinner. Meals have become more than punctuation marks in his day, they have become events in themselves. When he was a young man, doing his training in the hospital, there were times when he would forget to eat. While he was preparing for his doctorate he would leave his books to run across the road and buy a slice of pizza from the takeaway opposite; unwilling even to wait the minutes it took the Greek owner to warm it, he would eat it as he made his way back to his study, cold congealed cheese and curled ham.

He closes the window, trapping the sounds on the other side of the glass. There is dust from the sill on his palms, a fine, red, ubiquitous dust that covers everything. At this time of year it hangs in the air, a red mist, obscuring the hills behind the city, hovering above the horizon. Adrian

22

feels the dust in the back of his throat every time he breathes; his skin and nose itch, the wind sucks the moisture out of his pores. He finds a handkerchief in his pocket, he has taken to carrying one again, dampens it with bottled water and rubs at his palms. And though rust-coloured stains rise on the white cloth, he feels as if all he is doing is working the dust into the layers of skin. There are days he feels constantly soiled, can feel the dust trapped beneath his shirt, clinging to his damp skin.

The canteen is still empty, save for two men in porter's uniforms hunched over scattered Lotto tickets and a newspaper. The woman behind the counter heaps rice upon his plate and then, turning to the two tureens behind her, lifts the lid of the nearest and spoons chicken and sauce on top of the rice. A fortnight or so before Adrian had noticed how the woman served the local staff in the queue from the other tureen. He had asked the woman behind the counter what was inside the other pot.

'Chicken.'

Her unhelpfulness had provoked his insistence.

'I'll have some of that, please.' The woman had duly served him with what appeared to be identical chicken stew. At the table Adrian ate a spoonful. The food was fiery with pepper. Glad to be alone, he'd reached for a glass of water and another, returned to his office without finishing his meal, his mouth and lips still smarting.

Since then the woman behind the counter nods at him, and sometimes smiles. She appears to gain no particular satisfaction from what occurred, rather it seems to give their daily encounters a modest intimacy. Adrian remembers that day for the chicken stew and also because it was the day the new patient sent for him.

That the new patient was a man of some standing was evidenced by the fact he had a private room. Adrian passed the room every day on his way to his office. Never had he seen any visitors, save a retainer carrying sometimes a cloth-covered basket, sometimes a knotted sheet of soiled bedlinen, sometimes a pile of laundered clothes. Another time Adrian had glimpsed, through the slit of the partially opened door, the retainer sitting on the bed, fanning the torpid air with a raffia fan, chasing flies and adjusting the bed sheets with a twitch of the fingers, just like the mothers on the children's ward.

The day Adrian returned to his office, his lips smarting, he had found the retainer squatting on his haunches outside his office door.

'Can I help you?' Adrian unlocked the heavy door and the man rose and followed him into the room. Once inside he handed Adrian a folded slip of paper. Adrian opened the paper. It contained no more than a few lines, faint pencil strokes that meandered slowly across the page and spoke of an elderly hand.

Dear Sir,

I wish to request some time alone with you. I would be grateful if you gave Babagaleh, the bearer of this note, a date and hour convenient to yourself. I have no particular restriction on my own time, though it is, by nature of my condition, somewhat limited.

Yours faithfully,

Elias Cole Esq.

★

Out of the night, a scream. Adrian wakes, sweating and disorientated. The fan is still, the air in the room is hot. He lies and listens. The whirr of crickets, a truck somewhere in the distance, the call of a night bird. The window above his bed is open and the air carries the scent of woodsmoke, fragrant, like burning cedar. Adrian wonders if perhaps the scream belonged in his sleep, but then hears it again, plainly. A woman's cry.

He reaches under the mosquito net and switches on the lamp at his bedside, lets his eyes adjust to the light, from the chair takes a T-shirt, slips it over his head and opens the door on to the courtyard his bungalow apartment faces. A commotion is unfolding by the hospital gates. Out of the darkness a gurney pushed by two orderlies bearing a great, bulbous shape appears beneath the greenish glow of the security lights. A nurse holds up a drip. The trolley hurtles in the direction of the operating theatre. Adrian moves forward a few paces, peering through the dim light. As the group move closer he sees the form on top of the trolley is, in fact, two people: a man crouching astride an inert form. The man is pushing down with the heels of his hands, using his entire weight – or so it seems – to press down upon the patient's abdomen. The patient is a woman, hugely pregnant.

Someone shouts an order to stop. As Adrian watches the doctor continues to bear down upon the woman, at the same time exhorting her to push. It seems unthinkable to Adrian that a woman in her condition could possibly tolerate such treatment. His eyes are drawn to the child's head just visible, half in, half out of this world.

The one birth Adrian witnessed took place inside a room overlooking the Thames and the Houses of Parliament. Nothing prepared him for the terror – which he tried vainly to conceal. He sensed, or thought he sensed, his wife's forgiveness reach him from inside her cavern of pain. Later a retrospective guilt grew inside him, like the guilt of a soldier caught running away from enemy fire. Nevertheless, with or without his courage, it had happened. One moment the two of them were on one side of something huge. The next, tumbling down the other side. His daughter was born.

In the half-lit corridor, on a narrow trolley and in the dead of night, another child is being born before Adrian's eyes. The doctor on top of the woman gives a final, mighty push. At the same time the woman utters a long, low groan. A gush of liquid, the child slips out. Adrian watches, waits for someone to step forward and pick the infant up, slap his bottom, or blow into his airways. There is a terrible stillness about the child, lying there between his mother's legs. Adrian, who knows so little of such matters, knows this much. The life being saved belongs to the woman.

Inside the apartment he leans against the door frame and lets the breath out of his body, listens to the sound of the trolley, slower now, fade away. He pulls off his T-shirt and crawls back underneath the mosquito net. For a while he lies on his back, eyes closed. Behind his lids he sees the scene, the baby's head, the eyes: closed and peaceful, as though he had taken a look at the world he was about to enter and changed his mind.

Sleepless now, he turns on the light for a second time and climbs out of bed. In the kitchen he pours himself a glass of water from the bottle in the fridge. Tiny red ants mass around a half-biscuit on a plate, the edges of a patch of spilled guava juice, like beasts around a vanishing water hole. He picks up the plate; the ants swarm over his fingers delivering fiery bites. He swings around, drops the plate into the sink and holds his hand under the tap, watches the flailing ants sucked into the vortex.

In the sitting room he sits upon the crumbling foam cushions of the couch and picks up a book from the shelf beneath the coffee table. It is an English novel, of the kind taught in schools and left by the previous occupant. Adrian opens it randomly and begins to read, has difficulty concentrating, becomes entangled by words and their meaning. Then, before he can reach the end of the paragraph, the lights fail. For a moment he sits, insufficiently bothered to move, lets himself give in to the inertia and finds it comforting. A minute passes, then another. The thought occurs to him to sleep on the settee, when a series of rapid knocks on the door jerks him into alertness.

The man on the doorstep is dressed in green hospital scrubs, a T-shirt pulled over the top, on his feet a pair of rubber flip-flops. His face is lost in the darkness.

'Hey,' he says.

'Hello.'

'Sorry to bother you. Thought I might crash here a few hours, hope you don't mind.' A pause. The man points beyond Adrian's head, to the interior of the room. 'The light was on.'

Adrian blinks and, not knowing what else to do, moves aside.

'Thanks,' says the man, as he steps over the threshold into the apartment. His movements are exact, assured, unlike Adrian, who fumbles to find a candle and matches, light the candle's wick and set it on the table. In the trembling yellow light he sees something familiar in the man's profile.

'You were attending the woman just now?'

The visitor nods.

'What happened?'

'What happened?' The man looks up at Adrian. 'The baby was stuck. The woman was in labour for two days.'

'And now?'

He shrugs. 'Well, now it's out.'

Adrian is silent at that.

The man scratches his ear, but ventures nothing further. Then, 'So you live here?'

'That's right.'

'Yeah, I think I heard that. We used to use this place, you know. In-between times, after a late call. Mind if I crash?'

'I'll fetch some linen.'

'Don't trouble yourself.'

Adrian goes into the bedroom anyhow, where he locates a pair of sheets and takes a pillow from his own bed. When he returns the man is sitting, barefoot now, thumbing through the volume Adrian has left open on the table, squinting at the print in the inconstant light and pinching the place between his eyebrows. At the sound of Adrian's tread, he replaces the book carefully, face down as he had found it.

For some reason Adrian wants to tell him it doesn't matter, the book doesn't belong to him, but he says nothing. As he bends to put the sheets and pillow down, the man looks up and extends his hand.

'Kai Mansaray,' in an exhausted voice.

'Adrian Lockheart.'

'Pleased to meet you.' He places the pillow against the wooden arm of the settee, punches a hole in it to create a hollow and lies down.

With no more apparently forthcoming, Adrian carries the candle through to his bedroom, the shadows rearing up and shrinking back around him, and climbs into bed.

In this country there is no dawn. No spring or autumn. Nature is an abrupt timekeeper. About daybreak there is nothing in the least ambiguous, it is dark or it is light, with barely a sliver in between. Adrian wakes to the light. The air is heavy and carries the faint odour of mould, like a cricket pavilion entered for the first time in the season. It is always there, stronger in the morning and on some days more than others. It pervades everything, the bed sheets, towels, his clothes. Dust and mould.

Outside his window somebody is talking in a loud voice. He has no idea what they are saying. For a moment his mind drifts with the thought. To be surrounded by languages you don't understand. Of how it must, in some ways, be like being deaf. The deaf children he knew, whose parents sometimes came to see him, became remote, cut off, even inside their own families. Silent islands. By the time they were diagnosed the damage to the relationship with their parents and siblings was already done. No wonder, he thinks, that the deaf create their own communities. Deliberately turning their backs on the hearing world.

In the kitchen Kai Mansaray, barefoot but dressed in the clothes of the night before, is opening and closing cupboard doors. He doesn't turn when Adrian greets him.

'Hey, man. Not much here. Tell me you have coffee!'

Adrian opens a cupboard on the opposite wall and finds the tin of instant coffee. He fills the kettle with water from the plastic bottle and lights the gas ring.

Kai Mansaray watches him.

'Boiling sterilises it.'

'Yes, I know,' says Adrian, feeling the other's gaze. He fetches down the only two mugs he possesses and prises the lid of the coffee tin open with the end of a teaspoon. 'How did you find the couch? I hope it was all right.'

'Yeah, fine, fine. Me and your couch go back a long time. I'm not a big sleeper anyhow. I had to check on my patient.'

'How is she doing?' When there is no reply, Adrian glances up. Kai Mansaray is studying the label on the coffee tin. Adrian can't be sure whether he has heard the question or not. Suddenly the other man looks up at him.

'I could eat,' he announces. 'I'll make us breakfast.'

'There's nothing much here.'

'You don't say.' For the first time since they met, Kai Mansaray smiles. 'You relax.' He steps around Adrian, so nimbly Adrian doesn't have time to move out of the way, opens the door of the apartment. 'Sssss! I say! Come!' he beckons. A hospital porter hurries over. Kai hands him a few coins and a short time later the porter reappears carrying a plastic bag and two freshly baked loaves of bread wrapped in newspaper. Kai passes him a coin in return and the porter nods gratefully and retreats. On the kitchen counter Kai lays down the loaves of bread and unpacks the bag: a tin of powdered milk, another of Kraft cheese, onions, a dozen eggs, a fruit: large, oval and green with a ridged skin, a single lime.

Adrian dresses to the sounds of his visitor preparing breakfast in the kitchen. Efficient sounds, that relay a deftness of hand, a certainty of procedure. Still he dresses quickly. By the time Adrian reappears the apartment has been overtaken by the smell of frying onions. In the kitchen Kai Mansaray breaks eggs with one hand into a soup bowl, and whisks them into a froth. He has made coffee in the teapot and replaced the broken lid with a saucer. Adrian pours two cups, and sets one where the visitor can reach it, then leans back on the counter. In the silence a prickle of self-consciousness touches him. He shifts from one foot to the other. Watching the newcomer move around the kitchen, his kitchen, as though he were a man entirely alone in his own space, it is Adrian who feels like the intruder.

He has yet to become used to it, the silences between people. In Britain people came, or were sent, to see him. He learned to examine their silence, to see if it was tinted with shame, or pain, or guilt, coloured with reluctance or tainted with anger. He himself used silence as a lure, pitting his own silence against theirs, until they were compelled to fill the void. Here those tricks have no place,

28

even with those whom he calls his patients. If Adrian falls silent, so too do they, waiting patiently and without embarrassment. Here the silences have a different quality, are entirely devoid of expectation. And so he watches Kai Mansaray shaving curls of cheese with a knife blade. Swift, deft movements. Next Kai spoons two teaspoons of powdered milk into a tea cup, dribbles a little water from the tap into it and mixes the powder and water into a paste. This he adds to the eggs along with the cheese, relights the gas ring beneath the frying pan and pours the mixture into it. While the eggs cook he divides the fruit, scooping out shiny grey-black seeds, cuts a lime in half and squeezes the juice over the orange flesh. They sit down at the table to eat.

'Papaya!' says Adrian, recognising the fruit; he has never seen one so large.

'Pawpaw,' replies the other.

'Pawpaw. Is that what you call papaya?'

Kai Mansaray turns and looks at him briefly. 'That's what it is.' He takes a bite. 'Netherlands?'

'I beg your pardon?'

Kai Mansaray eats rapidly, hunched over the table, arms either side of his plate, as though ready to defend his food. 'Where you're from.' He tears a hunk of bread from the loaf and points it at Adrian's chest.

'I'm English.' Adrian frowns. Obvious, surely.

'OK. Only we get a lot of Dutch. Medical or emergency? You're not in surgical.'

'Actually, neither.' Adrian takes a sip of his coffee. 'I'm a psychologist.'

The other man looks up from his food at that, raises his eyebrows momentarily, inclines his head by slowly tilting his chin to one side. 'Ok-ay.' The word is spoken in two parts, split down the centre as neatly as if he'd used an axe. As though he is considering the statement carefully, examining its likelihood. Adrian might just have confessed to being the Grand Old Duke of York. 'So do they make you pay for this place?' he says, changing the subject.

Adrian tells him and Kai snorts by way of response. 'For how long? I mean, I take it you haven't immigrated.'

'I'm seconded for a year.'

'So you don't plan on coming to live here for good. No, well, I thought not. If you did you'd be the first immigrant in two hundred

29

years.' Kai Mansaray laughs at his own joke, a raucous, ear-splitting sound. 'We don't even have any tourists. Except your sort, that is.'

'My sort?'

The visitor takes another bite of bread. 'Nothing. What I meant to say to you was, "Welcome!" ' He raises his coffee cup.

'Thank you,' says Adrian, and sips at the cold remnants of his cup.

Silence for the rest of the meal, more or less. When they are through eating, Adrian picks up the plates and moves towards the dustbin.

'Hold it!' The other man reaches out, removes the plates from Adrian's hands and scrapes the remainders of the meal into the discarded plastic bag. For a moment he holds it over the dustbin in his outstretched hand, then bends over and peers into the hollow of the bin and grunts, 'Ants.'

He scoops up the bin, unties the plastic bag and upends the entire contents into the bag, juice bottle, biscuit pieces, ants and all, ties the handles of the bag and drops it into the bin. At the sink Adrian watches him wash his hands with meticulous care, examining the cuticles and searching under the fingernails for grains of dirt.

From the doorway he raises his hand in a salute. 'So. Next time.' He slides his feet into his flip-flops.

'Yes,' nods Adrian. 'Next time.'

And watches the door close.

CHAPTER 3

The house where Saffia and Julius lived was in a web of narrow streets
in the hills above the city. The paintwork was pale pink, sun-streaked,
with dark-pink recesses and a tin roof. An orange tree, laden with
fruit, bent over the house, which was reached through an open iron
gate. I was early, I knew – but nonetheless I climbed the steps. Still
sweating from the uphill walk, I paused and ran my finger around the
inside of my collar. A band of stray dogs raced past the gate. I knocked.
Moments later there was Saffia, running her palm over her hair and
smoothing her skirt. Julius was not yet back from the university. I
made an offer to walk a little and return. Naturally she demurred.

'No, no. You're welcome. Please, come in,' she said and stepped
back.

I followed her through to a verandah at the back. The house looked
directly out over the city.

'A beautiful home.' My own voice rang in my ears, the words had
come out too loudly, a declamation. Moreover, strictly speaking, it
was not the house, which was a modest affair, so much as the view
that commanded attention.

'*I* like it,' she replied, as though she recognised my compliment for
the hollow thing it was. 'We chose it for the garden, really.'

I hadn't noticed the garden as such, but now I could see what
she meant. It stretched out from below us, and swept one's gaze up
towards the view, rather in the way, or so I am told, an artist composes
a painting to draw the eye in a particular direction.

'Let me perhaps show you before the others get here.'

For a moment I had no idea what she was talking about until I
remembered the ostensible reason for my visit. Saffia picked up a
basket and a pair of secateurs and led the way down a spiral staircase
into the garden.

A pair of fan palms marked the two far corners of the garden and
were reached by a network of shaded gravel paths which led down
descending terraces. Travellers' palms, she told me, the leaves always

pointed east and west. There were ferns, some the size of trees. Fruit trees: almonds, lime, guava, a great breadfruit tree. Cumuli of white bougainvillea darkly edged with another kind of climbing flower, sweet-smelling with heavy violet heads. Here and there, perhaps where a path divided, or between the roots of a tree, clay pots of plants. And along the far wall more differently sized pots, some holding a single specimen, others containing artful arrangements of flowers and shrubs. She raised them, she told me as we walked, for weddings and the like.

Presently we reached an opening and there, a crowd of lushly dressed aristocrats, the Harmattan lilies. They stood magnificent, multi-hued, every shade of a dying sun. Their stems were fleshy, muscular, naked without the modesty of leaves. The flowers thick-petalled and brazenly open, revealing sweeping filaments and shiny, sticky stigmas.

'The Portuguese brought them from South America. The owners of sugar plantations in Brazil and the West Indies liked to plant them around their houses. The bulbs were very valuable.'

I had never known that and said so.

'They grow like weeds,' she continued lightly. 'No matter where you put them. No matter at all. In fact when these ones have finished flowering I'll have to dig a few of them out. I can give you some bulbs.'

'I'd like that,' I replied. 'I'd like that very much indeed.' There was a moment of silence between us. Our eyes met. She looked away. Somewhere inside me, an emotion bloomed.

Saffia began to cut stems of flowers, for the table. I watched her with her back turned to me, standing against the light. The shape of her neck, the angle of her head, her braids of hair which she smoothed from time to time with the back of her hand. When she turned to look at me, I forced my gaze back to the flowers.

We settled on the verandah watching the light slip from the sky. The scent of night blooms drifted up from the garden. Saffia served me a Star beer and poured herself a glass of ginger ale. I heard the sound of the door and Julius's voice. Laughter rolled through the empty house. I stood up quickly.

'I should organise a sweepstake,' Julius was saying. 'I could make money from people like you.' And he appeared accompanied by two other men. One of them he slapped so heartily on the back the chap was fairly propelled out on to the verandah. I recognised him vaguely from the campus.

If Julius was surprised to see me already there he gave no hint of it. Introductions followed. Ade Yansaneh, the one I thought I knew. Kekura Conteh, who worked for the state broadcasting station. They greeted Saffia with familiarity. Julius bent and kissed the top of her head. Without turning she raised a hand and lightly touched his cheek. They demonstrated their affection in the way Europeans did. I found it strange Julius was unembarrassed by it. Saffia stood up and slipped away, returning with three beers and glasses upon a tray. I sat back down. Julius produced extra chairs. Saffia opened the bottles. The general shuffling subsided.

Julius turned to me, he was grinning. 'Ade doesn't believe the Americans will make it to the moon.'

'It's not possible,' said Ade firmly, though without elaborating. Instead he shook his head for emphasis.

'Why not? The technology is there. The Russians have proved it. Several times.'

'A man was nearly lost in space.' This from Kekura. I realised I recognised his voice from the radio, high and hectoring.

'Come now! What is it they say? How do you make an omelette without breaking a few eggs? There's risk in everything. The point is he succeeded. He walked in space!' Julius, who alone drank straight from the bottle, wagged his Guinness bottle at Kekura.

'It is no place for Man,' said Ade ponderously, as though he were repeating it now for the umpteenth time. I noticed he possessed a hairline that was almost perfectly straight. It cut across his forehead, so that the top of his head looked like a lid. A pedant's hairline.

'Ah Ade. You disappoint me.'

'I can't see what good will come of it,' said Kekura. 'Big men doing battle.'

'Well, *there* you might have a point.' Julius, who had been leaning so far back in his chair that it was balanced only upon the two rear legs, now leaned forward letting the chair fall back into place. He put his bottle on the table in front of him and surveyed it closely, as though it were a miniature spaceship. Under him the chair creaked. Beneath his bulk it looked unworthy of its task. 'For them maybe. But not for the men working to build these machines. They're doing it knowing that every day they are making discoveries – in science,

33

technology, engineering. Not to reach the moon first, though that is what unites them. But because what they learn along the way will add to the sum of human knowledge. A century of work in a single decade.' With his thumb he caught a drop of condensation as it slid down the side of the bottle. In the pause that followed I took my chance to enter the conversation.

'They say we will be able to watch it on television.'

'That's right! Hey, Kekura, what do you say? We'll go to your offices and watch it.'

Kekura inclined his head. 'It would be my pleasure, certainly.'

'History in the making. But I tell you something I would like to see more,' Julius said, still staring at the bottle.

'What's that?' I asked.

Julius looked up, his face solemn. He reached out and picked up his beer. Suddenly his face cracked into a great grin. 'The day the first African lands on the moon!'

The laughter erupted just as Saffia opened the sliding door to call us to eat. Julius stood up holding his Guinness bottle aloft. 'To the first black man on the moon!'

'To the first black man on the moon,' we echoed and drank.

I can't remember all that was discussed that night at Saffia and Julius's table. There was no talk of politics, as I recall. Not in the immediate sense. Later, I wondered what the conversation would have been had they not had a stranger in their midst. I ate without noticing the food. Time passed. The conversation went back and forth. A new Chinese restaurant. The road-building scheme. A new comedy show on the radio of which Kekura was producer and therefore in constant search of new material. A story was told – by Ade, I believe. It went like this: three men visited a car dealership, one an aristocratic fellow dressed in a fine gown and carrying an attaché case. A Nigerian prince looking to buy a fleet of cars. The manager of the salesroom hurried out to greet them personally. The prince shook hands, but did not deign to utter a word, leaving it to his assistants to handle the discussions. They were ready to make a cash deal. Indeed the prince had brought the money with him in his attaché case. The manager, keen to oblige, hastily agreed to allow the two retainers to take one of the latest models for a test drive. Reassured by the presence of the taciturn prince, who sat in the waiting area with his briefcase of cash upon his knee, he decided not to bother to accompany them. Time passed.

One hour turned into two. The car and the two retainers showed no sign of returning. The manager decided to speak to the prince and soon realised the magnitude of his error. For this was no prince at all, but a local beggar, deaf and mute, cajoled into unwittingly acting a role for which he was perfectly suited. The attaché case was found to be filled with newspaper.

Everybody laughed, Julius so vigorously he began to wheeze. To my mind it did not seem anything in particular, but I saw a change come over Saffia. She watched with concern and seemed about to rise and go to him when Julius recovered himself. I would have given the episode no heed but for Saffia's reaction, in the indication it gave of the quality and nature of their relationship.

When the general laughter had subsided, she asked, 'What became of the beggar, the prince?'

Ade replied he didn't know.

'Well, at least he got a bath and a haircut,' said Saffia. 'And a new suit.'

'He probably masterminded the whole damned thing,' said Julius and everybody laughed again. 'He could be driving over the border right now.'

'That's it! That's it!' cried Kekura. He grabbed Julius's hand and shook it enthusiastically. 'There's the punchline. Thank you, my friend. I owe you. Whatever you want, I owe you.'

Julius smiled. Kekura stood up, almost overbalancing his chair, wiped his mouth and replaced the napkin at the side of his plate, straightened his jacket and said, 'Well, good people, until next time.' He turned and bowed to Saffia. 'Another exquisite meal, madam. I thank you.' He patted his stomach, which prompted a smile from Saffia.

I wished I had thought to praise the meal.

It was close on eleven o'clock. The curfew no longer applied; still people maintained the habit of returning home reasonably early of an evening. By midnight the streets were empty. Ade asked Kekura for a lift. Julius and Saffia rose to see them out. I stood up to shake hands. Very probably I was expected to take my leave too, but I did not.

After the door had closed the three of us remained standing. Then Julius invited me to join him for a whisky on the verandah. From a bottle of Red Label he poured us a half-tumbler of Scotch each. He handed me a glass and sat down, sideways to me, his legs stretched out in front of him. From where I sat I had a view of his profile in repose. He kept a beard, did I mention that? In those days it was a mildly unconventional act. For a long time he said nothing but stared out over the balcony railing.

I wondered where in the house Saffia was.

'See that?' said Julius, waving his glass at the view. Scattered lights marked the city and, farther away, the shape of the peninsula. Above us the stars. The moon was hidden behind the eaves of the house. A single, far-off light burned a tiny hole in the thick layer of black that separated earth from sky, a foreign trawler most likely. A row of moving lights made its way across a strip of blackness to and away from the peninsula.

'When I was a child I came to live in the city with one of my aunts for a few years. My mother had passed on, you know. My aunt, she was a strict woman. Yes indeed,' and he laughed. 'I'd like to say I was fond of her but that would be lying. The woman was a bully. A greedy bully. She took me out of the school my father was paying fees for and she used me as her errand boy. Every day she would send me across the bay into town to deliver messages. There was a ferry in those days, a passenger ferry.'

'I remember,' I said. The ferry was in fact a fishing canoe, poled by a single man. I had taken it once or twice that I could remember, on the way to visit relatives. The currents in the water could be perilous.

'Almost always I was the only child on board. The other passengers, the ones I saw every day, were protective of me. Some of them believed there was an evil spirit living under the water. You know how people are – they believed such spirits were especially drawn to children. One day, after some heavy rain, we were caught in vicious currents. The boat swung like a compass needle.' He took a swig from his glass, leaned forward for the bottle and poured himself some more. Then he pushed it across the table towards me. 'It lasted a few minutes. Not even that. Seconds. But everyone in the boat was terrified. I was terrified. When we reached the other side they helped me down and set me on the shore. We were all safe, but something had galvanised their mood. I don't know why. Possibly there were those who were afraid for themselves. Anyway, whatever the cause, something happened in those moments. One of the regular passengers, a woman, insisted on accompanying me home at the end of the day to speak to my aunt. I was nervous of my aunt's reaction, but I dared not disobey an adult. I led the woman to the house where I lived. Compared to my aunt, this woman was well-to-do. My aunt could see it. She invited the woman in while I waited outside. I have no idea what was said. But from that day on my aunt stopped sending me across the bay, in fact stopped using me as her errand boy and sent me back to school to continue learning. She honoured the arrangement my father had made with her.'

He sat still for a moment or two, thinking his own thoughts. Then grunted softly, as if he had made sense of the story or recalled his reason for telling it.

'Now there's a bridge. Built by the Germans. You can drive across to the city. Doesn't take a minute. How about that?'

'I know,' I said. 'I cross that bridge every day.'

'Ah, you live on the peninsula.'

'Who was she? The woman?' I asked.

'No idea,' he answered. 'A good soul. Or maybe not. Just an ordinary woman who did one good thing. Either way, without her I wouldn't be here now. I would have been more grateful if I'd had any idea of the favour she had done me.' He jumped up, suddenly animated. 'Let's have some music!'

'I should be going.' I stood up.

'I'll drive you,' he said. 'In just a few minutes.' He turned and disappeared into the house. 'What do you like?' he called over his shoulder. 'Fela Kuti?'

Music was not something I cared for. I didn't own a record player, only a radio. I replied, 'Yes, why not. Fela Kuti.'

'Or your namesake?'

'Who's that?'

'Oh come on, Elias!' He slipped a record from its sleeve, placed it on the turntable and carefully set the needle on the vinyl. Saffia entered the room, just as it was filled with the sound of Nat King Cole's voice. Julius reached out his arm to catch her as she passed behind him, spun her around and back towards him. Even caught off guard like that, in Julius's arms Saffia didn't miss a beat.

'You like the music, Elias?' Julius called over to me.

'Yes indeed,' I managed. 'Very much.'

'Then you'll come out with us one of these days. We'll go to the Talk of the Town. Bring somebody.'

Half an hour later, side by side in the Variant, we drove across the bridge. Either side the moon glittered darkly on the water. Julius said nothing but whistled the Nat King Cole tune. His whistling was off key, but he didn't seem to mind or even notice. He dropped me outside my house and I thanked him.

'Any time. Any time at all, my friend.' He waved as he pulled away. Rather than turn the car, though, he continued straight ahead along the length of the peninsula, the long way round.

At two in the morning I was still awake. My heart was thudding drily in my chest. Thoughts traced circles in my mind. I rehearsed different moments, parts of the evening's conversation. For whatever reason I found myself thinking of Julius almost as much as of Saffia. Eventually I got up out of bed. I groped my way to the kitchen, found the light and turned it on and poured myself a glass of water from the tap. My notebook was there on the table. I sat down and jotted down a few details, in part because I feared I might forget them, but mainly because I needed to exorcise them from my mind.

Finally I went back to bed and fell into a fitful sleep.

Is that where it began? In the garden before the splendour of the Harmattan lilies? Or afterwards, as I watched the two of them dance together? Or weeks before at the faculty wives' dinner? It's difficult to say. Beginnings are so hard to trace. Perhaps we three would each put the beginning in a different place, like blindfolded players trying to pin the tail on a donkey.

Three different beginnings. Three different endings, one for each of us.

CHAPTER 4

The Talk of the Town. I forget what brought me to pass by there a few years ago, but I found myself in the vicinity and wandered in through an unlocked door. It goes by some other name now, the fourth or fifth in however many years. I forget exactly. The Ruby Rooms, the Ruby Lounge? Otherwise nothing had changed.

Inside, the same red carpet, mapped with dark stains and chewed at the edges. In the half-light the pockmarked velvet of the banquettes, peeling fake-wood surfaces of the tables, like one of the girls from outside the City Hotel in the cold light of morning. The dance floor seemed ludicrously small and even empty the place felt cramped; the air was foul, dense with the odour of sweat, sour beer and urinals. A piano stool stood alone on the platform, but no evidence of the piano. A man was stacking empty drink crates. He did not look up or take the trouble to greet me, sparing me the obligation of having to explain myself.

Julius and Saffia and Vanessa and I. Thirty years ago. Together we stepped through the door and on to the lush red carpet. Four old friends to anyone looking from the outside. The atmosphere redolent with cigarette smoke, the vapour of strong spirits. Julius, carrying his jacket over his shoulder, led the way; Saffia and Vanessa followed close behind. I came last. I had heard of the Talk of the Town, though this was my first visit. Vanessa had been before, of course. Truth to tell I preferred bars, and visited them when I wanted to get out of my own space. Not to seek companionship; I preferred contemplation to conversation. And I had never liked, even feared a little, these kinds of public places. As I say, I cared little for music, and though I was a competent dancer, my talents in that direction had certainly never been remarked upon.

Vanessa turned her head this way and that, trying to see who was there and also to reassure herself of the effect of her entrance. She wore a strapless yellow dress I had seen before, though on someone else. On her head she wore some kind of hair adornment held in place by pins stuck into her scalp. The whole arrangement was spiky and dangerous-looking. As she swung her head around it seemed, at any moment, as if Vanessa might catch a stranger's eye, though not perhaps in the way she imagined.

Someone who knew Julius stopped him and so I guided (herded) the two women onwards looking out for a table. It was moments such as these I disliked about being out in public. Thankfully Vanessa took charge of the moment, shooting ahead to where a group were just vacating a table. As they gathered themselves together she slipped through the throng, slid her bottom along the banquette and plopped her handbag on the table in front of her like a trophy. I followed, stepping aside to allow Saffia into the banquette, and then sat down opposite her on one of the stools.

It was the first time I'd been able to look at Saffia properly all evening. They had collected us in the Variant, Saffia switching places to sit next to Vanessa in the back, while I sat up front with Julius. Now she leaned forward on to the table, pausing to inspect the surface and wipe it with a spare serviette before resting her forearms on the surface. Her arms were bare, she wore a cream dress with a scooped neck, large black polka dots, caught at the waist with a black belt, a matching scarf draped behind her. I noticed such things, most men don't. Or so we maintain, at any rate, for fear it would diminish us to admit it, I suppose. But more than that, I remember every moment of that evening.

Next to Saffia, Vanessa sat looking around, wearing a slightly sullen expression she imagined passed for sophistication. Saffia leaned forward and whispered something in Vanessa's ear. And judging by the smirk that appeared on Vanessa's face, I dare say Saffia was congratulating her upon her wits in securing the table.

We ordered drinks. Saffia asked for a ginger ale. I urged her to accept a real drink. She shook her head. I told the man to bring her a rum and Coke, whisky for me. Saffia requested a Guinness for Julius, who had yet to reappear. My back was to the room, to the dance floor. The room throbbed with sound. Impossible to talk over the din. Saffia, seemingly unconcerned, leant forward, smiling, watching the dancers behind my head.

Presently the waiter arrived with our drinks. Something scarlet and sticky, for Vanessa, imported and doubly expensive for it. I watched as Saffia sipped her drink, bending her head to the glass. She leaned back, caught my eye and smiled.

'How is it?'

Yes, she nodded and began to hum, moving her head to the beat of the music. 'Julius says I have no head for drink. It's true. Not like him. When we were students I used to drive them all home at the end of the evening. I never really acquired a tolerance for it. Now I am stuck with driving.'

At least that is more or less what I think she said; what I caught were phrases, punctuated by the bass beat. 'You studied together?'

She nodded.

'Engineering?'

She cupped her hand around an ear for me to repeat myself. She laughed, leaning back into the seat, shaking her head. I felt foolish.

'Botany,' she said.

'Flowers?'

'Well, plants really. Plant systems, soil. That sort of thing.' Her eyes slid sideways again, over my shoulder. Watching the dancers, or looking for Julius? Her hands were clasped on the table in front of her, the fingers interlaced. With the nail of her forefinger she began to trace an imaginary circle on the table. I looked at her and our eyes met, for the second time. I held her gaze, as long as I dared. She smiled and looked back at me, and then looked away. For a moment I was unable to breathe. I studied her profile and took a sip from my drink. From a different direction I felt the heat of Vanessa's glare. I swivelled my stool around, showing her my back, and studied the people dancing.

So you see moments later when Julius joined us at the table the currents between us all were fractionally altered.

Vanessa began to flirt with Julius, of course. Touching his forearm, whispering in his ear, wriggling upon the banquette in time to the music. Julius responded, after a fashion. The record changed, Julius and Saffia stood up to dance, and I, following his lead, asked Vanessa. I accompanied this request with a show of courtesy, helping her out from behind the table, and this mollified her somewhat. We followed the other two on to the crowded floor.

Later we strolled on to the terrace, easing our way through tables of people taking a respite from the music, their faces glowing beneath the clarity of the moon. Julius seemed to recognise a good few people, or at any rate they knew him. He was the kind of person they call the life and soul of the party. Life and soul. Life *and* soul, without whom the rest of us collectively comprised nothing more than an inert corpse. Vanessa had found somebody, an age mate, a girl in a shiny black dress, and they were standing a distance away, whispering, shielding their lips from view behind the backs of their hands.

Saffia and I were alone.

A blind man sat with his back against the wall. She said, 'Look at his smile. Why do you think he's smiling like that?'

'The music?' I replied.

'Yes, perhaps.'

We both watched the blind man. He sat, a great smile on his upturned face. He wasn't tapping his feet, or marking the beat with his hand. He was just smiling.

Saffia said, 'But do you notice how often blind people smile? Or don't. Sometimes cry. I once saw a blind man in the street, the tears pouring down his face, he was quite alone. I thought about him for a long time; perhaps it's a lack of self-consciousness, you know. They don't realise people are watching them.'

'Does that make it better or worse?'

'I can't help thinking it could only improve things if we all said and did exactly what we felt.'

'I'm not so sure,' I said. 'Do you really believe that? About the blind?'

'Yes. I do.' She watched the blind man, frowned slightly and then added, 'And of course, he doesn't even know I'm looking at him now.'

Saffia watched the blind man and I watched her.

'Dance with me,' I said, because it was uppermost in my mind. I could think of nothing else until I had voiced that one thought.

And so we danced. The way she danced with me, as though the act required concentration. Or perhaps it was just the rum, perhaps it had gone to her head, though with the effect of forcing her to focus rather than relaxing her. Her hand on my shoulder. My hand at her waist. I had taken her to be taller. Between our bodies, a few inches of warm air. She kept her eyes averted from me.

As we danced I tried to inhabit the moment to remember it for later. I had it in my hand, and then it was gone. I walked her back out on to the terrace.

There was Vanessa. Mouth like a wet prune, wearing an expression that made her face look as though the skin was stretched over a substructure of granite. Not a word all the way home. I remember Julius passing silent comment, the way men do. A surreptitious slap on the back as we parted. He slipped into the passenger seat next to Saffia, and as he did so he wagged his finger, grinned, raised an eyebrow and shot a glance at Vanessa and then back at me, as if to say, 'Elias, you old rascal.'

CHAPTER 5

Thursday, he is called to attend a child. The address he is given is the local police station. Inside a row of people wait upon a bench. Through a door left partly ajar Adrian can see several police officers. One, a fat woman officer with a hairstyle as elaborate as a prom queen's, sits at a desk. A male officer is perched on the edge talking to her. Two others stand close by. There is the occasional sound of laughter. Adrian hovers outside, waiting to be noticed. Someone glances in his direction, and away again. He raps on the door. Soft, even-spaced knocks. The woman at the desk waves at him to wait. He moves away to lean against the wall. When, finally, he is called inside and states his name, they exclaim and apologise. Not a crime victim then, somebody important. He should have said so.

Adrian follows the woman officer down the corridor, in silence except for the sound of her uniform trousers rubbing together between her enormous thighs. By a door she stops and gestures to Adrian to enter. He peers through the glass. A child sits alone in the empty room.

'What do you want me to do?' he asks.

'Well.' She shrugs as though she wonders why *he* should be asking *her*. 'They want you to examine him.'

Adrian approaches the boy and squats down in front of him.

'What's your name?' The boy looks at Adrian through dark, unblinking eyes. He doesn't answer though his gaze is steady.

'Your name?' bawls the woman from the doorway. The sound makes Adrian start. He turns and holds up a hand, but fails to impress her. 'An idiot.' And shakes her head, sucking her teeth as she does so. When Adrian turns back the child is still watching him. Adrian regards him for a few moments. He wonders what kind of trouble the boy is in.

'Excuse me,' he says to the officer, keeping the dislike out of his voice. 'Can you leave us a moment?'

She shakes her head. 'This is a police station.'

Adrian nods, pulls out his notebooks and pens. Under the eye of the policewoman he circles the child scribbling notes until he sees her lose interest and begin to examine the polish work on her nails. Then he moves behind the child and drops his notebook, swearing loudly as he does so. The policewoman straightens up. The child doesn't move.

The child is a simpleton, Adrian tells the officer in charge. The policeman wants to know what he is supposed to do with the boy. Something in his manner suggests the problem is of Adrian's making. So Adrian tells him to release the child into his custody and signs off on the paperwork as though he had done so many times before. A flurry of rubber stamping and countersignatures and he is shown the door.

Minutes later, hand in hand with the boy, he stands outside the police station. Adrian's heart is beating. His armpits are damp, the sweat like ice water. He has no real idea what to do with the boy, he simply couldn't bear to leave him in that place. Suddenly the child pulls away and darts off into the traffic. Before Adrian can even think of following, he is gone. Adrian turns and looks up at the police station, but nobody seems to be looking.

Four people are jammed into the back seat of the taxi on the way to the hospital. The woman next to him carries a basket containing some kind of fermented food; the yeasty odour mingles with her own smell and that of her perfume. Adrian has never uncovered the alchemic combination of words and fare that would secure him hire of a taxi on his own.

Inside the hospital the staff room is empty. On the two-ring electric hob coffee is simmering in a long-handled, stainless-steel pot. The bubbles rise and burst on the surface like lava. Among the mugs Adrian finds one less stained than the others and rinses it. The coffee is grainy and bitter, reminds him of the pretend coffee he made from acorns as a child. It coats his tongue and turns his saliva sour.

In this heat, he feels like a sleepwalker. His movements are laboured, he can feel the ponderous workings of his brain. He leans back and waits for the caffeine to snap through his system, the nerve endings quivering into life, prickling his skin.

Right now he'd like to talk to somebody, but who? From the desk he dials his home telephone number, listens to the ringing echo hollowly down the line. He counts. A click and Lisa's voice comes on the line. He listens to her cool, chirpy voice telling callers to leave a name and number. He replaces the receiver without speaking. What would he have said, anyway? To Lisa foreign countries were as alien and remote as Venus. World events revolved continuously, independent of human agency. War, coups, poverty – these existed on a par with viruses, cyclones and black holes in space. One expended emotion with economy. He could have told her about the deaf boy at the police station, anticipated the pause, the deft change of subject on to some more positive, more easily comprehensible matter. It had attracted him at first, brought him back to himself, her brisk, upbeat way of being. He had mistaken it, at first, for a certain tender-heartedness, a tendency to easy bruising.

Later he showers. Standing beneath the spout of water, he feels the urge to urinate. He stands at the edge of the tiled shower cubicle and aims at the toilet bowl. Success brings with it his first sense of achievement of the day.

The shower leaves him only temporarily refreshed. The heat soon takes over again, covering his skin and turning it clammy. In the kitchen he surveys the contents of the fridge, takes a can of evaporated milk, holds it up and lets it trickle into his open mouth.

How quickly one reverts.

He makes himself a cup of instant coffee and then pours into it two fingers of whisky. What he'd really like is a bottle of wine. The satisfying pull of the cork, the guarantee of a long evening suffused in an alcoholic glow. He settles on the couch, takes a cushion from one of the other chairs and places it behind his back. But the inertia prevents him even from reading; instead he stares at a spot on the floor and sips his drink. It is not quite eight o'clock. The evening rolls out ahead of him, like an unlit road.

A knock on the door. The laundry man delivering his clothes. At the third knock Adrian levers himself to his feet.

On the doorstep is Kai Mansaray, dressed much the same as before, only this time he is holding a glass-covered wooden board.

'Sorry, I thought it was somebody else.' Adrian steps aside to allow him inside.

'Oh yeah? Who do you owe money?' Kai laughs.

'No. Just my clothes back from the laundry, that's all.'

'Well, if that's what you have to look forward to, it's as well I came around.' He steps forward and places the board on the coffee table.

Adrian can't remember when he last saw a Ludo board. The one

Kai sets on the table carries with it the taste of tomato soup, the scent of wax crayons, the rubber-and-sweat smell of the school gymnasium. This is the game he has seen grown men playing in the street, on outsize boards decorated with photographs of footballers and actors.

Adrian pours Kai a tumbler of whisky. They open with the best of three. Kai wins easily and challenges Adrian again. Adrian, who has watched Kai's strategy closely, has worked out a thing or two, takes the fifth game and the sixth as well. They play double colours. Blue and green: Kai. Red and yellow: Adrian. Adrian mixes the whisky with water to stretch it. Kai plays intensely. Adrian is grateful for the company. In the kitchen he finds a packet of chocolate chip cookies. The cookies are soft and dusty. The chocolate has melted, seeped into the stratum and hardened. They eat the cookies in place of supper, washing the taste away with whisky.

Six sets later, Adrian concedes and leans back in his chair. Fleetingly the events of the morning come back into his mind. For a moment he considers raising the subject of the deaf boy, but chooses not to. If Kai had been a European, it might have been different. Conversation here can be challenging, language is a blunter instrument, each word a heavy black strike with a single meaning. To say exactly what you mean, to ask precisely the right question, this is what has to be done. For the bluntness of the language doesn't mean people speak their minds. Rather, they use the spaces to escape into.

Besides, he is enjoying the sense of oblivion seeping into him, a result of the whisky and the pleasing monotony of the board game. He feels as close to content as he has done since he arrived. He pours more whisky. The bottle is almost finished.

For a while they sit together in silence. Adrian leaves the room to use the bathroom; when he comes back Kai is leafing through the papers on the side table. He does this in an entirely natural way, unperturbed by Adrian's reappearance. He extracts a sheet.

'Yours?'

Adrian nods.

The sketch is of a songbird, made by Adrian the previous day. Since he came here he has resumed this schoolboy pastime. Among his junior-school friends, in that fleeting phase of boyhood when the tide of energy is still displaced into the wholesome, while his friends collected football cards and stamps, Adrian drew the birds he saw from his window: sparrows, blackbirds, crows, thrushes, robins at different times of day, weathers and seasons, in all their moods and guises.

The birds here are extraordinary, even the ones that sit on the telegraph post visible from his window: sunbirds, flycatchers, shrikes, kingfishers, pied crows. In the distance kites and the occasional vulture spiral down on currents of air above the city. Birds that would have been buried treasure to his thirteen-year-old self. He fumbled through the first sketches, frequently flexing his fingers, knowing enough to keep adding lines, resist the eraser. Gradually his talent has grown back. He wants to buy some paints. Yesterday he saw a bird whose wing feathers were of a near neon orange. He would never have believed such a colour existed in nature.

Kai replaces the sketch in silence and picks up a photograph in a green leather frame, of the kind that close upon themselves, a travelling photograph frame. A gift from Lisa. 'This your wife?'

'Yes,' replies Adrian. 'Lisa.'

A pause. And because he is trying not to show how discomfited he is by Kai's lack of niceties and because the notion that a conversation is a continuous act is bred into his bones and silences like nudity should be covered up lest they offend, Adrian asks, 'How long have you worked here?'

Kai puts Lisa's picture back upon the shelf. 'Four years. Something like that.'

'And before?'

'There was no before.' He cranes his neck sideways to read the titles of the books on the shelf; his back is to Adrian, who persists. 'You were studying?'

'Yup.'

'Of course. So where did you do your medical studies?' Adrian expects Kai to name an overseas university, in the United States or Britain, possibly one of the former Soviet bloc countries.

'Here.'

'Oh.'

'Yup. Local boy.'

'The whole lot?'

Kai nods.

'So you've never visited Britain?'

'Nope.' Kai accents the word, shaking his head, turns and places his whisky glass on the table.

Why this is such a surprise Adrian cannot quite say, something in Kai's manner, he struggles to put his finger on it. 'Have you ever been outside the country?'

Kai shakes his head. 'Leave? When we have so much here?' He laughs and drains his glass.

Adrian pours the last of the whisky, leaving the empty bottle on the table. He takes a sip, and then another, pacing the drink. The whisky has gone to his head. He remembers he hasn't eaten properly and closes his eyes. Behind his lids the blackness turns liquid. He wonders if he doesn't feel faintly unwell. He opens his eyes, feels the stab of light against his retina before his pupils have time to contract. Coffee is what he needs. He rises and makes his way to the kitchenette, tinkers with the kettle and cups. It is later than he thought. Outside invisible dust thickens the air. Tomorrow the hills above the city will have disappeared from view. He remembers the flight across the Sahara, watching the dust rolling across the dunes, gathering force and height until it extinguished the view from the window.

When he returns Kai is lying with his head back and his eyes closed. Adrian stands with the two cups in his hand. There is something compelling in looking at a sleeping person. In the early days he would watch Lisa asleep, right up close, feeling her breath on his face. If she woke up, when she woke up, their eyes met. She didn't start or flinch. And so with strangers, even a stranger on a bus, there is a shadow of that same intimacy. Something in the freedom of the gaze, to look without being seen, a kind of power, a stolen intimacy. Kai's skin, bright and unblemished. Unshaven; the hair grows on Kai's face in sparse, erratic bursts. He wears his hair in an unfashionable style for the times. In contrast to the cropped or smooth-shaved heads of many black men Kai's hair grows thickly and tufted to an inch or two.

The beard and the hair conceal his youth; he is much younger, Adrian thinks, much younger than at first imagined. This makes Adrian by far the senior. He realises why he was surprised to learn Kai had never left his country, never left Africa. It is the worldliness he carries with him, all the more noticeable now for being momentarily dissipated.

On the arm of the settee a single finger taps out an unheard rhythm.

'Coffee?' says Adrian, suddenly awkward.

'Sure, why not?' Kai answers. He does not open his eyes. Adrian places a cup on the table, where the liquid sloshes gently in the cup. Kai opens his eyes, reaches for it.

The middle of the night. Adrian wakes. His mouth is dry from the whisky. The water bottle on the bedside table is empty. He starts through to the kitchen, turning on lights as he goes. Too late, he remembers Kai, hastily turns the light off and is forced to stand still for a few moments while his eyes readjust to the darkness. He wonders if he has woken the other man, listens for Kai's breathing and finds it. Slowly he gropes his way along the walls towards the kitchen.

In the kitchen he opens the fridge, takes a plastic bottle of water and raises it to his lips. He pushes back the cotton curtain. No sign of a moon. From the other room he hears sounds. A murmuring. Muttering. He lowers the bottle from his lips and listens.

Conscious of the tread of his bare feet he crosses the kitchen to the doorway. Kai is sitting on the edge of the couch.

'Oh. I woke you,' says Adrian. 'Sorry.'

When there is no reply, he ventures forward, peering through the darkness. Kai is sitting on the couch, his arms squeezed to his sides, his face turned upwards, eyes open. He is speaking, though Adrian can distinguish none of the words, which come in a gabbled monotone. Faster now. And louder. Followed by a gasp, as if he had been hit in the chest. Silence. Then the murmuring begins again, softly rising.

Adrian reaches out to touch him, pushes him gently back down on to the couch. 'You're dreaming,' he says in a normal voice. 'You're asleep and dreaming.' He stays until the murmuring subsides, then makes his way back to his room.

In the morning Adrian wakes to a clattering. His head is buzzing. From above come loud scratching sounds of birds trying to gain purchase on the corrugated-iron roof with their claws. He rises and knocks experimentally on the door to the sitting room, pushes at the door. There are the pillow and sheets rumpled on the settee, the Ludo board and scattered coloured counters, the empty whisky bottle. He stands and surveys the scene, then turns and heads in the direction of the kitchen.

Boiling water for coffee Adrian hears the sound of the door and fetches down a second cup from the cupboard. He realises, suddenly, how empty he has felt these past weeks.

★   ★   ★

In the days and weeks that follow, the rhythms of their lives begin to intertwine. Kai takes to passing by at those times when he has a few minutes spare and sometimes to shower in Adrian's apartment. One day Kai arrives just as Adrian is leaving. Adrian lets him in, and gives him a key to lock behind him. Suggests he may as well hold on to it.

Certain days Adrian comes home to find Kai in the apartment, settled in the front room, going through papers or writing up notes. The pattern of Kai's breaks from the operating theatre becomes familiar to Adrian, and he will, on occasion, endeavour to stop work at the same time. He finds he looks forward to the other man's companionship in the evenings.

So a new friendship is formed.

CHAPTER 6

A high wall surrounds the hospital, built of rough, bare blocks through which hardened floes of concrete spill. Lizards dance between shards of broken bottles planted in a bed of concrete. A ruff of razor wire encircles the building.

Outside Elias Cole's room a kite is caught. A black kite with a bamboo frame, wings of black plastic and a tail of torn strips. It twists and turns, like a snared bird. The more it struggles to break free, the more hopelessly entangled it becomes.

In a moment of silence the old man's eyes follow Adrian's, and both watch the agonies of the kite.

'Does the kite mean something to you?' asks Adrian.

★

It reminds me of my brother. You were asking me about my family. We once built kites just like that, though in those days we made the wings from paper.

Once I was given a real kite; my father bought it for me with his clerk's salary the week I passed my school certificate. I ran out to test it on the bank behind our house. But the season was wrong, there was not so much as a whisper of wind. Running to and fro, I became frustrated, finally I threw it down and burst into tears. My crying angered my father. He told me to bring the kite to him and in front of him he made me hand it to my brother.

Within two days an unseasonable wind blew up. Who knows from where? I watched my brother playing with the kite. He called me to join him, but I refused. I would die rather than admit how much I wanted to play with that kite.

My brother was strong-limbed and solid, hard as a rubber ball, so when he first fell ill you couldn't notice it. I left him sleeping in the bed we shared. Afterwards he went about his chores, never complaining, only his usual boisterousness was tempered by the sickness. In a family of men doubtless nobody would have noticed. My mother had enough to do in a day, as she often said. She made all our clothes and some embroidery as well, to sell. But she had a fondness for him. Late in the morning she found him curled up in a corner of the room, complaining of the cold while outside the sun burned in the sky.

I was moved out of the bed soon afterwards, to sleep in the sitting room with an older cousin. I loved my brother, but still there were those times I would go into his room with the sole purpose of taunting him. If he asked for water, I would walk in and hold on to the mug and refuse to let him have it. There was a point in his sickness when his voice failed, and so there was nothing he could do but whimper little words and make stuttering sounds. Then I would imitate him and when I had had enough I would place the tin mug just beyond his reach and leave the room. Another time I pulled the bedclothes down and delivered bruising little pinches across his body, knowing he hadn't the strength to fight me. None of it made any difference. Whenever I entered his room he looked at me without fear or hate, rather with something like expectation. As if waiting to see what I might do next. And there were days I sensed he felt something like pity for me, though it was he who lay there with limbs as useless as a straw doll's.

In time he recovered though his walk maintained an uneven keel. My mother had made me fetch and carry for him during his sickness, and so it continued. Look after your brother, you're the eldest! All the responsibility came to me, though I never asked for it. And there were times his happiness seemed designed to goad me, and I confess, occasions when left alone I vented my frustration on him.

Don't ask me why I did it. A little childish jealousy. As an invalid he drew more of my mother's attention. The good thing is that my brother forgave me. Even after he no longer depended on me, when I left home to pursue my studies and left him behind.

And if you asked me did I love my brother, I would have said yes. I would say yes. I had spent more nights lying in the warmth from his body than in that from any lover's. Only during the time when he was sick did I ever sleep anywhere else.

At any rate, I digress.

A change in the season. Surreptitious at first. At night the rain tapped on the windowpanes, scores of hesitant fingers. Dawn brought bright skies, washed of the desert dust, and the hard, coppery smell of earth. For the first time in months you had a clear view of the hills from the city. As the weeks passed, the rain became emboldened, abandoned the sanctuary of the night and came by day, blindingly, accompanied by dark clouds. The blue skies that arrived with the morning by the afternoon had vanished.

One such a day, trapped indoors by the rain, I sat at my desk, trying to concentrate on the outline of a paper for the faculty journal. 'Reflections on Changing Political Dynamics'. I was looking for an arena in which to make my name, to put recent political events into perspective. The drumming of the rain, the tapping of the typewriter keys combined to unsettle my thoughts and I struggled to maintain the logic of my argument. The light was grainy and grey; I went into a neighbouring office to fetch a small lamp and when I returned I paused for a moment to gaze out of the window. People were scurrying across the courtyard, running from one doorway to the next as though there was a sniper on the roof. I saw Julius. He was walking along the diagonal path, bareheaded and without an umbrella. With him was another person, who I took to be one of his students; they were both deeply absorbed in conversation. Julius was gesticulating with both hands. It was a habit of his, he drew sketches in the air and even traced out mathematical problems of some complexity on an invisible blackboard. At one juncture they paused, heedless of the rain, better to conduct the conversation face to face. I stayed and watched from the window. They shook hands vigorously, as though they had arrived at some agreement. Julius left his companion at the door and walked on, ambling. I saw him shake the raindrops from his head, like a dog, and watched until he disappeared into the doorway beneath me. I went back to sit at my desk. Sure enough his face, glistening wet and grinning, popped around my door moments later.

'Borrow me twenty-five cents, Cole. I need a soft drink.'

I brought my change purse from my pocket and counted out the money. Julius had got into the habit of dropping by my office. Sometimes it was to borrow small amounts of money. At first I kept a running total of how much he owed me, until I realised he had no intention of paying it back, no intention even of expending the effort required to remember the debt. Once I came back to find three brand-new packs of cigarettes on my desk. From Julius, or at least so I assumed. Recompense for all the twenty-five-cent loans.

He had an appetite for history and frequently borrowed books. One or two he returned with phrases underscored and comments pencilled into the margin. Not for my benefit, or the benefit of any future reader, but as a record of his own thoughts.

There were other days when he sat in the spare chair, or rested his backside on the windowsill, and began to expand whatever was on his mind, something he had read in the papers, a thought, or a theory – seeing what I made of it. On days when he had use of the car he would invite me for a drive and he would continue to expound his ideas from behind the wheel. In front of my eyes he pulled down the city and rebuilt it. Drainage systems. Buildings. Bridges. Highways. Driving along, humming and singing off key.

The peninsula bridge. He told me how, when he was fifteen or so, he had watched its construction every day for months. The columns of the support towers being raised one by one. The superstructure, then the deck, one section at a time, transported and hoisted upwards on a crane and swung into place. The men who did the work knew him by name. Kru mostly, a hundred years ago they worked the ships going and coming from here, were used to the proximity of water, of heights and ropes. They seemed to understand, elementally, the nature of the construction, though none could so much as read or write. Once, at the close of the day's work, Julius told me he crept to the edge of the new section, crawling on his belly, and peered over, exhilarated by the drop down to the water, the possibility of being blown away. The day before the official opening they lowered him, dangerously, over the side on a trapeze and he wrote all the workers' names in the wet concrete, adding his own initials at the end. *J.K.*

For my part, I listened, which was my role. And anyway, Julius was a talker and I am not so prone to it. I am circumspect by nature. Julius was not. He was a man possessed of great ardour. The whiff of naivety, of wonderment was all about him. He had a way of seeing the world, full of glory, that served only to obscure the reality of it.

'So, Snoopy met with Charlie Brown.'

'What?'

He was talking, it transpired, about the moon landing, the subject of which continued to impress him. The proposed attempt was then just a few weeks away. Snoopy was one kind of craft, Charlie Brown another. Two astronauts had taken a trip outside their craft, and spacewalked close to the surface of the moon. They had made it safely back to the mother ship. From his pocket Julius drew an article cut from a news magazine. In the foreground of a black-and-white photograph was a stretch of milky land, in the distance the arc of a horizon upon which hovered a planet.

'What is it?' Julius demanded.

I shrugged. 'Outer space?'

'Yes, but what exactly? Look closely.'

I peered at the image. There was something faintly familiar about the far planet. You must remember, though such images are commonplace nowadays, at the time none of us had seen anything of its kind.

Julius tired of waiting for me. 'It's the earth, Elias! It's an earthrise. Like a sunrise.'

And for a moment I was caught by his ardour. By the sight of the earth hovering above a pale lunar horizon.

'There's no place we can't eventually go, and there's nothing we can't eventually do,' one of the astronauts had said. Julius took it, jokingly, as his mantra, repeating it often over the next few weeks. 'There's nothing we can't eventually do,' he said, when a bottle-opener could not be found, as he expertly flipped the metal top off his beer on the edge of a table.

Yes, he was quick to friendship, in a way I was not, neither was I used to. It was a quality I might have mistrusted, but I couldn't think what Julius might want from me. Or at least, put another way, since he never seemed to hesitate to ask for what he wanted, I could think of no ulterior motive in his befriending me. And on that basis, I suppose you could say we had become friends.

But for Saffia, we had become friends.

Saffia.

More than anything in those weeks and months, I desired time alone with Saffia, something I dreamt of constantly and how I might manage it. An evening, Julius asked for the loan of my office. It wasn't the first time. As I say, he was in the habit of asking, when he craved a quiet place to work, or somewhere to hold a meeting with other members of his faculty. He remarked, in a teasing way, on my good fortune in acquiring a space of my own, especially in light of my relatively junior status on the campus. His own faculty was undergoing building works and the staff members crammed into every available remaining space. That day it was easy enough to agree. I was happy to be offered a way out. Work on my article had stalled, I needed to do more thinking, which I could just as easily do at home. I capped my pen, collected my papers and left the room to him.

But I didn't go home.

There'd been a lull in the rain. In the last light of the day people were making their way home, passing me as I stood and smoked a cigarette across the road from the pink house. I threw the stub into a puddle, searched in my pocket for the packet, drew out another and lit it. When I had smoked the second cigarette, I crossed the road, stepping around the puddles and the other pedestrians. I stood before the front door, conscious I could yet turn back. At that moment I heard distinctly, on the other side of the door, the sound of her voice. My heart thudded to hear her thus, so close, unaware of my presence. I wondered who she might be talking to. Not Julius, who was in my office where I had left him. I thought I detected in her voice a note one might describe as controlled exasperation, the kind of voice a teacher might use to address a dull-witted child, or in this case a hapless servant. I raised my fist to the door and rapped. The footsteps changed direction and a moment later she stood before me.

'Elias!'

She was surprised to see me, and the smile she gave me, though she did her best to cover it, had been preceded fleetingly by a frown. 'I'm sorry,' she said. 'We're just rearranging a few things. Come in, come in!' She stepped backwards into the hall.

Inside the dining-room table was covered in papers and what I took to be botanical specimens, some labelled and bagged, others pressed on to paper. On the floor were piles of books, magazines, a stack of dressmaking material and patterns. She was clearing herself a workspace, she told me, as she led the way out on to the verandah, hoping to complete her PhD thesis. She'd been putting it off since their return home from Britain.

She sat down on the edge of a chair, tucked her hands in between her knees and leaned forward with a mild air of expectancy.

'Julius isn't home then?' I asked.

'No, I'm sorry. He's not. He's rarely back at this time. Did you want to talk to him?'

In not replying, I avoided the need to lie. She took my silence for assent.

'I'd offer to let you call him, except, with all the disruption at the department, he doesn't have an office.'

'It's not that important. I happened to be passing.'

'You're welcome to wait.'

I said, 'I'm disturbing you.'

'Oh, I welcome the distraction. What would you like? A beer?' And she disappeared into the house.

When she returned Saffia asked after Vanessa. In my answer, I told her Vanessa was well, which I expect was true. We talked a while of unimportant matters. At some point – I can't remember how we got there – Saffia told me she had newly acquired a camera and asked if she could take my picture.

'Of course,' I replied.

By the time she left the room and returned I had risen in readiness and was hovering, somewhat self-consciously, considering how best to position myself. The truth is I am an uncomfortable photographic subject. There is nothing about the experience I can find to like.

'Over here.' She patted the railing. 'With the view behind you.' I obliged and stood facing her.

'Like this?' I put my hat on my head and tipped it backwards, swung my jacket over my shoulder. An attempt to be jocular. Pathetic, I dare say. She didn't smile. Instead she stood gazing at me, the camera held loosely in her hands. I waited, unnerved and excited at the same time. There was a boldness in the nakedness of her gaze, the way she eschewed the use of the camera either as prop or buffer. Finally she shook her head. The light was behind me, she said. She moved me to a chair.

One or two clicks of the camera shutter. She paused and fiddled with the lens, moved a foot or two closer and depressed the shutter release. Closer again. From the middle of the floor to the arm of a chair. From the chair arm to the edge of the coffee table. Neither of us spoke. My palms had begun to sweat and I could feel the prickle of moisture under my arms. Saffia's proximity, the effort of maintaining my pose and of breathing through my nose was in danger of making me light-headed. I inhaled two or three times and forced myself to bring my breathing under control. Saffia for her part peered through the viewfinder and seemed to fidget with every knob and lever of the camera's apparatus. If she noticed any awkwardness on my part she gave no sign of it. When she looked at me, which she did frequently, it was as though a veil had dropped in front of her eyes. Looking not seeing. I had transformed into a thing to be photographed. I saw how the power of the camera could be disinhibiting, too. So close to me now, I swear I caught a scent of her, a combination of her perfume and a warm, animal smell.

Somewhere inside the house a door opened. A shadow slid across the wall, a door closed. I turned my head. The shutter clicked one last time. Saffia lowered the camera and followed my gaze.

'My aunt. You're lucky, Elias,' she laughed. 'You who are born in the city don't have to put up with relatives staying all the time.' At that she stood up and moved away. The camera's power had been dispelled.

An aunt then, of course. How I wished it had been a mere servant. The presence of an elder in the house, a chaperone, lent respectability to my visit, the reason Saffia was relaxed. I suspected it was important to her to do the right thing.

Below us, the cry from a minaret, and then another, the beginning of evening prayers across the city. For a while we both listened without speaking. Saffia rose to switch on a light or two above us and at the same time offered me another beer. As I was about to answer an old woman appeared carrying a rolled mat under her arm – the aunt, presumably. She eyed me narrowly and spoke a few words to Saffia in their language. Saffia responded. I have no idea what was being said. The old woman withdrew, walking with slow steps and continued mumblings, pulling a shawl from her shoulders over her head. At the edge of the verandah she spread the mat on the floor and began the movements associated with prayer.

It began to rain. A pattering at first, becoming faster, like running feet. Then the gentle moan of wind. Saffia watched the skies for a moment and suggested we move indoors.

'I must be going,' I said suddenly. I stood up, collecting my hat from the seat where I had laid it.

'Let the rain stop first.'

But I knew Julius was unafraid of the rain; I didn't want him to find me there.

'Really, I should go. I was supposed to meet somebody. I had quite forgotten.' I put my hat on.

Saffia offered to fetch me an umbrella. Immediately I saw in her offer not a mere umbrella, but a reason to return. I was about to accept, then shook my head. I might be expected to return the umbrella through Julius. Of course I would.

At the door she held out her hand. Her touch was almost painful to me. Some women offer you little more than the tips of their fingers. Not Saffia, she closed her hand around mine, the heat melted into me, seeped through my blood, filling it with a flash of white-hot hope.

Inside, her aunt's voice calling. Saffia withdrew her hand from mine.

'Come and visit us again soon, Elias.' *Us.*

I turned and fled into the rain. Out in the street I pushed my hand deep into my pocket, closing my fingers around the warmth of her touch, like an object I was afraid of losing. For a long time as I walked I wondered what it might be like to feel that touch, every day, whenever you felt the need. On an arm, on the back of your neck, on your cheek. A kiss. An embrace. I walked on, the rain filling the brim of my hat and pouring off, streaming down my neck. By now it was properly dark and I faced a long walk home.

I am a person generally happy in my own company; still I had no desire to spend the evening at home alone. I found myself passing an establishment I had once or twice frequented and stepped inside. I took a place at the bar. My hands were shaking and for some reason I felt unaccountably angry. The first whisky I ordered I knocked straight back. I ordered another and drank it neat and warm. The heat hit my belly, the alcohol warmed my blood, I felt the tension ease. I caught sight of myself in the fly-spotted mirror behind the bar; the shadow of my hat brim obscured my eyes. Behind me in the recesses of the room I saw a woman, alone and watching me. I removed my hat and allowed our eyes to meet in the mirror.

She was what you would call a working girl, though of course it never was that easy. They all expected to be paid for, but acted insulted if you suggested such a thing up front. It was always a fine line. Still, with the look we exchanged I felt we understood each other. I beckoned her over and offered her a drink. She accepted with a shrug. I ordered myself another whisky and put my hand on her knee.

Young. Nineteen, perhaps. Her youthfulness made up for what she lacked in beauty. She drank her beer fast and noisily, like a child, with her nose in the glass. I indicated to the barman to bring another and encouraged her to talk, to save me the bother of doing so myself. She lived in Murraytown, she told me, the old fishing village that was now part of the city. I remarked she was a long way from home. She was a friend of the owner, she said. With the subtlety of a mule, she peppered her conversation with references to her rent, her college fees – why do they always claim to be studying? – pointed to the broken heel of her shoe. Within a very short time she was tipsy. I helped her to her feet, told her I was going in her direction and offered her a lift home.

We climbed the stairs to my apartment. She sat down on the settee while I poured us both drinks. I sat down next to her and put my arm around the back of the seat.

'Don't you have any music?' she asked.

'Why don't we just talk,' I said. 'You're beautiful.' I put my hand under her chin, turned her to face me and kissed her. We moved to the bed.

I desired her. I wanted to lie with a woman. I also wanted, urgently and desperately, to rid my system of the still-nameless emotion that had overtaken it. As I raised myself above the girl and in the light of a passing car, I saw not her face but Saffia's face. When I touched her skin, I felt nothing but Saffia's skin. I entered her quickly.

The girl, who for her part had been more or less motionless, appeared to come to life and commenced writhing and moaning. No doubt she imagined it was what was expected of her. The truth was it had exactly the opposite effect to what was surely intended. I was forced to increase my activity in proportion to my wilting desire and she took this as a sign of her success, adding endearments and spoken encouragement to her repertoire. I would have liked to place a hand across her mouth, but doubtless she would have started screaming. I concentrated instead on blocking out the sounds. Finally, after some minutes, I managed a climax.

In the days following I applied myself to my article. I worked late most nights, hitting the keys until my fingers ached. In between Julius came and went, as before, borrowing twenty-five cents for a soft drink, updating me on the progress of Apollo 10, helping himself to my books. It seemed Saffia had said nothing to him of my visit. At the end of the week, after much drafting and redrafting, my paper was complete. I typed up a final copy and submitted it.

Two weeks later my paper was returned via my pigeonhole with an attached note from the Dean. It had been declined for publication.

CHAPTER 7

A morning. Adrian sits on the window ledge and surveys the patch of land between the back of the bungalow and the perimeter wall. On a length of surgical thread a plastic prescription bottle, filled with sugar solution and fashioned into a makeshift bird feeder, is suspended from a vine. Adrian finishes his cup of coffee, pours the dregs down the drain and goes to shower and shave. When he returns, a tiny sunbird, no bigger than a rosebud, is hovering next to the bird feeder. Its wings, held high above its back, beat so fast the bird is reduced to no more than a smudge of colour and a long, curved beak. Hastily Adrian picks up his sketch pad and block of watercolours and tries to capture the blur of violet-and-black feathers. He should, he knows, be on his way to his office. Instead he draws and watches the bird, weightless in the air, as if held by an invisible filament, and he considers how slender, how insubstantial his reasons for being here.

As a boy he had imagined his adult life as one of countless adventures. Early versions of the same vision saw him involved in the rescue of animals: a drowning dog, a horse with a broken leg. As his imagination roamed further from home, he saved wild animals from forest fires, or even from extinction. Later, the animals were replaced by a girl or a woman: his cousin Madeleine or his dark-haired art teacher. At night he dreamed of his art teacher, of acts of heroism, and of great journeys undertaken, of heights scaled, all with a kind of remote, fuzzy certainty. How exactly these adventures would come about was unclear; they simply lay ahead of him somewhere in a distant, amber-coloured future.

When he came to thinking about it much later, he saw the tint of his boyhood dreams had not been so much amber as sepia. Memories of his grandfather and grandmother, perhaps, of their faintly exotic ways, the ivory cigarette lighter and camphor-scented cigarette boxes, the polished wooden floors and rugs long before such furnishings became fashionable. Of his mother, who was so nearly born abroad. It used to impress him, how close she came to being foreign, as he thought of it. His pregnant grandmother stepping off the boat home in the run-up to war. His boyhood adventures took place not in the future, but in some fictional landscape of the past that could equally have been prompted by Tintin, Rider Haggard or any of the adventure books boys his age consumed. Adventures undertaken and survived, which would somehow solve all the things that had been puzzling him, and after which a quieter life began.

Sometime around Adrian's fifteenth year the imaginings faded, to be replaced by an anxiety, creeping and insidious. Life inside the house slowed and became suffused with a muted quality as his father's illness progressed. Adrian's mother's hopes gathered like clouds above her son's head. University followed exams. Adrian chose to study close to home to be on hand to help his mother. By the time he began his second year, those of his friends who had taken a year out returned coppery and newly confident, only to depart again to take up their places in university towns far from home.

When he left for Bristol to pursue his clinical training he did so alone in the knowledge of the post he had been offered and had declined at the hospital in a nearby town. At the railway station he turned and watched his mother's cloth coat disappear into the crowd, back to the closed walls of life with his father. His mother, who was nearly born in a foreign land.

The bird has been hovering for what seems to Adrian a remarkable length of time. With his brush he applies the paint straight on to the paper, sheet after sheet covered in images of the bird. Somebody — Adrian forgets who — once told him that if humans were to fly they would require chest muscles six feet deep to raise their own weight. He wonders now if this could possibly be right. Or if it is one of those beliefs of which there are so many small and large, carried from childhood to adulthood without question. He *did* know the birds expended such energy in flight they needed to drink twice their body weight in nectar each day. Such effort invested in the mere fact of existence. Sometimes nature's ways did not bear scrutiny, only the result: a beauty that burst the banks of logic.

Nine o'clock. He swirls his brush into the water, on to his palette, daubs the paper. At the end of the corridor his office awaits. Adrian paints on. The bird's feathers, now in full sun, appear black, though they are in fact the deepest purple with a metallic sheen he knows he lacks the expertise to capture.

Once his life was guided by train timetables, fifty-minute appointments that ended regardless of whether the timing was good or bad for his client (they were 'clients' now, 'patients' no longer). An hour for lunch, usually curtailed by staff matters. Two trains home. Twenty minutes and seven minutes, respectively. Perhaps an evening engagement, the hours in which hospitality would be dispensed neatly printed out in black-and-white and posted six weeks in advance. None of that here. In the months before his arrival, in those same hazy visions of his youth, he had imagined lines of patients – patients, not clients – and in responding to his patients' needs his workload would create itself and he would end each day gratifyingly exhausted. So he had thought. But they have stopped coming now, more or less entirely. And, he suspects, his colleagues have stopped bothering to make referrals. These are the thoughts that swirl in the back of his mind, like the colours of the paint in the water. He came here to help and he is not helping. *He is not helping.*

He glances at the clock on the wall above the shelf. Standing at the end of the uneven row of paperbacks is a neat group of thicker volumes: *Surviving Trauma, the Post-traumatic Stress Disorder Handbook,* the World Health Organisation's *Mental Health of Refugees, ICD-10 Classification of Mental and Behavioural Disorders, The Diagnostic and Statistical Manual of Mental Disorders.*

He begins to mix crimson paint and water, adds quantities of Prussian blue.

During his clinical years, Adrian had found himself drawn to the study of stress disorders. As a boy of twelve, around the same time as his adventurous imaginings began, he'd gone through a phase of reading books about the First World War. The stories he read and reread with morbid fascination were those of shell-shocked soldiers being forced back to face the guns or else being shot for cowardice. Once he'd recounted some of those stories for his mother. He remembered it distinctly, she standing making butterscotch pudding at the kitchen counter. In turn, she had recounted her own memories of the Second World War.

Once, Adrian's mother told him, when her mother was out and she was being minded by a neighbour, the air-raid sirens had sounded. The neighbour, a woman in her forties already yellowed with age and Capstan cigarettes, led her to the air-raid shelter. His mother remembered sitting huddled next to her neighbour upon the cold floor of the shelter, feeling the cold replaced by a flow of warmth, thinking she had wet herself until she realised the urine belonged not to her, but to the neighbour. The pool of liquid slowly turned chill. Sitting in the warm kitchen Adrian could smell the acrid tang of urine, the brick dust and stale air. Later, Adrian read how teams of psychiatrists had accompanied the men to the front during the Second World War. But none for the civilians back home, he thought. Nobody provided psychiatrists for them.

In the last month of Adrian's third year of clinical studies, a gas leak on an oil rig one hundred and twenty miles off the coast of Aberdeen caused an explosion late one night. The force of the explosion wrenched the platform in two, a torrent of flame rushed upwards into the northern skies. The men trapped on the rig escaped the flames by sliding down the support poles or jumping hundreds of feet into freezing seas overlaid with a slick of burning oil. One hundred and sixty men died. The survivors, who were few in number, struggled to return to their lives. They visited their doctors complaining of nightmares and flashbacks, of sleeplessness, panic attacks, of moods that swung from fear to fury. Several took to drink, one would not be touched by water, stopped washing and hid in his house behind locked doors, another saw his wife and children wearing the faces of his dead colleagues, a third soiled himself at the sight of the sea.

Adrian wrote a paper arguing for a more proactive response from mental health professionals after major disasters and had it accepted for publication. At the time many among his colleagues still described traumatised patients as suffering from nervous shock. The paper won Adrian modest acclaim when it was cited by lawyers preparing a case for compensation against the rig's owners. What previously had not existed as a classified mental disease eight years earlier suddenly drew the attention of others in his field. Adrian knew he should feel pleased. Instead he felt cold and anxious, as though he had foolishly revealed the whereabouts of something precious.

The years ticked by. Adrian built up a steady private practice alongside his position as a senior clinical psychologist at a London hospital. In his mother's regard, he had outdone himself. Adrian, though, felt his career oscillate just short of its tipping point.

Meanwhile there were new developments. Stress inoculation. Rewind technique. A practitioner of neuro-linguistic programming made his name with the publication of a theory he named emotional freedom technique. In America a woman psychologist developed a method called eye movement desensitisation and reprocessing. Some among the fraternity dismissed it as quackery, though Adrian wondered if this wasn't, at least in part, because the originator of the technique was both a woman and based in California. Adrian read all the available writings including those of the dissenters. The results, as published, were dramatic and nobody, not even the psychologist herself, whose name was Francine Shapiro, could entirely account for them. Out of sight of his colleagues Adrian attended a training course and on occasion had even practised the technique upon his private clients.

Yet despite investing every effort in keeping abreast of new developments as his chosen field grew ever more populated, increasingly it felt to Adrian that the momentum of his career had dissipated.

So when he saw the advertisement in the back of a professional journal for a government-sponsored psychologist to work overseas, Adrian had mailed an application to the address of the international health agency the same afternoon. He hadn't mentioned it to Lisa. The post was for a six-week project. In the event his application failed and he'd not bothered Lisa with news of that either. Then, one Friday night, a voice faintly on the telephone from Rome. The successful applicant had been taken ill. Was Adrian free to go at short notice?

Why there? Lisa had asked him, when he finally told her. She'd seemed neither pleased nor displeased, simply baffled. A civil war had placed the country in the news in the last year or so. Several times in the conversation Lisa transposed the name of the country to 'Sri Lanka' where a civil war was also being fought, though on an entirely different continent.

The team had stuck together. Beneath a still surface upon which people shopped at the markets and went to work violence bubbled, erupting from time to time in the rural areas. There was a curfew from eight to eight. Nobody left the capital. Adrian enjoyed the camaraderie, the sensation of remote danger. On his return to England he had applied for a further posting and been accepted. When he told Lisa he included, in his account, the impression his return had been requested. She had not been happy and yet it could not be said she had been happy – for several years.

The second time the plane was crowded. Groups of Europeans held conversations outside the toilets, in the aisles, across the backs of the seats. The Africans, for the most part, remained seated. Adrian knew nobody, though one or two among them ventured to ask his business. Or more precisely, with which agency he was working. Adrian's brief amounted to not much more than the name of a hospital and the information they had requested an in-house psychologist. The hospital administrator, a woman in her forties, with hair pulled back into a knot from which it escaped at spiky angles, was new to her job and seemed unprepared for his arrival. Her brisk manner conveyed less regret at her own lack of readiness than a sense that his coming at this time was something of an inconvenience.

Why? Lisa had asked him. Why this place? He had shrugged and told her there had been no choice. And that was partly the truth. The real truth was he'd always known this country's name, never made the mistake of confusing it with an island nation thousands of miles away. When, for a few weeks one year, the country was briefly in the news, he knew a little more about it than most, at the very least he knew its correct location. Sierra Leone, the place where his mother had nearly been born.

Nine-thirty-five. He really must be gone. The bird is no longer feeding but sitting at the apex of a curl of razor wire. Adrian carries the plate he has been using as a palette to the sink, holds it under the tap, watches the colours as they run into each other. He leaves the plate upside down to dry on the draining board and goes around the flat turning off lights.

On his way out of the house he takes down several of the reference books from the shelf, tucks them under his arm. He steps outside, into the heat and light, closes the door carefully behind him, turns his key in the upside-down lock and slips it into his pocket.

CHAPTER 8

Adrian and Elias Cole meet each week, at the same hour. Around them the hospital is in constant motion day and night. Adrian finds he has to think, when writing up his notes, consciously, of the day and date, to count forwards from the moment of his arrival. Even the month he forgets. In England, the days would have begun, tentatively, to reach out with silver fingers in each direction. Here, the patterns of the sky elude him. *Red sky at night, shepherd's delight. Red sky in the morning, shepherd's warning.* But what is one to make of a violet sunset? Or a white evening sun? The one thing of which he is certain is that it is getting hotter. Instead of becoming used to the heat, he is ever more tormented by it.

Adrian is still in the occasional habit of bringing something to each session. Once it was a novel, Huxley's *Antic Hay*, from the collection in his rooms. A newspaper bought from a roadside vendor, two thin leaves of dense, smudged text. A radio. He forgets the man's feelings about music. In time he removes it.

There are days when he must attend the Ministry to sort out his papers. The Labour Office is located on the sixth floor of a building without electricity and consequently no working lift. So far it has taken him several visits on different days to obtain the appropriate forms, establish who is the person who will process them. The man in question possesses a huge, shining bald head, is dressed, always, in a dark-blue safari-style suit and is never to be found in his office. Often he finds him sitting in the corridor talking with others of his kind, chewing matchsticks or cola nuts and watching people like Adrian come and go.

Thursday Adrian arrives back at the hospital exhausted and yet full of nervous energy. He sits down by the old man's bed. Elias Cole turns and watches him, but doesn't speak. Together they inhabit the amniotic stillness of the room, silent save for the old man's breathing, the muted sounds from outside.

His private clients in England, from the moment they left the room they ceased to exist. He did not allow their lives to spill into his.

Here it is different. From the moment he enters the old man's room it is his own, Adrian's, life outside that seems remote and unreal. His life in England even more so.

★

Exams had begun. The campus was quiet. Behind the windows rows of students, heads bent, dressed in the obligatory black trousers or skirts and white shirts. Along with the other staff members I took my turn invigilating. I enjoyed the peace, walking the aisles, handing out extra paper, warning the passing of another hour.

In those periods of enforced idleness I thought often of Saffia. The smooth mask of her beauty in repose. The rapid succession of her expressions as she listened to a story, at such times her face had an extraordinary mobility. She was not much given to talking, a listener by nature and by marriage. Julius and Saffia were like the sun and the moon. Everything revolved around Julius, or he behaved as though it did, you were drawn into his orbit. But Saffia was the moon, emanating her own clear, magnetic energy. The one to whom all our stories were told.

Though when Saffia had something to say, it's true she didn't hesitate to speak her mind, which was a sufficiently unusual quality in a woman that I was unused to it. She chided me once, for my languor. It was during one of their Sunday-night suppers. We were discussing the price of commodities, of rice. It was a subject I knew little about, but Saffia was full of stirring opinions. She felt an affinity with the farmers, you know. I must have been slow to respond because she berated me. For being too comfortable, she said, like a cat with its own place by the fire.

A married woman. Now when I think of it, I wonder if that isn't where the answer lay. It gave her a confidence other women lacked or better say 'could not afford'. Women in those days accorded more readily with what was expected of them. This seemed less true of Saffia. Julius gave her everything. Those evenings we spent at their house, Ade, Kekura and I, she needed nothing from us, and so we were drawn to her all the more, competing among ourselves like performing monkeys.

Those days, in the exam halls, I let our conversations run through my mind like a looped tape. I rehearsed in its entirety my last visit, when she had taken my photograph, adding a remembered detail here and there. I turned over each moment, examining it from different angles, for new meanings. I wondered if she had taken the film to be developed, whether she was, at this moment, looking at my image. She had not told Julius of my visit, I felt certain. And that meant something. What possible reason could there be for her to keep the fact of it from him, but that she intended it to happen again.

In this way I indulged myself, exquisitely, achingly. I had never been in love before. I had no idea. Hopes building up, fragile and heavy as crystals upon a filament. I was without caution.

Outside the routine of exams I took the opportunity to pursue my efforts to see the Dean. What Saffia had said, about my languor, was not entirely true. I had submitted and had rejected my paper, 'Reflections on Changing Political Dynamics'. That week I stopped by his office and spoke to his secretary, who guarded him like the Oracle at Delphi. I was apportioned a thin slot of time at the end of the day. I arrived with my arguments rehearsed and ready.

The Dean was a small man, dark-skinned, balding and possessed of a quicksilver energy, with tiny hands and feet, and high round buttocks which pitched him forward, so he appeared to approach the world at a trot. Stacked upon his desk were piles of papers, each wrapped around with a rubber band. The desk itself was a massive affair, dark wood with the high gloss of the reproduction, the surface of which was inlaid with green leather with a border of tooled gold. A green onyx paperweight and a pen in a matching stand, an ivory letter-opener and a brass nameplate, similar to the one on the door. Behind the Dean's chair on a stand stood a massive globe of the world, *Typus orbis terrarum* scripted above the tropic of Cancer. A ship scurried across the line of the Equator to Africa, hastened by a puff of wind to its sails.

'How is everything, Cole?'

I replied that everything was fine, as well as could be expected.

'Good, good. All to your liking?' He sounded like a hotel manager. I nodded and gave a version of the same reply.

'Good, good.'

A pause. He offered me a drink. I accepted. He swivelled around in his chair and flipped open the top of the globe. Inside were several decanters, an ice bucket, tongs, highball glasses and tumblers.

'What will you have?'

'I'll have whatever you're having,' I said. 'Thank you.' I had read somewhere ordering the same drink as your boss was a sure way to impress, a tacit endorsement of their own choice.

'Hmm?' he said, as though he hadn't been listening. His back to me, I couldn't get a glimpse of his face. 'Tell me what you'd like.'

Better perhaps to be my own man. 'I'll have a whisky, please.'

The Dean occupied himself in a search, lifting and replacing decanters, inspecting the contents inscribed upon silver plates suspended around their necks. Several were empty. He gave the impression of a child at play with a new toy. Finally he lifted out a decanter in which an inch of gold-coloured liquid swirled, removed the stopper, froze for a moment as though interrupted by a new and startling thought, shook his head slightly, replaced the stopper and returned the decanter to the globe.

'I think I'll send out for some soft drinks.'

I said, 'Thank you.'

He picked up the telephone and called the secretary, who arrived momentarily with two bottles on a tray, opened them and handed us one each. The Dean raised a bottle to his lips and sucked reflectively at the top. I followed suit.

'How are you finding the office? Comfortable enough for you?'

Again I nodded. Ten minutes had passed and all we had covered were the pleasantries. He leaned back in his chair and the leather squeaked beneath his buttocks. I imagined his feet, below the enormous desk, the tips of his shoes hovering an inch above the floor.

'Good. Good.' He placed his hands on the desk in front of him and spread his fingers. His next remark appeared to come out of nowhere.

'It's a real responsibility, you know, administration.'

'Of course.' What else but to agree?

'Oh, it doesn't attract the accolades of academia. You know that. I know that. And yet great societies are built on their administrators. We are historians. It's not us who make history. Nor the generals. It's the administrators. Who were the first administrators in this country, Cole?' He had been staring dreamily out of the window. Now his neck snapped back and his gaze was redirected to a spot in the centre of my forehead. Before I could reply he was wagging his finger at me in warning, as though I was about to give the wrong answer. 'Not the British, though they like to take the credit. It was the Fula! Yes. Cattlemen and shopkeepers. And, I know and so do you, Cole,' that gimlet eye daring me to say otherwise, 'once rulers of the largest empire in West Africa. I should say *arguably* the largest, because of course records as such are scant.'

He pushed himself back into his chair; the leather sighed again as it accommodated his movements. I waited, still perplexed by this turn in the conversation.

'Their gift didn't lie in superior fighting skills. Those they subjugated were mostly farmers, not warriors. Their gift, their trick,' and here his voice grew louder until he shouted out, 'their *brilliance*, was to leave an administrator in every town and village they passed through. Somebody to keep the local rulers in check, and to make sure the right taxes were paid at the right time. All without the benefit of a filing system. Less red tape that way. Ha!' And he gave a bark like a cough. 'Native administration, you see. The British didn't invent it after all! But red tape, now that really was their contribution. Ha!' He barked again. 'Forget the politicians and the soldiers. Learn to respect the administrators!' And he wagged a finger at me again, but less threateningly this time, as though to assure me of the levity of this last remark. Then he shook himself slightly. 'But I don't have to tell you that. Your father was a civil servant.'

I nodded.

In a relative frenzy of creaking the Dean swung himself out of his chair and went to the window.

'You're generous with use of your office space. Excellent. I feel I made the right choice in you. Not enough space, the university was never built for so many students. Nobody stopped to consider the consequences of all these decisions when they made them. Only how popular they would be.'

'Yes,' I replied, the only thing I had really said so far. I was beginning to wonder if we'd ever get around to the matter of my paper. I ventured, 'I submitted a paper for the journal. I was wondering if we might . . .'

The Dean interrupted me with a wave of his hand. 'Ah yes, yes. Not really your best. I'm sorry, Cole. And space in the journal was tight.'

'I was hoping we could discuss the particular aspects you considered problematic.'

'Are you sure you want to discuss it?' I could see the reflection of his frown in the window. 'Very well. You started with the wrong question, hence the argument was flawed from the start.' He continued to stand with his back to me. I waited, but he added nothing more.

'Your written comments would be very welcome.'

He turned from the window, without looking at me, and resumed his seat, spreading his tiny hands out on the table again, as though inspecting his fingernails.

'My advice? The work it would take, you may as well start again. The journal committee are really looking for a different kind of thing.' Everybody knew the journal committee and the Dean were one and the same. 'Now if you were to take a look through the archives, we're lucky to have them at the university and they're an undervalued resource in my opinion. In Europe, as you know, modern history is taken to begin at the end of the Middle Ages. Not quite applicable to us here. Still, it gives one a lot of scope.'

And that, once I had finished my drink, was more or less where we left it. As I reached the door he made one more remark, with perfect casualness.

'Dr Kamara, from engineering. A friend of yours.'

'Yes,' I replied. 'Though I haven't known him for long.'

'No,' he replied. 'Of course not. Well, have a good evening.'

That same week my old friend Banville Jones invited me to a party on campus, and though at first I demurred, after another night home on my own the idea struck me as more attractive. On the Friday in question I popped my head round his door and said I would join him. There were more parties in those days. Or perhaps it just seems so to me now. No, I believe it was a time of parties. We were happy, at least we thought so. Rushing headlong into the open space. The euphoria was a long time dying. We partied through the curfews, arriving late and staying until dawn. Even when the curfews were over, because by then we were in the habit of it.

The space was crowded by the time we arrived, the party in full swing; people spilled out on to the verandah and into the garden, moving in and out of the light and shadows. On a low table, open bottles of Johnnie Walker and Bacardi, a bucket of ice.

Inside people shouted at each other, above the music and the laughter. In a corner next to the record player a few couples swayed, snapping their fingers. Banville Jones plunged ahead while I stopped a yard inside the door. The atmosphere in the room was hot and sticky; within a few moments the sweat began to rise on my upper lip.

Banville Jones and I had already left the campus for a few beers and it's true to say I was already a little drunk by the time I arrived. I'd forgotten whose party it was. Not that it mattered. The crowd was drawn by word of mouth. Hearing about the party constituted its own invitation. I helped myself to a glass of whisky and squeezed through the crowd until I reached the patio doors. Insinuating myself into somebody else's conversation seemed like an uphill task and I began to review my judgement in coming. I moved outside and stood with my back against the wall of the house, found myself in the glare of a light and moved away. A moth, dancing around the light, cast bird-sized shadows. I made my way towards the steps leading down to the garden. There was a weight in the air, heavy and metallic. The outline of the hills, like a crouching animal, lit by distant lightning. I could see one or two people I vaguely knew, but could not be bothered to expend the energy of saying hello. I took a sip of the whisky. A low verandah wall offered a prop. I placed my drink upon it. There was an abundance of women, and lazily I considered engaging one of them in conversation. I thought of Vanessa, of whom I had seen little since the evening at the Talk of the Town. My decision. She would have forgiven me, though it would have cost me the price of a new dress.

Beneath the overhang of a large shrub, I thought I caught sight of Ade, the distinctive block-shaped head. Yes, it was he. And next to him, Saffia! She was standing straight, like a schoolgirl, holding her handbag with both hands before her, no drink – at least none that I could see. It was impossible to tell, in that moment, whether she had just arrived or was on the verge of departure. My heart sprang ahead of me as I moved towards them taking careful steps, to disguise my condition.

'Elias,' she said, seeing me first of the two; her smile was open and happy. Ade pressed a hand upon my shoulder.

'Hey, man.'

'I didn't know you were here,' I said. I don't know why I said that. Saffia was never one for small talk. I lit a cigarette, my hands shook slightly.

'We were talking,' she said, 'about which one of your senses you would give up, if you had to.'

It seemed a reprise of our conversation at the Talk of the Town. 'Hearing,' I said immediately. And she laughed.

'Yes. I believe that about you. But you wouldn't be able to talk to people either, of course.'

I shrugged. 'Sight, then. And you?'

74

'Well, that's what we were just discussing. I don't seem to be able to give up any of them.'

'Smell?' I said. 'It could even be an advantage at times.'

'The smell of a flower, of the rain, of your own children. So much of taste is based on our ability to smell. So think what else you would be giving up. Anyway . . .' She let the thoughts trail away. 'We were just being silly. How are you, Elias?'

I replied I was well. At that moment Ade took the opportunity to move away and talk to another of the guests, leaving Saffia in my care, an unspoken thing, as though she were a precious object that required guarding.

'Where is Julius tonight?'

'He should be on his way.'

'He let you come here alone?' Irresistible, to take a swipe at one's rival.

'Ade came with me. Oh, you know Julius.' She laughed lightly and added, 'Or maybe you don't. My husband has many strong points. Timekeeping isn't one of them.'

And so we stood, making conversation against the barrage of noise, at other times simply watching the people around us. I fetched her one Coke and another. Of Julius there was no sign. Next to me, I felt her shoulders drop. Rain began to fall out of the black. To avoid a soaking, we moved indoors, where even more people were crammed into the room.

An argument started, between two men, one of whom was Ade. In a moment Kekura, who I had not even known was present, had waded in, on the side of his friend. I believe they were discussing the situation in Nigeria, where secessionists were seeking recognition for their illegal state. Ade thought our faculty should call a strike in support of our colleagues over there. I suppose Ade might have had some Nigerian ancestry, as suggested by his name, though I have no idea which parent or even which part of that country. The energy expended between them could have defeated the national armed forces of Nigeria, gesticulating and pointing at the ceiling, each participant raising his voice above the other in an effort to press home their advantage. In the corner the dancers turned up the music. I had sobered up quite a bit by then. I turned to Saffia and offered to take her home.

'Actually I drove myself here,' she said. 'I could drop you off if you like.'

As we walked to the car, it began to rain hard. Windless, the water dropped vertically out of the sky. Saffia pulled a plastic rain scarf from her bag and tied it under her chin. The rain brought forth the smell of the soil, and lent a freshness to the note of jasmine in the midnight air, a reminder of our earlier conversation. As we walked, she talked about the university grounds, how they contained so many species of plants, some quite rare, others imported. She had been involved in cataloguing them, collecting specimens to be dried and labelled.

Inside the car the windscreen was opaque with condensation and our breath, the wipers working furiously. Beyond the gates the rain and the dark had driven people indoors, doused the oil lamps of the street sellers, cleared the rubbish and the pedestrians off the streets. She drove leaning forward to peer through the windscreen, as though she were peering down a well. At a crossroads we nearly missed a roadblock and the figure of a soldier swaddled in a plastic cape appeared before us. A flashlight and a tap on the glass. Saffia wound down her window.

'Yes, sir. Sorry oh!' I leaned across Saffia, smiled and touched my hat. I reckoned on a night like this he wouldn't want to bother with us. It was a matter of speaking to him in the right way. I could make out nothing of his face, just a dark shape behind the glare of the torch. I was wrong. He was having none of it, irritated by the wet, I suppose, and the irksome nature of his duty.

Saffia handed over her documentation, and finding no satisfaction there, the man next wanted to search the boot. I told Saffia to stay where she was and stepped out of the car. I told him I admired the job he was doing, and his thoroughness. I brought out my packet of cigarettes and offered him one, as well as a little something to buy some food. It's easy when you know how, no more than the seduction of a woman who desires to be seduced. Soon enough we were on our way.

In the passing lights, I caught glimpses of Saffia's profile as she stared ahead, her brows drawn together. After a time she spoke.

'Did you give him something?'

'Just a few cigarettes.' Actually, the best part of the packet.

'You shouldn't have.'

'It was nothing.' I shrugged. I thought she was thanking me.

Minutes later the rain eased. At the junction to my house she pulled over.

'Elias, would you mind? I think maybe I should get home.'

'Of course. It's stopped raining. I'll walk from here.'

I stood and watched the tail lights of the car shimmer on the wet road, grow small and disappear. I felt exhilarated. At the same time I had a sense of having somehow mis-stepped. I lit a cigarette from what remained of my packet. And I set off towards the bridge and home.

CHAPTER 9

There are lawns and it is such a long time since Adrian has seen a lawn. True, there is lushness in the trees and the foliage, the hills behind the city are densely green, but the soil is cracked and the earth raw. Adrian craves the sensation of soft grass beneath his feet, the dampness of dew. He would like to take his shoes off and walk across the lawn, feeling the blades between his toes, the hems of his trousers grow heavy and damp. It is an illusion. The grass here is spiky, and sharp. Walking across it would be like walking on hot coals.

And it is quiet. At first the silence, abrupt and arresting, pervaded everything. Now, as Adrian walks alongside the woman, he becomes aware for the first time of different sounds, murmurings and mutterings, muted sounds. He can hear the wind in the tops of palm trees, reminding him of spinnakers in the breeze. And he can hear the sea.

They stop at the door of a long, low building. 'OK. Ready?' the woman, who is called Ileana and works here, asks. Adrian nods. She pushes open the door.

The smell hits him and clots in the back of his throat – fermented and feral, the smell of hiding places and of stale fear. He begins to breathe in short, shallow breaths, drawing air in through his mouth. The room is in twilight. Presently he is able to make out two rows of beds and mattresses, each one with a figure lying or sitting on it. Ileana walks up the centre aisle. Adrian follows her, aware of the stark sound of his shoes on the concrete floor, looking from side to side, taking in the stained mattresses, the marks on the walls, shadows of those who have leant there. At their approach some of the patients begin to stir. In front of a tall iron bed Ileana halts and so does Adrian. A man lies on his side on the bed, his head resting upon a coverless pillow.

'Hello, John, how are you?'

At the sound of her voice, the man hauls himself around to face them both. 'I am well, Doctor,' he answers and begins to lever himself slowly up. 'How are you, too?'

'I'm fine, thank you, John. I have somebody with me today. Another doctor, from England. He'd like to know about us.'

The man on the bed turns his head to take Adrian into view, at the same time as he pulls himself up into the sitting position. There is an intermittent scraping sound of metal upon metal. The noise seems tremendous in the quiet of the ward. Once he has righted himself, the man extends his hands and the noise starts again, as of something unravelling. For some reason it makes Adrian think of ships. He looks down at the man's hands: wrists wrapped in rags, metal cuffs, hands clasped together in greeting. The sound stops abruptly, leaving a faint ringing in the air, as the man on the bed reaches the full extent of his chains.

Wednesday. The call had come that morning from the police station. Adrian arrived to be taken to the same room by the same woman officer as when he had examined the young deaf boy. This time she stood some distance from the door and allowed him to go forward alone. Inside the room was a man, apparently sleeping, curled up with his back to the door, his hands tucked between his knees.

'What's he doing here?' Adrian asked, glancing at her over his shoulder.

She shrugged. 'The family brought him.'

'Has he been violent?'

'This is what they are saying,' she said, in an offended tone. 'They don't want him there. They say they're afraid of him. That he barricaded the door and wanted to attack anybody who came in. They worry he'll break the whole place down.'

'But the problem, exactly? Why did you call me?'

She hadn't even been bothered to look at him except for a fleeting glance, her eyes empty, face suffused with boredom. She tapped her temple with her forefinger.

Adrian knocked on the door and entered the room, noting the rapid retreat of the policewoman.

Once inside he closed the door and stood with his back to it. There was the sound of heavy breathing.

'Hello,' he said. At the sound of his voice the figure on the other side of the room moved an inch or so further to the wall. The breathing hastened, a stream of garbled words.

Adrian paused, then continued moving forward, announcing each action. 'I hope you don't mind if I come a bit closer. I want to talk to you. Is that OK? I'll keep coming until you tell me to stop.'

The babbling grew in pitch and fervour with every step, but the man no longer seemed to be trying to move away. A few feet short of him, Adrian dropped down, so he was squatting almost level to the figure.

'My name is Adrian. I'm a doctor. What's your name?'

A response, of sorts, in that the sounds grew quieter.

Adrian waited.

'I'm sure you must be hungry. Are you hungry? Would you like something to eat?'

The murmuring quieted and ceased, silence but for the sound of breathing. The figure began first to strain and then to rock, until with a great effort it flopped over, like a fish. In front of Adrian lay a young man, bound hand and foot.

They wanted rid of him. Adrian made it clear that the provision of water and some food might hasten that eventuality. Using his own money, he managed to secure a loaf of bread and a small plastic bag of water and drinking straw. Not one of the police officers would acquiesce to run the errand himself, so Adrian had to wait until a person of sufficient insignificance – one of the ubiquitous small boys of the city – could be found.

Adrian agreed to accompany the prisoner to the mental hospital. With the help of two male officers, he bundled the young man into a taxi, propping him up on the back seat. By then he'd resumed his babbled discourse, as though complaining about his treatment, and was shivering violently. Adrian slid in alongside him. The young man flinched and huddled further away.

'It's OK,' said Adrian as he bent and undid the ropes that bound the young man's feet.

The taxi driver, reluctant and sullen, demanded double the fare. The policeman's answering laugh contained not a trace of humour as he banged the roof of the vehicle with the flat of his hand. The thunderous sound reverberated around the inside of the vehicle, setting the young man off again. The taxi pulled away.

Reluctant to leave his charge alone, Adrian waited inside the gates of the mental hospital, seated on a wooden bench. Next to him the young man drew his knees up to his chin and pulled his T-shirt up over his face. At an open window a woman, naked to the waist, stood shouting to unseen persons. There were people milling inside and outside the gates, though none appeared to be figures of authority. A couple of men were talking, bickering in the manner of long-term acquaintances. One had shown Adrian to the seat, but otherwise left him unattended. A bitch stealthily attempted to gain entry through the gates.

Adrian was uncertain what to do next. He called to one of the pair of men. Yes, yes, said the man, smiling and holding up his hand, telling Adrian to wait. Adrian resumed his seat on the bench. The heat had risen, he was beginning to sweat. A man stood outside the gate, his ears and nose plugged with paper, and shouted, 'Don't talk to me like that! I am not a patient any more.' Next to Adrian the young man rocked from side to side.

In time a man in a white short-sleeved shirt and white trousers appeared from around the corner. A nurse. He called to the woman at the window to be quiet. The woman promptly disappeared. One of the men standing at the gate gave him a broad wave, encompassing Adrian in the same gesture. Finally, Adrian got to his feet.

The nurse led the way, impassively, at a metronomic pace. To Adrian was left the task of coaxing the young man along. As soon as they left the gateway the silence began, which combined with the manner of the nurse seemed to quieten the young man, whose anxiety gave way to bewilderment. They were shown into a room, empty save for a desk, a chair and a glass cabinet containing a number of textbooks. The nurse fetched another chair from outside. He pointed first at the young man and then at the chair. Remarkably, the young man obeyed, shamblingly, sat keening from side to side. Adrian noticed how extraordinarily clean the nurse was, the evenness of his hair, the burnished skin. His clothes pristine. He watched him leave, closing the door behind him, all without a single word.

A few minutes later and the door opened again. The nurse held the door open for a sallow-skinned European woman. 'Thank you, Salia,' she said. She wore a smocked top over a skirt, a pair of slip-on casual shoes, dark-red lipstick and carried with her the smell of fresh cigarette smoke. Adrian covered his relief at seeing another white person by explaining what he knew of the patient.

The woman stood listening, her hands in the deep pocket at the front of her smock, and looked him up and down. 'Who the hell are you?' she asked.

Together they watched as the impeccable nurse supervised the removal of the patient by two attendants in blue overalls, standing balanced on the balls of his feet, arms crossed, a consistent two paces away. Not afraid of the patient, afraid of getting dirty, thought Adrian. The woman introduced herself as Ileana. She was the second-in-charge, a psychologist.

'We'll check for malaria first,' Ileana said. 'Sometimes it's as simple as that. The disease can cause hallucinations, as I'm sure you know. Though families usually recognise the symptoms for themselves. Then we'll check for all the rest, starting with drug abuse. He seems to have calmed down at any rate and we can give him some haloperidol to keep him quiet.'

Since Adrian had nowhere else to go, he'd asked to be shown around. Ileana glanced at her watch and then led the way outside. 'The facility survived pretty well. None of the buildings were destroyed. Ah, Dr Attila!'

Coming towards them, the senior psychiatrist returning from his rounds. Adrian recognised the name from a report in the *International Journal of Social Psychiatry*. And though he often imagined the authors of reports, imprecisely, in some vague way, invariably and archetypically as thin, colourless, reedy academics, of the man approaching them he had been able to produce no mental image whatsoever. A certain awe attached itself to Attila's name. Adrian saw a broad-chested man, in a collarless shirt, slacks and open sandals, gesturing to his left and right with huge hands, flanked by a blue-clad attendant as well as a number of others, who from their demeanour Adrian judged to be patients.

'Let me introduce you,' said Ileana, placing herself in the path of the psychiatrist, who had so far showed no particular signs of slowing. As she introduced Adrian Attila glanced his way briefly, but did not offer his hand.

Finally he scratched his ear and said, 'In whatever way we can help you, you're most welcome.'

'Thank you.'

'Just let Salia know.'

'Salia?'

'Our head nurse.'

Adrian thanked him again. Then added he'd wait until he had looked around, he wanted to know about services: occupational, psychotherapeutic, recreational. Perhaps he could talk to all the staff?

He'd welcome the opportunity to come back. And the social workers, naturally. As he talked, Adrian wondered why he had never thought to come here before.

'Of course. Ileana can deal with all that. Anything else you want, just ask.'

Despite the generosity of the words, there was something faintly bullish about the man's manner, in his posture perhaps, the broad body, which never inclined towards Adrian. He waved his huge hand, had already begun to move away. Adrian would have liked the opportunity to continue the conversation, though perhaps not so publicly. All those people listening in, even the patients, as though they were part of it. It bothered him, this absence of privacy.

They walked on. 'Sorry about that,' said Ileana. 'He can be that way sometimes. We'll begin at Ward Three.' She drew a packet of London cigarettes from the pocket of her smock, waved the packet at Adrian, who shook his head. She lit up and walked ahead, puffing. 'As I was saying, and as far as I know, most of the inmates survived. There's not a place in the world − rich or poor, frankly − where madness doesn't make people afraid. Call it fear. Though part of it's respect, too. After the invasion of the city the rebels left them alone. Attila was in charge all that time. They looted everywhere and set fire to people's houses, burned hundreds alive. The poorest people, of course. Always. Forced them to march into the city, to act as a human shield for the fighters. There were atrocities on all sides. So when things turned even worse, especially during the occupation, people hid inside these walls, pretending to be crazy. Poetic, don't you think? This is, after all, an asylum. There were a couple of peacekeepers in here as well.'

'I didn't read any of that in the reports.'

'No, well . . .'

'And what about you? I mean, how long have you been here? Which agency are you with?'

She looked at him, threw her cigarette down, went to grind it with the toe of her shoe, but missed as the cigarette rolled away down a faint incline. She didn't bother to pursue it. Nor to answer his question. They had reached the door, grey-painted, of a long, low building, the shape of a barn. She paused with her hand on the handle.

'OK. Ready?' she said.

Adrian nodded.

*　　*　　*

83

He is not ready, though. For this. He isn't yet able to make sense of it, but he will. Attila's manner. The silence that overlays the entire place. They keep the patients drugged. Drugged and chained. The man in front of him has his hands out and clasped together; it is a way people here have of saying hello, a shorthand to an actual handshake. From the man chained to the bed the gesture looks remarkably like prayer.

'Tell the doctor what brought you here,' Ileana says.

'I cut my father. My father brought me here.'

'Why did you cut your father?'

'He was sitting on the verandah. It was one night. A bad night. I was afraid. I didn't cut him.'

'So why do you say that you did?'

'I saw the wound.'

Afterwards, as they leave the ward, Adrian asks, 'What's his diagnosis?'

'Psychosis. Drug-induced.'

'And the drug of choice?'

'Cannabis mostly. There isn't much else anyone can afford. There's a bit of heroin. Brown brown, it's called here. But that's a lot more expensive, obviously, and has to come in from elsewhere. Most of them on this ward are the same.'

'All cannabis?'

'Yes,' she replies, turning to meet his gaze as she says the word. And then, 'He was transferred from the military hospital after Attila intervened. "Wounded in Action." I think the father sought Attila's help.'

'So he saw action?'

'I believe so, though I'm not sure of the details. You'd have to ask Dr Attila about that. John's been in and out of here for the best part of a decade. The war began in '91 and I'm not sure exactly when he was discharged. Certainly the army was where he began to use drugs. It was encouraged among the new recruits. They called it Booster Morale. As far as Dr Attila is concerned, he's a casualty of war.'

'So now his answer is to keep the man chained.'

She regards him for a moment in silence, dips her chin and looks at the floor.

'Looks like you dropped something,' she says, pointing.

His eye travels to the floor. There is nothing he can see.

'Where?'

84

'Right there.' She points.

Adrian sees nothing but a patch of lino, curled and broken. He frowns. 'What is it?'

'Oh, about two million dollars, I think.'

'I don't understand.'

'What it would cost to put in a proper security system: infrastructure, staff, training.'

They are on the other side of the door. Ileana reaches into her pocket for her cigarettes and lighter. She turns away, trailing smoke.

'I'm sorry. I just want to know about the treatment methods.'

'We have a method,' she says. 'We call it cold turkey.'

Ileana walks and smokes. Adrian, unsure of his response, walks alongside her, waiting for her to say something more, realising she does not intend to.

'So why did Dr Attila say . . .?'

'Exactly,' she says, laughs briefly and gives him a humourless smile. 'Now you get it. You should have been here at the start. But of course you weren't. Nobody was. You all turn up when it's over. Shit!' And throws her butt into a flowerbed.

At her office Ileana unlocks the door with a key she draws from her smock pocket, crosses the room and plugs a kettle into the wall.

'Back in the 1980s the country was being run into the ground. Attila was already working here by then. On his own. He trained abroad and came back after his studies were over. I think there was a Brit in charge up until that point, but gradually they were leaving and being replaced by Africans. He must have been pretty young to take on such a responsibility. At that time the population he was treating was pretty much the same as anywhere else: schizophrenics, psychotics, depressives. The usual breakdown of nutcases. Then, at some point, that began to change.'

Ileana makes tea in a small silvered pot. Lipton Yellow Label, it takes an age to brew and even then the tea achieves no more than a pale gold.

'In the early 1980s there was an influx of new admissions; Attila saw it first. He was the one admitting them. They were mostly young men, late teens and early twenties. They came from the city but also from the provinces, either without family or thrown out by their families. All with drug-related disorders. Within a few years, the make-up of

85

his population had inverted. Those who'd once made up no more than a tenth were now the overwhelming majority.'

She pauses to stir and then to pour the tea, hands Adrian a cup. There is no air conditioning in the room, no fridge either. The windows are all closed. What he'd in fact really like is a glass of cold water, but he accepts the tea without complaint. He wants to get over the bad start he seems to have made with Ileana.

'He wrote to the government, the newspapers. Something was coming. Of course no one took him seriously. The government ministers laughed and said he was as batty as his patients. But he went on, to the World Health Organisation. The government began to get irritated with him. Fuckers. He was trying to warn them. And then in the 1990s. Whoosh!' She throws both hands dramatically up in the air. 'Hundreds, thousands of young men, high on drugs and very, very angry. No jobs. No families. No futures. Nothing to lose. The thing that was coming had arrived.'

In the silence Adrian drinks his tea. Ileana fetches a tin from the top of a filing cabinet and offers him a biscuit from a selection. He takes one with jam in the middle, like the ones he used to enjoy as a child, licking out the sticky, synthetic centre. He hasn't had one in years. Ileana opens a window and a faint trickle of breeze reaches him. On the wall behind her desk a sign reads: *Some days it's just not worth chewing through the straps.* The conversation picks up and strays on to other subjects. He asks her where she trained, as a way of trying to locate where in Eastern Europe she is from.

'Tel Aviv.'

'Ah.'

She smiles for the first time, knowing she has confounded him. 'My initial training was in Bucharest.'

On the way back to the front gate they pass a building, smaller than the rest, and set slightly apart. Outside it is a washing line upon which are strung several *lappas*, lengths of printed cloth, limp with age and wear. At the back a woman is bent over a cooking fire. The women's quarters.

'Can we take a look?' asks Adrian.

'Don't see why not,' Ileana shrugs, tosses her half-smoked cigarette on to the ground and leads the way, introducing Adrian to the female attendant at the door.

Inside the room the beds are fewer and therefore more widely spaced than inside the men's ward. The rank odour is less present, possibly because the windows are open. None of the patients is restrained. Some are sitting or lying on their beds, at the far end a woman is folding clothes, nearest the door another sits cross-legged on her bed. She looks up at Adrian and smiles suddenly and warmly; one eye is cloudy, her hand plucks at the bedclothes as she babbles nonsense. They are, Ileana explains, mostly schizophrenics, some personality disorders. Few are violent, though they have to keep an eye on them.

'With women the families will try to keep them at home, seek treatment through local healers or religious leaders. So there are relatively few of them here.'

'Do they help? The local methods?' he asks.

'It's just care in the community under another name,' she replies.

The attendant, who has been shadowing them ever since they entered the room, says something to Ileana, who stops, holds up her hand, signalling for Adrian to wait. She moves forward, stopping a few paces in front of a woman who is standing facing them from the other side of a bed, sullen and motionless, a hairbrush in her hand. Ileana speaks to her for a moment. She turns to Adrian.

'This one's not good with men. They had a bit of trouble with her the other day, apparently. I hadn't heard about it. If you've seen enough we may as well go.'

'Sure.'

Ileana gives instructions regarding the patient's medication to the attendant. Adrian waits, looking around him. There is a woman lying in one of the beds, curled upon her side, hands under her chin, her eyes open, staring into the middle distance. He takes a step forward and peers at her, but moves no nearer, less concerned with his own safety than subverting Ileana's authority.

When Ileana joins him again he asks, 'What do you know about this woman?' It is her, he is sure of it, the woman who came to see him in the hospital and who approached him later on the street. She had fled then and never returned.

Ileana tilts her head on one side and peers at the woman's face. 'I've never seen her before, I don't think. Mostly it's Attila who deals with the women's ward.' She turns to the attendant, speaking the local dialect.

'She was admitted two days ago.' She interprets haltingly, her attention given to listening to the attendant. 'Somebody brought her. She's not sure who, but it wasn't a family member. Somebody off the street. She's confused, apparently.' A pause. 'That's it.' She is about to continue walking when the attendant speaks again, saying something which causes Ileana to raise her eyebrows and grunt with faint surprise. 'Every few months or so. She reappears every few months. It's a regular occurrence, apparently.'

Through the open office door Adrian can see Attila bent over his desk. Thankfully he is alone. Adrian knocks softly on the door. He is suddenly nervous, the memory of the man's earlier manner and also now the possibility of being refused. There is no reason, after all, for the man to say yes except as a professional courtesy. Adrian's sliver of hope rests on Attila seeing it that way. At the second knock Attila waves him in without looking up and points at an empty chair. Adrian obeys. Attila signs off on the document in front of him and rises, paper in hand.

'One moment,' he says to Adrian. 'Salia!'

A moment later the nurse glides into view and Attila hands him the document, issuing instructions as he does so. He returns and sits down behind the desk, regarding Adrian with no particular sign of warmth.

'How may I help you?'

Suddenly Adrian is in two minds whether to ask about the woman at all, but now he is expected to say something.

'Thanks for letting me look around.'

'My pleasure,' replies Attila, and inclines his head without smiling, as though he means nothing of the sort. He leans back with his hands spread out on the desk in front of him and waits for Adrian.

'There's a patient on the women's ward.' Adrian plunges straight in. 'She was admitted a few days ago. I'm told not for the first time.' He describes the woman he has just seen. Attila nods once, yes, he is aware of the patient. Adrian continues, telling Attila how the same woman had been to see him at the hospital. In the moment he decides to omit any mention of the encounter in the street. The psychiatrist listens expressionlessly and without comment until Adrian finishes.

'So what is it you think I can help you with?'

Adrian takes a breath. 'I'd like your permission to examine her, if I may.'

'By all means.'

It had been that easy. Adrian realises he has been holding his breath and exhales, wondering why he'd allowed himself to become so tense.

'Come back when it suits you. I will inform Salia. Her notes will be made available to you.'

'Thank you. Thank you very much.'

'We are,' says Attila, turning upon Adrian a fathomless look, 'at your service.'

It is enough for Adrian, who rises to go. By the time he reaches the door, Attila's attention has shifted back to the paperwork on his desk.

For the second time in the same day and with Ileana's help, Adrian succeeds in securing a taxi to himself. Despite the heat and the speakers relaying rap music directly behind his head, he luxuriates across the plastic-covered back seat.

For the first time since his arrival he feels a small sense of triumph.

At a T-junction next to a garage a traffic policeman is waving his arms in the air, rotating them like windmills. It seems to be a fashion among the new recruits to develop an individual style, a kind of a semaphoric signature. On three sides the traffic stops and starts in confusion. Inevitably, there is a collision, minor, but chaos ensues as the two drivers get out of their vehicles and a crowd, including the traffic policeman, gathers.

Adrian's driver exhales huffily, turns up the music and pulls out around the fracas, skirting the cars and people, turning right down a road Adrian has never been before. Suddenly the way ahead of them is clear. Adrian winds down the window and lets in the air, salt and marshy. In between the speed bumps, the driver accelerates. The houses come to an end. There is an expanse of scrub, a view of the sea and a bridge, stretching out ahead of them. As they cross it Adrian sees, to the left, an inlet leading to swampy, open land. To the right, the horizon, a straight blue-grey line. His thoughts are brought back from the mental hospital.

The bridge; he sits up and looks around properly. Over there, the peninsula. And this bridge is the one Elias Cole described. Exactly as he described, Adrian is certain of it.

Julius's bridge.

CHAPTER 10

It is something Kai enjoys. Keeps his fingers dextrous, like a piano player practising scales. And it entertains children. He holds up the single piece of orange peel, the entire skin of the fruit, so it falls into a natural helix, and hands it to the girl pressed up next to him on the bench. He places a segment of the fruit in his mouth, gives the next one to one of the children, sharing the segments out until the orange is finished. The last piece he hands to the girl next to him. When he stands, she stands alongside him. When he walks, she shadows him, one step behind. Bump, scrape, pushing her bamboo walking frame ahead of her. He turns and squats, pushes a forefinger experimentally into the space between her leg and the plaster.

'Good?'

A nod.

He moves away. She watches him go, leaning across her frame, like an old woman at the garden gate.

He passes through the children's ward, still decorated with the remnants of Christmas, tinsel and twists of coloured paper. There'd been presents this time, donated by a Western charity, who sent a photographer along to capture the occasion. The children sat unsmiling, clutching the presents on their knees. The photographer, a middle-aged German, had tried to press them into unwrapping their gifts. The children weepily resisted his encouragements. Finally he had removed – wrenched – the gift from the arms of a five-year-old, and begun to tear the paper away. The child's distress reached a new pitch, to cease suddenly when the man drew from the box a small wooden house. In moments the room was filled with the sound of tearing paper, scrabbling fingers. The photographer, happy now, clicked away for minutes. Kai stood smiling in a white coat and stethoscope he rarely wore, clapping along with the other staff members.

One parcel contained a plastic gun. A scuffle broke out between two of the boys. One of them, in fact the smaller of the two, wrestled the gun successfully from the other, forced his companion to his knees, hands behind his head, and shot him in the back of the skull. The rhythm of the clapping grew ragged. Mrs Mara stepped forward and removed the weapon, gave the child another toy and resumed her place in the line, the gun held behind her back.

Outside the swing doors of the outpatient department a boy, long-limbed and languid, is sitting in a wheelbarrow. His right knee and lower leg, massively distorted, is bandaged and propped out in front of him. Next to the boy his uncle fans flies away from the leg. Even at this distance the odour reaches Kai, sweet and high like rotted flowers. The amputation would take place in the evening. He pauses in front of the pair, asks the uncle who is to give blood for the operation. The man taps himself on the chest. The boy, feverishly beautiful with cheekbones cut across his face and huge, heavy-lidded eyes, stares into the middle distance, dreamy and preoccupied. He looks other-worldly. It strikes Kai how death, so often ugly, can sometimes arrive in the guise of such beauty.

Diagnosis: Sarcoma. Advanced. Proposed Treatment. Kai had written on the admission form, *Surgery. Amputation of left leg. ATK. Grounds: Compassionate.*

In the antechamber to the operating theatre he changes his clothes, tossing the used greens into the bin, kicking off his flip–flops and slipping his feet into one of the pairs of rubber clogs. Some of the visiting foreign surgeons have their own pairs, initialled in black marker pen upon the toe. Kai is content with one of the general pairs; they are a luxury, still.

He takes a cap from the shelf and sits down on the bench, flexes his fingers. Sometimes he remains in the changing room for minutes at a time, opening himself for the state to arrive. He read something once, on artists, performers, and their relationship with their work, and recognised himself in the description. One of the writers had commented that it was not so much a matter of waiting for the muse to descend, as opening oneself to receive it. Kai knows that when the sounds around him begin to recede, when the edges of his mind draw in and the horizon comes closer, he is ready to begin. In that state he had learned to work under almost any conditions. As he had for months under flickering lights, a generator roaring in the corner of the room, pausing motionless with his instruments held in the air, like a conductor at the start of an overture, each time the machine broke down and somebody was sent to coax it back into life. As he had when there were no anaesthetists available, when the patients were tied to the table and told to clamp down on a twisted sheet. Kai lost himself amid their screaming, failed to notice when and if they finally fainted. All the time making do with whatever instruments were available, even kitchen utensils.

During emergencies he is rushed, spinning on adrenalin, into the maze, racing down the paths, left and right, trusting his judgement to avoid the dead ends and wrong turnings, searching for those pinpoints of light. Now the hospital has money, some at any rate. The buildings have been renovated, there are doctors on sabbatical from overseas.

Today a letter from Tejani. Kai slips it from his back pocket and smoothes out the creases over his knee. In the computer age, they stick to this old-world form of correspondence. Tejani, he assumes, has a computer at home. But for him it means a trek into town to an Internet café, the long wait for a connection, the ponderous typing of his message – his fingers never having acquired the agility over the keys they possess when handling medical instruments – only to lose it when the server crashes or the electricity cuts out. The blue aerogramme bears a date some two weeks prior. The postal services are erratic, yet this is how they both seem to prefer it.

The anaesthetist puts her head around the door.

'Ready when you are.'

'Coming.' Kai places the letter on top of his clothes, closes the locker door and follows her out.

First thing in the day they deal with the scheduled operations, then perhaps an elective and then whatever emergency has brought in. Keeping busy is the one way he knows to keep things under control. When he is not operating he writes up his notes meticulously and drinks coffee, or volunteers to help in the second theatre where a surgeon is often working alone. Other times he writes to Tejani, details of the procedures he has carried out. He has few friends among the staff. The African staff, who comprise almost all the nurses but only a few of the doctors, all have homes and families. The Western staff live and socialise in their own cliques, arranged by language mostly, sometimes age or ethnicity. Generally they stay only a few months and in that time Kai will extract from them whatever threads of knowledge he can: the Scottish expert in pain who demonstrated how patients felt phantom pains in limbs they no longer possessed, the plastic surgeons who arrived in teams of four and worked around the clock for two weeks, the eye surgeon who rotated between the hospitals in the city and upcountry and who set a stopwatch for each operation to remove cataracts and liked to joke, to relax his patients, that he could perform with his own eyes shut.

And when, finally, Kai can extend his day no longer he will pass outside the staff room, where the doctors gather at the end of the afternoon, and head to the empty apartment, which few know exists. He will lie on the sofa, hating the prospect of sleep, checking the luminous numerals of his watch and counting off the hours of darkness. Sleep, when it comes, arrives in flights, accompanied by a rush of images or sometimes lingering dreams. He wakes, often, bathed in sweat. In the morning he stands beneath the shower waiting to feel restored, then he begins to work again.

Inside the theatre they are ready to start, but for the fly. Now hovering above the lights, now perched upon the window frame. A masked nurse flicks at it with a cloth. Some joker has posted a sign on the OR door: *No Fly Zone*. Kai waits while efforts are made to remove the insect. On the shelves are stacked bottles of saline solution, rolls of cotton, catheters, IV lines, braided silk, needles, polyester suture and boxes of gloves. Unimaginable a few years ago. He thinks of Tejani.

Once, as students, they travelled together to a town upcountry to find a doctor of whom they had heard, who was conducting research into Lassa fever. The man and his work had achieved a mythological status among the student body. The fever affected populations only in rural parts of West Africa, peasants and farmers. No drug companies had ever funded programmes into its cure, though the virus, which was carried in rats' urine, had been identified in 1969. The infection started with a headache, ended in death, blood pouring from the body orifices. Some claimed the doctor had a world-class reputation. Others that he didn't exist. They'd hitched up one Saturday morning, Tejani and Kai, chased by the momentum of a late-night drinking session, and a handshake bet. Neither had travelled outside the city for several years, and neither could tell if the other was serious. The roads were appalling, nervous truck drivers insisted by then on travelling in convoy. They arrived after darkness. In the town they searched for a bar in which to relieve their hangovers, the edge of the thrill already blunted, their minds turned to getting back for Monday lectures. Two soldiers, stepping out of the black, asked to see their papers and what their business was in town. Tejani had spoken for both of them, as was the way in their friendship. He was honest, he told the soldiers they were students, of the doctor for whom they had come. There was nowhere in the world where doctors weren't cherished. The soldiers had led them to him.

They found the doctor still at work, late into the night beneath a lone, insect-spotted, forty-watt bulb. He worked with a single assistant. Tejani and Kai waited in silence until he was ready for them. A small man, who seemed uncomfortable in his skin and baffled by their visit, though gracious enough. Kai remembered seeing a picture of him some time later, at an awards ceremony for his work, wearing an outsize suit and the same expression of bafflement, surrounded by European faces. Two images of him: that one, which came later, and the first, of him working on the other side of the room, handling samples of contaminated matter, wearing a snorkel and mask, and a pair of household rubber gloves.

In those days they had learned to make do. Throughout the whole of their medical training, it had been the same. One would perform a procedure, the others watch. It has become part of him, this lack of need. And there is always a fly. So they decide to proceed, as they always do. Time in the operating theatre is marked out in precious minutes.

The amputation patient is lying on the table, arms outstretched, one arm hooked up to the blood-pressure monitor, the other to a line into which the nurse is pumping ketamine. He is strapped to the table to prevent him moving should he begin to hallucinate. Kai has seen a patient try to stand up in the middle of a procedure, heard another talk to his dead mother. Tejani had written to him of nightclubs in America where people lay in darkened rooms, knocked out on ketamine. During the war commanders had given the drug to child combatants just before they sent them into battle.

In this most recent letter, Kai thinks he detects a new mood of confidence. Tejani's letters of the first two years have been full of laments. It has been Kai's job to reassure him. Now, for the first time, something different. Come, Tejani is saying to his old friend. *Come.* The word acts upon him all day, making him restless, like a grain of sand between skin and shirt.

Kai swabs the area where the first incision will be made with a mixture of water, iodine and ampicillin.

Seligmann, the Canadian surgeon whom Kai is assisting, is ready to begin.

'Cutting now.'

Kai closes his eyes and opens them. He breathes in, lets all the sounds behind him fall away, all except the voices of the team and the sound of the instruments.

CHAPTER 11

A photograph.

'I had Babagaleh bring this in. I hadn't seen it myself for years. It was among the things we were packing up a few weeks ago.'

The garden, a vast sweep of foliage, seems to merge with the sky, heavy black-and-white clouds, brightened by a glint of silver, like far-off lightning. By contrast, beneath his hat the face of the man in the pale suit is shadowed. Adrian can see, though, that it is Elias Cole. Elias Cole thirty years ago.

★

I think it would be wrong to say I ever *followed* Saffia. In conversation the names of places she liked to visit or where she did her shopping might arise. Later, I might jot the detail down in my notebook. And if I happened to find myself there at any of those times, naturally I would look to see if she happened to be there also. Sometimes I might say hello. Other times, I thought it better not to intrude on her thoughts. I might have watched her from a distance. That was all.

In Victoria Park I saw her walking towards the library carrying a small pile of books shadowed by the shambling figure of a lunatic. I stepped up alongside her and shooed him away.

'Oh, Elias! You frightened me.' And then when she saw the man with his matted hair and beard, thick curling fingernails, she said, 'Oh, there's no harm in him.' She reached into her handbag and found a few cents. 'Come. Come.'

The man edged closer, keeping me in the periphery of his vision, until he was close enough to reach out and take the coin from Saffia. He smelled appallingly of piss.

'Thank you, Ma. God bless you,' and he bowed and retreated, somewhat as a waiter might.

'All the same you should be careful,' I said when he had gone.

We walked on, passing the statue of the British queen, along the pathways of cracked concrete. She lowered her chin, smiling to herself.

'Look at this. Have you seen this before?' She reached up, bent down a stem of bougainvillea, its head crowded with papery petals. 'See. Three different colours. No, four. On the same shrub. There are a few like this on campus, too. Have you ever noticed? Somebody took a great deal of trouble once upon a time.'

We reached the library steps. There she stopped and half turned towards me, one hand shielding her eyes from the sun.

I groaned and smacked my forehead with my palm. 'Oh, no! Excuse me, please. I hope he hasn't let it go. A volume by Sayer. The library copy has been out for weeks. Missing, probably. You'd be amazed what you can find at the second-hand stalls down here.'

She smiled. 'I must take a look one of these days.' She raised her free hand. 'Well, let me not keep you.'

At the top of the stairs she turned around and caught me watching her, lowered her head and quickly pushed through the revolving doors. I turned, walked past the second-hand bookstalls without stopping and made my way home.

The first thing to go, in matters of this kind, is judgement. I yearned for her. I lived in constant frustration. As soon as one meeting was over, I began to plan where and when the next might occur.

It is true to say no woman had ever produced such a restlessness in me. I had never been in love. Once or twice I'd whispered the words, idly, to certain women. Always in the moments before the act of love itself. But I knew, if I had not known before, that the affection I had felt for those creatures was like comparing the pleasure of a summer's day to the terror of a storm. I was lost in the darkness amid thunder, blinding flashes, the madness of the wind. I was caught up in a tempest, I had lost all sense of direction. If Saffia found my appearance in various places unusual, she had never commented upon it. This single fact I now allowed to lend a recklessness to my warped judgement.

Friday. Four days after our meeting in Victoria Park. I stood at the side of the road and watched the people pass in groups on their way to the mosque. It had just stopped raining, the sky was pale and clear, stripped bare. The voices of the passers-by rang out, lent clarity by the purity of the air. Nobody paid me much attention. After a few minutes the door to the pink house opened and the crone stepped out and paused there for a moment, framed by the darkness of the hall. Swaddled in green cloth, her prayer beads entwined in her head covering, she tweaked the folds of her gown, tightened the grip on her purse and launched herself down the street. I watched her figure dwarf in the distance, then I crossed the street and knocked at the door.

Saffia regarded me in silence for several moments.

'Hello, Elias,' a note in her voice, of weariness or caution. She did not open the door, but held on to the handle.

'I'm sorry. I woke you. You were sleeping, perhaps.'

'No, no,' hurriedly, for I dare say Saffia couldn't stomach such a notion of herself as the kind of woman who slept in the afternoon.

'Then you were on your way out.'

She wore a simple house dress and at that she glanced down at it. Quite plainly she was going nowhere. In the end she had no option but to move aside. 'Come in, Elias.' Her tone was less than welcoming, but I did not let that stop me, as perhaps I should have. 'I don't have very long. I have to go into town,' she lied. Not a natural liar, too vague, too slow off the mark.

I sat in my customary chair on the verandah. Even dressed as she was in a loose house dress, a batik design of greys and greens, her hair in plain braids, no woman I had ever met could match her beauty. The telephone rang and she went to answer it. Her voice drifted back to me and I listened to her end of the conversation, trying to work out who she was speaking to. Whoever it was I was jealous of them, of the presumption they owned in calling her whenever they pleased.

In front of me, the sky, vast and empty. Pools of water had gathered in the garden and were beginning to hum with insect life. The rains had set the frogs off, like a chorus of drunks. Solitary drops fell from the ends of the leaves and from somewhere the sound of running water. When Saffia returned to the verandah she did not offer me coffee or a glass of water, she sat down and placed her hands in her lap. I was tempted to ask her who'd been on the telephone; instead I said something about the garden, something vaguely complimentary, about its appearance after the rain.

'Except for the Harmattan lilies,' she responded. She was happiest talking about her garden. 'They prefer the dry. It's the end of the season for them.'

There came the sound of the door and of somebody entering the house. I thought it was Julius even though I had left him in my office less than an hour before. He was in the habit now of using it when he

98

pleased. The door swung open. I steeled myself. Saffia jumped up and hurried across the sitting room.

'Auntie? What have you forgotten? Let me fetch it for you.'

Not Julius then, but the crone, muttering and shuffling past Saffia on her way to her room. Saffia followed her, placing her body between the woman and the verandah where I was sitting, hovering outside the woman's door. In time the woman emerged and, as she did so, seemed to catch sight of me, for she stopped, turned and shuffled forward, peering through the glass. I nodded to her, but if she noticed she ignored me. I heard her say something to Saffia, I can't tell you what, because I didn't, don't speak their language, but it was all there, in the scolding tone. Saffia closed the door behind her and stood holding on to the handle, her back to me.

When she returned she had withdrawn from me further still. My visit had become untenable. Even so, I couldn't bring myself to leave. What I did next I did out of desperation. It wasn't what I wanted. I'd imagined it differently, over lunch or in a café, perhaps. Or in the dark hollows of a garden, at a party, left alone for a few minutes. Or walking side by side through Victoria Park. Not the Victoria Park of madmen, beggars and second-hand books salesmen. Another Victoria Park, peopled by students reading in the shade of the frangipani trees and couples like ourselves, one that existed only in the landscape of my imagination.

I had no idea when I would next get the chance to be alone with her. I panicked. I reached out my hand and would have touched her arm, had she not risen swiftly to her feet.

'Forgive me, Elias, I really must get ready to go.'

Some days later I was in my office. Julius entered. It did me no good at all to see him.

'Cole, Cole, Cole.' He was shaking his head. 'My wife . . .' And he wagged his finger at me.

I confess it gave me a jolt, but then I saw he was grinning. I forced myself to smile back, and to greet him. I could hear my voice, cracked and hollow.

'Oh, Cole, Cole,' he said. 'My wife is very upset with me. She asked me to give you this a long while back. And I forgot all about it. I've had to beg her forgiveness.'

He placed upon my desk an envelope, yellow with black squares, of the kind you get when you have a film developed. And inside – the images of me, taken at their house the day of my first visit.

So she had told him. Julius had known all the time.

He sat, perched on the edge of my desk; by then he was talking about something else. I forced myself into the appearance of listening. I was distantly aware of him punching my shoulder, of the door closing behind him. I murmured something, I let him go. I sat still, gazing at the surface of my desk. I felt a flicker of something burning in my bowels. Not dislike, it was impossible to dislike a man like Julius. Not dislike, then. A small flicker of hate.

CHAPTER 12

An evening, Friday, Adrian waits for Kai. It is early still and the bar is close to empty. His beer, a local brand, is gassy and pale. Adrian watches the other customers: a pair of African men, friends of the bartender, a small group of expatriate men at the bar. Two local girls keep company with the expats.

A trail of sea air reaches him through the other, darker odours. The beer is his second on an empty stomach. As Adrian looks around his eyes come to rest on one of the women. She is wearing a purple top, leaning her body against the man in front of her, her head over his shoulder. Of her companion Adrian can see little more than an expanse of back, a striped shirt, a tanned forearm. The woman is pretty by any standards, resting against the man with feline languor. Adrian watches her, mentally positions himself in place of the man against whose chest she leans, imagines the feel of her breasts, and wonders what it would be like to have sex with her. He takes a moment to speculate how such a thing might be managed. Would he come here alone, wait for her to approach him? Sit at the bar, perhaps?

Now he realises that she has shifted her gaze and is looking directly at him. She holds his eyes unabashed. A long, dark, opaque stare. Embarrassed, Adrian turns away.

Adrian has spent the better part of the morning at the mental hospital talking to the attendants and staff, those who might have more information on the woman patient. Accompanied at first by Salia, he had eventually managed to persuade the nurse to leave him to his own devices.

From the staff and from the hospital records, Adrian learned there was a pattern to the woman's admissions. Loosely speaking they occurred every six or seven months. On each occasion she'd been found wandering. Hardly extraordinary in a country where so much of the population had been displaced, still the woman had been brought to the hospital by a stranger or strangers, whose names had sometimes but not always been recorded. Her psychiatric records were neatly kept though scant. No more luck, either, with the ward notes. The attendants had little in the way of formal training. Adrian had spoken to them all, careful to show due deference. A few more details had emerged. Once she had been found outside the gutted ruin of a department store. Twice she'd been examined by the visiting physician, who found her to be in good physical health. No evidence of substance abuse or epilepsy. Her sojourns at the hospital lasted a few days, two weeks at most, and concluded, Adrian was surprised to read, with a self-discharge on each occasion. Her name was Agnes.

When he was as satisfied as he could be, Adrian had gone along to the women's ward. It was lunchtime. An attendant stood in the middle of the ward ladling rice out of steel vats on to plastic plates. The women moved forward, forming a semicircle around the trolley. From the other side of the room a woman crossed the floor with a stiff-legged gait, the Thorazine shuffle. A long time now since Adrian had seen it. In the trembling hands of others, he recognised, too, the side effects of Haldol. Agnes was sitting on the edge of her bed, holding the plate in her left hand, eating carefully with her right hand, wrist held high, delicately gathering the food with her fingers. He noticed she didn't lick her fingers clean like most of the others, but poured water over them into a basin from a plastic kettle by the side of her bed.

Adrian approached her from where she could see him. She gave no indication of having heard him. He positioned himself so that he was standing in front of her, leaving her no choice but to look at him.

'I am Dr Lockheart.' Not strictly true, but he'd learned how it worked here. She looked up unblinking, the light of her eyes unchanged, either by recognition, or confusion. 'Come,' he said, and indicated to her to stand up. He turned and walked away, slowly at first, until he felt her following.

'Do you know who I am?' Adrian was sitting in Ileana's chair, the woman opposite him. Salia had come to act as interpreter. Now he put Adrian's words into Creole. They had discussed this already; if the woman was from the city she would understand. If she was from elsewhere Salia might or might not be able to help.

Agnes sat, curled upon herself. She offered no answer.

'Can you tell me your own name?'

She was silent still, though she had moved her head slightly at the sound of his voice. Her fingers worried at a loose thread in her dress. He repeated the question. This time there came a sound, a murmuring, as though she was trying out sounds. In this way she failed to answer any of the basic questions Adrian put to her. The date, day or time, a knowledge of where she was. He watched her carefully, the sideways motion of the head, the pauses in the plucking of the thread. He gathered an impression that she was at some level computing the questions. She hadn't yet looked at him.

'Do you know how you came to be here?' She looked up, rolling her head back on her shoulders, and gazed somewhere into the space between him and Salia leaning against the window ledge. A dark line appeared between her eyebrows, her breathing quickened momentarily. She rubbed her hand across her face.

'Did you come here on your own or did somebody bring you?'

The plucking stopped and started again furiously. Adrian paused, aware of Salia watching from the sidelines. All this would be reported straight back to Attila, for sure. Agnes's fingernails were trimmed, he observed, her hair was neatly braided. Either somebody did these things for her, or she did them herself. He doubted anybody in this place was responsible for such a degree of care.

He altered his tone to one of brisk impersonality. 'Can you count your fingers for me?' She looked down at her hands and moved the fingers one by one.

'One. Two. Three. Four. Five,' she whispered.

'Good. And the other hand.'

This time she missed her thumb, finished up on four and sat staring at her hand.

'Try again.'

'One. Two. Three. Four. Five.'

So she was in there, somewhere. And she understood English.

Later, in the same room, he drank tea with Ileana and described the woman and their session. He had concluded it after fifteen minutes, long enough to gain an initial impression. To Ileana he gave an account of what had occurred.

'My guess is that she's from a reasonable background.' Her appearance, composure, the fact she understood English. 'I'd certainly like to know who brought her here. Maybe they could be of some use.'

'Quite probably. Or not. If her appearance is as you say, then that might encourage someone to bring her to a safe place like this. Hoping for a reward or a tip, either from us or the family.'

'Has anyone made enquiries with the police?'

'I doubt it very much. Even if we thought they'd be cooperative, who here has the time?'

They'd left it there. Adrian would examine her again in two days' time.

He is on his third beer when Kai arrives and drops into the chair next to him without apology. He lifts a hand at a passing waiter, indicates Adrian's beer, holds up two fingers. Adrian has grown used to the silences, their textures and shades. Around them the bar is filling. A mass of insects thickens around the fluorescent lights, their humming resonating with the buzz of the lights. By the time Kai is on his third beer, Adrian is hungry. They order skewers of roast meat, smeared with crushed groundnuts and pepper. Elated and now somewhat drunk, Adrian orders another round. He is tired, and he savours the feeling, the exhaustion that comes from a hard day's work.

He hums along to the music. Another beer. And another. A woman standing at the bar is watching Kai. Square-shouldered, blonde hair, the skin on her back and shoulders faintly pink and filmed with moisture, exposed by a blue halter-neck top. He can see the pale outline of her bikini straps, the red swelling of an insect bite. Her mouth is open, eyes narrowed, head angled. Her pose is one of concentrated desire, such that Adrian, shocked, looks to see whether Kai has noticed. Kai drains his bottle and gets to his feet, headed for the toilet. As he does so he staggers slightly.

'Watch how you go.'

The woman pushes away from the bar, moving towards Kai, never once taking her eyes from him. When he straightens himself she is there in front of him, her breasts pointed at his chest, so close her body almost touches his.

'Hi,' she says and puts out her hand, into the narrow space between them. 'I'm Candy.' Or was it Sherrie? Some such, later Adrian cannot be sure. He is taken aback by her boldness. 'Can I buy you a drink?'

Kai looks down at the woman, who waits in the moment of silence that wells briefly up in the wake of her question.

'No thanks.' He places his empty bottle carefully on the table.

The woman makes the best of the rebuff, pushes her lips into a moue of mock disappointment, lifts her shoulders, puts her head on one side and looks up at him. But Kai is already off, headed for the toilets. She shrugs and saunters back to her friends, resumes her place by the bar. A moment later two Middle Eastern–looking men, swarthy and tight, move from the other side of the bar to take up positions either side of the woman and lean across her, breathing into her neck, touching her hair. And she is laughing again.

Adrian turns away, thinks again about his friend, about the wall inside him. Kai occupies only the present, reveals little of his past. Of the manner of his existence when he is not at the hospital, Adrian has no real idea, imagines only a house with relatives, a shared room, cloths strung up against the light. He is adept at taking care of himself, though, so perhaps a houseful of bachelors. Where else does he spend his evenings? In places like this? No. This is for Adrian's benefit. At night Adrian hears the sounds from Kai's dreams, footsteps late into the night that begin and end in no place, has lost count of the times he has come through to find Kai awake and dressed, while the stars still glimmered in the sky outside.

Kai returns; he has stopped at the bar on his way and purchased two more bottles of beer. Adrian, because he has been thinking about these things, asks, 'Ever been married?'

'Who, me?' Kai deflects the question.

'Yes, ever been married?'

'Nope.' He upends his bottle of beer, tipping the liquid down his throat, his eyes on a point somewhere past Adrian's shoulder.

Adrian takes a sip from his own bottle. The food has helped and his head is, for a while at least, clear again.

'Once, nearly. I thought about it,' says Kai.

'And?'

Kai shakes his head. 'We were too young. At least so I thought. I'd set myself a lot of things to do when I graduated. A few things got in the way of that.' He belches.

'Like what?'

'A little thing like a war.'

'What did you want to do?'

'Plans, man. I had big plans.'

'To do what?'

'To be the best, I guess. Just that. Me and Tejani, he was my friend back then. We never imagined it any other way.'

'What happened to him?'

'Gone.' He waved vaguely as though he were swatting a mosquito. 'And the girl?'

'Ah.' He swallows from the bottle until he has to stop for air. 'The girl? She's still out there.'

It is midnight. The crowd has thickened into a mass. Inside the fluorescence illuminates some faces like moons, while outside other faces slip in and out of the darkness. On the dance floor a coloured ball transforms the sweat of the dancers into glistening trails of red. Adrian and Kai sit alone at their table, marooned in the middle of so much noise and heat, like shipwreck survivors, exhausted, pleased to be alive. A song begins, with a South African rhythm. *Congo maway, congo. Congo mama.*

'Come on.' Kai is up and swaying on his feet. He is on his way to the dance floor. Adrian is drunk enough to follow. Together they dance, nobody cares. The blood and alcohol in his body, the lights, cause Adrian's head to begin to spin again. He feels certain if he let himself go limp he would be buoyed along by the welter of bodies. After a while the dizziness overwhelms him and he makes his way back to the table, where he sits and watches Kai, his head tilted back, eyes half closed, dancing on.

CHAPTER 13

Julius. What would you like me to tell you about him? He was a person who believed in himself, in the purpose of his existence, in his own good fortune. Julius didn't like to be alone, he required companionship. He sought out my company, and in many ways, it seemed to me, he had come to depend upon it.

Once we made a trip to the casino. We were together without either of our women. By that time my relationship with Vanessa had shrivelled to virtually nothing and I was still at odds as to how best to conduct myself around Saffia given the unfortunate outcome of my last visit. Julius, unaware of all of this, came to my office looking for entertainment.

We had been drinking. The suggestion was his, as most suggestions were. He grew exuberant under the influence. In that way, as in so many, we were opposites, for drink has always caused me to close in upon myself and, if bothered, I am prone to lash out. Julius felt lucky, and he declared it aloud to the empty street as we stepped out of a bar and headed in the direction of the casino. He stacked his chips on a single number. I spread my chips carefully. The wheel spun. I won, modestly. Julius lost, royally. He celebrated his losses at the bar.

That was the night I learned Julius was an asthmatic. While we were in the casino, something, I forget what, struck him as amusing. He began to laugh. The illness showed in his laughter, laughing was apt to set off an attack. That was why Saffia had looked at him with such concern that first dinner at their house. This time the laugh turned into a cough, he had been coughing a lot recently. The change in the seasons, perhaps. The dust in the air had lessened as the harmattan drew to a close. But the rains brought their own hazards. Spores and pollens filled the air as new life burst forth. Within moments he was wheezing, a see-sawing sound, broken with intermittent bursts of coughing. He reached into his pocket, drew out an inhaler. I was surprised. I suppose in my mind I always thought of asthmatics as carrying considerably less weight than a man like Julius. I remember he had once told me that as a child he had nearly died. I believe he must have been talking about his asthma. He was the youngest, the only boy. I could see it all. He behaved as though the world had been made for him alone, a result of being constantly indulged, no doubt. Or perhaps also for so nearly having left it.

In the weeks that followed I was a guest at their house on two occasions. Both times at Julius's behest, and at the risk of drawing myself to his attention with a sudden display of reticence, I acquiesced. I could not resist the opportunity to be near her. I sought solace in the very thing that caused me pain.

Saffia's withdrawal from me took the form of unerring good manners. I alone noticed the way her eyes never sought mine, as they had before, unselfconsciously. And should our eyes meet by chance, her smile never broadened as it used to, but remained fixed in depth and width, quickly supplanted by an offer of more beer, an enquiry as to whether I was being bothered by mosquitoes, a suggestion to visit this place or that place, or meet this person or that person. She asked after Vanessa frequently. It is a way women have, or perhaps learn, of repositioning a man at arm's length.

On the second occasion I dined at their house, Saffia and I were left momentarily alone at the table. Julius and Ade had set out to fetch more beer. Kekura had disappeared into the toilet. She would not have desired it, this sudden abandonment by the others, but was left little choice but to entertain me. She filled the silence with a question, another one, about Vanessa's well-being.

'Well, that's just it,' I said. 'I'm afraid to tell you Vanessa and I won't be marrying after all.'

'Oh.' She was genuinely taken aback by this, as of course she would be. Wary still, though. 'I didn't realise. I mean I didn't know you two were engaged.'

'No, of course you wouldn't. And we weren't, not formally. I had hoped it would be so; Vanessa decided differently.'

'You should have come to see me.' Her face was full of concern.

'I did. I mean I tried. But your aunt . . . It wasn't the right time.'

A white lie. Essential to our friendship, to the delicate negotiations that kept it within the framework of the acceptable. I watched her face as the shades of knowledge deepened, the shift in emotions, the flare of relief, the flush of embarrassment that came with the realisation she had mistaken the purpose to my last visit.

'Perhaps I could talk to Vanessa.' She was keen to help now.

'Thank you, Saffia. But I don't think it would do any good. Any good at all.' I shook my head and stared down at my plate. A moment of silence. From somewhere in the back of the house came the singing of the cistern. 'There's just one thing.' One last tap, I couldn't resist but drive my advantage all the way.

'Of course.'

'If you wouldn't mind, I'd prefer we kept it between us. Not even Julius.'

'No, no. Don't worry. You won't have to put up with any of Julius's teasing.' She leant across and squeezed my forearm.

Friendship restored.

Moments later Kekura appeared, attending to the buckle of his belt and waving his damp hands in the air to dry them. I watched Saffia, who sat, the shadow of a crease upon her brow, still trying to compute what I'd told her and most of all, I suspect, the fact that she had apparently been wrong about my motives. Ah, the vanity of women! She'd allowed herself to believe I was attracted to her and so the freshness of relief contained a chill of rejection.

June. And the rains had settled into their stride. The water ran off the hills and out to sea staining the blue with a dark shadow of silt. In those hours in the late morning and afternoon when the rain let up and the sun shone, you could see the hills above the city, vibrant and green. With the students revising or else in exams, and many lectures and classes consequently suspended until the new academic year, the campus had the atmosphere of a seaside town out of season. With the exception of the holidays, this was the time I enjoyed the most. Space to think, time alone. These were the things I cherished. Not so Julius who, without the daily performance of his lectures and the adoration of his students, seemed bored.

I was at work, once more, on a paper for publication in the faculty journal. This time I had taken stock of my conversation with the Dean and come to the conclusion he was inviting me, if one could put it like that, under his wing – to become his protégé. In addition I had absorbed his advice over the choice of subject for my paper. We had spoken once more on the topic; he had passed me in the corridor, 'Ah, Cole!' and ushered me into his office. I was gazing at the objects on his desk, fixing them in my memory. Onyx paperweight. Pen stand. Ivory letter-opener. Nameplate. The Dean stood facing the window, his stiff little buttocks pointed at me.

'Are you a political man, Cole?'

I answered, honestly, I believe, that I was not.

'Good. In my view the job of we academics is to provide the perspective of the past. Leave the present to others.'

I mumbled a demurral, adding that surely the study of one period did not preclude the simultaneous study of another.

'I'm not suggesting anything of the sort,' the Dean had answered, somewhat testily. 'I'm saying we are historians, that's what we are.'

'Of course.' Frankly, I had no wish to get into a row. I needed several more publications to my name to stay on track to tenure. If the Dean offered me an administrative post as well, so much the better.

'A university is a place of learning, not of politics. And I like to run a tight ship. You see what I'm saying, Cole?'

He was referring, I think, or at least thought so then, to what was going on in Europe and in America, the demonstrations which seemed to be erupting everywhere. The year before was 1968. There'd been riots in Paris, strikes and student occupations in Rome. At Harvard the next year the administration building had been overrun. The same in Berkeley, in May. A student had been shot by the police. In his outrage Julius had burst into my office, shaking a copy of the newspaper. 'Kids, Cole!' he'd said. 'They were kids. If they're going to have the courage to question kicked out of them, who is there who will do it?' For a man of his size, he was quite excitable. He sat down, blinking. I believe there were tears in his eyes. I knew little of the riots or indeed what exactly had provoked them. Communist sympathisers, if you believed the authorities. Free speech, if you were with the students. I didn't put much store by either account. The students were troublemakers. The police were doing their job, with relish, undoubtedly. But doing it all the same. For me such antics were a world away. This was Africa. The 1960s had not reached us here. Well, that's not quite true. Some of the academics in other countries like Nigeria had involved themselves in politics, kicking up a ruckus over things they didn't like. But they were the exception rather than the rule. All it achieved was to lose them their jobs. And I wasn't sure I agreed with some of Julius's ideas about education. It was our job to get the students through their exams, that was all. In that respect you could say I was a traditionalist, like the Dean.

I steered the conversation back on track by raising the subject of my proposed new paper, 'Direct Taxation in the Early History of the Province'. The Dean, as he had already made clear to me, had the soul of a bean counter. Much as I expected, he was delighted with my proposal. There then followed a thoroughly enjoyable conversation between the two of us on the subject, during which he addressed me throughout as his equal. In time I rose and made to depart.

'Good talking to you, Cole.' And then, 'Cole?' I turned, my hand on the door. The Dean didn't look up at me as he rummaged around the papers on his desk. 'Your room. Weren't you going to give me a list of people who used it outside hours? Other than yourself, of course.'

'I don't think so.'

'Oh. I thought I'd asked you.'

I shook my head.

'Well, anyway, there's a meeting coming up about office space on the campus. It would be good to have some figures, to give me a picture. If not an overview, then an example to better our case.' He raised his head and looked at me directly as he said this.

'Of course. No problem.'

'Leave it in my pigeonhole.'

I assured him I would, and with that I made my departure.

CHAPTER 14

There, on the opposite path, Attila. It is the morning of Adrian's third visit to the asylum. He cannot help himself, he estimates the distance to the stairway to Ileana's office and calculates that an encounter is unavoidable. He feels a faint flush, something about the man unnerves him.

Attila seems not to remember his name.

'Of course,' he says when Adrian has supplied it, accompanied by a small deadly smile. 'So you're back. How are you finding things?'

'Fine. Thank you. Salia is being most helpful.'

Adrian doesn't want to say more until he has had the chance to examine Agnes again, until he has a greater sense of her condition. Here Attila is all powerful, his grace everything. The Minotaur inside his labyrinth. Adrian moves aside to make way for the older man.

Agnes is an enigma, still. The clues he has to work with are few. There is no evidence of delusions, she is calm. The attendants say she is one of the better patients, meaning she is not disruptive, complaining only of a headache. She seems to be in a constant state of readiness, as if waiting for someone or something.

Twice Adrian has interviewed her, both times in Salia's presence. On the last occasion Adrian borrowed from Ileana an orange, a sugar cube and a biscuit with a jam centre. 'Can you tell me the name of this?' he said, rolling the orange across the table towards her. He offered to let her keep each item she correctly identified. She'd been more responsive, and though still did not look directly at Adrian, she answered his questions. To Agnes he would likely seem a figure of some authority, an impression he decided to preserve. She could not remember how she came to be here or who brought her. Her voice was halting, he struggled to hear her and required Salia's intervention. From time to time she rubbed a hand across her face. Other times she twisted the corner of her *lappa*. And though she could not answer all his questions, everything about her manner was compliant.

Though he despises cheap tricks he picked up a mirror from Ileana's desk and turned it round to her. 'Tell me what you see.'

One minute rolled over into two; she continued to gaze at her image. Once she rubbed her thumb over it. She leaned forward and placed the mirror upon the table.

'What did you see?' he repeated.

She shook her head and frowned. 'The glass is no good.'

There'd been one other significant moment. It occurred as Agnes was leaving and passed Salia, in his customary stance, back to the window, hands folded behind him. She'd raised her chin and gazed out of the window. And then she had enquired of Salia, in an entirely conversational manner, why the harmattan had come so early this year. Were the rains over so quickly? And Salia had replied, softly and with deference, that the rains had ended several months past. That had been three days ago.

Today Salia reports he had been called to attend Agnes during the night. After the progress of the last few days she has taken a turn for the worse. A disturbance on the ward in the early hours of the morning. She'd been agitated and upset, talked of the loss of a gold chain and became frantic in her efforts to leave. He'd had no choice but to sedate her. Adrian listens to Salia, who stands silhouetted against the window, against splinters of white sunlight. Together they go to the female ward, where Agnes lies, still sleeping.

'Should we constrain her when she wakes?' asks Salia.

But Adrian cannot abide the idea. 'Just keep her quiet. Let her sleep it off.'

Salia's silent assent conveys a sense that he would do it differently, though it will be as Adrian wishes.

Afternoon. Salia and Adrian are in town. Salia steps across the choked and foul gutter in his unblemished nurse's shoes. Tradesmen sit behind open wooden cases balanced upon stools. Salia passes between them, stops in front of a building and allows Adrian to take the lead. The stairway is unlit, the air sulphurous. At the first floor the door opens into a large hall. Inside the shapes of people move around in noise and shadows between cubicles delineated by lines of washing and makeshift cardboard screens. From outside, less than ten yards away, there is no evidence of this second city within the halls of the old department store. Adrian's foot knocks against a bucket, water sloshes over his shoe, the noise bounces dully off the walls. A woman's voice softly curses him. Adrian hesitates and Salia takes the lead once more. 'Excuse me, Ma?' to the woman as she rescues her bucket. He asks her where they might find the person they have come to find. Bent over her bucket, she raises her head and points.

They find the man, dressed in a vest and a pair of shorts, sitting upon a plinth once used to display mannequins. Yes, he says. It was he who brought the woman to the crazy hospital. He knew about Dr Attila. He hadn't wanted to leave her on the streets.

'You live here now?' Adrian asks.

The man nods. To Adrian's relief he speaks English. 'I was doorman here,' he adds. 'Before.' He says it as others do, in a way that conveys a sense of timelessness. Before. There was before. And there is now. And in between a dreamless void.

'Do you know her?'

'Yes. Her daughter worked here once, the ma would pass by from time to time.'

Sometimes he would go and call her daughter for her. A fine girl, the daughter. He and the woman would pass the time of day as she waited. The woman lived a way outside the city, he remembered, because when there was nothing else to say they discussed the state of the roads. That is as much as he remembers. Many years have passed. So much has changed. People say the woman has become possessed.

'Is that what you think? That she is possessed?'

The man stands up from the plinth to address Adrian: strained, slow movements.

'I have seen her here before. Sometimes, for some of us, they say spirits call. She is not possessed, but she is crossed, yes. And that makes some people afraid. I am not afraid, because I knew her before. But people now are not as they were, they are more fearful.'

The man accompanies them back to the stairwell. Adrian thanks him and shakes his hand. Salia leans forward and presses a few notes into his palm, and the man nods and closes his fingers around them. Silently he watches them go.

Outside they make their way back through the glare and the dust. Salia, two steps ahead of Adrian, walks like a dancer with his shoulders and chin straight, seeming almost to glide an inch above the ground. Adrian wonders how to engage him in conversation.

'What exactly did he mean when he said she was crossed?' he asks.

Salia turns to look at him. 'Why do you worry about this woman?'

The question, upon the lips of a psychiatric nurse, stops Adrian short. One of the attendants had asked the same thing, chuckling secretively as she waddled down the ward sprinkling disinfectant upon the floor, her manner suggestive of something faintly improper about his interest. Why this one? Why not? he wants to answer back. But he cannot think of any other answer apart from one that is true, because apart from the patient in the hospital, the dying Elias Cole, she is all he has. He has no desire to have to justify himself. Still, Salia is Attila's henchman.

'Shall we get something cold?' Adrian points to a seller with an ice box sitting upon his haunches under a tree. He needs to be in the shade, out of this unrelenting heat. Salia nods and orders crushed ice, choosing a topping in a lurid shade of yellow. Adrian asks for a Coke and searches in his pocket for the change. While Salia spoons crushed ice into his mouth, Adrian repeats his question.

'It is to say,' answers Salia. 'When a spirit enters a person sometimes it makes them act a certain way, what people call crazy. So he is trying to tell you the woman was acting crazy when he found her. That is all.'

Later, in Ileana's office, Adrian carefully rereads Agnes's notes. On the wall he stares at a map of the country. Holding on to the patterns, the order of vowels and consonants of the unfamiliar place names mentioned in her notes, he locates them one by one. In an ashtray on Ileana's desk he finds a small number of coloured drawing pins, also three earrings and a safety pin with a ribbon tied to it; he uses them all, pressing them through the paper. In this way he marks each separate location, including the place where he saw Agnes in the street his first week in the country. He is standing back, reviewing his work, when Ileana enters and stands next to him smelling of smoke and perfume.

'Art therapy?'

Adrian smiles. 'Guess.'

'Something to do with your patient, right?'

'Yes.'

She gazes at the map, then shakes her head. 'Tell me.'

'They're all the places she was found before she was brought here.'

'Jesus fucking Christ!' says Ileana.

Side by side they stand and stare at Agnes's journeys mapped in colours and jewels.

Agnes sleeps. Both her hands are tucked under her chin, her body curled into a question mark. She is completely still, no fluttering of eyelids, a dreamless sleep. Adrian stands at the foot of her bed. He can barely discern her breathing. In the corner of the room a woman smiles and sings to herself.

Afterwards he walks through the gardens, past the lawns to a small cluster of trees in a hidden corner. The Patients' Garden, as it once was, has gone wild. Crazy paving. Anywhere else he might have imagined it as somebody's idea of a joke. The paths are overgrown, the air carries an odour of dead flowers mingled with the freshness of the sea. The ground is covered with long, curved pods, some of which have opened and spilt their seeds. An orchid, dark and dense, crouches on a branch above him. He ponders Agnes and her journeys. Fugue, they call it in his profession, a condition in which the body and the disturbed spirit are joined in shadowy wanderings.

Agnes is searching for something. Something she goes out looking for and fails to find. Time after time.

CHAPTER 15

The man on the table has dreams, he dreams of marrying. The most Kai usually knows about a patient is a name and a medical history, sometimes not even that much. But this patient is Kai's elective. His dream is to walk straight and find a bride, or perhaps it would be truer to say to become a groom. There are few who would give their daughter to a cripple, especially a poor one. His name is Foday. This will be his first operation.

Kai works the pedal of the diathermy with his foot, cauterising the blood vessels at the point of incision. In contrast to his youthful face, Foday's body is muscular and bears old scars, one on the heel of his right hand, another on the back of the leg upon which they are operating, upon his right buttock two small disc-shaped scars.

'Looks like he's been through the wars, this one,' says Seligmann. And then, 'Sorry,' as he catches the anaesthetist's glance. She is, Kai knows, merely confused by Seligmann's use of idiom. But he says nothing.

Foday lies on the table, asleep and naked. He has placed his dreams in the hands of the surgeons and his balls in the hand of a nurse, who holds them aloft, out of danger of the scorching end of the diathermy wand. He expects miracles, Kai knows.

An hour and a half later Kai, alone in the theatre, works on, soaking the plaster of Paris bandages in water and wrapping them around Foday's leg. The leg is straight now. Kai's hands work dextrously, smoothing the slippery plaster. Foday's other leg slides off the table. Kai moves around and replaces it carefully, leaving plaster of Paris handprints on the upper thigh. He is as intimate with Foday's body as with a lover. He takes a damp cloth and dabs at the chalky prints on Foday's thighs. There are splashes of wet plaster on his genitals and Kai wipes them too. If he has time, when he has seen how things are going in emergency, maybe he will stop by the ward, try and get there soon after Foday wakes up.

A hillside. How many years ago? Five, six. Kai, Tejani and Nenebah. Two of them revising for a test: textbooks and lecture notes, a picnic of peppered chicken and Vimto. They hadn't gone far, just the hills above the campus. There they had a view of the city, of the sprawling docks. The smell of dried grass. Tejani and he rehearsing mnemonics upon Nenebah's person. C5, 6, 7,' said Kai. 'Raise your wings up to heaven.' His fingers walked up Nenebah's back between her shoulder blades, using her vertebrae as stepping stones, feeling the muscles quicken at his touch before she let her arms float upwards like a bird in flight. 'Injury causes inability to raise arms past ninety degrees,' replied Tejani, lying on his back with his hands across his eyes. Kai laid the flat of his hand against Nenebah's back. And results in, Tejani spoke each word slowly, pushing against the effort of remembering. 'Winging of the scapula.' He lifted his hands from his eyes. Nenebah clapped.

'Don't Exercise in Quicksand,' said Kai. 'Diaphragm, External Intercostals, Internal Intercostals, Quadratus,' Tejani responded. Kai's fingers traced maps across Nenebah's ribs.

'I Long for Spinach.' Kai bent to Nenebah's ear and whispered, 'I Love Sex.' Her soft snort and giggle as she elbowed him in the ribs. 'Iliocostalis, Longissimus, Spinals,' Tejani recited. 'And I heard that, by the way, you two.'

Kai sitting facing Nenebah and Tejani. The sky behind them. Watching his face drift into hers, and back again, until he can no longer tell one from the other. A cloud passes in front of the sun, the shadows spread across their faces obliterating their features.

Another time. Before or after, he cannot be sure. The two of them alone, he lying on his back with his head in her lap, savouring the warmth and scent of her and of their recent lovemaking, gazing at an upward-tilted nipple. 'Nenebah,' he says. And she leans back on her hands, puts her head on one side, the better to peruse him and asks, 'Why do you call me that? Nobody else does.' And he replies, 'Because it is your name. Nenebah. That is your name, isn't it? Or am I getting you confused with somebody else?' And she grabs a T-shirt and hits him with it. And when he opens his mouth, the better to laugh at his own joke, she stuffs the shirt inside. It tastes of her.

He gives the finished plaster an experimental knock, pulls the cord for the porters. Afterwards, in the surgeons' rest room, he writes up notes of the operation. There is nothing for him yet in emergency. Mid-morning and the staff room is crowded. A year or so ago somebody had brought a miniature croquet game and the medics sometimes passed their breaks knocking balls across the lino. Now the miniature croquet has been superseded by miniature boules, though the balls are prone to skid and bounce. He is in no mood either for boules or for conversation. He passes by the window on his way to Adrian's apartment and lets himself in. Nobody is home. In the kitchen he switches on the kettle, and waits for it to come to the boil. A sunbird is perched on the feeder outside, hanging upside down, angling its head to reach the pipette. From the fridge Kai takes a plastic jar of coffee creamer and the box of sugar cubes, stirs one and then the other into his cup and carries it to the sitting room. He rarely eats until surgery is over for the day.

And today, another letter from Tejani, the second in just a few days. He has yet to reply to the last, though he has composed several different versions in his head. The timing of the letters' arrival is down to the vagaries of the post, the actual dates are two weeks apart. He spreads them both out on the coffee table in front of him, helps himself to a pen and paper from Adrian's store and sits down to write. In his first letter Tejani writes of awaiting the results of his first-stage professional surgical exams, of which he is tentatively hopeful. The second letter is much shorter:

Well, I did it, bro! I did it! Christ, though, I wish you'd been here. I had to put in a couple of all-nighters there at the end. Remember that time we did three in one week, until we ran out of candles? We sneaked into Mo's room and took his battery light and got it back in the cupboard in the morning. Man couldn't figure why the thing had run out of juice. And the palaver in front of the Vice Chancellor's office, when we went to hand in the petition. Those were the days, I was telling Helena about it. She can relate, being from Belarus. But I tell you, you should be here. You've got the qualifications and they're crying out for people like you and me, man. I can give you any help you need, but the agency handles it all anyway. Don't worry about where to stay. This place has a couch with your name on it. But seriously, if I get this job, I (we) am going to buy us a place and then you'll be welcome any time. Don't leave it too late. Kai man, I miss you.

If you go down to Mary's have a beer for me. Tell her 'how do' and that I'm doing good. Tell her I miss her food. Tell her I miss her big, beautiful tumbu.
  Your brother,
  Tejani.

At the bottom of the page, a postscript had been added using the same pen, but in a different hand.

PS. This is Helena, TJ's friend. TJ tells me about you all the time. This is true. I very much look forward to one day when we meet.

Kai starts to write and stops. It has been two years now and still he feels Tejani's absence, feels it in his soul, a yearning, cold and hollow. When Tejani left for America, they'd punched fists at the ferry port, making believe Tejani was going away for a few weeks. 'When you get there send something small for me,' Kai joked. They had turned away from each other. Kai thought of nothing but the next hour, the next day. He did not let himself think, was incapable of thinking, further than that. Tejani could, though. He had gone.

They'd always planned to leave together.

In the end he pens a paragraph congratulating Tejani on his exam pass, on being one step closer to membership of the elite professional body, which is his ambition.

He lays down the pen and sips his coffee, not knowing how to finish the letter. He should just take up Tejani's offer, send over his résumé. The coffee is tepid. He drinks it hastily, a half-hour has passed. From the table he picks up and pockets all three letters and lets himself out.

Minutes later he enters the ward. A nurse passes carrying a kidney bowl of swabs and a pair of forceps. She nods at him.

'He just opened his eyes. I was on my way to get him something to drink. Over there.'

'Hello, Dr Mansaray.' Foday's voice is husky.

'How are you?'

'I'm fine, thank you, Doctor.' A small grin. Kai can see how hard Foday is struggling to keep his eyes open.

'I just wanted to tell you everything went well. So fingers crossed, hey?'

'I will pray for that.'

'We'll take a look at that leg in a day or two, just to make sure everything's all right. May I?' Kai pulls the sheet down to uncover Foday's leg. The young man pulls himself up using his powerful arms and shoulders. From there he looks down at his legs, reaches to touch the cast. 'And we'll get you a wheelchair for the time being.' With those arms Kai doesn't doubt Foday will be able to wheel himself anywhere he wants to go.

'Yes, Doctor. May God bless you.'

Above the bed a photograph is tacked to the wall, one Kai has seen before. A Polaroid, taken around the time Foday was admitted to the hospital. It shows his legs from the waist down before the two operations. The weak calves, angulated from the knee, the feet below turned in upon themselves. Not one but two congenital abnormalities of the lower limbs. Blount's disease and talipes in both legs, plus a dislocated kneecap, which had floated around the side of his left leg. By contrast, above the knee, the thighs had the muscularity of a sprinter. His chest and his arms were massive. Unbelievably, Foday walked.

Four operations, then. Two to straighten the calves. Two to correct the ankles. And then the months of physiotherapy. Kai has no doubt Foday will see it through. He is a fighter.

A surgeon, recently arrived from Geneva, had passed by as Kai was examining the X-rays, stopped to look. He had been both shocked and excited.

'Do you know how often we see this in Switzerland?'

'How often?' Kai obliged.

'Never. Not once in my career. Tell me when you're operating. I'd like the opportunity to observe. If I may?' And he had bowed slightly, as though Kai was the senior of the two.

The war was medieval neither in concept nor in tactics, whatever the view from elsewhere, only in the hardware. From the outset the patients came in two classes. There were the soldiers and foreign peacekeepers, victims mostly of gunshot wounds, sometimes grenade and mortar wounds. In the second class were the peasants, the ones who somehow made it from their villages and were admitted with a *C* scrawled heavily on their charts. Unarmed and poor, the waste of a bullet wasn't so much resented as simply unnecessary. They were the victims of attacks using machetes and cutlasses. *C*. The doctor's own shorthand adapted to the circumstances. *C. Cleaved.* Kai gained hundreds of hours of experience in repairs, stitching layers of muscle, sewing skin, patching holes with pieces from elsewhere. Surgical housekeeping. Late in the war, the rebels advanced upon the capital and in advance of them came the first of the amputees. Mostly the team of surgeons concerned themselves with saving lives, cutting away necrotised flesh, repairing the 'hatchet jobs', the way they once, in peacetime, referred to the work of lesser surgeons. Though there were occasions, a few, when the attackers had been either merciful or inept, when it had been possible to reattach a tendon and restore a walk. Later a team of surgeons including Kai practised the Krukenberg intervention, unused since the First World War, fashioning out of the muscles and two bones of the wrist a pair of blunted pincers: a hand. Ugly, it was true. But Kai had seen a man once again able to hold his own penis when he pissed, a mother place a nipple into her child's mouth. In those months of turmoil, Kai had discovered a new and enduring love, of orthopaedic surgery. Still a junior surgeon, he had seen and dealt with more than some consultants of thirty years.

Six o'clock now. Kai heads for the men's changing room, where he exchanges his scrubs for day clothes. Now he is hungry. On the way home he stops at the roadside and buys okra, onions, peppers and smoked fish from the women traders. No meat, too late for the butchers. He hails a taxi, a shared one, and checks the route. The driver is going via the peninsula bridge. Kai lets him go, waves the next taxi down.

On his way up the road towards the house he sees Abass hanging over the verandah railings. Kai raises a hand. The boy turns to rush down the stairs. As Kai opens the door in the metal gate, the child hurtles towards him throwing his full weight against his stomach, arms around his waist. Kai braces; all the same the impact very nearly winds him.

'Hey, my man. You're almost too big for that. How goes it?'

The child doesn't reply, but pulls Kai's arm around him and buries his face in his side. Together they walk up to the house.

'Is your mother home?'

'Yes. But she's gone out again. She told me to tell you. To Yeama,' Abass answers in his deep, little man's voice.

Yeama is a neighbour whose sister-in-law died in childbirth. Yeama has been left with the infant. The father, serving with the army on the northern border, has no idea yet of either the arrival of his daughter or the death of his new wife. Abass's mother, Kai's cousin, makes visits bearing baby clothes and tins of formula to Yeama's tiny house. The child was born prematurely: Kai doesn't imagine she'll live too long.

'How hungry are you? Can you eat again?'

Abass nods.

'Good,' says Kai, squeezing the boy's skinny shoulder.

In the kitchen an aunt sits on a stool in the corner, her chin in her hand, nodding in sleep. At the sound of him she grunts and rises to help, but Kai gently resists and she shuffles off, wrapping her *lappa* about her, still half asleep. Doubtless they've left something in the pot for him, but today he wants to cook. At the worktop he unpacks his purchases. He slices the onions, chops each finger of okra into a dozen pieces. He loves the routine and rhythm of preparing food. It brings him to a feeling of peace, being able to close off a part of his mind, just as he was in surgery, putting the cast on Foday's leg, or is sometimes suturing a wound, tying off the ends stitch after stitch. Operating affords him a privacy, an escape from the world into a place which has its own narratives, its own emergencies, but which is a less random world, one he can control with his skills. Cooking, though less absorbing, does something similar.

In the corner of the room Abass sits on the stool in the corner, twirling a piece of string around his fingers.

'So what did you do at school today?'

The child shrugs. 'Nothing.'

'Nothing at all?'

Abass shrugs again.

'So how did it go, this doing nothing? You sat at your desk and stared out of the window.' Kai takes a pepper, halves it and dices it swiftly.

'Yes,' says Abass, grinning. 'That's exactly what we did.'

'Ah, so you did do something. You sat and you stared. Was that good? What did you see?'

A giggle. 'I don't know.'

'I was looking out of the window this morning. Do you know what I saw?'

'No.'

'I saw fifty orange monkeys racing by. Did they come your way?'

Abass's grin widens. 'Yes. They did. They ran past the school window.'

'That sounds interesting. Did your teacher see them, too?'

'Mrs Turay? No. Because she was facing the blackboard.'

'What about the other kids?'

'They were looking at the teacher.'

'So it was just you. Lucky old you. What else did you see?'

123

'Umm.'

'When I saw the orange monkeys, I noticed they were being followed by a brass band.'

'Yes. I saw the brass band, too. And . . .'

'The Pied Piper of Hamelin?'

'And all the rats and all the children,' Abass claps and bounces on the stool. 'The angry townspeople, the mayor.'

'One Foot Jombee. The Hunting Devil.'

'Umm. Umm. A talking sheep!'

'Now that's a good one. Can it predict the future?'

'Yes.'

'And do arithmetic?'

'Yes. It can do everything.'

'Well, maybe you should have given the talking, mathematically-minded sheep your seat in the class while you went and joined the parade. Do you think Mrs Turay would have noticed?'

This last sends Abass into a fit of giggles. Kai carries the pot outside and places it on the fire. There is a stove in the kitchen, but cooking gas is frequently in short supply. And anyway, Kai's aunts prefer to cook on charcoal. For Kai there is something elemental about it, like bathing in a stream or making a journey by foot.

While the food cooks he goes to wash, dousing himself in water from the bucket in the corner of the bathroom. In his room he slips on a clean T-shirt and a pair of cotton drawstring trousers. Abass sits and waits for him, perched on a set of drawers crammed with papers.

'Can I sleep here tonight?'

'Do you want to?'

'Yes.'

Kai laughs. Abass regards it as a privilege to sleep in Kai's room and dreams of the day when the room will be his.

'OK, well, let's see.'

Together they carry plates of food out to the bench on the verandah, where they eat and watch the world as it goes by.

A rush of air, he can feel his cheeks distort with the force of it. His stomach flips over. He is falling. Falling. The stinging slap of water.

He wakes with a jolt convinced he has levitated, that he may actually have felt the impact of the bed. It takes several minutes for his breathing and his heart rate to return to normal. When it does he can hear the ticking of his watch on the night stand, the howl of dogs calling to one another in the night, the same wavering notes endlessly repeated. He gets up and picks his way through the house. The odd murmur, the occasional sigh accompany his passage. By his reckoning it is around four, the darkness has begun to lift. This is the third night in a row and the lack of sleep is beginning to tell on him. If tonight he doesn't get a few more hours it will start to affect his work, his concentration, even his hands. He sits and waits for sleep, though he knows it may be as far off as the coming dawn. After an hour he rises and goes back into the house, only partially retracing his steps, to Abass's room. The child lies asleep on the bed. He picks up the child's light body and leaves the room. Abass's thumb falls from his mouth, his hand trails over Kai's shoulder.

Never waking, the child tucks himself into the crook of Kai's body and replaces his thumb. Kai lies still and lets his mind follow the rhythm of the child's breathing until it drowns the howling of the dogs. Until he sleeps.

CHAPTER 16

The static on the line sounds like the breathing of unseen listeners.

'Can you hear me?' Adrian's words, relayed six thousand miles, bounce straight back to him.

A pause, then Lisa's voice. 'Yes, I can hear you.' Around the sound of her voice images cluster. He sees her standing in the yellow light of the kitchen, her arm wrapped around her waist, leaning against the worktop, one leg bent, cradling the phone in her neck, smoothing out a strand of her hair with her hand, the way she used to when they first married.

'Sorry about the line,' he says.

'It's OK.'

'How is everything?'

'Everything's fine.' They talk for a few minutes. Kate has chipped a tooth, an appointment at the orthodontist made for Tuesday week. The old apple tree behind the conservatory might need to come down. Dinner the night before with friends of theirs, some of whom had asked after him, had asked what he was doing. The way she reports this makes it clear she was unable to come up with a satisfactory answer.

Adrian says nothing, instead he tells her the reason for his call. 'You'll have to go up to my office. Pick up the phone in there.'

'I'm already in your office. Go ahead and tell me what you want. I have you on speakerphone.'

The image he has been holding of her fragments. He closes his eyes, scans the shelves of his office from memory and directs her to each book. When she is finished, she comes back to the phone, her breathing quickened by the exertion. He adds the names of several other texts and asks her to order them up for him. He pauses, he wants to tell her what is happening to him here. The man in the private room. The woman at the hospital. What he is looking out upon now. A dying sun, a transparent orb against a grainy sky.

'I was thinking,' she says, before he can begin. 'Do you want me to redecorate in here while you're away?'

Though he can visualise the place of every book on the shelves he barely remembers the wallpaper.

'Sure,' he replies.

Another day Adrian talks to Kai about the man in the room. He is not Kai's patient, though Kai volunteers what he knows of the man's condition. In another country they would be looking for a lung donor. Impossible here, it goes without saying. Oxygen might extend his life by years, but the oxygen plant in the city has been destroyed. The hospital's two concentrators are both in constant use. And though it is a fool's errand, Adrian searches out the hospital administrator and asks her if anything can be done, knowing all the while that if she had an extra machine Elias Cole would still not rank in the hierarchy of the meek. It wouldn't have surprised him had she chosen to deliver him a lecture, but instead she saves her breath, looks him straight in the eye and boldly utters the lie that she will do what she can.

A day later she puts her head around the door of his office. This is more than Adrian has seen of her since his arrival, but it is only to say that a package has arrived and is waiting for him in her office. He rises. For a moment she stands in the doorway in front of him, not moving. She has a way of regarding Adrian, as though perplexed by precisely what sort of being he is. Any minute now she will promise that talk, he thinks.

'Yes,' she says as though listening to his thoughts. 'When things are a bit easier, stop by for a chat, won't you?' And she turns and hurries off, gunshot heels resounding in the corridor.

In the evening Adrian carries the parcel of books back to his apartment and sets them on the coffee table. He lights several candles (the generator has been playing up), opens a fresh bottle of whisky and sits down. He orders the books into a pile on the table and selects a slim volume, subtitled, *A History of Mental Illness*. Searching the list of chapters and then the index for the word 'fugue', he finds the reference he wants, turns to the page and begins to read.

1887. A time of vagabonds and gypsies, of travellers, wayfarers and tramps. A French psychiatrist working in Bordeaux treated for a number of years a patient by the name of Albert Dada. Dada was not a drifter or a tramp, he was something else – an obsessive traveller. At regular intervals he would abandon his family and his work to journey on foot as far as Constantinople and Moscow. At times he ran out of money, at others he was arrested for vagrancy, thrown into jail and made to return home. But within a few months, always, he set out again. Dada could not say why he travelled, or what he planned to do when he reached the end of his journey. At times he couldn't even remember his own name. He knew nothing, save his destination. The psychiatrist published a paper, *Les Aliens Voyageurs*, which brought him a modest fame. Albert Dada became the world's first recognised fuguer.

A spate of fugues followed the publication of *Les Aliens Voyageurs*, Adrian reads. Most accounts related to missing servicemen between the First and Second World Wars. The men eventually turned up hundreds of miles from home. All claimed to suffer memory loss, not to know who they were, or how they had ended up in the place in which they were found. Some were using other names and pursuing new occupations. All appeared to inhabit a state of obscured consciousness from which they eventually emerged with no memory of the weeks, months or even years they had spent away. These were not isolated incidents in the lives of these men, but a constant, a pattern of behaviour, of journey, of wanderings, of compulsive travelling. The suspicion, on the part of the psychiatrists treating the servicemen, was of malingering. The men were shot as deserters.

With no single case of fugue identified for decades a small lobby within the profession was arguing for it to be recognised for what it was – a hoax perpetrated by cowards and shirkers which ought to be removed from the official classification of mental diseases.

Three hours after he began reading, Adrian sets the book on the coffee table, stands and stretches. He heads into the kitchen to make himself a sandwich, slices open a loaf of bread to find dead ants baked into the honeycomb, shakes them out on to the kitchen surface, spreads the bread with margarine and layers on slices of bright-pink salami and processed cheese. He yearns for Caerphilly and ham sliced from the bone. From the fridge he takes a bottle of Heineken. The fridge has been on and off all day, the bottle is barely cold. He eats the sandwich standing at the worktop, in front of his reflection in the black glass of the window. What he feels is a sense of anxious euphoria, of a person who happens upon what they think might be a lost treasure in a field, brushing away the mud to see what they have found, hoping, but not daring to hope, fearful of scrutinising their find in case it turns out not to be what they had thought.

Something Salia said, the day of the visit to the old department store, the thing that had prompted Adrian to take a second look at the woman's notes. They had returned to the mental hospital from their trip into town. Adrian had pressed Salia on the former doorman's words. He'd said, Adrian repeated, that the woman was not possessed, rather that she was crossed.

'He was making a distinction,' said Adrian. 'At least that is how it seemed to me.'

Walking ahead of him, his shoes squeaking faintly on the floor, Salia had stopped and turned to face Adrian. For a few seconds he appeared to consider whether or not to answer Adrian, or perhaps was just weighing his answer.

When he spoke he said, 'If a spirit possess you, you become another person, it is a bad thing. Only bad spirits possess the living. I am telling you what some people believe, you understand.'

'Yes.'

'But sometimes a person may be able to cross back and forth between this world and the spirit world. That is to say, a living person, a real person. And when they are in between the worlds, in neither world, then we say they are crossed. This woman is travelling between worlds. It is something that happens. When I was a small boy there was a woman who became crossed, she was my aunt, in fact. There were times she would move from one village to another, alone, even as far as Guinea and Liberia. People saw her, they said she did not recognise them. Her hair grew long. People believed she had special powers.'

'Did you ever hear of anybody else like that?'

'There were people, yes.'

'Who were they?'

'Women.'

'All of them?'

Salia inclined his head. 'All of them.'

In his mind's eye Adrian sees the map on the wall of Ileana's office, the coloured pins of Agnes's destinations superimposed on the dark window.

The European fuguers one hundred years ago were all men.

Here they are women.

129

CHAPTER 17

Julius entered my office carrying a briefcase of whisky. His shirt was linen, short-sleeved with stitching upon the lapels, highly starched and only slightly wrinkled in the heat. Next to him I felt dull and rumpled. I was wearing a suit, one of the two I possessed, given to me by my father and shiny at the trouser seat and elbows. The other I should have collected from the cleaner's on my way in, but had been diverted by a fracas involving a hustler, one of those men who approach you on the street, their illicit wares hidden inside their coats. This fellow had newspapers. They were no more than gossip sheets really, though they were theoretically banned. Their stock-in-trade comprised half-baked conspiracy theories, political scandals, murders served up with especially gruesome or bizarre details and often a graphic photograph, obtained from a police source for the price of a bribe. Once or twice I had found a copy of one of those papers in my office after Julius had been there. I might cast an eye over the front page before I tossed it into the bin.

I barely registered the vendor as he passed me. I noticed he tried to catch my eye. I shifted my gaze and he moved on. Moments later he was seized by three men who seemed to come out of nowhere. The vendor tried to make his escape, but today wasn't his day. The place was full of plain-clothes police. A sweep of the whole street at rush hour when the vendors were busiest. They gave him a thrashing and tossed him in the back of a Land Rover.

That and the rain held the traffic up for hours. I passed the time in a barber's shop. Some weeks before I had been persuaded by the owner to try a moustache. I sat back in the chair while he soaped my face and scraped at the stray hairs, shaping the line of hairs on my upper lip into a neat bar, divided by a parting. I faced myself in the mirror. I was pleased with the result.

And now here was Julius, stockpiling booty in my office, crates of soft drinks and mixers, bottles of spirits. He was planning a party for the moon landing, which threatened to overwhelm the event itself.

'Hey, Cole!'

I was hot, damp and vaguely irritated to see him. He leaned over the desk, and I caught, mixed in with his own smell, a scent of Saffia. It almost winded me.

I know how we looked. People couldn't understand what he saw in me, I'm sure. For I had the same thought. I was, am, a careful man. Julius's presumptuousness was breathtaking. He had no fear of life. It was there in his fluid attitude to the ownership of possessions, in the way he spent whatever money he had in his pocket. He possessed the ability to drink himself to incoherence and back to lucidity. He would go on, carrying you with him, until all the tiredness had gone. And when, with the new light stretched across the horizon, he would drive the two of us home though he was in no fit state to do so. He would bang the bonnet of the car. 'No fear, Cole,' he'd shout, 'she knows the way home by now.' Of religion he had no need. He believed in himself. A confidence that extended even to his singing, so that years later when he was remembered, it was as a musical man. Yet the only quality you could say his voice possessed was force. Yes, Julius believed in himself. He didn't fear death — for death was too insignificant, too small, it resided below the level of his contempt. He had survived a serious childhood illness that killed many others. He drew power from the fact of it, as though it proved he was blessed.

He believed in his own destiny and he made others believe it too. He was a seducer. Of woman, man, child or dog. To him I was company, someone to be won over, simple as that. Plus, he was easily bored.

'Give me five, Cole!' Our palms slapped together and slid across each other, our thumbs and forefingers clicked. He hefted a buttock up on to the edge of my desk.

'What's up, my friend?'

'Nothing.'

He bent over for a closer look at me, put out his hand and lifted my chin, his face a mere six inches away. I could feel his warm breath. He gave a low whistle.

'Suits you, Cole.'

'Thank you.' I decided to respond as though he was serious.

He sat back and regarded me thoughtfully a moment. 'What have you done with Vanessa? That was one fine-looking lady. You need a woman, Cole.' For some reason he kept using my surname, an occasional habit of his.

I shrugged. 'I'm fine.'

'I'm serious, Cole. I may be a married man but I still know a few of the ladies.' He winked at me.

I didn't want to enquire too closely what he meant by that. I felt vaguely unwell.

'I shall make sure I invite somebody to the party for you. Some fine woman.'

'Not on my account, please.'

Julius laughed at that. 'You know, among the Mende, Cole, there is a practice that when a stranger arrives in a village he is given a woman to keep him company at night, often a daughter of the chief himself. The Europeans made much of this custom, to them it proved what people of low morals we all were. But you know why the Mende had this custom, Cole?'

I shook my head.

'Because they know full well a man needs a woman. It is in the nature of things. A single man is trouble, a hungry jackal. So the village provides a chicken. To me, Cole, this is surely the more civilised approach. And besides, by providing a chicken of their own choosing, now they had a spy in the jackal's lair! And the European traders thought they were being generous. They kept on coming back. Beware chickens bearing gifts, my friend.' His laughter rolled like applause around the room.

I swallowed and pasted the facsimile of a smile upon my face.

'You need a woman, my friend, to cheer you up. Whose *tumbu* you can tickle with that new moustache of yours.'

Julius's worry beads, the way I thought of them then. He often carried, in his pockets, some piece of metal, an engine part or piece of some structure, something used to demonstrate a principle to his students or perhaps just something picked up and pocketed in the course of the day. That afternoon it was a nut and bolt he spun on the surface of my desk. I watched his hands, spinning the bolt round and round. Fingers. Knuckles. Fingertips. Nails. The smooth brown surface of the desk. Smooth like skin. Julius's fingers playing, grazing, stroking, touching. Saffia.

Exams over, the students headed home for the summer break, although, of course, in our country it was the height of the rains. We had, since Independence, stuck with the British scholastic timetable. I had nowhere to go, no family to visit, and I lacked the funds to travel. Banville Jones had secured for himself a fellowship overseas, recommended by the Dean. I wondered how he had managed it. A vacancy had arisen within the department with the departure of another colleague. Some months earlier I would have assumed it was mine for the asking, but now I was less confident. I decided to devote the holidays to completing at least two more papers, and to this end I spent hours each week going through the archives in the university library. I planned to keep myself busy.

Still, I faced the thought of the long break with apprehension. I relied on my regular contact with Julius to see Saffia. Julius was a spontaneous sort of fellow, incapable of planning ahead by more than a few minutes. He would doubtless eschew the mundane rituals involved in keeping in touch. And there were only so many times I could contrive encounters with Saffia, especially in the light of recent, dismaying events.

Meanwhile the day of the moon landing approached. That at least afforded me an evening in Saffia's company. Julius was as excited as a small child on his birthday. My office had become a drinks store. Kekura was charged with setting up the equipment for the broadcast. I had promised to secure extra chairs, to which end I had placed a request with the Dean to borrow some from the lecture theatre.

In the streets, the fever spread. Women clothed themselves in commemorative batiks and threaded their hair into concoctions contrived to produce the illusion of upward velocity, named their male offspring Apollo. The chief Imam included a denunciation of the mission in his call to prayers. Our own pastor called the enterprise godless, warned against the perils of man's egotism and pointed, if proof were needed, to the fact of the craft's pagan name. Julius thought the whole thing hilarious and begged me to invite my pastor to the house for the party. He would invite the Imam, for the pleasure, he said, of hearing them agree on something.

That afternoon in town I collected my suit from the cleaner's and, on the spur of the moment, I entered a tailor's shop. At some level I think I felt emboldened by my new moustache, though I would never describe myself as a vain man. I had not the physique to encourage vanity. Still, that day I decided I'd had enough of the starched white shirts I was in the habit of ordering three at a time. The tailor took my measurements and showed me a number of different styles, flicking through the pages of the catalogue. I pointed one out, he smiled and complimented me on my choice. Discussion of the price, as ever, turned out to be a somewhat lengthier business. We reached a compromise on the understanding the shirts would be ready for collection within forty-eight hours, in time for the party.

Organising the delivery of the chairs proved considerably more problematic. I had arranged transport through a contact of Banville Jones, a Syrian, who owned a haulage company. The company turned out to consist of a single open-back lorry. I left the man a deposit and made a booking for the morning of the party, overlooking the fact the event was to take place on a Sunday. The university buildings would be closed. I switched the booking to the Friday, but the lorry, I was informed, would be going upcountry earlier in the week. It was due back on Friday. I could have use of it as soon as it arrived.

'How do I know your driver will be back in time?'

The owner looked at me. 'He'll be there,' and smiled. 'Inshalla.'

As luck had it the man was true to his word. I was sitting in my office when the lorry arrived; the driver parked up on the other side of the faculty building. For a few cents I had secured the labour of two of the night watchmen and we set about loading stacks of chairs. The driver sat picking his teeth with a matchstick and watching us from his cabin, his labour apparently not being part of the agreement. It was slow going. By chance two of my students passed by. One was a Ghanaian fellow, another from the provinces. They were staying on campus for the duration of the break. I called to them and within half an hour we were done. I realised I'd given no consideration to how the chairs were to be unloaded. I could scarcely remove the watchmen from their posts. Fortunately the two students offered their services and hopped into the back, while I climbed into the cab to direct the driver.

As we drove through the streets, a warm wind entered the cab. Darkness was falling over the houses. We passed through the streets of the city and began to climb up the winding road into the hills, the engine straining under the load. The two students sitting on the tailgate raised their voices against the wind. At a traffic light one of them leaned over and purchased several sticks of roast meat from a street seller and for the rest of the journey they sat sharing the meat between them and tossing the sticks over the side.

The house was in darkness. I had told Julius when I was coming. Feeling exasperated I instructed the driver and the two students to wait while I went to knock on the door.

My first knock went unanswered, as did my second. I tried one more time. Behind me I was aware of the driver sitting, worrying at the spaces between his teeth with a matchstick. He turned off the engine and dimmed the headlights. I heard him suck his teeth with impatience. The students had lapsed into silence, watching me idly.

'Come on! Where are your people?' called the driver.

It wasn't something I would ordinarily do, but the weight of the man's insistence was at my back. I reached out and turned the doorknob. The door was open. So somebody was home. Saffia's aunt? Quite possibly she was at the back of the house and hadn't heard the door. I moved hesitantly forward. There was no light, except that of the dying day. Too early still for a moon. I moved like a blind man. I didn't want to give the aunt a stroke by coming up at her out of the darkness. I searched for a lamp or light switch. Another step and another, I moved forward into the house. From somewhere I thought I heard a sound, though the timing coincided so exactly with my own tread I felt unsure. I waited and listened until it came again.

Louder this time. A moan. I stood, covered by the darkness, and listened as it came, over and over. My heart began to beat, the blood rushed to my head. I felt I must leave, but I could not move. My body was rigid.

The sound of footsteps behind me. The truck driver, come to find out what was going on. As he moved towards me, I saw his face split into an obscene grin; his teeth glinted in the half-light and he uttered a filthy laugh. I turned and pushed him towards the door. He went, but with reluctance, chuckling as he allowed himself to be propelled outside. I closed the door behind us. The driver passed a remark to the students accompanied by a filthy gesture.

'Shut your mouth!' I would have hit him, I could scarcely hold on to my rage. He was quiet, but the insolent smile stayed on his face.

We unloaded the chairs and piled them up outside the door. When I felt sufficient time had passed, I told the driver to sound the horn. At the same time I rapped smartly on the door. The combined noise would have woken the dead. Sure enough, Julius appeared, barefoot, his shirt unbuttoned. Suddenly I found I could hardly look him in the eye. He disappeared to fetch a pair of shoes and helped us move the chairs into the house, where we stacked them on the verandah.

I told Julius I was unable to stay as I must accompany the students back to campus and make sure the truck driver returned to his place of employment. At the door I asked him to give my regards to Saffia.

'Of course,' he replied. 'She's resting.'

We returned as we had come. I kept my eyes on the road in front of me. One of the students banged on the top of the cab for us to stop; they had changed their minds about returning to campus and wanted to be dropped off in town. They bowed slightly as they thanked me and touched their fingers to their foreheads. I watched them go, the coins I had given them burning a hole in their back pockets. Ten minutes later outside the offices of the truck company, I dispatched the driver – I decided he could forgo his tip and derived some small measure of satisfaction from seeing the grin finally fall off his face. I went to look for a taxi or a bus to take me home.

A light, hot wind. As I walked the currents of air wrapped themselves around me, touching my face and filling my ears with sounds. I fancied I could hear the sea from a mile away, the sound of the waves thrashing the shore, clawing the sand as the water was dragged backwards. I walked on the road, there was no pavement. I could feel the soles of my shoes striking the tarmac, the hard ground sending shudders through my body. I walked fast, wanting to leave the events of the evening behind.

But I could not shake one sound from my head. Later that night, in the silence of my bedroom, it would torment and excite me, leave me sleepless, exhausted yet kept alert by the emotions that crackled through my being. The only relief I could find was physical, and afterwards I fell into a wretched sleep, which brought no respite. I woke early, the feelings of the previous evening as alive as ever.

CHAPTER 18

The first time Adrian sees the young woman, she is standing with Babagaleh at the gate. But it is Babagaleh he is focused upon. Only when he turns to nod at the manservant out of good manners and a little awkwardness – for he is on his way to the asylum and has postponed his visit to Elias Cole – he casts a nod in her direction, too. The gesture, seen from the outside, must seem oddly brisk, a dry gesture in this warm liquid atmosphere, where people move slowly through the day like long-distance swimmers. She is slim, with wide-spaced eyes, and a wry tilt to her mouth. Her hair is pulled back and hidden under a scarf knotted at the nape of her neck. Later, waiting for a funeral procession to pass, Adrian watches the mourners move, as unhurriedly as midday shadows. His mind returns to the woman at the hospital gates. Babagaleh's daughter or niece, perhaps? Another servant? She hadn't responded to his nod, only looked at him, her eyes travelling the length of his body. The physical impact of that look had left a mark upon his body as painful as a graze. As he walked away, he had been suddenly and shockingly aware of something fleetingly and exquisitely possible. So much so, he almost turned back, to say something to Babagaleh – anything – to find a reason to look at her again.

At the mental hospital Ileana greets him. 'Hey, you! I've got good news for you. Your lady is back in the real world.' She grins, showing dark-red lipstick on her teeth.

'Christ! When did this happen? You should have called me.'

Ileana shrugs. 'You're here now. Do you want to see her?'

At the window, the silhouette of Salia, the sentinel. Agnes sits opposite Adrian. Her eyes rest on a point midway across the table. She will, he notes, look Salia in the eye, but still not him. His palms are sweating. He is nervous with anticipation.

'Hello. My name is Adrian. This is Salia, who I think you already know. Salia is going to stay in the room for the duration of our conversation, in case we need help understanding each other. Is that all right?'

The woman glances at Salia and nods.

'I'm going to make sure we aren't disturbed. I'm going to switch off the telephones and Salia is going to lock the door – just to make sure nobody interrupts us. Is it OK if he does that?'

She nods again. Salia complies.

'We have met before. Do you remember me?'

She looks at him, directly this time, and away again, frowns and shakes her head.

'My name is Adrian. Do you remember that you came to see me? Not here. At the medical hospital?'

She looks up at him at that but her gaze wavers and drops. 'A white doctor.'

'Yes, that was me.'

In a low voice Salia says a few words, to which the woman responds keeping her eyes on the table.

Salia speaks. 'Excuse me. She says she does remember. But not if it was you. It was a white doctor. For some of us it is difficult, you understand.'

'I understand,' says Adrian. Turning back to Agnes, he continues, 'I would like to see if I can help you. Will you let me try to help you?'

Once more she nods.

'OK.' He takes a breath and in a clear voice he says to Agnes, 'Perhaps we can start by you telling me your name and where you live?'

To his surprise, in an equally clear tone, though in a quiet voice, she replies, 'My name is Agnes. I live in Port Loko.'

'Who do you live with there?'

'With family.'

'What were you doing in the city? Do you know?'

She shakes her head.

'Do you know where you are now?'

This time she gives a nod and glances at Salia, as if for confirmation.

'Can you tell me how you came to be here?'

She cannot remember.

It is slow going, with frequent low-voiced interjections from Salia, for the woman speaks so softly, and her words are heavily accented. Her voice drags on occasion and on others catches, as though tripping on uncertain thoughts. From time to time she steps out of English and takes several paces in her own language. Adrian wishes he could understand. He feels the air thick with his desperation. To get her to a certain place is all he needs to accomplish right now, to trust him a little. He continues with simple questions, lets her know they can stop any time, offers her a drink of water.

Gradually he returns her to the days before her last journey.

The end of the rains was in sight, she tells him. There hadn't been as much to eat. She shopped for smoked fish and for the few vegetables available in the market, at least there was still rice and salt in sacks in the storeroom. She had been suffering aches in her joints. Her daughter had bought her some mentholated ointment and arranged for her to see the doctor, but he found nothing wrong with her. Anyway she was well enough to be able to do her work in the house, taking care of her daughter's son and cooking on alternate days. She had help from a young girl who lived with them. One day she had a headache; she went and lay down on her bed, calling the girl to bring her a cup of water. The headache persisted, like the blade of a cold knife laid at the back of her skull.

Some days later she was heating a pan of oil to fry plantains. The next thing she knew the pan was smoking heavily and almost in flames. She managed to remove it from the fire just in time. The oil was burnt, she had to clean the pan and begin again. Her daughter was away from home for a few days, otherwise she would have called her to come and take over the cooking. She had no idea where the time went. One moment she was placing the pan upon the flame, next it was almost in flames.

'Who else was in the house?'

She doesn't know, she shakes her head.

'Where was the girl? What about your grandchild?'

She shakes her head. She doesn't remember. Perhaps they were outside.

'What about your son-in-law?'

Silence. Perhaps she has not heard him. Adrian repeats the question. And then, thinking too that maybe the phrase has not translated well, he adds, 'Your daughter's husband, I mean.'

Agnes looks distracted. She puts her hand up to her throat, feeling with her fingers around the base of her neck. She seems upset about something.

'What is it?' asks Adrian.

'Where is my gold chain? I cannot find my gold chain. Somebody's taken it. Has this matter been reported? Why has nobody returned the chain to me?' Her voice has acquired weight.

'Tell me about the chain.'

'It is gold. Somebody's taken it.'

'Was it a special chain?'

'It was gold.'

Adrian listens. He reassures Agnes everything possible will be done to find her chain. He doesn't want to let her stray too far from the path of their discussion. The mention of the chain may be significant, then again it may not. He makes a mental note of the detail, of where in the conversation it arose, like one of the pins he left upon the map of her travels.

'What else do you remember? From before you left home.'

She shakes her head and turns her hands over in her lap. She seems to have lost her place.

He urges her gently on. 'What do you remember? Tell me one thing you remember. Just one.'

A dog barking, over and over again. It woke her from her dreams. The sound was bothersome, adding to her headache. She was lying on her bed thinking she should get up, but couldn't seem to rouse herself. She kept being drawn back into her dreams. Somewhere somebody was burning rice fields, even though it was the wrong time of the year. The smoke entered her room and her lungs. It tasted bitter, made her nauseous. Outside the sun was rising, the shadows shifted at the window. She knew she had to get out of the house, but she remained in the grip of her dreams.

'What were the dreams?'

She cannot remember.

Adrian waits, not wanting to interrupt more than necessary. Sitting before him in the heat of the room, Agnes twitches slightly, her shoulders and head slump and her eyelids flutter. Adrian leans forward. Though he can't be sure, it looks very much as though she is asleep.

'Agnes?' he says softly. At the sound of his voice she pulls herself up. 'You can go back to the ward now.'

It is nearly time for lunch. Salia steps forward and helps Agnes to her feet. She seems very frail.

At the door, Adrian says, 'Salia will see about your chain.'

Agnes looks at him.

'Your chain.'

'What chain?' Her face is blank.

'The gold chain you lost.'

She does not reply. She blinks and moves on.

Adrian watches her as she leaves, guiding herself around the desk and towards the door. She does not look back. There is no element of performance in her shuffling steps, the head that sways slightly as she makes her way down the corridor and out towards the women's ward. He stands at the window and watches, sees Salia stop to talk to another staff member and Agnes shuffle on oblivious, Salia walk smartly to catch her up.

If she had been faking, Adrian would have to ask himself why. But he is quite sure what he saw was real. He watched her cross from one state to another, one in which she was concerned about the loss of a gold chain, the other in which she appeared to have no memory of the loss of the same item. He remembers the words of the man in the old department store, the one who had brought Agnes to the hospital. Salia had used the same words and tried to explain them to Adrian.

Agnes is crossed.

They are in the Patients' Garden, the smoke from Ileana's cigarette curling upward, entwining with the branches of the trees. Her elbow rests on the arm of the wooden bench, half an inch of ash droops from the end of the cigarette. Inside the pocket of her smock she fiddles with her lighter. Adrian can hear the rasping of the wheel against the flint. She is listening with her eyes upon him.

When he stops speaking she says, without taking her eyes away from him, 'You are considering schizophrenia, of course?'

'Of course,' Adrian replies. 'Though she's clearly confused. And there are lapses. I don't think I'm dealing with a psychotic. In fact, I'm as sure as I can be.' And then, 'You've never examined her?'

Ileana shakes her head, a movement which causes the ash to drop from her cigarette; she raises the remainder of it to her lips and draws deeply before discarding the butt among the fallen flowers.

'What about Attila?' says Adrian.

'He tries to see all the patients, but there are so many. Besides, she doesn't stay long. It would have amounted to an intake interview. Nothing more.'

Adrian picks a pod up from the ground and begins to pull it apart. The seeds fall out, clattering faintly on to the stones. He doesn't want to say anything to Ileana just yet, about what he is thinking, the books he has been reading. He wants to wait until he is a little more certain. He needs to hold off talking to Attila, too. For now he is enjoying Ileana's company, sitting here in the shade of the garden, the most peaceful place in the city. He'd like to carry on talking to her, to invite her for a beer. He realises he has no idea of her home life, whether she is here alone, married or single. He struggles to picture her anywhere else but here.

'Where do you live? I mean here, in this place.'

'A bungalow. By Malaika beach. I've been there about six months. Before that I had an apartment in town, a real dump. What I have now is so much better. You should come and see it.'

'Are you there alone? I mean . . .' He is fumbling a little now. 'Sorry. I wasn't prying. I was just thinking about safety.' He finishes abruptly.

She laughs and looks at him; in her dark eyes there is genuine amusement. 'I know what you mean. And the answer is yes, I'm on my own. And I feel safer here than anywhere in Israel, or Romania for that matter. I don't suppose anybody back home would believe it if I told them.' She laughs. 'Last time I was in your bloody country I was followed round Haringey by some fucking pervert. I could have screamed my head off and nobody would have heard me.'

Ileana lights another cigarette and stands up. Together they leave the garden.

'Tea?'

'Yes, please.'

On the way home he asks the driver to stop at the supermarket. Inside he moves up and down the aisles, perusing the imported products, savouring the air conditioning. The prices are almost beyond reach, the owners must be making a fortune. He selects two large packets of crisps, takes some beers from the cold cabinet and pays, counting out grubby notes. It is the end of the day, his mind is unwinding, he performs the task slowly, loses count and begins again.

Back in the taxi, heading out to the hospital, not across Julius's bridge this time, but through the thick of the town. There is a song on the radio. Adrian can't place it exactly, but it takes him back decades.

The title track to a film, maybe. The rhythm lifts his mood. Not for the first time the face of the woman he saw talking to Babagaleh rises before him. This time he does nothing to suppress it, remembers the look she gave him, the way it touched his skin, leaving him exposed as he tried to slip past. He tries to focus upon the features of her face, but they elude him. He sees only the expression she wore, as if she knew exactly what he was doing as he tried to slip past Babagaleh. But then, all good-looking women possessed the same power, or so it seemed.

He presses a beer can against his forehead, feels the cool seep through his body. Six o'clock. The day is over.

CHAPTER 19

'What's the time, please?'

Elias Cole was asleep when Adrian arrived, his eyelids fractionally open. For once his breathing was inaudible, causing a momentary hesitation in Adrian accompanied by a double beat of his heart. Of death, he had no experience, except that of his own father. Pneumonia, the official version. It had been a slow death, an awkward lingering. Adrian knew enough to know how these matters were generally handled. A dose of penicillin withheld, the gentle, cold kiss of the morphine needle. By the time Adrian arrived the bed sheets had already been changed. All the time his father was in the home, Adrian chided himself for not visiting more often. Not for his father, who barely recognised him. Or for his mother, who believed, or maintained, that Adrian's job was extremely demanding. But for himself. He knew he'd regret it. He chided himself. He'd done it anyway.

Adrian walks to the window and draws the curtain against the sunlight.

'It's two o'clock.'

He helps the old man to a glass of water. From elsewhere the sound of the expatriate medical staff singing 'Happy Birthday' to a German colleague. Minutes before Adrian had stood with them in the staff room, sipping vinegary, dusty wine. He'd slipped away before the cutting of the cake.

Adrian sits, the other man's eyes upon him. 'You told me people often wondered what Julius saw in you.'

'Yes.'

'And that you yourself often wondered the same thing.'

'I have no illusions.'

'But what did you see in him, in Julius?'

'I saw Saffia. Nothing but Saffia.'

★

20 July 1969. The Sea of Tranquillity.

It was all done for the Americans, of course. So they could take the afternoon off and watch at home with beer and barbecues. It was, after all, their money, their president, their rocket, their show. They were the winners. The rest of the world could but watch. The American Embassy on my way to the Ocean Club was alive with light and noise, dignitaries arriving by the score. The Soviet Embassy by contrast was closed and dark, a house of mourning. Winner takes all. The Soviets had even lost the loyalty of an insignificant state such as ours. Our Prime Minister – or was that the year he made himself President? Our President was at that moment rubbing shoulders with the Americans, basking in their glory, despite years of Soviet munificence.

The taxi I was travelling in came to a halt behind a long line of traffic. I took my chances and climbed down. Moments later it started to rain, but by then somebody had already claimed the empty taxi. No choice but to keep walking. I'd forgotten my umbrella. As luck would have it I passed a bar I knew and decided to stop for a drink to escape the rain. The bartender had the radio tuned to the World Service with all the preamble, the discussions and interviews, the expert opinion that would fill the hours up until the attempt. Who cared? Not I. I finished my first drink. I thought of Saffia and felt the familiar jolt of yearning.

My second whisky was followed by a third. They watered down the spirits in this place, I'd be hard-pressed to get drunk. So I stayed and drank. I drank to avoid the rain. I drank to avoid too early an arrival. I drank to keep my new shirt from getting wet. Most of all I drank to postpone, painfully, exquisitely, the moment when I would be in Saffia's company again.

All talk in the bar was of the evening's events. The same all over town, no escaping it. The mood of confidence was unshakeable; do you believe me when I say that? Men had died, it's true. But America was the superpower. It was a time of gods and we in Africa were mere mortals.

'I thought maybe you had forgotten me.' A woman's voice, soft and ingratiating.

I swivelled round. It took me a moment to place the young woman standing next to me. She spotted my hesitation, her eyes flickered in the direction of the barman, as if to check whether he was watching. Her smile though remained turned upon me. It was the girl from the bar, the one with whom I had spent the night the day of my first visit alone with Saffia. I had taken her home with me. I'd given her no thought from the moment I put her in a taxi and gave her a sum of money that amounted to somewhat more than the fare. Still, in my present state the thought of her company, the distraction it offered, was moderately appealing.

'Hello,' I said. 'How nice to see you.'

She replied, 'I have thought about you. I hoped you would come and find me.'

'Well, here I am. What would you like to drink?' I didn't bother with excuses, what was the point? We both knew what it had all been about. She could play coy all she wanted. I clicked my fingers for the barman.

Why I invited the girl to the Ocean Club, I don't know. An anger licking at my insides. Perhaps I wanted to spite Saffia. Her love for her husband, her immaculate coolness, her honour that seemed designed to keep me at a distance and yet allowed her friendships with men as she pleased.

And then, of course, the sound of her, the day I went to deliver the chairs. It burned. It burned.

Kekura was leaning against the bar when we entered.

'Cool shirt, man. I thought for a moment Julius had just walked in.' He looked at the girl, waiting to be introduced. I had forgotten her name, if I had ever known it.

'Hello, my name is Kekura. Kekura Conteh.' He extended his hand to her.

'Hello,' she replied shyly. She didn't proffer her name, so neither of us were any the wiser. Kekura slipped off his stool and the girl sat down.

'Are the others here?' I asked.

'Only Ade. I won't be staying too long myself. I need to get up to the house and make sure everything is working.'

I remembered Kekura had been charged with providing the audio-visual entertainment because of his job with the state broadcasting station. I nodded. My head throbbed slightly. I was just considering what might fix it better, another whisky or a glass of water, when I saw Julius and Saffia.

The Ocean Club. Let me sketch it for you. A semicircular bar. A dance floor, vast and open to the sky. Sometimes they played live music there. Tables scattered all around. The sea was only a few yards away, you could walk straight on to the sand. The inside of the club was reached by a stairway of curved steps, which led almost directly on to the dance floor, so whoever had just arrived drew the eye of everyone in the room. Saffia was wearing a blue gown, the same dress as the day I first laid eyes upon her. I watched them descend, Julius one pace ahead, exactly as he'd been the day of the faculty wives' dinner, when he was minded to skip the receiving line and she had drawn him back with the touch of her fingertips.

Kekura, too, stopped talking, and watched. I had the impression everyone in the room was engaged in the same act. Suddenly Saffia was standing next to me, greeting me, laying her hand upon my arm. No woman I knew had the power to alter my mood by such simple gestures. Where previously I had felt irritable, I was now elated.

'Aren't you excited, Elias?' she said. I could smell her scent on the warm air, just for a moment.

'Of course,' I replied, taking the opportunity to look at her, aware of her hand still resting on my bare arm, the touch of her fingers. 'It's an historic moment.'

'I wonder what the significance of this will be?' Kekura said. 'In ten years' time, when we look back.'

'I do, too,' I said.

Saffia removed her hand. I was aware of her turning away to see who else was there.

'Well, I pray it puts an end to this race between Russia and America. Perhaps the Americans will stop what they are doing in Vietnam.'

'I doubt that,' I said. I had no desire to be forced by Kekura into a discussion; my brain was slowly liquefying.

Saffia rejoined us. 'Everyone else is wondering whether they'll find men on the moon.'

'There are not,' Kekura replied flatly. 'Otherwise we would surely see them waving at us.'

Saffia laughed. 'No. But who is to say there aren't other life forms, micro-organisms, plant life?'

She was a scientist, of course.

Julius joined us then, back from working the tables. Kekura called the barman and ordered more drinks. The conversation broke and re-formed around Julius, who raised his glass and proposed a toast.

'My friends, after today nothing will ever be the same again.' And we all drank, not knowing how true his words would be for all of us.

I'd forgotten the girl, who was still sitting on the stool. We'd all shifted slightly to accommodate the arrival of first Saffia and then Julius, gradually forming a circle from which the girl was now excluded. She stood up and came over to stand next to me. I gave no response, the way I acted she might have been a stranger. I was aware of Saffia and Julius watching me. I wondered what on earth had possessed me to bring the girl? Perhaps if she'd stayed where she was I could have quietly dispatched her before the party. But now, in the wake of this act of presumption, I had no choice but to bow to the inevitable.

'This is Adline, a friend.' Adline was another girl I had once known, a girl of similar character; in the moment I seized her name out of the air.

Saffia nodded. Julius, his eyebrows fractionally raised, said, 'Hello, Adline.'

'My name is Yamba,' the girl said loudly, as though broadcasting a public statement. She emphasised the two syllables of her name. *Yam-ba.* 'And I am very pleased to make the acquaintance of you people.' *Pee-pool.* I realised I had barely ever listened to her. She was not from the city as I had assumed, but from the provinces. Saffia and Julius stared at her politely, faintly nonplussed, as did Kekura, nobody quite knowing how to follow her statement. It was Saffia who broke the spell of the moment.

'Well, very nice to meet you. Are you at the university?'

'What university is that?'

I butted in. 'Maybe we should think about going. The traffic is bad, you know.'

'We've got plenty of time,' said Julius.

'Actually, I'm glad you reminded me. I should be going. Is there somebody at the house to let me in?' Kekura, mercifully, helped bring the conversation round to another tack and in a few moments we had moved on to other things.

Julius, as I have told you before, attracted people and soon others in the bar migrated towards our group. A woman I recognised from the campus. I didn't know anything about her, except that she was a black American. She was with a mulatto fellow, a writer who also ran a dance troupe, with some success or so I had been told. Saffia asked him whether he felt inspired by the night's events.

All over the city people were gathering together in homes, in compounds, in bars to listen to news of Apollo 11's progress on the radio. We were still at the Ocean Club when the announcement came that the lunar module would soon make the attempt to land. The proprietor ordered the music turned down, the room fell silent. Nothing except the hiss of static and the sound of the waves. I could see the water, faintly phosphorescent, advancing and retreating to the call of the very moon upon whose surface mankind would shortly arrive. The announcement came, followed by a short, black space and then the voice of the astronaut: 'Houston. Tranquillity Base here. The Eagle has landed.' Everyone in the room began to applaud and to congratulate each other. Even the proprietor, a miserly fellow by nature, was moved to order drinks on the house. The bartender sprang from stillness into life.

Julius punched the air and shouted, 'The Eagle has landed!'

The girl Yamba, gazing at him from atop a barstool, asked, 'What eagle?'

'The name of the lunar module,' I explained. When she looked at me as though I had spoken in Dutch, I added, 'The spaceship.'

'What spaceship are you talking about?'

I explained the mission to the moon, which had evidently completely passed her alone in the world by, she continued to regard me in disbelief. Some part of our conversation caught Julius's attention and he turned to listen, as did others. At the end of my account, she pointed to the night sky.

'This small moon here.'

'Of course, that moon.'

She drew in her chin, put her hands to her hips and her head to one side, assessing me for the possibility I was making a fool of her. 'Well, tell me one thing,' she said.

'Of course.'

'What kind of person would want to do a thing like that?'

At that Julius shouted with laughter and slapped his thigh, slopping his drink around in his glass.

'Excellent! I should let you talk to some of my pupils. First principles. Why?'

'To humiliate the Soviets,' said Kekura. 'This is the new scramble for Africa. The scramble for space. A hundred years ago it was us they were fighting over. Our land, our wealth, our souls.'

'Yes, indeed.' It was Ade, who had joined us in the last ten minutes. 'And to stop the newspapers talking always about Vietnam, Vietnam.'

'It's hard to disagree.' The writer-dancer spoke next. 'But if it were me I know why I would do it.'

'Why?' asked Saffia.

'To fly.'

Saffia said, 'I like that.'

'To fly,' repeated Julius. 'To test the limits of our endeavour, of our courage.' He was serious. 'Otherwise what point is there in being alive?'

Did I mention to you how young we were then? How very young?

A piece of street theatre was going on outside. The dancer called for Julius to stop the car and we all descended. He went on to achieve some degree of fame as a choreographer, as I recall, until he fell foul of the authorities. I believe he died abroad. But that is by the by.

Outside a store two men dressed in improvised space suits moved about the interior of a makeshift module. Behind them was a television screen too small to be viewed by the crowd. So the performers were mimicking the astronauts, replicating for the audience what was taking place on Apollo 11. The dancer was enthralled and we stood and watched for a few minutes, until Saffia, made anxious by the possibility of guests arriving in our absence, said we must go and so we left him to catch us up later.

A few people had indeed already arrived. Julius went directly to the bar and began to serve drinks. Saffia disappeared into the kitchen. Kekura moved around the room holding up an aerial, while Ade monitored the quality of the picture. Kekura found a chair, placed the aerial on a shelf and stepped back to check his handiwork. Julius went to the record player, slipped a record from its sleeve and placed it on the turntable. The sound of a man's voice accompanied by the rhythms of a guitar filled the room. Next to me the girl began to dance.

Nowadays every person you speak to who was alive at the time of the moon landing will tell you they can remember precisely where they were. My own recollections of that night are as shabby and ill-lit as the image that appeared on the screen Kekura and Ade had set up. A good part of that evening is lost to me now, lost to me moments after they occurred, lost in self-pity, frustration and alcohol. Here's what I do remember:

At midnight people were still arriving. I wandered from the verandah to the main room and back again, for the most part avoiding becoming embroiled in conversation, drinking steadily. I picked up scraps of talk here and there as I moved by, like remote radio stations.

'Keep a dog. Better than insurance.'

'I hear Boston is as cold as hell. Yes, please. Campari.'

'They are challenging the opposition MPs' election one by one. Through the courts, so no one can complain. But it amounts to the same thing. Soon there will be none left.' Kekura, who else?

'And if something goes wrong with the spaceship?'

'If they run out of oxygen, they will die.' Ade Yansaneh, frowning under the lid of his hairline.

'Eggplant. What is it you call them here? Garden eggs. I like that.' The black American woman.

All the time I kept surreptitious watch on Saffia. Oh, she was an excellent hostess, as I think I have mentioned before; she attended to her guests in every matter, calling over the steward – whom I recognised from the university canteen – to refill a glass here, empty an ashtray there. There were dishes of spiced cashew nuts and Twiglets, as the evening wore on trays of *olele* wrapped in leaves. I ate nothing.

The moon walk was scheduled to take place at two o'clock in the morning. I helped myself to a cigarette from the box on the coffee table. The television, largely ignored once the initial buzz had worn off, glowed silently on one side of the room. Men talking behind desks and reruns of footage we had seen already. I stood gazing at images of the astronauts. The music had changed to something slow and melodic.

Next to me the dancer appeared: 'Watch them for long enough and they begin to move in time to the music.'

Rubbish, I thought, though in fact he was not too far from the truth. The astronauts stepping into the craft, turning and waving, their weightless antics in space did indeed seem to correspond to the rhythm of the music. The same became true even of the programme hosts as they gestured and swivelled. The more I watched, the more it seemed so. After a few minutes I laughed out loud and turned to the fellow, but he had moved away. I watched for a few more minutes and laughed again. At some point I began to feel a little dizzy. I shook my head and looked at the picture again. Air. I needed air. I went out to the verandah, passing Ade, who asked me if I was all right. I brushed his hand away. I saw the back of Saffia. Did I mention to you her very resolute posture? Yes, quite unyielding, in fact. I turned and headed in the other direction, knocking against a chair, which caused a small amount of my drink to spill on to the back of the woman sitting in it. She shrieked and snapped her head around to glare at me. I mumbled an apology, but didn't stop.

Then I remembered the girl. Who cared if I couldn't have Saffia? There were other women. I had half a mind to call Vanessa, though the practicalities of doing so eluded me. I made a promise to myself I would do it the very next day. Not too late, it could all yet be mended. For now there was the girl. Where was the girl?

I was in the garden. I have no memory of taking the stairs. It was as though I floated down: an ethereal, alcohol-fuelled descent. I wandered through the maze of paths, my drink in my hand. The moon hovered protectively overhead. From indoors I could hear the sound of the music, livelier now. I stopped and listened. Dizzy Gillespie, I could say with some certainty, one of Julius's favourites. The music though did not have a cheering effect upon me, standing where I was, removed from the party. At one point I stood under a tree and gazed up at the milky swathes of stars. Standing thus, with my head tilted as far back as it could go, caused me some loss of balance. I staggered and reached out for the tree with my one free arm and stood there holding on to it whilst I took the precautionary measure of taking another slug or two of my drink.

After a while I felt better and decided to get going. I followed the scent of the flowers and the earth, I fancied I could smell the moonlight, pure oxygen. I reached the place where the Harmattan lilies grew. By now, of course, the season was well and truly past. I could make out forms, upright and angular as insects, black against the moonlight. I knocked back the remainder of my drink and stood there clutching my empty glass pressed against my chest, staring at the silhouetted flowers.

The truth, if you want it, is that I have a tendency to become maudlin when I am drunk. Did I tell you that? I stood there, in front of the Harmattan lilies, and for some reason I thought of my mother, of her last illness. And then I thought of my brother, my mother's favourite, who had written to me when I was in England with news of her death. I realised I was still holding on to my empty glass and I tossed it into the flowerbed.

A movement. Somebody close by. A couple had entered the space. Seemingly unaware of my presence, they stopped and seemed to embrace. There was shuffling and breathing, a giggle and a few words of encouragement disguised as protest as women make. I moved over and peered at them through the darkness. The ground was soft and silent underfoot, after so many weeks of rain. By the time they looked up and saw me, I was only a few feet away. It was exactly as I thought: the giggle, the voice. It was the girl I had brought to the party and who I had been searching for this last half-hour. She was with some lowlife. I was furious.

Parts of what happened next remain fuzzily bright. I remember I provoked him. You could say I had already *been* provoked by him. For what kind of man is supposed to stand by and tolerate another man's hands upon his girlfriend? Somehow, anyway, the whole thing escalated. I remember lunging forward and grabbing the girl's arm when she failed to move away from him, as I ordered her to do. Her insolence heightened my sense of outrage. Some words were exchanged. I picked up a stick and threatened to beat him. The girl must have taken fright and run into the house, because the next I remember is that Julius was there and the other chap began to make excuses, claiming to have no idea what had got into me. The girl stood by emitting weeping noises. Entirely unnecessary. The sound of her and the sight of Julius only served to goad me further. I swore at them all. I raised the arm with the stick in it – not to brandish it as such, but to fling it over their heads. Julius tried to placate me, arms outstretched. I can't remember whether any kind of tussle followed. I believe not. At that point I lost my footing and fell over backwards.

All at once indignation turned to solicitation. I was pulled on to my feet – by Julius – and dusted down. More than anything else he seemed to find it funny. He repeated my name over and over. *Elias. Elias. Elias.* But I was in no mood to be appeased, or to be the butt of his humour. Inside I felt the pressure of my growing rage. I wanted to lower my head and charge at him, to throw my weight upon him and to punch and kick. Instead I knocked away his hand and stumbled towards the house, crashing through flowerbeds and shrubs. More than once I knocked into a tree. I remember, vaguely, passing through the living room. The stabbing lights. The chaotic chatter. The volume on the television was up and people were gathered around it. I passed behind them towards the front door and pushed it open.

Everybody the world over knows where they were the night the first man walked on the moon. I have always said I was at a party at Julius and Saffia's house. In time I created a version of the truth for myself, which even included my memory of that grainy grey film, Armstrong's first sentence complete with internal hesitation. *One small step.* Pause. *One giant leap.*

The truth is I have no real idea how or at what time I reached home. I passed many bars. I may even have had a drink in one or more of them. It is possible that I watched, or more likely listened to, the moon walk. I may have seen the two actors in front of the store, dressed in their tinfoil suits, combined sound and image in my own mind to create an ersatz memory.

All I know is that somehow I reached home alone. I lay in bed sweating, the ceiling spinning above me. Once I crawled out and vomited into the toilet. I went back to bed and curled up in the foetal position. At some point I slept.

I had fallen asleep without drawing the curtains and through the window I could see the sky, dense with purplish cloud that weighed low over the rooftops. Something, I knew not what, had awoken me abruptly. I lay back on the pillow, free-floating in a moment of perfect blankness, of temporary disorientation, my brain doubtless slowed by the amounts of whisky I had consumed, so for a moment, lying there, I experienced only a sense of serenity. I could not remember what day it was, it felt like a Sunday. All too soon I became aware that my mouth was so dry it was glued shut. When I opened it my breath – even to myself – smelled foul. I became aware too that I was lying on top of my bed, still dressed in my clothes. An odour of vomit hung in the air. The first memory of the night before hit me with a hot jolt. And as I continued to lie there, dislocated memories came creeping back, cloaked in shame.

I rose to use the bathroom. My shoulder throbbed faintly. I remembered my crashing progress through the garden, the immovable solidity of a tree trunk. There were a few scratches here and there, otherwise I was unhurt. The mirror displayed no further evidence. I looked the same as any other day, with the exception of an ashy cast to my skin and a smear of dark under my eyes. I would shake off the hangover soon enough with some food and coffee and in that way I might delay the effort and emotion involved in thinking about what

154

I had done. I splashed water on my face, rinsed out my mouth and spat into the basin. Then I went to set some water on the stove to fill a bath.

I was returning from the bathroom with the emptied pan of water when I noticed a woman standing on the opposite side of the street. By then it was drizzling. The rain came in thin, viscous loops that seemed to hang from the sky. The woman had an umbrella up and gave the impression of a person waiting for something. It was her stillness, I suppose, she looked neither right nor left, but gripped the stem of the umbrella with both hands.

I refilled the pan under the tap, listening to the hiss of the cold water hitting the scalding metal. As I was about to carry the pan back to the bathroom the woman raised her head. I caught a glimpse of her profile, the tilt of her chin and nose. It was enough to stop me in my tracks. I put the pan in the sink, opened the window and looked out. What on earth could she be doing here? My first reaction was alarm: her visit must be connected to my behaviour of the previous evening.

I drew back. I did a turn of the room and went once more to the window. No doubt about it. Despite myself, hope, foolish and desperate, mingled with the fear. My heart thudded in my chest, my head reeled to the point of nausea. A memory of the altercation in the garden surfaced, like a drowned corpse from beneath the swamp. What had I said? What had I done? And why had Julius not come? Or Kekura or Ade Yansaneh on a diplomatic mission to mend bridges?

Hastily I threw the covers back over the bed and pulled on some clothes. I stepped outside on to the landing of the outside stairs just at the point Saffia looked up.

If I have never described my apartment to you, I should say now that to use the word apartment was to overstate the case. It was in reality a single though largish room, with a sink and stove at one end, a bed and a bathroom at the other. It is strange to admit but as Saffia hurried up the stairs all I could think was that this was not the way I had imagined her visiting me. She reached the top step, her face unsmiling and her gaze shifting as though she was searching for something.

'Oh Elias!' she said. 'I'm sorry. I'm so sorry. I've been waiting.'

'You should have come up,' I said, moving aside to let her in.

'I did. I think I woke up your landlady.'

155

I followed her inside, sensitive to the smell in the room, of sweat and stale breath, the residual odour of vomit. Two steps into the room she turned to me, her voice as hollow as dead wood. What she said next swept my mind clear of thoughts.

'Julius has been arrested.'

On the drive to the house Saffia told me what had happened. Two men had arrived at the house in the wake of the party, just after the last of the guests had departed. Plain clothes, it seemed, for neither wore uniforms. Julius and Saffia had not yet gone to bed. No reason had been given for the arrest, no warrant, no explanation. Julius protested, of course, but in the end had seen no other choice but to comply. Saffia had tried to telephone Ade and Kekura, but failing to reach either she had come to me. I'd flattered myself, thinking I was the first place she had turned. I watched her while she tried the telephone again, listening to the faint, maddening ringing. Nobody answered. She stood with her hands covering her face, shaking her head.

'I'm sure it's a mistake,' I said. 'What else could it be?'

I suppose I had imagined we would simply wait it out. God knows I had no experience of these things, but I was – I am – by nature inclined to caution. There seemed no point in getting worked up by what could yet turn out to be a false alarm. We might even be sitting down together in a few hours laughing about it. I genuinely believed it. What I wanted to do was to stay with Saffia, here in this house. I could offer her comfort, I could offer her strength. I could be her protector. We would wait it out, and when it was over – well, I didn't think that far ahead, only of the possibility of the hours between.

Saffia picked up her car keys and proposed we drive to Ade and Kekura's homes.

No sign of Ade. A neighbour told us he had been taken away in the early morning. Ade had been one of the last to leave the party; they'd been waiting for him when he arrived home. From Ade's place we hastened to Kekura. There we found neither Kekura, nor news of him. There were three police stations within reasonable proximity of Saffia and Julius's house and we visited each in turn. The officer in charge at the first station tried to reassure Saffia that missing husbands had a habit of turning up. Saffia described the men who had come to the house that morning. He'd looked at her then, a narrow, curious stare, shrugged his shoulders and turned his back to us. I took Saffia by the arm and pulled her away.

We drove through silent streets. Back at the house Saffia continued to make calls. We discovered nothing new. Nothing on the radio either, just the usual round-up of births, deaths and marriages. All news was of the successful moon landing.

Saffia told me her aunt was away. I went into the kitchen and found some food left over from the night before. There was a new throbbing in my temple and I drank several glasses of water. I carried some cold *olele* and plantain back into the sitting room.

There was still then, at least in me, the certainty that this was not as serious as it appeared, that Julius would yet stride through the door any minute and turn the whole thing into a huge laugh, a story to tell against himself. I even, astonishingly, entertained quite seriously for several minutes the notion of kidnap, and then the idea that this was a practical joke on the part of Kekura and Ade. No doubt it was the bizarre nature of the previous evening: the moon landing, my own fall from grace, the residual alcohol in my bloodstream; anything had begun to seem possible.

One o'clock. Julius was not back. Two o'clock. Julius was not back. Four-thirty. Julius was not back. Five o'clock. Six-forty-five. Eight o'clock.

The hours dragged by, at other times sped bumpily past. At the sound of the telephone bell Saffia jumped up and snatched the receiver only to slump in disappointment when it was not Julius. Darkness came, encroaching upon hope. Somewhere a child was being beaten, the cries seemed to go on for minutes. Between Saffia and me, silence. Then Saffia rose and as she did so uttered a long sigh, of which she seemed entirely unaware. When it was over her physicality was altered; her shoulders sagged as though she was literally deflated. She moved around the room turning on the lights.

I said, 'Is there anything at all Julius might have been arrested for?'
'Of course not.'

We rehearsed the events of the morning, the possibilities – of which there were few. At the end of it she repeated what she had said at the start. None of it made any sense.

I poured us drinks. Saffia protested she didn't want anything. I persuaded her it would help. She had not touched food all day. After a single sip she set the glass back upon the table. As for me, the action of the alcohol, the hair of the dog, had an immediate and soothing effect upon my nervous system.

'We don't even know where he is,' she said. 'I should have followed them. I didn't think. It was all so confusing.'

'How could you have known?'

'No,' she said. 'I couldn't have known. You don't know until it happens. And something like this has never happened before.'

At eleven I went home promising to be back in the morning. An offer to stay had been declined. My route home took me through several checkpoints. Like so many others I'd ceased to see them other than a momentary inconvenience, that is unless your luck went against you, or you handled an exchange badly. Bullish behaviour provoked the soldiers. I wondered if something of the sort had unfolded between Julius and the men who came to the house that morning, that what began as some sort of mistake had escalated into something more for no good reason.

I nodded at the soldier manning the roadblock. He loosed the rope in his hand and eased the barrier upwards.

CHAPTER 20

Some names he knows.

Lamin says he worked colouring Easter eggs in a factory in Germany. He uses the occasional German word: *Frau. Haus. Osterei*. Diagnosed with dissocial personality disorder. Attila does not believe Lamin has ever been to Germany, Ileana tells Adrian. Lamin is making progress, Attila has allowed him to be unshackled from his bed, the chains remain around his ankles and wrists. Lamin shambles around in the sunlight, the mass of his chains gathered up and looped over one arm, like a bride's train. He raises his free hand in salute to Adrian.

In the bed next to Lamin is Kapuwa. Adrian has read his notes. Paid a bowl of rice in exchange for twelve hours a day in a diamond pit. In the evenings the men curbed their hunger with ganja. The mines were overrun by rebel soldiers, who worked them just as hard, for less food. Kapuwa escaped, but left his mind behind. His family brought a healer to wash him and recite prayers once a week. His violent outbursts frightened his family, who kept him chained to a bamboo pole in the yard.

Borbor occupies the bed in the centre of the ward. Borbor is mentally retarded and epileptic. He turns his back to Adrian and bends over waving his backside, which Adrian can see plainly through the rent in Borbor's trousers. Adrian pretends to be horrified, Borbor laughs and claps. The other patients complain Borbor is crazy. Adrian suspects Borbor is less demented than he would have others believe.

And then there is the Professor. One in every asylum, thinks Adrian. The mentally retarded and the brilliant, together in madness. The Professor is a manic-depressive, the walls around whose bed are covered in chalked words: poetic, nonsensical, obscene. The father of one of the new patients, a religious man, has complained. The Professor does not wear chains, and has the freedom of the grounds. Adrian recognises him as the man he spoke to at the front gate that first morning.

These four are long-term residents. Then there are the others, who come and go. They lie in bed all day, sleeping or in various stages of withdrawal. At night the sound of their deliriums upsets the other patients. Occasionally there is a ruckus. Many of them were once fighters, who faced each other as enemies. Now they lie side by side. The young man Adrian brought is one of them. They come and go. Come and go.

Today Lisa had called in the early morning to remind him of Kate's eleven-plus exam. Adrian hung up and called back after ten minutes to speak to Kate. If his daughter was at all nervous, it had not shown. 'It's very sweet of you to call, Daddy.' A careful, conservative child, six pounds at birth, petite and china fragile. Lisa had stayed home to look after her for the first year, and then a second, then a third, after which all talk of returning to work had ceased. Sometimes, it seemed to Adrian, he had difficulty telling where his wife ended and his daughter began, as if birth had failed to separate them. Secretly he wished Lisa would go back to work. Meanwhile Kate had grown into a child measured in thought and deed, whose transition to adulthood looked seamless, with none of the messy mistakes other children suffered.

On the telephone Adrian wished Kate luck. He was just about to tell her about the sunbird, when she interrupted him. 'I'd better go now. So I shan't be late.' At times her poise unsettled him, as though she found his efforts wanting. It had not always been so. When Kate was two she'd been prone to nightmares and would insist he — not Lisa — sit by her bed until she went back to sleep. Later he would watch her sleep, wondering what such a tiny creature could possibly be dreaming about.

On the way through town he'd bought several packets of biscuits from a roadside seller. He gives them now to Kapuwa, who takes them to a table in the middle of the room, allotting them carefully among the residents of the ward. Those who can step forward do so quietly to receive their share. Kapuwa carries biscuits over to the chained men. Lamin shambles in. The whole affair is conducted with solemnity and in silence. Kapuwa moving along the line of bunks, the men raising both chained hands to receive the biscuit, followed by a nod or grunt of thanks. Adrian wonders what it reminds him of, then realises. Kapuwa looks like a priest giving communion.

And afterwards, passing through the ward, he no longer notices the smell. The sound of his footsteps reassuringly solid. Adrian feels happier than he has in many weeks, months. Years.

Today she is dressed in a patterned blue *lappa* and a T-shirt bearing a picture of a dolphin. The T-shirt is too big for her and slips from one shoulder, a slender bone to which flesh and skin cling. Her feet are bare. Forty-three. Two years older than Adrian, the same age as Lisa. Adrian thinks of the fine lines on Lisa's skin. Agnes's face is unblemished, she weighs no more than a girl. She could be twenty or she could be sixty. The years are carried not upon her body, but in the light of her eyes.

Today, too, another development. Salia, who must have been waiting for him to arrive, intercepted him within yards of the gate and handed him a gold chain.

She sits facing him, her forearms on the armrests of the chair. This time she looks less often at Salia. She is calm, her voice contains little inflection or emotion. Adrian has less trouble understanding. Time spent helping Ileana with her rounds in the hospital has familiarised him to accents and patterns of the language.

Agnes. She was born and married, she tells him, in a town to the north of the city; her husband worked at the government agricultural project raising different varieties of fruit and vegetables. Dwarf bananas, whose yield equalled and even surpassed the ordinary ones. Pawpaws, larger than the local variety. Guavas, limes, tomatoes and vegetables. He kept a few seeds back for her and she grew them on her own plot at the back of the house and traded them in the market. In time she began to carry them to the city once a week to sell outside the supermarkets to white women. She bore five children, of whom two returned. Both were boys. The girls all survived. Naasu. Yalie. Marian.

Naasu, the eldest, was a helpful child and clever. When she passed her school certificate they gave her a party with sweets and drinks of coloured water. As soon as she finished with school Naasu got a job at the department store in the city. By then, a bag of rice had become so much more expensive. And some months too, Agnes's husband's salary at the government nurseries went unpaid.

Sometimes Agnes visited Naasu at the store on days when she went into town to sell her produce. Naasu would leave the counter where she sold cosmetics and take her to the places she and the other girls had lunch, one place in particular called the Red Rooster. Agnes enjoyed herself although it seemed wrong to spend money on food cooked by somebody else. They ate the food out of paper boxes. Afterwards Agnes would collect up the boxes and take them home, though Naasu laughed and tried to persuade her to leave them. Other times Naasu brought home tiny bottles of perfume she said were for giving out to the customers. Agnes saved them to wear on special occasions. Ah, Naasu looked so fine in the clothes she wore to work, though Alfred didn't like the way she painted her face. Naasu explained she must wear the cosmetics herself, so that the customers could see how they looked. However, in deference to her father, she left home with her face bare. She had to pay for the cosmetics out of her own money; for some reason this knowledge appeased Alfred.

Agnes had never been inside the shop during opening hours, but there were times Naasu let her in through the back after the store was closed. She walked through the empty halls gazing at the displays, the imported fabrics, the shoes with long, narrow heels, the pale dummies with pink pouting mouths. She touched them all, except the dummies, which for some reason frightened her. Naasu laughed and showed her the storeroom, where the disembodied arms and legs were stacked in piles.

Another time a bird flew in. It swooped through the wide doorways from hall to hall and perched on the shoulder of a mannequin.

Naasu no longer works at the store, Agnes tells him. She herself has not been back to the store for many years.

She is not dissembling, this Adrian can see. In turn he doesn't contradict her, but says, 'Tell me about the first trip you made, the first one you remember making that you didn't plan to make.'

It was maybe a year ago. Harmattan time again. It began in the same way as every one since, with dreams so real she could not escape them. She woke in the morning with the soles of her feet dirty; she must have gone out of the house to use the toilet and forgotten her slippers, though she had no memory of doing so. The dreams brought on a headache and she remembered waking in the morning with a blurred patch in the centre of her vision. Then suddenly everything turned black, leaving only a circle of light. She sent the girl out to buy medicine because Naasu wasn't at home, she had travelled to the wedding of a classmate in another town, she had been gone for two days and was not due for two more.

All that morning Agnes had a strong sense something was about to happen. She went to the door to see if the girl was on her way back from the pharmacy. But even after the child had returned, Agnes found herself rising to go and check at the door over and over. She forced herself to sit down. Anxiety beat in her breast like a bird's wings, like the bird trapped in the department store. Still she couldn't stay in the chair for long. She called the child to come and they set about preparing the evening meal. The pressure in Agnes's skull was joined by a sound like the rushing of air. Her own voice as she gave instructions to the child sounded like somebody else calling from another room. She wished Naasu was home. She tried to block out the sounds and concentrate on what she was doing, but all the time she felt as if she were dreaming, as if standing there cooking with the child, watching her hands slicing meat, was all part of the dream.

She does not remember leaving the house. Later, the child described what happened. Agnes had sent her on an errand in the afternoon, into town to buy fruit for Naasu's return. The child did as she was bid. She was standing at the market when she saw Agnes hurrying in the direction of the main road. The girl thought maybe Naasu was coming back early and Agnes was going to meet the bus.

Naasu found Agnes five days later. She followed her mother's footsteps, asking people in every village. In one town, somebody – a niece by marriage – had recognised Agnes, and spoken to her, but Agnes seemed not to remember her. She pointed Naasu in the direction Agnes had taken.

Agnes remembers fragments from those days. But she cannot tell Adrian whether those things truly occurred or were part of her dreams. She remembers taking a foot road, seeing the dust form a whirlwind ahead of her, spinning away. One night she slept in a farm worker's hut. Another day she watched the clouds moving across the sky, and noticed they were both heading in the same direction, but when Naasu asked her where she had been going she could not say. She was forty miles from the place they both lived. After Naasu brought her home Agnes slept for two whole days.

Agnes reaches the end of her account. She sits facing Adrian, who in turn regards her in silence. He is right, he knows he is right. Everything she has told him today supports his notion. He would not dare to make a diagnosis at this early stage. But nonetheless he is sure of himself in a way he has rarely had occasion to be before.

163

From under a sheet of paper Adrian draws the gold chain Salia had given him and hands it to Agnes.

'Thank you,' she says courteously.

'It is yours, then?'

'Yes. This is the one I lost in the ward. I thought maybe it had been stolen.'

Adrian inclines his head. He is aware of Salia watching. Adrian doesn't tell Agnes what Salia has told him. That the chain had been brought by the man from the old department store, who'd redeemed it from a pawnbroker, one of the many who sat with weighing scales and jeweller's loupes in the street outside the store.

Agnes herself had pawned it.

Sunday lunchtime. Adrian has managed to borrow a vehicle to go to Ileana's for lunch. It is the first time he has been behind the wheel of a car in weeks and he sets off, uncertainly at first. The Land Cruiser is much larger than anything he has handled, as well as being left-hand drive. It takes his hands and feet time to recover the memory of driving. Soon he is moving at speed, savouring the mood of independence. He drives in the opposite direction to the instructions Ileana has given him, towards the city, through the dense throng at the roundabout. The heat is rising, he is grateful for the air conditioning, both for the cool and the insulating effect from the dust and noise on the other side of the glass. He turns the wheel of the vehicle to the left and the traffic eases up. On the right is an open stretch of ground, a golf course; directly ahead he can see the sea. The road swings around to the right and Adrian follows it, driving the full length of the beach. Here there is no traffic at all. He turns off the air conditioning and winds down the window, lets the breeze touch his face. At the far end he doubles back at another roundabout. When he reaches the left turn at the end he sees a small road he had missed when he had come from the other direction. Behind a pair of concrete pillars a crescent driveway curves under the arch of a building. Adrian turns in and drives to the car park at the back, descends and makes his way across the uneven tarmac to the building. Three steps lead up to a fountain, an art deco figure of a girl, head tilted back, outstretched arms holding aloft a torch. A trickle of water from the torch runs down the girl's arms and belly into a small pool of green at her feet, from which a scab-eared dog laps. Behind her, a sign painted upon the wall, in faded letters: *Ocean Club Patrons Only.*

Parquet floors, bleached and water-stained, a few blocks missing in places. Adrian reaches the top of the short flight of stairs. On one side of the vast space a horseshoe bar, ahead clusters of tables and chairs, to the right a sweeping dance floor capable of holding a hundred couples or more. Morning sun and shadows shimmer on the tabletops, the walls, the stilled ceiling fans. On the far side of the dance floor the building is entirely open to the seafront. All is quiet, save for the sound of the waves. There is nobody in sight as he wanders across the dance floor, feeling strangely vulnerable as he always does crossing an empty dance floor, as though at any moment he might hear a drum roll or the clash of cymbals or find himself suddenly illuminated by a spotlight.

On the beach a score of translucent crabs scuttle from his shadow. Down by the water tiny seabirds, sandpipers, follow the movement of the waves, scurrying after the retreating water, inspecting the sand for whatever has been left in its wake. Hurrying back as the water advances. Detectives scanning the beach for evidence, wings like hands clasped self-importantly behind backs. Adrian is tempted to remove his shoes and socks and walk down to the water, but the practicalities are off-putting. So he heads instead for the bar, pulling up one of the old stools to sit on. Within moments a man appears.

'Yes, sir?'

'Beer, please.' It is only eleven, what the hell.

The barman opens a bottle and slides the beer down the inside of a tilted glass. He flips a beer mat, places the glass upon it and pushes it towards Adrian, who takes a sip enjoying the bite of the cold beer at the back of his throat. The man goes away and comes back with a stainless-steel dish of peanuts. They are tiny, delicious, with salty pink papery skins, a fragment of which gets caught in Adrian's throat causing him to cough and cough again.

'Be careful, sir.'

'Yes, thank you.' Adrian drains his glass, but is left still coughing. 'Another beer, please.'

'First time here?' says the waiter as he pours the second bottle.

'Yes.' It is a question he has grown to dislike. He feels patronised, a new arrival, wet behind the gills – particularly if the questioner is another Westerner.

'And how do you find us here?'

Adrian nods. 'I like it very much.'

The bartender nods gravely as though this is as he would have expected. He replies, 'Maybe you will tell others. And then they will come.'

Adrian drinks his beer. The barman departs and returns with a basin of ice, which he positions on a shelf beneath the bar.

'Actually,' says Adrian, 'I already knew a bit about the country. From my grandfather.' This is not strictly true, and he is not quite sure why he says it. Perhaps because he is tired of being treated like a beginner. The barman looks up.

'Your grandfather was here?'

'Yes,' says Adrian. 'A long time ago. Before the war. He was a district commissioner.'

'What was his name, your grandfather?'

'Silk.'

'District Commissioner Silk, yes.' Neither the barman's tone of voice nor his expression convey a thing, not even whether he recognises the name or is merely politely concurring. Adrian finishes his beer. By the time he comes to pay the barman has gone again. He counts the money and looks around for the man, noticing for the first time a poster on a pillar behind him. He slips from the stool for a closer look; *Mamba Blues. 6 p.m. to 8 p.m. First Monday of the Month. At the Ocean Club.* There is an image of a woman's face partly in profile. It looks like the woman he saw outside the hospital talking to Babagaleh; the angle of the photograph makes it hard to be certain. Adrian looks around for the barman, but there's still no sign of him, so he places the correct money on the counter and leaves.

The road to Ileana's house is straight and the distance no more than a few miles; nevertheless it takes Adrian thirty minutes to drive there because of the road's treacherous condition. Two dogs, collarless and slender, lie by the door. One of them cautiously sniffs Adrian's hand as he waits for Ileana to answer his knock. Through the fly screen he can see the living room: old rattan sofa, coffee table, books. Bright shawls cover the furniture. On the wall a mirror bordered by a mosaic frame, sharp fragments of glass. There is piano music playing. In time he sees Ileana cross the sitting room, smoking a cigarette. As he watches she performs a few steps of a dance. Her lips are pale, bare of lipstick. She does not see him. Adrian waits until she is out of sight before knocking a second time. This time Ileana appears down the short passage, and briskly throws open the fly screen.

'The door is open. You should have come in.' She smiles and kisses him on each of his cheeks, stands back and regards him for a moment, like a mother looking to see how much her son has grown. Her lips are dark red, freshly painted. 'Welcome!'

The house, a compact bungalow, sits squarely on the beach. Ileana goes to the kitchen and returns with a cold beer for Adrian.

'If this was my place, I'd knock down all the walls and keep it as one space, like a studio,' she says.

'It's great.' He removes his shoes, slides open the screen and steps on to springy grass and sand. 'How did you find it?'

'It was leased by a mining company, for their foreign workers to take weekend breaks. I took it over at a bargain rent. You could say there was a bit of a glut in the property market at that time.' Ileana laughs. 'You'd never get something like this now, and not at that price. All the ones along this stretch are rented for a fortune to one NGO or another.'

She places a pair of plastic chairs and they sit, enjoying for a few moments a companionable silence and the sound of the sea.

A group are walking up the beach against the sun. Three fat silhouettes and three thin. Each of the fat figures appears conjoined to a thin one. As they approach, Adrian sees that they are three men, each with a young black girl. The girls seem exceptionally young, narrow and pretty.

Ileana and Adrian watch them pass.

'How differently we behave in other people's countries,' says Ileana. She raises her beer bottle to her lips. 'It just goes to show.'

'Show what?'

'No sooner than we think we can get away with it, we do as we please. It doesn't require the breakdown of a social order. It takes a six-hour plane flight.'

'I see what you mean.' Adrian watches the receding figures.

Here and there groups of bathers sit on the sand, or under an umbrella. Children move between them selling peanuts and fruit.

'I hope you like crab,' says Ileana.

They carry salad, plates and cutlery outside. There is fried rice and a bottle of cold white wine. Ileana throws a pair of giant crabs on top of a coal pot, where they pop and sizzle. While they eat Adrian talks to Ileana about Agnes, of the progress she is making.

'She's still pretty confused, though that's improving. A few days ago she couldn't recognise herself in a mirror. Now she's able to hold a conversation. There are gaps but my guess is that in a few days she'll be back to herself.'

'And the journeys?'

'So far as I know they started after the war, not before. That much seems clear. I need to find the trigger. I'm working on the premise that something occurred during the war.'

'You think she's suffering from post-traumatic stress disorder?'

'That's what I'm looking at,' Adrian says carefully.

Adrian is aware of Ileana's steady gaze upon him. He can't fool her, she knows exactly what's in his mind. If he's right he will have achieved something considerable. To prove the existence of fugue in a population would be a professional coup. But if he could also demonstrate a clear link to post-traumatic stress disorder? Well, that could make his name.

Moving on, he tells Ileana about the gold chain, how they had got to the bottom of that particular mystery. Agnes had pawned it and forgotten.

'Dissociation,' says Ileana, standing up. 'She does things she can't remember doing. More wine?'

'Yes please,' says Adrian.

He looks out at the horizon. In his mind he replays the second interview with Agnes, during which she'd complained about the theft of her gold chain. This followed the night Salia had been forced to sedate her. Adrian had prompted Agnes into recalling the events leading up to her most recent journey. She'd mentioned her daughter had been away. And again, in the last interview, when they had talked about her first journey, the daughter had been away from home that time, too. With this realisation his heart skips a beat, he leans forward in the chair, peruses the connection he has just made. It cannot simply be a coincidence. Naasu is the only daughter she talks about, he'd already noted that. The journeys occur when Naasu is away from home. He exhales and leans back in his chair. He can hardly wait to interview Agnes again. He must be careful not to rush her. What had they been talking about when she'd brought up the gold chain again? He asked her who was in the house with her. He mentioned the girl, her son-in-law. He ponders whether there is meaning in that. Sudden switches of subject were sometimes a marker of a patient wanting to avoid something: the subconscious steered them away.

Ileana returns with the wine.

'It could take a long time,' she says, continuing their early conversation. 'I mean for you to discover the trigger, if there is one. Years of investigation. Therapy. And even then there are no guarantees. After all, it was us Europeans who invented the talking cure. And most of the maladies it's designed to treat.' She snorts faintly.

'There are other ways,' says Adrian.

'Like what, hypnosis?'

'Yes. Have you ever tried it?'

'No,' replies Ileana. 'I don't know what Attila would make of it. I know I think it's a bit early in the game.'

'Of course,' concedes Adrian. 'It was just a thought.'

Ileana stands and scrapes the contents of one plate to the other, the debris of crab shells and empty claws. Out at sea a fishing canoe sits high upon the shallow waves, a line of buoys marks the shape of the net. Ileana is in the kitchen. Two women are walking along the beach; one of them waves at Adrian. A moment later she waves again. Politely, Adrian waves back thinking she must have mistaken him for somebody else. The women change direction and come up the beach towards him.

'Hiya,' says the one who waved. She is tall, her shoulders almost as broad as his, an athlete's body, blonde hair and prominent teeth. Her companion is shorter, small-breasted though with a good figure, reddish hair and a red bikini, the pale skin of a true redhead.

'Hello,' says Adrian, shielding his eyes against the sun as he looks up at them.

'We saw you and thought we'd come and say hello. Pedro's, a couple of weeks ago.' Her accent is American.

'Of course,' Adrian replies. He recognises her now as the woman from the bar the evening he drank beers with Kai. Kai had given her the brush-off, though she hadn't seemed to mind.

'Been having a good day?'

'Absolutely.'

'Isn't the beach great? But there are others that are even better, with some great beach bars, well, if you can call them that. Of course it takes them for ever to bring the food. And half the time they don't have what you order. But then isn't that the same every place? You get used to it. The lobster is to die for and just about two dollars for a whole one. Can't get that at home. Some guy dives from the rocks for fresh oysters while you wait. They're a dollar a dozen.' She sits in Ileana's chair. 'Have you tried the Shangri-La?'

'This is my first day out at the beach.'

'You're kidding! By the way, I'm Candy. This is Elle.' They are both in the country working for aid agencies. In turn Adrian tells them about his position at the hospital.

'So this isn't your place then?'

'No.' Adrian mentions Ileana. Candy shrugs and shakes her head. Two men selling sarongs and souvenirs approach and begin to display their wares, batik cloths, haematite necklaces and glossy, carved animals. One of the men is in his fifties, the other in his twenties, shirtless with a smooth muscular chest. Neither Candy nor Elle pays attention to the men or their wares. Elle sits on the sand and, turning her back on them, rolls over on to her stomach on the sand; as she does so, she reaches down to adjust her bikini bottoms, flicking the elastic. There is no self-consciousness in the gesture, as if the men behind her don't exist. Candy is still talking. Adrian looks at her, remembers the expression on her face the night she had approached Kai: self-confident, hungry. He thanks the two men, tells them they are not interested in buying.

'Don't bother, they never give up,' says Candy. 'So how long have you been here?' For the second time that day Adrian is asked the question. He tells them and Candy laughs.

'I thought you looked saner than the rest of us,' and she laughs again.

'I'm sorry?'

'You haven't heard the joke?' says Candy, flicking a look at Elle.

Adrian shakes his head, bemused.

'You know the joke? About the tourist?'

He still has no idea what she is talking about.

'What's the difference between a tourist and a racist?'

'I don't know,' he responds automatically.

'Two weeks!'

Elle laughs supportively, though she has clearly heard the joke before. Candy is grinning at him. Adrian has no idea how to respond. He is silent.

Behind Candy the sellers are folding sarongs, putting them away. Adrian thinks of the obtuse police officers and the deaf boy, his frustration with the hospital administrator, the power cuts and water shortages, the heat, the clogged gutters and traffic jams in the city, the beggars. He thinks of the pregnant woman with the dead baby between her legs, of Kai, then of Agnes, of the young man he first brought to the hospital, of his friends among the patients at the hospital, the calm and beauty of the Patients' Garden. Of Attila's unbroken determination. Of his own strange happiness in that place. He is still unsure what to say when he realises the attention of both women has been redirected.

'Oh, hi,' Candy says, in a tone noticeably flatter to the one with which she had greeted Adrian. Ileana has reappeared with a dish of sliced fruit, mango and pineapple. She greets the two women and sets the plate down on the table.

'Hey, that looks great!' Candy says, her tone gushing now. 'And this place, too.'

'Thank you. I'll get some more plates.'

To Adrian's relief the moment has passed. He wonders if Ileana heard Candy's joke, though if she did she gives no sign of it, disappearing for a second time to re-emerge with extra plates and cutlery. The fruit is fresh, sharp and clean, clears his taste buds of the residual flavour of crab.

Suddenly Ileana sets her plate back on the table and stands up. 'I'm so sorry,' she says to the two women. 'You don't have anything to drink. What would you like? There's wine.'

'Hey. Awesome! We've lucked out here. Could a day get any better?'

Ileana nods graciously. She takes the bottle from the cool box beside Adrian and pours two more glasses.

'This is really good.' Elle, this time.

'Do you know what the most popular white wine here is?' asks Ileana.

'No,' say Candy and Elle and turn to her, Adrian as well. The two women open-faced and smiling.

'It goes like this,' says Ileana, and she affects a grating, high-pitched voice, a clear imitation of Candy's nasal accents. 'Christ, what's wrong with these people? Can't they do anything for themselves? If it wasn't

171

for us they'd still be in the trees.' And with that she sits down heavily in her chair, takes a sip from her own glass. 'Cheers! Good, isn't it? The most popular white whine.'

That night it turns cold. There is no wind, no rain and yet, lying in his bed, Adrian feels a chill in the air. He gets up from his bed and switches off the ceiling fan. The movement sets his stomach churning. The crab perhaps, though it had tasted fresh enough. With these things one seldom knew until it was too late. And yet, if his memory serves, seafood poisoning came on quickly. He calculates how long it has been since he left Ileana's. About five hours. Candy and Elle had stayed only a few minutes after Ileana's remarks. 'Silly tarts,' she'd said as they watched the two women walk away. 'Do you know how much they get as a hardship allowance?' Fortunately, the tension caused by the women's visit had vanished with them, Adrian and Ileana once more at ease between themselves. He had admired the sharpness of her response, and felt grateful for her apparent willingness to overlook the failure of his own.

They had swum, the shock of the water – the warmth rather than the cold – dispelling any awkwardness resulting from seeing each other, two professional colleagues, in their swimwear. Ileana, hair tucked up inside a tight rubber cap, turned out to be a strong, serious swimmer and a match for Adrian. They had both cut through the soupy water for fifty yards, and stayed there riding the ebb and flow of the waves, as the sun went down. And afterwards they'd walked down the beach, where Ileana had shown Adrian a hotel, deserted since the war. There was the bar, the card tables: torn felt and broken glass, as though a wind had blown through them.

Later Adrian had driven home through the rapidly gathering dusk, not wanting to test his driving skills in the dark. He arrived exhausted and with the beginnings of a headache, had drunk some water and gone soon to bed, to wake a few hours later to this unseasonal coolness. The cotton sheet, which he usually pushes from his body during the night, is not enough. He searches the cupboards, finds a blanket and lies back down, pulling the stiff, stale wool up around his shoulders.

Dawn finds him shivering. Far away he hears the key turn in the door, wonders what Kai is doing here so early. He pulls the blanket around his body and stumbles to the bedroom door.

'Hey, man,' says Kai. 'How's the morning?'

Adrian tries to answer, his voice emerges weakly. He sees Kai turn to look more closely, take a few steps towards him. Standing there Adrian feels the sweat rising, seeping from his pores, bringing with it a flush of heat. He pushes the blanket away, suddenly he is thirsty. He puts out a hand to steady himself. Kai is in front of him, blocking his way, his hands on his shoulders, peering into his face.

'Woah, man.' He hears Kai's voice distantly. 'Man, you are sick!'

CHAPTER 21

Two hours after the end of his shift and Kai has cleaned the kitchen, washed the dishes, thrown out all the old food in the fridge, wiped the surfaces and emptied the bin of rubbish and ants. Next he rearranged the front room, punching the cushions and shaking the mats. With a switch broom borrowed from the caretaker he swept the dust out of the door. Then he stripped the soiled sheets from under Adrian, tipping a porter to remove them and return with clean ones, and made up the bed, moving Adrian from one side of the bed to the other with practised efficiency. Minutes later the porter returned with a bag of food, and Kai entered the kitchen and set about making soup: a clean, clear broth to which he added an entire Scotch bonnet pepper, crushed on the back of a wooden spoon, and a dash of lime.

Now he sits on the settee, while the soup simmers, glances through some of the papers on the coffee table, flicks through a reference book reading a sentence here, a chapter heading there. He lays his head back and closes his eyes. In a moment images begin to rise, fragments of dreams. He shakes his head and forces his eyes open. He is not sleeping well and sleep, when it comes, chooses inopportune moments. He hasn't been home in three days, going instead straight from the theatre to Adrian's apartment.

He enters the bedroom carrying a bowl of soup. At the sound of the bowl being set upon the night stand, Adrian opens his eyes. Kai leaves and returns with another bowl, this time of water, plus soap and a towel.

'I can use the bathroom, you know.'

'Sure you can. Easier for me to carry the bowl than you, that's all.'

Adrian smiles and pulls himself up. He washes his hands. In the three days he has grown leaner, the bones of his face thrown into relief.

Kai hands him the bowl and spoon. 'Pepper soup. All-time cure. Everything from hangovers to malaria. Good for the soul, too. Like

Jewish chicken soup, only better. Both have proven curative and restorative powers.'

'I believe you.'

'Good.'

'I was dreaming,' says Adrian, in between sips. 'Swimming underwater. The fish. The colours, my God. Is this what it's like?'

Kai nods. 'Mild deliriums, maybe. The medication can sometimes have that effect, not just the illness.'

A movement at the window on the other side of the room causes them both to turn. It is the sunbird. The bird's body is curved, his wings work so fast as to be invisible to the naked eye, just the slender body of the bird, a comma hanging in the air, or a pause in a moment in time. Kai has moved the feeder to a place outside the window of the bedroom. Earlier in the day the sight of it from the kitchen window had revived a memory from childhood – he must have been very young indeed, for the memory came without accompanying thoughts, only physical sensations – of following a bird such as this through a garden. Not to catch it, but to imitate it. He remembered picking a flower and putting it in his mouth, the dustiness of the pollen, the taste of crushed petals, and finally, the sweetness.

Adrian's sketchbook and paints are on the floor next to the bed, where Kai has placed them. 'I feel too much like shit to be bored,' Adrian says.

'You wait. You'll need to rest at least a week before you go back to work. You'll be bored.'

'I can't afford a week.'

'Listen.' Kai sits on the edge of the bed. 'The last guy who declined the advice I've just given you we shipped back home three months later. He didn't work again for a year. It's not just the malaria. Your body is fighting on all fronts in this climate. If you're born here you get used to it. On the other hand, there's a reason life expectancy is so short. So take my advice.'

On Adrian's behalf, Kai telephones Ileana and also sends a message to the old man's room. Afterwards he collects some medicine from the hospital pharmacy and makes his way along to Adrian's apartment again.

'The guy in the private room. You told me about him. Pulmonary fibrosis, right?'

'Right.'

'I guess I didn't bother to read the name on the notes.'

'Why? Do you know him?'

'Yes. Well, *knew* him. From the university.'

'He was a lecturer, is that right?'

'More than that, he was Dean of Humanities in my time.'

'Oh?' says Adrian. 'Is there a reason you ask?'

Kai takes a breath. 'Not really. How are you doing with that soup?'

'I feel better already.'

'I'll let you finish it,' says Kai. He leaves the bedroom, crosses the living room, opens the front door and looks out at the hospital quadrangle.

Elias Cole. How that name takes Kai back to another time, drops him down into a place in the past he doesn't want to go. He casts around for something else to think about, fastens on a picture sent to him by his sister some years back of the whole family, minus Kai, of course, whale watching in Vancouver. In the picture his parents made uncertain, lumpish tourists, wearing zipped cardigans and solemn expressions, like overgrown children. In between them his sister's two kids mugged for the camera; the boy had pushed himself forward of the group so that his head was absurdly large within the frame. His sister's Canadian husband must have been behind the camera. Doubtless the excursion was his idea. It would never occur to Kai's parents to go whale watching. They didn't understand those kinds of activities: climbing a hill for the view, sending postcards containing a single line of text. Besides there were whales right here; you could see them from the beach at certain times of the year.

With his parents gone Kai inhabited the house less and less, and then only in the hours of darkness. On weekends, when not with Nenebah, he was with Tejani, and when he was with neither of them he simply returned to the hospital.

A Sunday they'd operated upon a miner. The man, a Guinean, spoke only French. He'd been given an epidural rather than a full anaesthetic, nobody anticipating quite how awkward the procedure would prove to be. A steel pin, a repair to an earlier fracture, had slipped downwards into the knee joint and needed to be removed. They'd struggled to locate the tip of it within the femur. All the while the man had lain upon his back, gazing at the ceiling, apparently indifferent to the bone-jarring drill.

Afterwards they'd emerged to a darkened city, thinking at first it was later than it was. In the staff room there was talk of a coup. The Europeans went to the phones and began to dial their embassy switchboards. Kai left the hospital and entered the curfew-quiet streets. On his way he saw others, ghosts flitting through the narrow lanes away from the main roads. On a corner he collided with somebody's shoulder. The other man reached out to steady him, a moment later Kai was on his way. Not a word had been spoken, the only sound the softly uttered grunt at first contact.

The moon was a waning crescent, a sliver of light escaping through a slit in the sky. Just enough to outline, faintly, the edges of the house. Kai waited outside until he saw Nenebah leave the sitting room. He stood up and skirted the house, walking in parallel to her, she inside, he outside, they both reached the bedroom at the same time. His fingers found the edge of the shutter. When she returned from washing, still drying her face with one end of the towel, he was lying on his stomach across her bed. A quick breath, her eyes darted towards the door. Silently she let the towel drop and slid into his embrace.

'You're crazy,' she told him. 'What if my father finds you? You're not supposed to do this. You're supposed to say the password.'

'Sorry.' He pressed his face against her belly, his chin rested in shower-damp hair.

'Go on.' She lay back and placed her arms above her head. And then, a small giggle. 'Not that. I mean say the word.'

So he'd whispered their password, there and then, but she didn't hear it, rather felt his breath, and arched her back slightly to meet him, placing her hands on his shoulders, pressing down with open palms. He loved the even pacing of her breathing, the intake and release, until the rhythm fell away, like a musician missing a string of notes, crashing down upon the keyboard.

Later, tracing her form with the back of his hand, feeling the new dampness upon her skin, he caught her nipple between his index finger and middle finger and held it the way one would hold a cigarette.

'You'll have to stay,' she said. 'You can't go now. It's too dangerous.'

'I know,' he replied. Not knowing if she were talking about her father or the coup. From Kai's room in the student halls of residence, the return to their family homes restricted their lovemaking, bringing to it a new anticipation. Many times he had knocked on the shutter, whispered their password; never had he slept there. That night he

177

had not slept, either, but lain awake and watched the changing light upon the bare wall, dawn slowly highlighting the shape of her beside him. It had rained hard in the night, the pattern of the rain played out upon the wall; the sound wrapped itself around them as they lay in the huddle of each other's arms.

In the morning he had slipped out, the air clammy with dew and the exhaled breath of sleepers. By then there was a new order.

Kai awakens from dreaming of her. From outside comes the sound of rain. For a while he imagines it is some part of the dream, surely it is too early in the year for rain. The water resounds upon the roof. Kai rises and crosses the sitting room to turn up the music, Jimmy Cliff. 'Wonderful World, Beautiful People.' He goes to the door and opens it, watching the rain, feeling the water splash up and touch his feet, his ankles. Gradually the glory of the music, the soothing sounds of the rain absorb the memory of the dream.

On the fifth day Kai opens the door of the bedroom to find Adrian up and half dressed. At Kai's entrance he slumps on to the bed, apparently defeated by the effort of buttoning his trousers. There are faint shadows between his ribs, tracks of purplish veins run beneath translucent skin.

'Where do you think you're going?'

'I have to go in.' Adrian struggles with the buckle of his belt.

Kai shakes his head. 'Man, you can barely stand.'

'Just for two hours. That's all. I have to see her.'

'Who?'

'My patient.'

Kai stands regarding Adrian's efforts for a moment. Then he crosses the room, takes a striped cotton shirt from the cupboard, hands it to Adrian and watches as he forces one arm and then the other through the sleeves, a sheen of sweat upon his forehead. Kai steps forward to help with the buttons.

'I'll drive you,' he says.

Kai recognises Ileana from her voice over the telephone.

She takes one look at Adrian. 'My God, you look awful.'

'Don't worry. I've brought my doctor.' Adrian smiles faintly and waves his arm at Kai, a lolling gesture, like a barely animated rag doll. 'Kai, Ileana. Ileana, Kai.'

Ileana looks at Kai and nods briskly. Her attention immediately returns to Adrian. 'Listen, I'm really sorry,' she says.

'It's malaria. Everyone gets it. Or so I'm told.'

'No. I mean I'm sorry, Adrian. Agnes's gone. I'm so sorry. I should have called, but you were sick.'

The drive back takes place in silence. Adrian, his head resting upon the glass, gazes sightlessly out of the window. Kai understands the dismay that goes with losing a patient, in whatever manner. Each time you start work on a patient, you begin – he does not know a surgeon who is different – with total belief. It is a belief in the possibility of life, almost a spiritual belief which dwarfs all scientific knowledge, all medical learning. No information about the chances for the patient can assail it. You tackle a one-in-a-hundred with the same vigour you bring to a one-in-three or a one-in-two. During the worst days of the war, the doctors would walk down the corridors picking the injured men and women who might have a chance, leaving the others to die. He had experienced less conflict over doing so than he imagined. Yet once a patient had become their own, once the team became united in that goal, the loss was bitterly felt by all.

In the event it is Adrian who speaks first, to ask if the air conditioning might be turned down. Kai reaches across and rests the back of his hand briefly on Adrian's brow.

'Your temperature is right back up. What you need is to cool down.' He leans back and gropes about on the rear seat until he finds a plastic bottle of water. He hands it to Adrian. Kai sees him take a few sips, bracing himself against the jolting of the vehicle on the uneven road. He slows the vehicle and says, 'From what you told me she'll be back in a few months.'

Adrian stares ahead and wipes his mouth. 'Yes. Only I don't know if I'll still be here when she does.'

When they reach the flat Adrian heads straight to the bedroom, and Kai into the kitchen. Presently Kai hears the sound of the cistern and Adrian returns to the sitting room.

'Christ, I'm exhausted. By the way, is that normal?'

'To be exhausted? Yes.'

'No, I mean my piss. It's the colour of orangeade.'

Kai laughs. 'I forgot to warn you about that.'

The telephone rings. Lisa. Kai listens to the restraint in Adrian's voice. He and Nenebah had never got to that place, the place where

179

politeness reasserts itself, had argued frequently. He notices Adrian makes no mention of his illness.

That morning, when Kai had left Nenebah's house and arrived back at the hospital, had been the first. There would be a lull. The storm would catch them all unawares. But all that was two years away from that morning. Right then he'd been twenty-six years old. On the walk to work he'd heard the sound of mortars for the first time, beginning with the cheerful whistling overhead and ending in an explosion. He began to run, arriving to find the hospital in chaos. His heart still pumped from the run, to him it was exhilarating. The army had mutinied and stormed the central prison, the prison gates had been torn down. The first casualties were prisoners. Burns mostly, and the effects of smoke inhalation, for the first wave of departing prisoners had set fire to their quarters, forgetting or perhaps heedless of the fate of the other inmates. Only the worst wounded came to the hospital, the others preferring to seize the opportunity which had presented itself. There were a few prison guards among them, who thought they should be treated first, and some of the staff were in agreement. Kai hadn't cared. He merely set to work on the patients, one after the other. The fires burned all night, the sacking of the city continued. That day, apart from burns, he had treated more gunshot wounds than he had seen in his career.

Late in the afternoon he had stepped outside the building. Somebody offered him a cigarette, and though he didn't smoke he placed it unlit between his lips. Rumours abounded. One, no, two of the hotels were under siege, packed full of fleeing politicians. The Americans were coming. The British were sending a gunship. The central bank had been raided, there was money lying in the streets. Inside the empty staff room a radio blared, the spokesman for the coup leaders issuing statements in broken English.

The next time Kai left the building it must have been around midnight. It was dark. For the last five hours he'd been working by the light of a camping lantern. He stood listening to the sound of gunfire. Later it would never fail to amaze him how innocuous a sound it was in reality, nothing like the loud bangs in the movies. A time would come when he would be able to identify the make and model of a weapon from the sound it made, match the resulting injuries to those weapon types. For now he stood and stared at the sky, the iron-rich scent of blood rising from the stains on his gown. He felt exhausted, and at the same time utterly content. He smiled.

Then he remembered Nenebah.

Evening comes. Kai is folding paper from memory: in half, a corner here, an edge turned over, he runs a fingernail down a fold, working quickly for speed is part of the purpose. His fingers move deftly, finally pulling the object into shape. A frog. He pulls it apart, smoothes out the creases and begins again. This time he fashions a long-necked camel, after that a swan. At home, origami animals line the windowsill in the room where Abass sleeps. Kai is about to dismantle the swan when Adrian comes into the room, clad only in his shorts. His hair is stuck in dark points to his forehead. He is holding a pair of scissors.

'Can you help me?'

'Sure.' Kai puts the swan back on the table.

'That's impressive.' Adrian picks up the swan. 'Where did you learn to do this?'

'I practise.' He shrugs. He takes the scissors from Adrian. 'What do you want me to do with those?'

'Cut my hair. It's driving me crazy.'

Kai rises and goes to stand behind Adrian, he picks up a strand of hair experimentally. 'Do you have a comb?'

'Yes.' Adrian fetches a comb from the bedroom. Kai selects a lock of hair; the texture is disconcertingly glassy, the small nail scissors scarcely gain purchase. He snips at a few strands of hair, stops, watches the trembling in the fingers of the hand holding the scissors. This morning, in surgery, he'd been obliged – almost – to ask another surgeon to handle a delicate task. He'd even gone so far as to imagine what he might say, pretend that a speck of something was caught under his eyelid, an excuse to leave the room. In the end it had been all right. Kai concentrated on breathing and managed to steady his hand; just once he thought he saw the nurse's eye upon him.

Sharp strands of hair fall to the floor.

'Your wife didn't want you to come here.'

'Not as such.'

Kai considers Adrian's reply for a moment. 'That means no.'

'I didn't really give her the opportunity to object, if I am honest.'

'OK.'

'I needed something else. I could look up and see my future rolling into the distance. I knew exactly what was going to happen every day. I used to wonder, too, whether if I disappeared it would make any difference to any of my clients' lives, I mean in reality as opposed to the short-term inconvenience. Probably it was a dangerous thing to do.' He laughs. 'But you know what I mean.'

Kai does not know what he means. Still, he chooses not to say. This is the way Europeans talk, as though everybody shared their experiences. Adrian's tone suggested that the desire for something was all it took. They all live with endless possibilities, leave their homes for the sake of something new. But the dream is woven from the fabric of freedom. For desire to exist it requires the element of possibility, and that for Kai has never existed, until now, with the arrival of Tejani's letters. There for the first time is the element of possibility, kindling for the small flame of his own desire. He looks at Adrian's hair, which now is about an uneven two inches long all over.

'I don't think this is working,' he says. And watches Adrian's tentative fingers appear over the horizon of his head. 'Wait. I'll go and get a pair of clippers from the store.'

When Kai walked away from the hospital the day of the coup nobody tried to stop him for the simple reason he told nobody he was going. The most direct route to Nenebah's house passed through the centre of town. He reasoned nobody else would think to go that way, which was the extent of his forethought. The hospital lay at the end of a street perpendicular to the main road. The street was empty as Kai had never seen it, even in the early hours of the morning. He kept moving, staying close to the walls of the buildings. A car, a Toyota packed with joyriding soldiers, crossed the intersection ahead of him. Kai stopped and crouched next to a stinking gutter. The vehicle passed by, leaving a trail of sound. The tune stayed in his mind. From behind a corrugated-iron yard door he saw a child's face, regarding him through rusted eyelets. Kai put a finger to his lips. He stood up, doubled back on himself. This time he took the bay road, slung like a hammock between one high point of the town and another, the lowest point sagging through the city slums. The air was heavy with smoke, the tart fumes of burning fuel. A car approached him, travelling at speed. Kai caught a glimpse of the driver, a man wearing a panama hat, driving with a ferocious concentration. Kai raised his hand to ask for a lift. The driver passed by without slowing. Kai had expected little else. By now he had settled into a slow jog, marking time to the sound of his own breathing.

At the roundabout, a roadblock, Kai slowed to a walk. Five roads met at this point. He could see a dozen or so soldiers, some checking vehicles, others standing around. He saw the man with the panama hat sitting behind the wheel of his car. A soldier opened the car door, the man climbed down and the soldier took his place behind the wheel. Kai could see the man's mouth, an oval of protest. A soldier patted the man on the shoulder. From inside the vehicle another soldier threw his briefcase to him. The man clumsily tried to catch it. The vehicle backed out, clutch screaming. Kai walked on with measured paces, his heart hammered in his chest, there was a ringing in his ears. He walked towards the checkpoint.

There were people – those desperate enough to venture out, or else with nothing to lose, street boys and madmen. The street boys cheered every time a military vehicle passed, the madmen cursed. When they saw Kai, several of the soldiers yelled at him to turn back. 'Curfew. Go to your home.' Kai stopped walking and raised his hands, then he approached slowly, he wanted them to see he was a doctor. Soldiers were almost superstitious about doctors, never knowing when they might need one. The smell of ganja was heavy in the air. Down each of the five roads fires burned, figures moved through the light and darkness, the sound of their calls like jackdaws.

'Mansaray!' somebody called him. A Bedford truck was slowing for the checkpoint. Kai looked up into darkness. 'Mansaray!' A hand reached out towards him through the wooden slats at the back of the truck. Automatically Kai stretched out his own hand. Up ahead the barrier was raised, the truck's engine revved and the vehicle began to gather speed again. Whoever it was called, 'I say, wait up! Wait up!' The truck stopped five yards on the other side of the barrier and Kai raced towards it. He had no idea who he was running to, simply that this was his only chance. He climbed up on to the tailgate of the truck and sat down opposite the man who had called to him, an army officer around the same age as himself. 'Lucky I saw you there, my friend.' Hindered by the darkness, Kai struggled to recognise the other man at first, then it came to him. Five-a-side football. Kai had been in the college team for a season. Lansana was his name. Lansana what? He couldn't remember.

'They've invited the rebels into the city. For talks, they say,' he told

Kai. 'But look at this. Most of these are not our men. Some of them, yes.' Around them drunken looters staggered under the weight of their bounty. Cars abandoned full of crates and boxes.

The Bedford dropped Kai two streets short of Nenebah's house. 'Take care, man.' Lansana gave him a high five as he prepared to climb out of the truck. A glimmer of light momentarily revealed the other man's face to Kai. Behind the smile his eyes were flat, almost without expression. The look stayed with Kai for a long time afterwards, until finally he saw it for what it was. Fear, nerves or excitement, these had all been absent. And that, in turn, spoke of something else – the absence of hope. Kai thanked Lansana and wished he knew his surname.

The army was divided, he told Nenebah. If the army was divided it was dangerous for everyone. The army, the rebels, whoever they were – were attacking homes now. Even the diplomatic missions and the houses of the whites.

'Funny, isn't it?' Nenebah had said once, not then, before. Before, before. When they were younger still, at university. What were they talking about? Some faraway atrocity reported in the news. The students passed a resolution condemning it. That was it, yes, he had dismissed the action with a joke. But she had a dislike of cynicism. 'Hitler, Pol Pot. Funny, isn't it? How it only seems to be evil people who think they can change the world? I wonder why that is.' And Kai had responded, 'Because they're mad.' She had dug a sharp elbow into his ribs. Then she shook her head. 'But they do, don't they? They do change the world.'

For the next three days Kai walked alone to the hospital, where the medical staff continued to report for work and treat the wounded with detached determination. This was their job, their life. At those times Kai was happy.

The memories come at unguarded moments, when he cannot sleep. In the past, at the height of it, he had attended to people whose limbs had been severed. Working with a Scottish pain expert years later, he treated some of those same patients again. They complained of feeling pain in the lost limbs, the aching ghost of a hewn hand or foot. It was a trick of the mind, the Scotsman explained to Kai: the nerves continued to transmit signals between the brain and the ghost limb. The pain is real, yes, but it is a memory of pain.

And when he wakes from dreaming of her, is it not the same for him? The hollowness in his chest, the tense yearning, the loneliness he braces against every morning until he can immerse himself in work and forget. Not love. Something else, something with a power that endures. Not love, but a memory of love.

CHAPTER 22

A day passed. Then another. The clouds hung thick over the city, only their patterns altered with the wind. It was as if we were trapped on the dark side of a mirror. We could see the world, people running through the rain, children playing in the puddles, but we could not hear them. The house was quiet. One or two of Julius's colleagues from the university called, his absence at a meeting had been noted. We told them he had been called away on a family matter. No news of Kekura. The dancer fellow, I remember, dropped by. Somehow he had heard what had happened and he arrived, throwing out offers of help, claiming to have various contacts here and there among the police. I did not like his familiarity, the way he sat, legs splayed, arms stretched out along the back of the chair, making a display of himself. Nor did I believe his claims. Were the police taking dancing lessons now? But Saffia would take help where she found it. I had a growing sense by then that no good would come of stirring things up. Better to sit it out. And anyway, sure enough, the fellow returned hours later, with nothing to show for his apparent efforts.

After the door closed behind him, Saffia began to cry.

I moved over to sit by her. I put my arm around her. She neither resisted nor made to move away. The sobs came, dry, uneven, causing her shoulders to shudder. Her head rested on my shoulder. From her hair rose a close, earthy scent. A tear landed upon my shirt, and I felt it soak through the cotton and touch my skin. I stayed sitting there as long as I could until I felt the shift in her. Any moment she would regain her composure and perhaps feel awkward with our proximity. I stood up.

'It will be over soon. There's a procedure for these things, soon enough we will know.'

My words provided the break. She sat up straight, wiped her eyes and blew her nose.

'Can I fetch you something?' I said. 'Shall we go and get something to eat?'

'No thanks, Elias. I should stay close to the phone. But I am terribly thirsty.'

In the kitchen I opened the fridge door and reached for a bottle of water, but instead took a bottle of Coca-Cola, poured half of it into a glass along with a slug of Julius's whisky. I put the glass on the table in front of her. She picked it up and took a sip.

'What's in here?'

'A little whisky,' I replied. 'Just to calm you.' She nodded and took another sip, began to rehearse aloud details from the previous days, starting with the morning after the party, a fingertip search through her own mind for whatever it was she had missed.

Outside the window, the blue of the sea turned grey and then black. In the garden the colours grew solemn and withdrew. The phone was silent. Between ourselves, little of consequence was said. I refilled Saffia's glass, once, twice. She did not move from her place on the settee.

I stepped outside on to the verandah to gaze at the sky, the lead-blue darkness settling over the city. I lit a cigarette and smoked it in the darkness. Through the glass of the sliding door I could see Saffia. She sat in a coin of bright light from the lamp, her head rested on her forearm across the back of the settee. I stood and watched, I shrouded by darkness, she in the light. Something in her pose struck me, the weight of her head where it rested upon her arm. I realised she was asleep, or else on the verge of it. For several minutes I remained where I was, quite still.

I wished I could stay there all night. I let go of my self-imposed restraints and allowed myself to fantasise, to think what it might be like. That this was all mine, my home, lit up against the night. The sleeping woman inside my wife. Not sleeping from exhaustion, fear and whisky. But slumbering in peace.

I wished Julius would never come back.

The next day, at eleven o'clock in the morning, I was arrested. Two plain-clothes policemen were waiting for me on the stairs outside my apartment as I returned home carrying a freshly purchased cake for my breakfast. We drove away through the city and from the back of the car I watched people going about their business; already I envied them the mundane ritual of their mornings.

After a few minutes the car pulled up outside an unobtrusive single-storey building and I was taken inside. Two men were standing in the lobby. They paused their conversation, their eyes followed me as I was led by. A remark was exchanged with one of my escorts. Something frivolous, followed by a laugh. We passed into a corridor, a series of grey-painted doors on either side. One of the doors was open. They pushed me inside. A cell, windowless apart from a letter-box slit of window high up a wall. Stains on the wall. The air heavy with the reek of body odour. A desk, a chair. No other furniture. I placed the cake upon the desk and sat down.

I waited. I took the time to review my situation calmly. No point panicking. Julius, Yansaneh, Kekura. No doubt whatsoever I had been arrested in connection with those three. But what were they involved in? And what did it have to do with me? I knew nothing. I would tell that to the police. But would they believe me? It seemed unlikely anything could be that simple. With the thought my heart beat harder. They must believe me. I counted my breaths. One, two, three, four.

Outside the temperature rose and so did the temperature in the room. I pinched at the cloth of my shirt. I felt sticky. I heard occasional sounds of people passing down the corridor. Nobody stopped. Nobody came to the door. I had been in need of the toilet when I arrived, and as I sat there the pressure inside my bladder began to mount. I considered my options. I could continue to wait. I could call someone. It occurred to me they had left me without locking the door. I could step outside at any time, though that seemed somehow reckless. I held on ten more minutes, then stood up and knocked on the door. I listened. I waited. I rapped again. Footsteps in the corridor. The door opened and I took a step backwards. A man leaned in, glanced at me, pushed the door fully open and held it for a second man, who stepped into the room.

'Mr Cole. Please sit down.'

The man in front of me was short, with very black skin, dressed in a charcoal-grey suit with short sleeves and button-down pockets; he was carrying a manila folder. The first man placed a chair inside the door and departed. The second man took the chair and placed it, not opposite me, as one might imagine, but on the same side of the desk. When he sat down our knees and elbows were practically touching. He placed the papers on the desk and folded his hands.

'I must apologise for having inconvenienced you, Mr Cole. I know you are a teacher at the university.'

'A lecturer.'

'Of course.' He smiled. 'I hope this will not make you late for classes.'

I replied that classes were over for the holidays. I relaxed slightly, relieved to hear the civil tone he was taking. I had begun to let my nervous imagination get to me. I smiled back to signal my cooperation.

'Good,' he replied.

From his pocket he drew a pencil and opened the folder. I watched while he wrote my name in capital letters across the top of a piece of paper. At his request I supplied my address.

'What is your position at the university?' he asked.

'I am a lecturer in modern history.'

'And how long have you taught there?'

I told him. He wrote the information down. He seemed to write at an interminable pace, like a child copying his letters.

'If I am to make a statement, could I perhaps write it?' I offered.

'It is quite all right, Mr Cole.' He glanced up, surveyed me momentarily. 'I know what I'm doing.' Something in the glance, the way he seemed to enjoy enunciating the syllables of my name, stopped me persisting. He added, 'This is not a formal statement. Just some notes for my own records.'

He asked me details about my life. The time I had lived at my present address, my landlady's name. Where I had been born and where I had studied. Which courses I taught at the university. At the mention of European history he stopped writing in order to share with me some observations on the Jacobean Wars, in which he claimed to have an interest. Amateur, naturally, he smiled. Guy Fawkes. Catholic Spain. The Gunpowder Plot. He'd become interested after observing the rituals of Bonfire Night while training in England. I could not see the relevance of any of this to my case. Though because he seemed friendly enough, I made a pretence of listening and kept my knees pressed together. I yearned for a cigarette, but I had none on me. He resumed writing. Broke off again to ask me about the contents of the box on the table. I told him the box contained a cake. His pencil lead broke, he called for a replacement. The minutes ground by.

After over an hour he had still not asked me anything of substance. I knew the time because I glanced at my watch.

Without looking up or interrupting his meticulous transcription of my answers, he said, 'Do you need to be somewhere?'

I replied that I did not, however I did need to use the bathroom.

He continued to write.

'I need to use the toilet,' I repeated.

He looked up at me appearing to focus, like a small creature emerging out of the darkness: 'Yes, of course.'

'Thank you.' I stood up. He waved me back down again.

'This won't take a minute. Please, Mr Cole, be patient. As soon as we are done here I will have somebody show you to the bathroom. You can relax. Enjoy some breakfast.' He smiled, indicating the cake with a nod.

And so it went on, the asking and careful annotating of one banal question after another. I answered as evenly as I could, repeating my answers once, twice as he struggled to write them down verbatim. Then, without warning, the nature of the questions altered. I had answered a question about which campus activities I supervised.

In the same opaque tone, he asked, 'Are you aware of any illegal activities taking place on campus?'

'What?' I said. 'No. I mean, what sort of activity? Students drinking? That happens all the time.'

'No,' he replied. 'I am not talking about drinking.' He waved his hand dismissively.

'In that case, no.'

'What would you say if I told you the reason you are here is because we believe that you are.'

'Well, I would have to say I'm not. I don't even know what you are talking about.'

'So you deny it?'

'No, I'm not denying anything, I'm just saying I don't know.'

'So you are *not* denying it, then?' He fixed me with a hard stare, at the same time holding up his pencil and giving it a triumphant twirl. He sounded almost cheerful. I wondered if, in his world, this was what passed for a sense of humour.

'I am simply saying I don't know.' The words came out louder than I had intended. I was frustrated, unamused by this petty wordplay. I could feel the beginnings of a headache. I watched as he added my most recent words to the bottom of my lengthy and growing statement. He was either an idiot or he was amusing himself with this pretence of being a boneheaded policeman. I suspected the latter.

'May I ask what this is about?' I said presently.

He looked at me for several moments and blinked as if trying to make sense of the string of sounds I had just uttered. 'What this is about?' he repeated.

'Yes,' I retorted somewhat testily. 'Why am I here?'

'Well,' he said. 'I cannot tell you. At this time we do not know whether you have any information, so we cannot say.' He was at it again.

I said, 'You're saying you don't *know* what this is about?'

'We are making enquiries, you understand.'

'You must know why you are making enquiries.' I tried to maintain my composure, but the obtuseness was grating on me. I smiled to hide my anger. He smiled back at me. There followed a deadly silence.

'Mr Cole,' he said. 'I am sure you have nothing to fear. Please let us continue.' He bent to his paper, as if reading the next question from it.

'You are a friend of Dr Kamara?'

'Which Dr Kamara?' Pathetic, but I couldn't help myself.

'Dr Julius Kamara. He teaches engineering. I am told he is a friend of yours.'

'I know him, yes.' I crossed my legs.

He asked about Julius. How long had I known him? Who were Julius's other friends? What might I know of Julius's background? I resisted any further temptation to parry with him, keeping my answers to a minimum, not least because of the intense pressure in my abdomen.

'Dr Kamara uses your study at the university.'

'From time to time, yes.'

'How often?'

'Not often.'

'Once a week, twice a week?'

'Once a week. No more.'

'And when was the last occasion you allowed him to use your study?'

'I can't recall exactly,' I said. I knew precisely. It was the day I had gone to see Saffia; though I recalled neither the day nor the date, I had them written down in my notebook.

'This week, last week?'

'During the exams, I believe. The Dean knows all about this. He was perfectly happy with the arrangement. There's a shortage of space for faculty on campus.'

He nodded and looked at me, a long-considered gaze before applying his pencil to the pad once more.

With sudden desperation I said, 'If I could use the toilet before we continue.'

Nothing, save the scratch of pencil upon paper.

'Perhaps I could have your name.'

He looked up. 'Johnson.'

'Mr Johnson. I am happy to help you in any way I can. But I would like to use the facilities before we continue.'

He put down his pencil. 'The problem is this,' he explained slowly, as if he was talking to a moron. 'The toilets on this floor are reserved for staff use. Somebody will have to take you to the correct floor to use the ones there.'

'Perhaps, then, I could have your permission to use the staff toilets?'

He stared at me, before replying, deadpan, 'I am afraid I do not have the authority to allow that. It is better we continue here,' he tapped the paper with the end of his pencil, 'and finish. Then you can go.' He continued to gaze at me. The man was a small-time sadist, pedantry his weapon of choice. I felt a trickle of rage in my belly. I wanted to hit him.

For an hour more he questioned me. I hid nothing. I had nothing to hide. Eventually he put away his pencil and his notes, opened the door and called somebody. I was led to the toilets. The junior officer who accompanied me insisted that the cubicle door remain open. I turned my back on him, unzipped my fly and urinated. I had held on so long there was as much pain as relief in the act. At first the piss was slow in coming; when it hit the bowl it was lurid and evil-smelling.

I was shown back to the same room, which was empty. No sign of Johnson, of his papers, or my cake.

'Am I free to go?' I said.

'One minute, please.' My guide trundled off. I waited. A long minute passed. The air in the room was hot now and the smell of sweat was my own. I could have removed my jacket, but I chose not to, for to do so felt like some sort of submission. Neither did I sit down again. I walked about a bit, as much as I could in the confined space. The room was five paces long. Four paces wide. A half-hour must have passed before Johnson reappeared.

At the sight of him I felt a cold gust of anger. I said, 'Are we through yet?'

'Oh yes.' His manner was amiable.

I was in no mood for it. 'Am I then free to go?'

'Yes, yes. There are one or two formalities to attend to. Forgive me if I delay you a few minutes further. None of it should take long. You did say you were not teaching today.' He was amusing himself at my expense. 'Do sit.'

'I'm perfectly fine as I am, thank you.'

'You will be more comfortable if you sit.'

I didn't move but remained standing in the same spot. Johnson, too, stayed where he was, arms folded in front of him, and watched me. The seconds ticked past. I could hear the sound of rain, a rushing in the distance, ponderous drops from the eaves of the building and from tree branches. I was aware of Johnson's eyes upon me, regarding me as though I were a querulous child. I felt petulant and aggrieved. My head ached and I experienced a strange and sudden urge to cry. He had even stolen my cake.

Johnson cleared his throat. 'You will be more comfortable if you sit.'

I was about to decline a second time when I changed my mind, seeing how absurdly I was behaving. I was only delaying my own departure.

'Fine.' I walked across the room, seized a chair and dragged it into the middle of the floor. I sat down.

Johnson crossed to the door. 'Be assured I'll try not to keep you waiting any longer than necessary, Mr Cole. Just a few minutes.' He smiled minimally, and as he left the room he turned the key in the lock behind him.

I had been wrong about Johnson. There was nothing civil about him at all.

I waited. Outside the rain eased off, slowing to a distant patter. I listened to the drip, drip of the run-off from the roof. I sat for an hour or so in the failing light until, without warning, the overhead light went on. A switch on the other side of the door. I called out, but nobody answered. A numbness was spreading across my buttocks. The heat had gone from the day and the room seemed suddenly cold. I stood up. I went to the door and banged. I counted to five. I banged again.

Nothing.

CHAPTER 23

'Is it true,' says the child Abass, voice juddering as he bounces on the car's back seat, 'that the number of stars in the sky is infinity?'

From the driving seat Kai glances back at him. 'Nobody knows how many stars are in the sky. Nobody knows where the universe ends, so you could say there are an infinite number of stars in the sky. Yes.'

'How many zeros does infinity have?'

'A never-ending number.'

'Never-ending,' echoes Abass, trying the words out for size, staring from the window as they pass a palm plantation. His eyes switch back and forth from one row to the next, he begins to experiment, closing one eye and then the other.

'Imagine you tried to drive to the ends of the earth,' continues Kai. 'You'd just go round and round, you'd never get to the end of your journey. Think of that as zeros.'

Silence for a while, between the three of them. Adrian can almost hear the whirring cogs of the kid's imagination. His mind turns to the old man in the room at the hospital and his memories of the moon walk. Adrian had been ten when the moon walk happened. He remembered being in his grandparents' house, sitting on the rug watching the television across the expanse of the coffee table. His father's voice explaining what was happening. Calling Adrian to sit by him. His father had been well then.

'When I was your age,' says Adrian, then clears his throat. It has been a while since he spoke to a child. Kai has an easy way with Abass, whom he treats as a smaller and more vulnerable version of himself. It's a matter of hitting the right note. 'I mean, my father once explained to me how to think of infinity, the only way you could keep the idea in your head.'

'What did he say?' Abass comes to lean between the seats; he smells of lemons and soap.

'He told me to think of a big block of stone a thousand miles long, a thousand miles high, and a thousand miles wide.'

'That's a *huge* block!'

'A huge block,' concurs Adrian. 'OK, now imagine a tiny bird, like a sparrow.'

'What's a sparrow?'

'Well, any tiny bird. Like that one!' Adrian points at a movement between trees. 'Now imagine that bird lands on the rock once every thousand years.'

'Every thousand years?'

'Yes.'

'And then imagine it wipes its beak once on one side, and once on the other side. How long do you think it would take for the whole rock to be worn away?'

Abass jumps up and down between the seats. 'A very, very long time.'

'Yes. Not quite infinity but very close to.'

'Yes,' agrees Abass. 'Only the bird would die first.'

Kai and Adrian laugh.

The road takes a series of tight turns down through one small village and then another. Here the houses are tall, wooden with narrow windows and shingled roofs, different from the concrete houses of the city and the clay-brick homes in the villages on the road out to Ileana's place.

'The first settlements,' says Kai. 'There's a church, too. It's worth seeing. But we'll have to come back another time. We've a long drive.'

The road dips down along the valley floor and rises again. Here the macadam has disappeared altogether, giving way to rough laterite and in some places huge moguls round which Kai steers the car, a thirty-year-old yellow Mercedes he calls Old Faithful. A white Land Cruiser races past them, kicking up clouds of red dust, briefly wiping out all visibility. At such a moment Adrian might have halted, but Kai drives on unperturbed. The side of the hill rises steeply on one side of them and falls away equally steeply on the other. Here and there, the smooth scars of landslides. On the far side water pours from high up the hillside on to a slope of sheer, dark rock.

'Look!' screams Abass, an inch from Adrian's ear. 'Waterfall!'

'Call that a waterfall?' says Kai. 'Wait until you see where we're going.'

'How long will it take us to get there?'

'About three hours.'

'Three hours!?' He flings himself back against the seat.

'Don't worry. It's worth it. It'll get faster once we're on the main road. Do you want to get some cassava bread and fish at Waterloo?'

'Yes please.'

A bridge, the width of the car. The railings have fallen away, leaving the sides unguarded. Opposite an oncoming vehicle hovers at the entrance to the bridge, waiting for them to make the crossing. Adrian holds his breath as they do so. They have now skirted the city entirely. It lies to the south of them, between the tail of the car and the Atlantic Ocean. Due north is Guinea, three hundred kilometres as the crow flies. Beyond Guinea – Mali, Mauritania, then sand, the Sahara. They pass a settlement of single-storey houses, open scrub, a scattering of rusted equipment and arrive at the junction for the main road. Here the pace shifts gears suddenly. Vehicles sweep past, swerving, overtaking, sometimes stopping abruptly to allow a passenger to descend or pick up another. Kai is silent, giving his concentration to the road.

Around the bend of the hill the road narrows suddenly, encroached upon by a marketplace. Kai pulls over and lowers the window. 'Sssssss!' He raises a hand and clicks his fingers. A woman approaches and lowers a tray from her head. She counts out six fish, golden and blackened, a dozen rounds of flat bread, separates the fish and bread into portions and ladles a deep-red sauce over each. Kai passes a portion to Adrian, to Abass another. Adrian eats with his fingers. The fish is smoky and dry, the cassava bread plain and unsalted – reminding him of unleavened bread. By contrast the sauce is rich, greasy and savoury. Kai starts the car and drives away, eating from his lap with one hand and steering with the other. The sauce stains the tips of Adrian's fingers saffron.

Up through the hills, trees closing in on either side of the road. The traffic is gone, the road is silent. The landscape flattens out. Rice fields, vegetable plots and tree plantations are gradually replaced by an unvarying wall of elephant grass. There is the occasional broken-down lorry but little else. The interval between settlements widens, children seemingly frozen in a single moment in time watch the passage of the vehicle. Once they pass what looks like a disused quarry. Abass lowers the window and sticks his head out, opens and closes his mouth to make popping sounds and occasionally shouts his name into the wind.

Kai presses a cassette into the tape player, the speakers hiss, a drum beat and then another.

> *Well they tell me of a pie up in the sky,*
> *Waiting for me when I die.*
> *But between the day you're born and when you die,*
> *They never seem to even hear your cry.*

Abass draws his head back inside the car, stands up between the seats, steadying himself between the headrests, and sings at the top of his voice, *The harder they come, the harder they'll fall, one and all!*

Kai taps the steering wheel. Adrian remembers Kai playing the same tape in the evenings in the apartment during his illness. Another song follows. Abass seems to know the words to each one. Kai leans across and flips open the glove compartment. 'Choose something.'

Adrian rummages through the space: Biros, latex gloves, matchsticks, cassettes. Next to him Kai takes a corner, swerves suddenly and comes to a halt. Out of the rear window Adrian sees a minibus on its roof in the ditch. A knot of people are gathered in the road. In front of them, a row of cloth-covered shapes.

Kai has the door open. 'Hold on here a moment.' He doesn't pause for an answer but steps out of the car, slamming the door behind him.

'Wait for me!' Abass scrabbles at the door handle. 'I'm coming, too.' But Kai is already twenty yards away.

'You know, I think we should wait here,' says Adrian. 'Like we were asked to.'

Abass's head snaps round, he is still tugging at the door. 'Why?'

'Well, I think they might need a doctor. They don't need us, either of us. You stay with me.'

Abass peruses Adrian's face for a moment, considering his response. Adrian smiles. Abass relaxes and lets go of the door. 'OK, then,' he says. Behind the boy's head Adrian can see Kai pause and squat at each of the covered shapes. There follows a brief conversation with the people by the roadside, Kai walks back to the car and swings himself into his seat, turning down the volume of the music before they drive away.

'What happened to the *poda poda*? Did it crash?' asks Abass.

'Yes,' says Kai.

'What happened to the people?'

'Some of them are dead. The ones who were injured have been taken away. The accident was a little while ago. They're waiting for someone to collect the bodies.'

'I want to see the dead people!' shouts Abass.

'Well, they didn't want to see you,' replies Kai equably.

Abass squirms around on the back seat and stares at the wreck out of the back window as it recedes into the distance. They drive in silence for a while. After a few minutes Kai turns the music up. He has moved on. It is their day out. Abass, too, is soon humming along and pointing out of the window. Adrian tries to erase from his mind the image of the survivors standing waiting, the bulky lozenges beside them, like an orchestra of double-bass players.

A half-hour on Kai turns off the highway on to a dirt road. They traverse a metal bridge high over a slow, wide river and pass through a town. From there they continue east down a long, straight dirt track. Here the landscape is different again, even less cultivated. There are scatterings of black boulders that seem to absorb the sunlight, so starkly black in the dazzling day that Adrian finds it hard to focus upon them. A short series of hills juts out of the flat landscape to cast a shadow over the surrounding earth.

They stop to stretch their legs, the men set off in opposite directions to urinate – Abbas follows Kai. The air is sweet and heavy. Adrian's clothes and skin are covered in a layer of dust. He shakes his head and dust falls from his cropped hair. The ground at his feet is cracked, and when he relieves his bladder the liquid sends up a small spurt of dust and a white butterfly. From the ice box in the boot Kai fetches cold drinks and the three drink them standing by the car. A man steps out of nowhere and exchanges greetings with Kai. His eyes flick over Adrian with interest, though it is to Kai he addresses his words. From what Adrian can guess, from the nods, the gestures, he is asking where they are going. Kai offers him the empty drink bottle and the man reaches out to accept it gravely. Again and again his eyes slip back towards Adrian. In time he moves on. To where? From where? Adrian cannot imagine. For on either side of them the road reaches out for miles.

It is one o'clock when they turn off the road down a descending and increasingly narrow and uneven track. The track is so overgrown that light is scarce. After ten minutes Kai pulls over and applies the handbrake. 'We'll walk from here.' So they gather their things and set off, Kai in the lead, the cooler from the boot on his shoulder.

'Have I been here before?' asks Abass.

'No, we used to come here before you were born.'

'How come you never brought me?'

'It was never possible,' says Kai, shifting the weight of the cooler, waving off Adrian's offer of help. 'There was a lot of fighting around here.' He turns to Adrian and points somewhere up into the trees ahead of them. 'There's a dam up there, a big hydroelectric project.'

'Are we going to see the dam?' Abass asks.

'Not this time.'

Abass runs up behind Kai and butts the small of Kai's back with his head. Kai catches hold of Abass and swings him around with his free arm. They walk, play-fighting as they go, Abass, head lowered like a small ram. Kai, catching him, swinging him, never breaking his stride.

The call of birds, footsteps on dry leaves, an occasional insect, nothing else. Sweat trickles down Adrian's back. How hot it is even in the shade! As he walks on Adrian hears a rushing in the air, a white noise. Ahead of them he can see light, muted by the leaves, transforming in the distance into pure, pale, shimmering brilliance. They are by a river. He can see the reflection of the sun upon water. Beneath his feet the way turns to rocks, and he picks his route over and between them. They follow the curve of the river. The noise fills Adrian's head. Kai turns and calls to him; Adrian can see Kai's mouth open and close, but hears nothing. He cups his ears. Kai points and Adrian stumbles towards him, his gaze following Kai's finger.

It is the height of a three-storey building. To Adrian the breadth is as impressive as the depth, for it is some fifty yards wide. Powerful, determined, inexorable, the water is like a great herd of animals, plunging from a cliff of rock into the silent pool.

They picnic on the rocks and then swim. Adrian feels the glow of the cool water enter him. The river is faster moving than it looks and they give in to the current, floating downstream on their backs and ending up in an eddy by the riverbank. They dry off in the sunlight. Adrian's skin feels clean and smells sweet and faintly brackish. Abass plays with the empty beer bottles in a rock pool, half filling them with water and watching them bob on the surface. Two boys appear with home-made fishing rods and come over to stare at Adrian. After a few minutes Kai tells them to go away. They obey, wordlessly and without apparent resentment, and join Abass at his rock pool. Later, when Adrian goes to relieve himself behind a bush, they will follow him and at his insistence depart, repeating his words between themselves, *Buggeroff, buggeroff.*

Adrian watches Abass sitting hunched over his knees, absorbed in the tiny underwater world of the rock pool, feels a surge of tenderness for him and says, 'He's a lucky kid.' Immediately he feels foolish, the absurdity of envying anybody here their luck, though somehow he does.

But Kai merely replies, 'Yes, I know. I was just like him.'

'In what way?'

'We used to come here a lot. Actually, probably it was less than half a dozen times, but then, in a kid's life, that's a tradition, right? Six years, as much as you can remember. This one time we'd come after the rains, you should see how much water there is then. I tried to swim under the waterfall. I thought I'd find a secret cave. I nearly drowned. My mother gave me such a whipping.'

Adrian thinks of his own childhood. He would never have dared do such a thing. Not for the danger to himself, but for fear of disappointing his mother. He stands up.

'Come on!' he says. And plunges into the water.

It is after four when Kai says, 'We'd better be going. It's not a good idea to drive too much into the dark. There are some crazy drivers.'

They pack up and head back to the car. Kai reverses up the track. Old Faithful's engine whines, the tyres spin on the gravel, but Kai doesn't stop until he finds a place to execute a tight three-point turn. They pass through and over the same series of towns and bridges, this time with the sun on the other side of the road. The earth is redder now, the light softer. It fills Adrian with well-being, now after a week of illness, a week spent recovering, he feels ready to get back to work.

An hour and a half into the journey they make a detour into a town to find petrol. There is a queue, the petrol pump is hand-operated and slow. So while Kai waits, Adrian allows Abass to lead him towards a stall selling cassettes, where four speakers relay music so loudly it is distorted. Unperturbed, the boy peruses cassettes. Adrian moves away from the noise to a distance where he can still keep an eye on Abass. Around him are stalls displaying trainers, plastic kerosene containers, hats. On the far side of the square a taxi pulls over, the driver takes his fare from the passenger and opens the boot, releasing three handsome, deep-brown goats. The ground is dusty and strewn with paper, like a fairground at the end of the evening.

He recalls his father in the nursing home towards the end. Adrian had taken Kate with him on the visit and they had stopped at a funfair on the way. The lights, the cool October air, the noise. By contrast the atmosphere inside the nursing home: overheated, static, hushed. They had stayed for an hour, during which Adrian had been unable to work out truly whether his father remembered any of the events Adrian described or even knew who he was. At the end of the visit he had turned at the door to say goodbye and the old man had raised his hand, fingers closed around his palm, and held up a wavering thumb. At first Adrian hadn't understood. And then he had seen it, the thumbs-up sign. It had once been their joke. There was a country somewhere in the world where the thumbs-up was the equivalent of the V sign. Where was that? Thailand? Iran? He'd read about it and told his father. Later his father had performed the gesture – emphatically – behind the back of a priggish waiter. By then the disease had already begun to strip his brain of cells, though none of them knew it yet. Adrian giggled into his Coke glass.

Watched by the stallholder, Abass is lingering over the cassettes in the manner of all small boys with no money of their own. Adrian decides to leave it a few minutes before he offers to buy one for him. Meanwhile he surveys the marketplace. He has no real idea of where they are.

Fifty yards away a woman and a young girl leave one of the stalls, and turn in his direction. The woman is tiny, the size of the girl. She is wearing a piece of light-coloured cloth wound around her body and over her head. The girl is wearing a cotton blouse and a denim skirt. Adrian watches them idly. The heat, the exertion of swimming, the beer, the recent illness have slowed him. Only when they are twenty yards from him does the realisation begin to trickle through his brain like a cold oil. The woman with the girl. The woman with the cloth covering her head, framing her face. It is Agnes.

Quickly he turns on his heel and returns to Abass. 'Tell your uncle I'll be two minutes.' He holds up two fingers. Abass stares at him uncomprehendingly, his hands closed around a cassette. 'Two minutes.' Adrian turns to the stallholder, who inclines his head slowly in assent. Satisfied, Adrian sets off, walking quickly. Ahead of him he sees the two women turn down one of the streets off the square. He slows his walk and follows. From the end of the road he watches them climb the steps up to a house. The house is identical to all the others on the street: square, single-storey, with a deep verandah at the front, a concrete balustrade, stairs leading up from either side.

On the verandah of the house Agnes entered a man, dressed only in a pair of cotton trousers, sits upon an old car seat.

'Hello,' says Adrian.

'Hello,' the man answers. 'What can I do for you?' His English is excellent. If he is surprised to see Adrian it does not show.

Adrian gives his name, asks if the woman who came in is called Agnes.

'She is Agnes, yes.' The man rises and positions himself on the balustrade, the better to hear, it seems, only now he is leaning over Adrian. He is handsome, unsmiling, with even white teeth and heavy, slanted cheekbones. His hair is knotted into short dreadlocks. 'What is your business with her?'

Adrian hesitates, unsure how to respond. He doesn't want to appear uncooperative, on the other hand there is the matter of patient confidentiality.

'I'm a doctor,' he says.

'Agnes is not sick.' A statement.

'Not exactly. I saw her some time ago. I just wanted to follow up. I didn't manage to see her before she was discharged.'

The man is watching him closely, the eyes never leave Adrian's face; his expression is indiscernible in the failing light. Adrian sees himself through the man's eyes, a strange white man from off the street. Perhaps he shouldn't have followed Agnes to her home, she had discharged herself. He just wants to talk to her. 'It'll take five minutes.'

The man eases himself off the balustrade. 'You are a doctor, you say?' He is still looking at Adrian, his speech is measured and deliberate, his manner unhurried.

'That's correct.'

'One moment. Let me find her for you.' He crosses to the door and enters the house, closing the door behind him. Adrian waits in the street. There are few passers-by, the day is over. In a short time it will be dark. Adrian hopes the young man is conveying the message accurately; for some reason he hesitates to trust him entirely, something in his manner. More curious about Adrian than concerned

202

for Agnes. When after several more minutes the man doesn't return, Adrian starts tentatively up the stairs. If Agnes sees him she'll recognise him, he's sure.

From behind him a woman's voice, 'Good evening.'

A young woman. A shallow, round pannier covered with a cloth and balanced on her head dictates her straight posture, the gentle rhythm of her steps. She walks past Adrian and up the stairs. 'Can I help you?'

Adrian explains, once again. He is a doctor, here to see Agnes, he saw her in the square as he was passing. He doesn't mean to alarm anybody over Agnes's health, just to help if he can.

'Agnes is my mother.'

Naasu. Agnes had told him she lived with her daughter and her son-in-law. That, presumably, was him.

The young woman who must be Naasu listens without interruption. 'I didn't know she had seen you. But if you can help her, it would be good. Let me go inside and find her.'

Adrian doesn't mention to the young woman that he has already spoken to her husband. She clearly has her mother's interests at heart.

She sets the pannier down on the floor. 'Please wait here. I'll bring her to you.'

Now Adrian is confident, clear-thinking. He knows where she lives. He'll be able to follow up on her, even if it means driving out here once a week or so. There's a lot he could do, especially with her daughter's help. That will make a big difference. Somebody reliable. Maybe they could get to the root of the matter. Once he has that, there's a chance. Everything else can follow.

The door opens and the daughter appears accompanied by Agnes. She has removed the cloth with which she had covered her hair. She is wearing a long cotton batik dress and a pair of slippers. Behind both women comes the son-in-law. He crosses to sit on the balustrade at Adrian's right shoulder, sitting close and yet out of Adrian's view. Adrian tries not to be unsettled by the man's manner. What matters is Agnes.

'Agnes,' he smiles. 'I'm very pleased to see you. I hope you don't mind me coming to your home. I saw you just now in the market.'

Agnes doesn't step forward or smile, but stands, hands clasped in front of her.

Adrian keeps talking. 'I'm sorry, Agnes, I was ill when you were discharged. I had malaria.' And then, 'I want you to come back and see me. There are some things we can do. I think we can make some real progress. Will you do that? Will you come and see me?'

It would have been better to have this conversation alone, he thinks, aware he's floundering. If he can just reach her. He waits for her response, but none comes. Perhaps she doesn't recognise him after all.

Naasu turns to her mother and speaks to her loudly and in English, for Adrian's benefit, as though Agnes is deaf. '*Oya*, a doctor. He says you have seen him. He wants you to see him again.' She continues to speak, this time more softly and in another language. Agnes replies. There is an exchange of some sort. Adrian waits, looking from one to the other, listening intently to a conversation he cannot understand. He can sense the daughter's husband motionless at his back. The daughter looks back at Adrian and shrugs. 'She says she is better, she doesn't need to see you.'

If he is honest he could have expected something of the sort. Shame attaches itself to these matters. To Agnes he says, 'Agnes, I really think it would be a good idea. Just one session.' Then to the daughter, 'If you can tell your mother, just one session.' Perhaps, if it came from her.

The young woman nods rapidly, translates. She appears to be genuinely trying to help. Agnes is shaking her head, actually shaking her head. He is anxious now. Naasu turns to him, frowning. 'I'm telling her what you told me. She says no, she doesn't want to.'

'If you can just make her understand. I can help her. Some of the things we talked about . . .' He turns to Agnes, but she interrupts him, speaking quietly and clearly in English.

'I am better now. The problems are gone. Thank you, Doctor.' She turns and steps inside the house, her daughter at her elbow.

Adrian remains where he is, standing on the verandah, utterly lost.

Agnes's son-in-law walks him back to the petrol station. The chap is friendlier now, apologising for Agnes, asking Adrian questions: whether he has visited the town before, questions about London. Adrian's responses are muted and automatic. He needs to get back to Kai and Abass. He's thinking about the next step with Agnes. Even if she believes she's better, she isn't, she'll go wandering again before too long. Who knew what the projection of her illness might be, or what harm could come to her? Perhaps he could return with Salia. Salia would be able to cross the divide.

The darkness has settled in now and Adrian is forced to concentrate on placing his feet. There are no street lights, the road is uneven. They are taking a different route to the petrol station, he notices, one that passes through the streets around the square. His companion has stopped talking. He can no longer hear the other man's footfall. He stops and turns.

The first blow pitches him forward. There follows the split–second delay before he realises he has been hit. The hot cold flush. Finally the pain, billowing through his body like ink in water. The blow to the back of his head is followed by a kick to the base of his spine, which forces the air out of his chest. A third blow lands on the back of his neck and his shoulders. Something hard, wood or metal. Adrian's knees buckle. He staggers. His impulse is to run. He tries and fails, his legs give way. He'd like to call out, but his lungs are airless. His face hits the dirt. The dirt is soft and cool. Sharp kicks to his side. Please, no more pain. Adrian concentrates on trying to speak, to say something, but he can only gasp. He starts to crawl away, aware even in the moment of the indignity. He doesn't care. He thinks of internal damage, his kidneys, his liver. Maybe whoever it is intends to kill him. If only they would say what they want he would give it to them. Nausea rises in the wake of the pain. His mouth fills with saliva. He wants to retch. Still on all fours, he heaves drily. The nausea overwhelms him. The last thing he sees, before he blacks out, is a street dog, watching from the side of the road.

He is dreaming. Swimming off a Norfolk beach, when he was a child. Except that there are black children fishing off the rocks. The dream has a soundtrack, the words of the song keep coming back to him. *The harder they come, the harder they'll fall, one and all.* He smiles in his sleep. It's funny.

Now Kai is in the dream, talking to him. What's Kai doing here? He tries to answer but his lips won't form the words. He can't speak. Adrian doesn't want Kai to go away, only he's trapped on the other side of the dream.

CHAPTER 24

I slept in the chair, unable – in both senses – to lower myself to the floor. I slept for perhaps two hours, doubled over myself. Nobody knew where I was except Johnson. I could see what he was doing. Leaving me to ruminate, to soften me up – the phrase they used in films.

I tried to focus on the facts at hand. I had not been arrested or charged with anything. So far I had cooperated. Johnson had trampled all over my goodwill. He was trying to drive me into a corner, provoke me into behaving as though I had something to hide. Well, there was nothing. So far Johnson had accused me of precisely nothing. Then again, how exactly do you prove *nothing*? How do you fight *nothing*? The thoughts turned over and over in my mind.

At one point, in the depth of the night, I had a sudden image of myself from the outside. A dark, untidy shape, hunched over itself on a chair in that small and empty room. My shape, my outline, in my mind's eye, was devoid of detail. It was not me, but the shadow of me, of what remained. It was as though I had already disappeared. I am not one given to flights of fancy, nevertheless I could not control the thoughts that emerged, indistinctly, from sulphurous places in my mind.

Once I woke from dozing with a start, certain I had heard the sound of a cry. I listened. From somewhere in the building I heard a thump, then nothing. Impossible to know whether I had imagined the sound, if it had come from outside or been part of my dreams.

When dawn came I was exhausted, relieved the night was over, even knowing that in all likelihood the day ahead would be a difficult one. At least it held some hope – if only for the prospect of progress. Today was Saturday. Friday morning, when I'd been brought here. Normally I would be drinking coffee at home, reviewing the newspapers. Nobody was expecting me, I had no social engagements.

At ten o'clock a guard came for me. I could smell the foulness of my own breath, felt the rough stubble on my chin, the flakes of dried sweat under my arms. My clothes were stained and crumpled. I'd eaten nothing since I was brought in the day before. The last drink I'd had was when I'd drunk some water out of my cupped hand at the basin when I went to the lavatory.

My escort didn't look at me but pushed me by the shoulder out of the door. We turned left back towards the entrance of the building. For a brief moment I dared to hope perhaps I was being released. I was wrong. We turned away from the entrance and went up two flights of stairs to another floor, another passage, another room. My guard opened the door and pushed me inside. I was in Johnson's office. He was seated at his desk.

His first words to me were, 'I am sorry, Mr Cole, it was not my intention to delay you overnight. A matter of some urgency arose. Please accept my apologies.' He didn't offer me a seat. I remained where I was, standing before him. He repeated his apology, placing the emphasis on the first word, '*Please*,' and then in a softer voice – a technique which served to heighten the sense of threat and to increase the impression he was giving an order, 'accept my apologies.'

'Very well.' If that was what was required.

'Please sit down.'

I sat.

'Can I get you anything?'

I was hoarse. I needed a drink of water. He called the guard and ordered him to bring a jug of water and a glass. Upon his desk lay an open pink folder containing a number of papers. While I drank, he leafed through them. All very theatrical. I remember his old man's hands, wizened and small, like those of an ancient Chinaman. He reminded me of my old headmaster, who was given to this sort of display, designed to demonstrate who was boss.

'I've been reviewing your file.'

What the hell? 'What file?'

He ignored me. 'You recently attempted to publish a political tract.'

'I've done nothing of the sort,' I replied.

'Is that so?' He looked at me directly.

'That's right,' I said. About this I was confident. A thought formed. No, I daren't allow myself to think it. There'd been a mix-up. A mistake. Quite possibly Johnson's. I might yet get one over him. But it wouldn't do to goad him, provoking him into justifying himself. I kept my voice neutral as I continued, 'I think there's some confusion, a mix-up. Perhaps somebody has mixed me up me with another person.' I deliberately avoided use of the second nominative pronoun. Not his mistake, someone's mistake. Men concerned with power and the display of it required some kind of face-saving device.

'Who?'

'I don't know, one of your investigating officers, perhaps.'

'I am not asking you who made this error, as you claim. I am asking who *you* are saying *I* have confused you with?'

That threw me, I confess, the way he took it right back to himself: 'I don't know,' I replied.

'You have somebody in mind? Somebody else who has published a political tract? A colleague, perhaps?'

'No. I don't.' He had a confounding way about him, as unreadable and unpredictable as a cat. I said, 'I'm just telling you I haven't attempted to publish any tract or manifesto, or any political writing of any sort. I don't involve myself in politics.'

All this time he had kept his gaze firmly upon my face. To my annoyance I found I was beginning to sweat, small prickles in my underarms, down the line of my spine. Now he looked down and read aloud from one of the sheets of paper in front of him, following the words with his forefinger. 'Reflections on Changing Political Dynamics'. It was the title of the paper I had submitted to the faculty journal. Despite myself I felt the muscles of my heart contract, a tiny pulse.

'That's the title of one of my papers,' I said. 'I submitted it to our journal at the university. It was turned down.'

'So you admit you are the author?'

Why did he insist on using this kind of language? In his paranoid world there were no simple facts. Everything was an accusation, a confession.

'Yes,' I conceded. And added, 'It's an academic paper, not a manifesto. Read it and you'll understand perfectly.'

He picked up the file, holding the edge between his thumb and forefinger; he gave it a shake to demonstrate its flimsiness.

'Your file doesn't appear to contain the text of the article. Perhaps you can explain it to me.'

'Yes, of course.' I drew a breath and began to outline the context of the paper, acutely aware of the sound of each sentence, each choice of word, how a mind like his, always on the search for the telling, the incriminating, would process each one. I concentrated on rehearsing the minutiae of certain uncontroversial constitutional changes and the creation of the instruments of state in the late 1950s. I steered clear of mentioning names. This is a small country, you never knew who was related to whom. You'd be surprised how even the lowliest person might have political connections, and one might very well ask how Johnson had acquired his present position – though it had to be said, his natural aptitude for the work would seem to dispense with any need for nepotism. As I spoke I revised, edited and modified the thrust of the piece. All the time I was aware of Johnson's eyes upon me. I kept my hands in my lap, to control any trembling. I slowed my speech as much as I dared, I focused on bringing my breathing under control.

I waited for Johnson to stop me, but he listened without interruption. I repeated myself once or twice, over the effects of the Stevenson Constitution in shifting power to the Protectorate. It didn't matter. Much worse, that ridiculous rhyme once taught to me by an erstwhile colleague from Scotland came to mind, *Beresford Stuke makes me puke*. I had the curious sensation of feeling my mind split into two. One part controlled the movement of my lips, like a ventriloquist's dummy, outlining my paper for Johnson's benefit, whilst in the other the absurd ditty repeated itself over and over. *Beresford Stuke makes me puke, But in the Protectorate they expectorate.* I tried to think precisely, to engage the necessary half of my brain. I was able to hold myself together sufficiently to briefly describe my conclusions and draw to a halt.

Johnson continued to engage my gaze: 'Well done, Mr Cole,' and he gave me one of his pared-down smiles.

I had been unaware of the pearls of sweat that had broken upon my brow; now I felt a drop begin its descent down my temple. I had not spoken a single untruth, and yet somehow I had failed. I knew then Johnson would never be persuaded. He knew what he wanted. He wanted me. There was no getting out of this so easily. I felt angry and overwhelmingly weary. I was tired of games.

I said, 'Why don't you let me telephone my dean? He can explain.' It was an imperfect strategy, not one I would have chosen freely. If news had not already reached him then I had no desire to alert the Dean to my arrest, certain it would count against me. I knew how his mind worked, I'd be marked as a troublemaker. It could have consequences for my career. But then, did that matter so very much? I was no high-flier. The very paper that was causing me so much trouble had even been declined for publication.

'Detainees are not permitted to make telephone calls, other than to their legal representatives.'

Was I now a detainee? Was he trying to intimidate me? I hesitated to pursue it, for fear of having it confirmed, made solid. Then there would be no going back. I said, 'It must be possible.'

'I assure you, I know the rules, Mr Cole.' He went on to quote the act and even the clause relating to communications with detainees.

I said, 'Those laws were passed during the state of emergency.' And by the previous regime. Reference to them was contained in my paper.

'That may be.' He flattened his palm on my file in front of him. 'I'm afraid I don't understand your point.'

The guard returned and escorted me back to my room. My room, as I had already begun to think of it. I sat on the chair. Once, twice I heard sounds of other people, steps in the corridor. I waited through the afternoon and evening. Again I reviewed my conversations with Johnson. I pondered the existence of a file on me. At times the fact of it seemed momentous, at other times insignificant. Quite likely it contained nothing more than my employment and social security records, all of which he could have acquired without difficulty. The title of the paper – how had Johnson come to have knowledge of that? Who had supplied it? I checked myself. I was beginning to think like Johnson. The paper had been unremarkable – an all too unremarkable work of academia. Possibly mention of it was contained in my employment records. And yet it was an unpublished paper. How could it have acquired such status?

I thought, too, of Johnson, the practised obtuseness, the implacability of his regard and strange old man's hands. Tiny, black and wrinkled, those searching fingertips. Monkey's hands. Nit-picking hands. What was it he wanted? I didn't know. If I had, I might have given it to him.

I wanted a smoke. The comforting task of lighting and inhaling. I was frightened. Nobody had hurt me so far, but one heard of things happening – to people who were activists, troublemakers. And wasn't that precisely what Johnson seemed insistent on trying to pin on me?

How quickly in such situations one searches out comfort where one will. A small rectangle of sun from the tiny window appeared on the wall. I moved the chair, took off my jacket and sat in it. I have always had a sharp sense of mortality. I had no wife, no children. I had no regrets, I was not being maudlin. I say simply that I had a sharp sense of my own mortality. I had never possessed the kind of fearlessness one finds so often in the very young – in my brother, before his illness. In Julius. *Julius*. What had he got me involved in?

That moment, during the night before, when I'd seen myself from the outside, not myself – the vacant space I occupied – I knew my limitations. I knew I was no hero.

I must have fallen asleep. I awoke on the hard floor, grit pressed into my face. My body ached, the points of my hip and shoulder felt bruised. For a moment I forgot where I was.

Who hasn't had one of those terrible dreams in which some unremembered crime has come to light, some dreadful act for which you know yourself to be responsible, because all the evidence is there in your own heart, and yet you can recall nothing of it? You wake up in your own bed awash with relief. That dawn, when I woke curled upon the floor of the cell, in the moment or two it took me to remember where I was, I waited in vain for the release that would tell me it had been a bad dream. I sat up. Somewhere out there people were going about their business, my colleagues, my landlady, Saffia. I'd barely thought about Saffia. I wondered what she was doing, whether she had understood the reason for my absence.

A guard came for me, just as one had the day before. I was shown into Johnson's office. He was standing with his back to me studying the noticeboard behind his desk. I had tried to steel myself for another bout of his questions, but the truth is I was lost. When he turned to me and I saw it was not Johnson but the Dean, I almost collapsed with relief. I believe I would have cried, were it not for the briskness of the Dean's manner. He made no remark on my appearance, though his gaze lingered over me. No doubt because of his own particularity regarding matters of personal hygiene, he looked faintly repelled. He sat down in Johnson's chair; the table in front of him had been cleared of papers. My knees buckled slightly and I sat down heavily in the chair opposite.

'I have spoken to Mr Johnson. He has explained some of the matter to me. I've told him that you are one of the most reliable members of the faculty. As a result he has been kind enough to allow the use of his office for us to have this conversation.'

'Thank you.'

'I see no reason why this should take very long at all.' His manner was devoid of the fractious energy and absent-mindedness he displayed at other times. I was pleased. He was taking it seriously. At last somebody to make sense of it all, to lead me out of this place.

'I have no idea what this is about,' I said. 'I can assure you.'

'Mr Johnson tells me the police are clamping down on illegal publications,' said the Dean. 'It seems you may have been swept up in somebody else's business.'

He pushed a newspaper across the desk towards me, one of those street sheets, with names like *Scope* and *Searchlight*. I thought of the vendor whose arrest I'd witnessed. The paper on the desk bore a date a month old; in terms of quality it was marginally better produced than most.

The Dean continued, 'It's simply a matter of cooperating with these people.'

I didn't have the strength to argue with the Dean, to tell him what kind of person Johnson was, how you could not believe anything he said. I waited.

The Dean pushed the paper an inch further towards me. 'He asks me to show you this.'

'What does this have to do with me?'

'Take a look.'

I opened the paper, and began to turn the leaves one by one. I could feel the Dean watching me. On the third page, on the right-hand side, a headline caused me to pause. I felt the same small electrical jolt to my heart as when Johnson had mentioned my essay. This article was entitled, 'A Black Man on the Moon'.

'Read it.'

I had paused too long. I should have continued turning the pages, maintained a pretence. Too late. So I did as the Dean had asked me and read the article. Put plainly, it consisted of a sustained attack upon the government, on the regime's failure to observe basic human rights during their time in power. Progress in the country was in danger of stalling because the elite had more interest in lining their pockets. The relevance of the headline was to indicate to the reader how distant we were as a nation from such an achievement. There was no byline, and I noticed none of the other articles had bylines either. I scanned the article quickly; one phrase came to the fore that still sticks: *At the present rate of development it will take a century to achieve what many nations manage in a decade.* An inversion of the words Julius had used, the very first evening we spent together. A century of work in a single decade. He'd been talking about the moon landing.

The Dean watched me, leaning back in Johnson's chair, balanced between the chair's two back legs and his toes. Before I had finished reading he interrupted. 'Not the kind of thing we want associated with the university, I think you'll agree.'

I nodded, I was scarcely in a position to do otherwise.

He let the chair drop forward and leaned his elbows on the desk. He was silent, tapping his pursed lips with his forefinger. Then he put his fingertips together, and looked at me over their steepled arch. 'Really, it's a matter of coming to some arrangement with these people. No more than that.'

CHAPTER 25

Kai watched the pump lever move up and down, the pink liquid slide from side to side within the glass tank as the level dropped, rising in Old Faithful's tank. To Kai the colour of petrol was a faint surprise, always. He stretched, felt the skin tight across his back from the swim. Driving with the car windows down, he'd retained the feeling of freshness from that first dive into the water. Somehow he had never expected to find their old haunt unchanged. Surely that was the true force of nature. When so much else lay in ruins, the waterfall, the rocks, the river: these things remained.

One station in town with petrol. Cars, motorbikes, people holding containers, all waited in a line – still, Kai's mood was good. He counted out the notes and gave them to the attendant. Afterwards he held his hands out in front of him and spread his fingers. No trembling. Good. He looked around for Abass and Adrian. The driver of the car next in line sounded his horn and gave a lazy wave. And so Kai slid into the driver's seat, started the engine and pulled out of the petrol station. He parked up, still looking around. Ah, there was Abass. The boy stood, fingering cassettes with all the awe and yearning of an archaeologist handling an ancient pot he knows he must return to the earth. Of Adrian there was no sign. Kai got out of the car and went over to the stall, where the stallholder, in his white djellaba and skullcap, perched upon his stool like a stork, one leg crossed over the other.

'Hey, little man.' But Abass, deafened by the music, didn't hear him. Kai put the palms of his hands on the child's head, Abass tried to swivel round, Kai applied pressure, pinning him to the spot. Abass giggled and squirmed.

The stallholder joined in, laughing oilily. 'Yes, sir. Your son has been safe with me.'

Kai nodded at him briefly and waited for Abass to correct the stallholder, to tell him Kai was his uncle. Children were particular like that. But Abass said nothing. Kai looked down at Abass, at his bowed head. The pattern of the hairs, near perfect concentric circles ending in a single hair in the centre of the crown. The curled rim of his ears. The unblemished skin. He wondered if Abass remembered anything about his father. He had never asked. And earlier that day, seeing the bodies by the side of the road, Abass had displayed only a child's morbid curiosity.

'Look!' Abass held the cassette box up for Kai's inspection.

'Is this the one you want?'

Abass nodded vigorously.

The vendor watched sideways on.

'How much?' Kai asked the vendor.

'Five thousand,' the man replied.

Kai dug in his pocket for the notes.

'What of this one?' The vendor held up a second cassette. Kai felt Abass's eyes upon him.

'No thanks. Just the one,' said Kai, then to Abass, 'Where's Adrian?'

'He's coming back soon. He said I should wait.'

'How long ago was that?'

'I don't know,' said Abass, shrugging as he inspected his purchase. 'Not very long, I don't think.' Then with more emphasis, 'Like a *minute*, maybe.'

'Twenty minutes now,' said the vendor as he took the money.

Kai looked at the man properly this time. 'Did he say where he was going?'

'No,' said Abass chirpily. 'He didn't say anything, except I was to stay here.'

The vendor didn't reply directly but pointed with his chin as he pushed the notes into his money belt. 'This road here. This is the one he took.'

'Thank you. Come on.' He reached out for Abass. 'Let's go find Adrian.' He released Abass's hand and watched the kid run ahead, his arms whirling, kicking up dust.

No sign of Adrian down the road the stallholder had indicated. The street was empty, the market extended no further than the square. Dusk was deepening. Houses were shuttered up, the occupants mostly out back, gathered around the cooking fires. Abass made a game of it, rushing to peer down every side road and calling out Adrian's name. When he heard Abass's cry, Kai began to run. By the time he reached the corner his heart was racing. He turned into the street.

In the half-light, Abass was standing staring ahead in the middle of the road, his hands hanging limply by his sides. Beyond him a man lay on the ground.

It took ten minutes to reach the car. Kai placed one of Adrian's arms around his shoulders and hoisted him to his feet after he'd checked to see if anything was broken, running expert fingers across Adrian's ribs. Abass ran ahead to open the door of the car so Adrian could lie on the back seat, but Adrian demurred, climbed gingerly into the front. Kai sent Abass to the boot to fetch water. The boy stood and watched, frowning and intent, while Adrian sipped from the bottle and then handed it back. Kai said little, but concentrated on finding his way back on to the main road. In the white light of the passing vehicles, Adrian's skin was bluish, covered in a sheen of sweat.

'Is Uncle Adrian going to be all right?' asked Abass. The boy sat pressed against the upholstery, clutching the water bottle in his lap.

Adrian turned his head stiffly. 'Yes. Don't worry about me, Abass. I'm going to be fine.' And then, 'I was hit by somebody on a bicycle. I don't suppose he saw me in the dark.'

'A bicycle?' repeated Abass wonderingly.

'Yes.'

Kai said nothing and they left it there, by silent mutual assent. An hour and a half later they dropped Abass at home. The boy pushed the water bottle into Adrian's hands, along with his new cassette. Adrian kept the water but handed the cassette back. 'We'll listen to it together another time. How about that?'

Abass nodded.

'Tell your mum I'll be back later,' said Kai. 'I need to take Adrian home.'

Kai listened to Adrian's account of what happened. Of seeing Agnes, following her to the house, the son-in-law, the daughter, Agnes's reluctance. Then had come the attack, by the son-in-law, Adrian had no doubt. The man had been with him one minute, gone the next. Kai drove in silence throughout.

'You went to her home?' he asked, when Adrian had finished.

'Yes,' replied Adrian. 'I shouldn't have. I mean, not strictly speaking. But these are unusual circumstances. She needs help.'

'I'm just saying you have to take some care, you don't understand this country. There are a lot of bad, bad people out there. You could have got yourself really hurt.'

216

In the apartment Adrian disappeared into the bathroom. Kai went to the kitchen, where he filled the kettle and put it on to boil. Though he wasn't hungry he began rummaging through the cupboards, purely out of habit. A life lived without fast food and snacks had made him an opportunistic eater. As a child he ate whatever was put in front of him, meat was a treat, he and his sister fought surreptitiously with their forks over the best pieces. Then later, training as a doctor and eating on the run. Years of half-eaten meals, finished cold often hours later. He never suffered indigestion. He decided against tea, lifted the kettle from the stove and helped himself to a beer from the fridge instead.

Adrian appeared.

'How do you feel?' asked Kai.

'I'll live.'

'Do you want me to take a look?'

Adrian shook his head. 'Actually what I really want now is a whisky.'

'Let me have a look at you.' He stood in front of Adrian, surveyed his face, reached for his wrist and checked his pulse, pressed on the ends of Adrian's fingers. Then he located one of the two tumblers Adrian possessed and poured a sizeable measure of whisky into it. He handed it to Adrian. 'I could run a couple of X-rays. Just to be sure.'

'No, really. I'm fine. He wasn't trying to kill me. I'm sure if he wanted to he could have.' Adrian poured a small amount of water from a bottle into his whisky, stared deep into the glass for a moment, swirled the contents and inhaled. 'Smell that. My father used to call it releasing the serpent, the water frees the flavour. He was a whisky man. I didn't really take to it until a few years ago. Funny, that.'

'What did he want?' asked Kai.

For a moment Adrian looked at him, perplexed.

'The guy back there, I mean,' said Kai.

'I don't know.' Adrian shook his head and stared into the glass. 'Money?'

'And yet he didn't steal anything from you?' Kai took a sip of his beer and shook his head. 'Makes no sense. He had every opportunity. You were out cold.'

'What then?'

'My guess? He just didn't want you around.'

'So it would seem.'

'For sure not.'

217

They were silent. Adrian continued looking into his whisky glass. Then, without warning, he said, 'I need to go back.'

Kai didn't answer. Instead he tipped the rest of his beer down his throat, opened the bin and dropped the bottle inside. Then he opened the fridge and brought out some eggs, set the frying pan on the flame. By the time he broke the first egg into the pan the oil was so hot the edges of the egg curled up and began to brown. When he cooked he could think more clearly. He flicked hot oil over the surface of the egg, watched the white grow opaque, the yolk stiffen.

Behind him Adrian repeated, 'I need to go back.'

Kai gave a slight shake of his head. 'Don't be fucking crazy.'

'I need to.'

'Listen,' said Kai, more sharply than he intended. 'You have no idea what you're getting into. A lot of things have happened here. During the war, a lot of people did a lot of things. Others used the opportunity to make a lot of money. War makes some people rich. That guy is mixed up in something heavy. Whatever is going on in that house – drugs, most likely – you don't want to know.'

'What about Agnes?'

'What *about* Agnes?'

'She's suffering post-traumatic stress. She's ill.'

'Jesus!' Angry now, Kai turned to face Adrian; oil dripped from the spatula on to the worktop and the floor following the sweep of his hand. 'How the hell can I explain this to you in a way you'll understand? How many months have you been here? Two, three? There's been a war. What do you expect? This isn't a game. The guy in that house doesn't give a damn that you're a British passport holder. If he needs to kill you, he will.'

Adrian took a piece of kitchen roll and wiped the oil from the counter, squatted down to wipe the floor. Kai saw the grimace, the juddering in his breathing, evidence of the effort it cost him. Now he felt bad. He shook his head. 'This isn't your country, man. I'm sorry. But this isn't your country.'

'I know that,' said Adrian. 'I know this isn't my country. But it *is* my job.' He stepped forward, reached for the whisky bottle and poured himself another glass before returning to his former position against the wall, only this time he slid down it and sat on the floor.

Kai removed one egg and cracked another into the pan. It was errantry that brought them here, flooding in through the gaping wound left by the war, lascivious in their eagerness. Kai had seen it in the feverish eyes of the women, the sweat on their upper lips, the smell of their breath as they pressed close to him. They came to get their newspaper stories, to save black babies, to spread the word, to make money, to fuck black bodies. They all had their own reasons. Modern-day knights, each after his or her trophy, their very own Holy Grail. Adrian's Grail was Agnes.

And yet.

And yet, for Kai it was simple. His patients came, an unending trail. If he worked as a surgeon his whole life it would never be enough. In that way his professional life was self-sufficient, possessed clarity. His achievements were measurable. The people he treated walked again, or breathed again, lived again. Kai knew something of Adrian's early experiences here at the hospital. When they first met, he remembered his sense of the other man as, what? Unanchored. Since then Kai had witnessed the shift in Adrian. Talk of Ileana, of the man who ran the mental hospital. What was his name? Attila. Kai had met Attila only once. At a funding conference he had found himself alone with Attila for a few minutes, the only two black faces in the room. Kai had been impressed, thinking Attila had got closer to a kind of truth than anyone else. Attila understood something which Adrian didn't. Not yet.

He looked at Adrian's face, narrow and pale. The lethargy in his friend, dispelled during the course of the day, had returned.

Kai thought, too, of the last time he'd been to that town, Port Loko. With Tejani, their last trip together, on their way to find the Lassa fever doctor. They'd done it against the odds, not even knowing if the man existed, the country on the brink of anarchy. For the hell of it. Ah, Tejani.

The second egg was cooked on the underside. Kai flipped it over. He said, 'So what's the plan? Go back when he's not around?'

Adrian lifted his head. 'Yes. Talk to the daughter. She wanted the best for her mother. It was the son-in-law who was the problem. Whatever he is involved in, she isn't a part of it. I'm certain.'

Kai removed the pan from the gas ring, slid the cooked egg out on to the plate, reached for another egg and rolled it around the palm of his right hand, contemplating possibilities. 'And how is that going to work? You can't just hang around on the street corner in a place like that. You, especially.' With one hand he cracked the egg into the pan.

'You're right,' said Adrian. He struggled to his feet, whisky in his hand. 'What if . . .? No, it's too much to ask.' Then, 'What if you came with me?'

Kai looked at Adrian and looked away. He took a deep breath and released it. A moment ago for some reason, he'd been on the brink of saying yes. Now he felt Adrian's hopes building, filling the space. The idea was reckless. He shook his head.

'It's just too dangerous. Look what this guy already did to you. You could end up making it worse for Agnes. Listen, man, I'm sorry. I know how you feel. But it isn't worth it.'

Kai could feel the disappointment in Adrian, the slackening of the shoulders. He didn't look at him. Too bad. What to do? There were too many like Adrian, here living out their unfinished dreams.

He reached up to the shelf above his head and brought down a bottle of ketchup. 'Come on. You should eat.'

CHAPTER 26

My first reaction, upon my release, was to rid myself of the odours of that vile place. I showered twice, then shaved. Later I called and arranged to see Saffia. She was thinner, the skin beneath her eyes puffy and darkened, strands of hair had loosened from her braids. She embraced me and for a few seconds she remained with her forehead pressed against my shoulder. I became overwhelmingly conscious of her physical presence. Her relief, of course, lay in knowing where Julius was being held, if not the exact reason why. In the account I gave of my own time in custody, I omitted mention of the visit to me by the Dean. I'm not sure why. I suppose I felt it would complicate matters unnecessarily.

First thing Monday Saffia visited the building where Johnson worked. She telephoned me later. Johnson, with his usual obtuseness, had kept her waiting for two hours then sent down a number of forms for her to complete. She'd had no option but to oblige. When she returned he promised to process them. It might take a few days.

'In a few days!' I could hear in her voice how close she was to tears.

'Shall I come over?' I asked.

She said she was going to bed.

Meanwhile I was having my own troubles. Earlier that day as I went to buy bread I noticed a man standing in the street. I would have thought nothing of it, only later, emerging from the bakery, I saw him again, on the opposite side of the street. I eased my pace, just to see what happened. I noted he let a vacant taxi pass him by. He was still there when I reached my door. Later, I checked the street. No sign of him. Instead there was another man standing at the cigarette kiosk. He had his back to me, but as he turned I was certain I caught him glancing up at my window.

All through that oppressive day I stayed in my apartment, seeking solace and distraction among my papers, but to read was impossible. Instead I smoked and paced, twitching, moving an object here or there. You'd think that after two sleepless nights I would be exhausted.

And I was. Exhausted and yet incapable of rest. Outside my window the sound of a workman's hammer played on my nerves. In an effort to regain control and try to put my thoughts in some sort of order, I wrote down everything that had happened. It helped, as it often did, to see it in black and white on the page.

I went to bed late, slept erratically and woke determined not to endure another day like the one before. I left the house and hailed a passing *poda poda*. As we drew away I watched from the window for a sign of anything suspicious. I switched vehicle twice during my journey and arrived at the university mid-morning.

Nothing unusual, either, on campus. It was my luck this whole episode had taken place during the holidays. Today was Tuesday. Friday, the day of my arrest, was always a slow day. It was likely few people had missed me. I made my way up to my office, checking my pigeonhole on the way, saw two of my colleagues and exchanged greetings. I reached my room and closed the door behind me, remained leaning against it for a moment or two. I looked around. Somebody had been in my room. Several items had been moved. Vitally, my typewriter was missing. I looked through cupboards and opened drawers. The typewriter was nowhere to be seen. It became apparent my room had been searched, the typewriter removed as some sort of evidence. I walked down the corridor to the Dean's office.

The Dean was facing the window. He stood with his legs apart, hands behind his back. He did not turn his head or acknowledge my presence, yet I had the sense, in that still figure at the window, of a tremendous alertness. He turned around to face me.

'Good to see you, Cole. How are you?'

I replied I was well.

'Excellent,' he said.

'I just came by to thank you for your help last week.'

He waved my words away and said, 'Bad, bad. These sorts of matters. No good for anyone.'

'Yes,' I said. 'I was wondering . . .' I hesitated and then continued, 'Is there any news of Dr Kamara? His wife is very worried.'

'Dr Kamara?'

'I wondered if you had any information. If, perhaps, you could use your good offices with Mr Johnson to enquire.'

But the Dean was already shaking his head. 'I barely know Mr Johnson.'

I tried again. 'I'd like to be able to reassure his wife.'

The warmth had left his face entirely. He moved to sit down behind his desk and began to straighten some of the piles of paper upon it. When he spoke his voice contained a slight but significant change of tone. 'My advice to you is to leave this matter alone, if you are not involved, as you maintain. The point of authority is not to question it.'

'That's why I have come to you. To see if there is anything you can do.'

'We have been through difficult times,' said the Dean, with some irritation. 'And nobody in this country wants a return to the problems of the past. The police have a job to do. Once trouble begins, it has a habit of spreading. Now it's the universities. Look at Europe. Students burning down their own libraries, taking to the streets, disobeying the law. Now the disease has come over here. Ibadan. Nairobi. Accra. The students are no longer interested in learning. They've turned into hooligans. I have no intention of allowing this university to go the same way.' As he spoke his gaze rested upon me; he was entirely still, his eyes reflected the light from the window. Just before his eyelids dropped down over his eyes, I saw the depths of the ambition in them.

I had the unerring sense the discussion was at an end. I rose to go.

'One moment.' He fetched something from the cupboard behind his desk. I saw it was my typewriter. He said, 'Unauthorised use of university property. It may seem unimportant to you, but then you do not have my job. Once you let something slide, it is just the beginning.' He handed it to me. 'In this case, though, I am willing to accept it was an honest mistake.'

'Thank you,' I said.

Just as I reached the door, he said my name. 'Cole.'

My hand was on the doorknob. I turned.

He was standing reading a document. He looked up fleetingly. 'Be careful of the company you keep, Cole.'

Kekura, as it turned out, had escaped arrest. He had spent the night with a woman friend and, stopping by Yansaneh's house early in the day, had got wind of the arrests. He'd decided to visit some friends who happened to live over the border until he deemed it safe to return. Saffia told me this on Wednesday when we met over coffee at the Red Rooster. She'd been busy pursuing her own lines of enquiry. Her face was serious, resolved. Delicate lines on the sides of her eyes I had never noticed before. Other lines — of determination — either side of her mouth. They did nothing to diminish her beauty. She seemed to have regained her poise: the news of Kekura delivered by a friend, the dancer apparently. For some reason it grated upon me that he should have played a part in the restoration of her confidence. I wondered about him. I wondered about Kekura, too.

A waitress brought Nescafé in stainless-steel pots, a small jug of evaporated milk, a bowl of sugar cubes and set them down without ceremony upon the chequered plastic cloth.

'So what's next?' I said.

She had been back to see Johnson each day. While he refused to officially verify Julius was in his custody, everything in his manner confirmed it to her. He had told her to go home and wait.

'Perhaps you should. You look exhausted.'

She looked up at me, her eyes flashed. 'What are you saying, Elias?'

'Only that some things are best left. If you rile them, you might end up making things worse for Julius.'

She looked at me steadily. 'I know you're just trying to help.' She drew a deep breath: 'I've been to see a lawyer,' she announced. 'The lawyer says to give Johnson two more days and then to issue a writ of habeas corpus. One for Julius. One for Ade.'

I listened, I said, 'I want Julius out of there as much as you do, believe me. Only if you do as you suggest you risk bringing the whole thing out into the open.'

'That's the point.'

'The trouble is,' I said gently, 'you'd end up putting Johnson on the defensive. He might have to justify himself by charging Julius. And that would be a worse outcome.'

'What would you suggest?' she asked.

'That we continue as we are. Do as Johnson says and wait. He can't keep Julius in there for ever, he just wants to show he's a big man. Perhaps I can speak to my pastor, see if he can bring any pressure to bear.'

She sipped her coffee. Thoughts shadowed her face. Finally, she said, 'It's not just that I can't sit and do nothing, it's that I won't. This isn't just about Julius, don't you see, Elias? This is about all of us. To tolerate this kind of thing, well, it would be just the beginning.'

Just the beginning. The second time inside the day somebody had said those words. Ten minutes later I watched her wind her orange scarf around her head and walk away from me. She declined my offer to accompany her home. She wasn't sure yet where she was going, whether back to Johnson or to the lawyer's office. She had a few errands to run in the meantime.

'Call me if you hear anything.'

'Of course, Elias.'

As it turned out events outpaced the lawyer's intervention. The writ of habeas corpus was drawn up on Thursday. Before it could be delivered, Yansaneh was released. In the light of this new development the lawyer suggested they hold off to see what happened next. Julius's release might be imminent. Later in the same day Saffia and I went to Yansaneh's place. He seemed, how can I describe it to you? Somehow slowed, even more so than before. His short brow furrowed beneath the straight hairline. There was an air of bewilderment about him. I held back and watched Saffia embrace him, couldn't help but measure the embrace for warmth and tenderness. But Yansaneh just stood, his arms by his sides. Afterwards he turned and walked to the settee, where he sat down heavily and shook his head. For some minutes the three of us remained bound together in silence. Yansaneh asked if there was news of Julius. No, Saffia replied. Shoulders bowed, eyes cast downwards, he seemed smaller. Somehow I expected Yansaneh, the good-natured pedant, to be more stoical.

You will imagine we questioned him about his experiences, that we dug around for facts to piece together, that we examined the thing this way and that to find answers. It wasn't like that. We listened as he recounted in a low voice those relevant parts of his ordeal. He spoke at his own pace, the sentences punctuated by long silences. He had been questioned, as I had been. The questions pursued more or less the same line. They seemed to be looking for agitators on the campus. Julius. His views, his movements, the company he kept. Yansaneh mentioned meetings in my room, though in the flow of his account they did not emerge as especially significant. None of what he said added much to what we already knew.

We left Yansaneh's place and drove back through the town. It was early evening. Saffia's fingers played upon the steering wheel. She said, 'One never expects to find oneself in this kind of situation. It's the sort of thing you read about, that happens to other people in other countries.'

I made no reply. A few years ago we'd had a coup, our first, followed by two years of military rule. Not what you hope for, but still. It had all seemed to take place at a different level, well above the lives of ordinary people. We'd woken up one morning to a new government. And in many ways the military were not the worst you could imagine. Though few people publicly supported them, quite a few did so privately. Now we had a civilian government again.

'In a building in this city, in a room or a cell, is my husband. I can't see him. I can't find my way to him. Yet I know he is there. And so do the people who put him there. Whatever the outcome, even if Julius is released tomorrow, things will never be the same again. This is something more. Don't you see?'

I shook my head. 'Let's not blow things out of proportion. You don't know Johnson like I do. I was with the man for the best part of two days. He's the one who's behind this. There's no great conspiracy. Johnson's got ahead of himself, that's all. Nothing more to it than that. But he's not all powerful. To take things further he'll have to consult someone higher up and they'll put a stop to it.'

She looked at me. I could see the hope in her eyes.

'Do you think so, Elias?' She wanted to believe.

'Yes,' I said firmly. 'I do.'

CHAPTER 27

Early morning, a month after his illness. Adrian is driving himself for once. He sees the young woman standing at the roadside, a pair of plastic containers at her feet. It is her, he is certain, the woman he saw talking to Babagaleh and whose face he saw again on the poster at the Ocean Club. He is peering through the windscreen, wanting to assure himself of the fact, when she steps out in front of the vehicle and waves. Adrian's first response is to wave back, until he realises she is flagging him down. He stops and she hoists the two containers into the back, opens the door and climbs up into the front seat.

'Thanks,' she says, as though she has been waiting for him all this time. 'Water.'

'Water?' he repeats.

'There isn't any water where I live. They haven't turned the pumps on for weeks.'

Adrian blinks. 'So what do people do?'

She jerks her head backwards in the direction of the containers.

Now he understands. He's seen the queues of people, or sometimes a line of differently shaped and coloured containers, marking places, waiting for the water to come when some government official deemed it. Next to him the young woman sits in silence, except to give occasional directions. Fifteen minutes later she asks him to stop. Before Adrian manages to open his door, she has already stepped out and lifted the two containers from the back. Drops of perspiration bead her forehead and she wipes them with the back of her arm.

'Thanks,' she says through the open passenger window.

For the first time he is able to look directly into her face.

'Is that you? On the poster at the Ocean Club?'

'Yes. It is.'

He doesn't want to let her go. 'You're a singer?'

She smiles. 'Oh no. There's a few of us. It isn't a living. More like something to do.'

227

He pauses to leave an opening, hoping for an invitation, but instead she bends down to pick up the containers. And so he says, 'Perhaps I could come and listen one evening.'

She smiles at him, properly this time. And though he feels faintly exposed, he also feels rewarded.

'I'm not sure when we're next playing at the Ocean Club,' she says. 'Oh.'

She continues, 'But if you're looking for something to do, we're at the Ruby Rooms. You know it?'

He nods. The name is familiar, though he's not sure exactly why. She walks away from him, not up the steps of a house, as he imagined, but down the street, labouring under the weight of her containers. He watches her for a few moments more, notices she doesn't turn once.

Later in the day Adrian gave an account of Agnes's case to Attila. He stuck to the clinical details, omitting mention of the visit to Port Loko and Agnes's house. Instead he concluded with her departure from the hospital. Attila's response had been to shrug and regard Adrian from his great height, those hawkish features atop the bulk of his body. They were standing in the hospital's courtyard, Attila for once without his retinue.

'Change takes time, my friend,' he'd said as he made to move on, a ship preparing to sail. 'And some of us here have more time than others.' The implication being, Adrian tells Ileana later, that Adrian was some sort of fly-by-night. The truth is that since arriving here his life has seemed more charged with meaning than it ever had in London. Here the boundaries are limitless, no horizon, no sky. He can feel his emotions, solid and weighty, like stones in the palm of his hands. Everything matters more.

Ileana exhales and at the same time sighs. 'Yeah, well.' Her voice is gritty with smoke. 'Shit happens.' She does not raise her head, or meet his eye, but smokes and shuffles papers.

Adrian is astonished. 'Ileana?'

She looks up, takes another pull at her cigarette, pinching the filter tight between her thumb and forefinger. Tiny tributaries of lipstick run down the lines around her mouth. Her eyes, inside the dark ring of mascara, are red-rimmed.

'I'm sorry,' she says. And shakes her head.

'Are you all right?'

'Nina. She was hit by a car. The bastard didn't even stop. She managed to crawl almost all the way home. She died outside the house.'

'Oh, Ileana. I'm sorry.'

'I've never told anyone else this, but when I worked at the mental hospital in Bucharest a patient was admitted one evening straight from the medical hospital. At the staff meeting the next day she was allocated to me. Apparently everybody else had a full caseload. I was delighted. I still only saw patients under supervision. I was desperate for a *real* case.

'She was young. Maybe a couple of years younger than me. She was on suicide watch. I mean, this was a long way off teaching inmates to make string bags and tea towels. I took it as a sign my supervisor had faith in me.' Ileana sets a pot of tea down on the desk along with the two flowered bone china cups and a box of sugar cubes. 'They had her on the full dose of drugs. Early on I fought to have her regime reduced. After that she started making progress. She was smart, educated. In another place she could have been my friend. Sugar?'

Adrian shakes his head.

'When I came back she wasn't there. She'd been transferred. Without any reference to me. Gone. They'd already given her bed to somebody else.'

'Christ!' said Adrian. 'What was that about?'

'I'd been set up. She was a political detainee. From us she was transferred to a high-security psychiatric hospital, where she was diagnosed paranoiac. Everyone in the country knew what was happening but pretended everything was perfectly normal. The ones who couldn't keep up the pretence we locked away.' She laughs and Adrian smiles. Ileana raises her tea cup. 'To Nina. Snappy little bitch, soul of a stray. Bit me more than once. I found her on the beach, did I ever tell you that? Seduced her with tinned salmon.' She sighs. 'I loved her.'

'To Nina,' Adrian concurs. The tea burns the roof of his mouth. He asks, 'Is that why you left Bucharest?'

'More or less. The fact is, soon after I didn't have a job. None of us did.'

'How?'

'Ceauşescu decided we were collaborators with Western spy

agencies. He sent a lot of people to prison. Banned the entire profession from practising.'

'But not you?'

'I was too junior. I didn't matter.'

'So what did you do?'

'I went to work as a cleaner until my family could emigrate. We dug up a Jewish grandmother, actually a dead step-grandmother. We used her to emigrate to Israel.' She raises her cup again. 'A toast to her, too. Whoever she was.'

'Have you been back since? To Bucharest?'

'Once. That was enough.'

He is quiet. She lights another cigarette and disappears briefly behind the smokescreen. 'My family, the ones who still lived there, they didn't want to talk about the past. All they wanted were watches, TVs, video recorders. Not one of them raised a finger to help after I lost my job. Fuck this! Come on!' She grinds out the stub of her cigarette into a saucer and slides the handle of her handbag off the back of the chair. 'Let's get out of here. I'll buy you a drink. In fact, I'll do better. I'll buy you tomorrow's hangover.'

Somehow, not before they have been to a couple of the bars along the way, they wind up at the Ruby Rooms. As soon as he enters, Adrian realises why the name seemed so familiar. The booths, the wine-coloured carpet and compact dance floor, the terrace overlooking the hills, the place is just as Elias Cole described it in their conversations, from a time when it was called the Talk of the Town.

Ileana is at the bar ordering drinks. Shouting Romanian-accented Creole at the barman above the din. He cannot imagine Lisa acting like that, or even agreeing to come to a place like this. The bass beat pounds through Adrian's guts. There are people on the dance floor, dark shapes, their edges illuminated by the strobe light. A DJ, trapped like a bird in a tiny booth above the dancers, announces each new song. Smells of sweat, beer and dry ice. He catches Ileana's eye, mouths to her at the same time as pointing to the door. She nods back. Outside on the terrace he finds a table, wet with beer, a couple of plastic chairs. Up this high there is a breeze. The music has settled to a more bearable level. He watches Ileana as she comes towards him carrying the drinks. In her high-necked floral blouse, white socks and sandals, she could scarcely look more incongruous.

As Adrian watches a tall, good-looking man in baggy jeans and an oversize T-shirt peels away from a wall and intercepts her, keeping pace with her as she walks. From what Adrian can make out he appears to be saying something to her under his breath. Ileana responds without breaking her stride. The young man stops dead in his tracks and stares at her with his mouth open. Then he draws back his chin, sucks his teeth so loudly even Adrian can hear it, turns on his heel and rejoins his companions. Adrian rises to help Ileana with the drinks.

'What was that about?'

'He offered to pleasure me. Apparently his cock is enormous. Can you believe it?'

Adrian can't quite, in fact. The young man can't be much past his twenties, if that. 'What was it you said to him?'

'I told him no thanks. But to come back when he could lick his eyebrows. *Noroc!*' She raises her glass of Jack Daniels.

Adrian, who has already taken a sip of his drink, nearly chokes.

Inside the music has quieted. People are leaving the verandah, moving back inside, in ones and twos.

'They must be starting,' he says. He feels nervous with anticipation.

They leave the table and follow the other guests inside. For the first time Adrian notices a small stage at the back of the room. Musical instruments. Drums. A guitar leaning on a chair. A clarinet. The DJ is speaking into the microphone. Adrian can't make out what he is saying, only the drama in the man's voice. Around Adrian people begin to clap. Three men and a woman come on to the stage. It is her. Adrian closes his lips, misses a breath, and inhales deeply with the next. A dress, of the same print as the men's shirts, is wrapped around her body. Her shoulders are bare, her hair pulled back from her face. She doesn't go to the microphone stand, as he expects, but crosses the stage and picks up the clarinet. One of the group steps forward to the microphone and begins to hum ascending notes. The sound is immense, reverberating through the density of bodies. Minutes, it seems, pass. The sound grows louder. Then enters the clarinet. Finally the guitar and the keyboard. But it is the clarinet, so close in sound to the human voice, that rises above the others. The man in the lead shifts his footing to lean closer in to the microphone and begins to sing. Afterwards Adrian would struggle to describe to himself the sort of music it was, whether jazz or soul, only the mood of it. It slows his heartbeat, his spirit is lifted and carried along on it, only to be set down and lifted again. Nobody dances, just listens. As each song finishes the sound of the last chord hangs in the air above the heads of the audience, is dispelled only by the sound of clapping. The band moves from one song to the next. Three songs in all. He watches her throughout, the sharp point of her elbow, the movement of her wrists and fingers, the way she rests the mouthpiece on her lower lip. Her playing is unostentatious, devoid of showmanship, she does not close her eyes or sway. Just the heel of a foot counting beats upon the wooden floor. From time to time she lifts her eyes and casts an appraising look over the crowd. Once she sees him, he thinks, and seems to smile. The singer leans into the microphone again, murmurs several thank yous, introduces the band one by one. There is clapping and whistling at each name. She holds her clarinet across her body. When her cue comes she raises the mouthpiece to her lips and plays a few notes of a solo. Three songs more. And then it is over. People drift back outside. The band leave. The instruments remain on the stage.

Ten minutes. Adrian watched the door to the club virtually the entire time. Finally the band come out on to the terrace, to be surrounded immediately by well-wishers. She is not among them. When she does appear she wends her way through the groups of people. A nod here, a handshake. She does not stop, clearly on her way somewhere else. Disappointed, he turns away. When next he looks up, she is standing by the table.

'Hello,' he says, rising quickly.

'So you came along,' she says. 'How did you like the music?'

'It was,' he opens his hands, 'really beautiful. Thank you.'

'Glad you enjoyed it.' She smiles at him, looks across at Ileana.

'This is my colleague, Ileana.' He stops. He doesn't know her name.

'Mamakay.'

'Mamakay,' he repeats. So he never forgets it.

'It's my house name,' she says, as if in reply to a question.

'Sorry?'

'It's my house name. You know, not your real name but the one everyone calls you. Sort of like a nickname. Mamakay is for my great-aunt. Mama Kay. She used to look after me. Terrible woman, actually. All she did was pray.' She grins. 'I used to ask her, Auntie, what are you praying for? Every time she gave me the same reply. For God's answer. One day, when I was older, I said to her, maybe he already

232

has answered. Maybe this *is* his answer!' And she gestured all around. 'Maybe he's telling us he doesn't give a damn!' She laughs. 'Bring me one Star, please,' she says over her shoulder to a passing waiter. When the beer comes she wipes the top with the flat of her palm and drinks straight from the bottle.

'Sit with us,' says Adrian.

Whereas earlier in the day he felt weary, now he feels energised. Between the three of them, over the hours of the evening, the conversation turns around and around. Mamakay tells them of an island fort, complete with cannons, that is there still. Ileana sings the first few lines of a Romanian folk song, with which she mourns the death and celebrates the life of her dog. They talk about the matriarchal nature of hyenas. The advantages of animals over humans. Of men over women, and women over men. Of how best to grow tomatoes from seed. Of being rained upon, which Adrian longs for.

Often it is just Ileana and Mamakay talking between themselves; the two women find something in each other. It amazes him how soon between women the talk goes to the next level. He is content to be an audience, and grateful to Ileana, whose presence makes this possible. It's a long time since he has sat with women. He looks from one to the other. Ileana's vivid features, the dry humour etched upon her face. Mamakay's suppressed energy, which erupts in hands that dance in the air in front of her. She stays and sits with them. Because he fears, with every passing minute, losing her company perversely he apologises for keeping her. She waves her beer bottle dismissively. Later, much later, they order food. She eats with her hands, without stopping or speaking except to praise the food. And chews the ends of her chicken bones.

That night he dreams of her. Of driving past her on the road with her water containers, towards Ileana further ahead. Of turning the vehicle before he reaches Ileana and returning for her. It is not an erotic dream as such, though as powerful as any he has had. And like the music, he is left less with images of the dream than the mood it creates in him. Such dreams in the past have left him bereft, wanting but unable to return to sleep to rediscover what he had lost. This time he awakes comforted, left with a different sense. One of utter certainty.

The next day he sees her, and again the day after. On each occasion he stops. He climbs down to help her with the heavy containers and she climbs up to take the seat next to him. For her work she wears a cotton dress, sleeveless with a small tear at the hem. A dress of sunflowers. She rubs her arms, hunches her shoulders. He turns off the air conditioning and she winds down the window. When he leans across to help with the door, he smells her sweat faintly. He inhales surreptitiously. After she is gone, he closes the window, to trap the scent inside.

In a short while it is again as it was on that first day. She stands on the street, as if she is waiting for him.

CHAPTER 28

War gave new intensity to their lovemaking. On the floor, facing him. Nenebah with her legs around Kai's waist. He, inside her, a nipple in his mouth. One hand squeezes the surrounding breast, his tongue flicks back and forth, round and round. The fingers of his other hand, in the warm V of her thighs, imitate the same motion. Her breathing rises and quickens. As she comes, he holds on to her, an arm around her shoulders, pressing her down on to his cock. With the slowing of her shudders he rolls Nenebah on to her back, his fingers in her hair, moving forward and back until he loses himself. Afterwards he lies, still inside her, slowly softening, her hand stroking the back of his neck. In time they both sleep held in the same position.

They meet when they can. Around the hours of curfew and surgery. It is dark, there is no light, no cooking gas. Sometimes they go without eating or speaking, making love is all they do.

The memory of their lovemaking comes to Kai out of nowhere. He is standing holding a paper cup of drink: purple, sweet and alcoholic. The room is hot and crowded. The memory of Nenebah's smell and taste, of the smooth skin and muscles of her back, the melting liquidness, hits him like a blast. Nothing he can do but stand still and wait for it to pass.

Mrs Mara is next to him, holding a cup of the same purple punch, dressed in a Swiss voile dress, a gathering at the hem and puff sleeves, in place of the usual suit. Her smile, too long held, has turned glassy. She is unable to smooth the furrow from between her brows. In front of them the two departing nurses are being photographed by a senior registrar. Arms around each other, heads together, the same shade of bright lipstick, mauve blusher – make-up bought and shared for the party. People have brought food and gifts: a scarf, bars of Lux soap, a plastic passport holder and an outsize card signed by each staff member. The two girls squirm in front of the registrar's camera, their giggles betraying their nervousness. They have managed to arrange to go together to the same hospital in Reading. Kai, in the staff room, overheard one of the foreign doctors correct their pronunciation. 'Reh-ding. Not Reeding.'

How many did that make this year? The operating theatres had lost an anaesthetist. He had attended at least three other parties for nurses, exactly like this one. Or was it three? They were beginning to merge. And now Wilhemina. The loss of Wilhemina, in particular, would be felt. She had the makings of an excellent theatre nurse.

Kai prepares to make his exit, goes up to say his goodbyes, kisses them both on the cheek. Squeezes Wilhemina's shoulder. Once she had a crush on him, or so he suspects. Something about Wilhemina reminds Kai of Balia. Balia was another young nurse he'd known once years ago and who had been sweet on him, too. But Kai mustn't think about her. He slips out of the door into the heat of the night.

Inside the ward Kai follows the trail of blue night lights to the corner of the room, to the bed with the wheelchair parked up by it. Scrawled upon a blackboard on the wall above are the letters *NBM*, nil by mouth. Foday is asleep. Kai is just preparing to leave when Foday opens his eyes.

'I thought you were sleeping,' says Kai.

'I was sleeping, yes. But I can still hear you, even in my sleep.' He grins and begins to struggle into a sitting position.

Kai presses him gently back down by the shoulders. 'Relax. I just came by to see how you are doing. All ready for tomorrow?'

Foday nods.

'Anything I can get you?'

Foday shakes his head. 'Except you bring me some rice and cassava leaves.'

Kai smiles and shakes his head. 'No, but afterwards you can eat all you want. You have someone from your family coming to give blood?'

'My uncle.'

'Good. Tell him to bring your fiancée. We're all waiting to meet her. Tell her we've heard so much about her. Must be some fine woman. Does she know the trouble you are going to for her?' It is their joke, the fictional fiancée, Foday's dreams of marriage and a family.

Foday laughs wheezily. 'So you can come and take her from me? When you get your own fiancée, then I let you meet mine.'

Kai smiles. 'Sleep well. And I'll see you tomorrow.'

On the way out he nods to the night nurse, sitting with her book of crossword puzzles on the desk before her. She raises her head and returns his nod.

That night he dreams of the bridge. The railings pressed into his back. A face close to his. There is shouting. And pain, like a claw hammer at the back of his skull. The pressure on his temple. The agonising paralysis. Then the sensation of weightlessness. He wakes with the taste of blood and metal in his mouth, a ringing in his ears, images crashing against the line of his consciousness. Only the sound of his cousin knocking gently on the door brings him back to himself.

'OK,' he calls. Hears her begin to move away, slow steps, in the direction of her own room. He sits up, frees himself from the tangled sheets and searches for the luminous light of his watch. Four-thirty. Two hours left. Through the sleeping house he makes his way to the kitchen, pours himself a glass of water from the steel container. The sound of the water trickling into the glass brings on the urge to urinate. He opens the back door. The moon is high in the sky. His squat black shadow tracks him across the yard like an animal at his heels. Under the banana trees he relieves his bladder. Heading back to the house he stops and for a few moments gazes up at the sky, the milky streaks of stars. He rolls his head around the back of his shoulders. He feels completely and utterly awake.

In his room he lies awake listening to the ticking of his watch and the sounds of the night, measuring off the remaining minutes. At six o'clock he is still there. Outside the sounds thicken with the approach of dawn as every household braces for the onslaught of another day.

Half an hour later he comes out of sleep to the sound of his cousin rapping on the door again, a louder, more insistent knock this time. In the kitchen he quarters a pawpaw deftly with a large knife, offers a slice to his cousin, who shakes her head. Abass is gone already, his satchel bouncing on his back. The two cousins eat together in silence for a few minutes, each with their own preoccupations.

'Will you help me with the chairs before you go?'

'Sure.'

'We can do it now, together.'

237

Kai waves his fork. 'Don't worry. You go ahead. I'll get it done before I go.'

She rinses her coffee cup at the sink. 'Will you join us this time?'

'Let me see how I get on.'

'You know, you'd be very welcome.'

'Thanks.'

They go through the same routine every time. Since the church meetings started to be held in the house, Kai makes sure he's rarely ever at home at the same time. In the beginning he was happy for his cousin, for the comfort she had found in the act of worship. But increasingly he finds the other members of the church irritating, the anxious and obsequious manner they affect around him. They are awed by his job at the hospital and desperate to recruit him to their cause, unaware of how much he despises them, their fevered fatalism. Everywhere you look in the city new churches are springing up, on every patch of bare earth, in the open air, under blue-and-white UN canvas, in houses and empty buildings.

After breakfast Kai carries the chairs through from the yard to the verandah and sets them out in rows. By seven-thirty he is on his way to the hospital. The traffic is light, he makes good time. In the staff room he pours himself his third cup of coffee and sits with it, watching his hands holding the cup, the surface of the black liquid vibrating, the reflections shimmering and shifting. The last few nights have not been good. Hard to know if the coffee improves matters or makes them worse. Another few sips and he sets the cup down. He needs to prepare. He makes his way to the changing rooms for the operating theatres. Nobody is there. Just Mrs Goma's wig hanging on a peg like a dead bird. Time alone is all he needs. It is an important day, the second operation of the elective, out of a total of four. When it is all over, and if everything goes according to plan, if no serious infections set in, and if all their projections are correct, a few months from now Foday will walk. Not the way he walks now, every step a flailing uphill struggle. Foday will walk tall.

In the first operation they had broken and reset the tibia of the right leg. Today they would perform the same operation on the left leg.

Kai strips off his day clothes and selects a green scrub suit from the shelves. He's restless, nervous and overly alert. At the sink he washes his face in cold water and inspects himself in the mirror, pulling down his bottom eyelid and inspecting his gums. His skin is dry and taut. He feels queasy. He runs the tap and drinks from his hand. The water is warm and only slightly refreshing.

He sits on the bench and holds his hands up to his face. The tremble is still there. He closes his eyes and leans back against the lockers, feels his breathing slow, his heart quieten. He spreads his fingers out upon his thighs; his body begins to feel lighter.

A knock on the door. He opens his eyes. 'Yes?'

'Dr Mansaray?'

'Yes?'

It is one of the theatre nurses with a message. 'You're wanted in emergency.'

'Did you tell them I'm about to go into surgery?'

'Yes. They say there's nobody else.'

He sighs, rises and opens the door, but she has already turned away. He sees her shoulder her way into the theatre where Mrs Goma is working. Swiftly he changes his shoes and makes his way upstairs and through the building to the emergency unit. The unit doesn't stay open all hours. They don't have the staff. Instead it opens at ten in the morning and people begin to gather long before. Most conditions can be treated routinely, even when they are serious. But those times there is a real emergency out of hours, you can be drafted in from anywhere.

A massive iron gate had fallen while being lowered into place by a crane, trapping three workmen beneath it. Two of the men had escaped with broken bones and were already being attended to. The third man is the one Kai has been called to look at. The nurse indicates a man lying on his back on the far side of the room. He is not yet forty by Kai's guess, though he is gaunt and this makes him appear older. He lies without speaking, his eyes open.

'Hello,' says Kai. 'How do you feel? Are you in pain?'

'Not so much pain, Doctor. Only I cannot feel my body.'

Kai reads the notes the nurse has given him. Suspected spinal injury. He examines the man briefly, calls the nurse and asks for a pin. Starting high on the man's chest, he delivers pinpricks at regular intervals. 'Tell me if you can feel this.' The man nods and whispers, 'Yes. Yes. Yes.' Then silence. Just above his navel. Kai backs up and repeats the pinpricks, this time to check the exact location where the sensation disappears. 'Yes, yes.' When he reaches the same spot, there is silence once again. Next he checks the deep-tendon reflexes at the Achilles tendon. Nothing.

239

'I'll be back,' he tells the man. 'Who is here with you? Family?'

He shakes his head. 'Mr Sesay.'

'Who's that, your boss?'

A nod.

At the nurse's station Kai gives his diagnosis. Likely severance of the spinal cord at T8. To be confirmed by X-ray.

'Shall I admit him?' asks the nurse.

Kai shakes his head. 'Ask him to let us call his family. Someone will need to explain to them.' He exhales. He hates this most of all. 'And to him.' He hands her the notes. She takes them without looking up.

'Who will explain to them?' No doubt she is already worried the job might fall to her.

'I'll do it. Call me when the X-rays are ready. Otherwise I'll come back and check after theatre.'

Outside he calls Mr Sesay's name. The foreman steps forward, pulling off his woollen hat. Kai explains to him, in a way he hopes he can understand, the nature of the injury. The foreman isn't stupid. He has lost a worker. He listens attentively, shakes his head, promises to bring the family himself. He is still standing there holding on to his woollen hat as Kai walks away. Kai thinks of all the things he has not told the foreman. In particular of Mrs Mara's decision not to admit any more spinal-injury patients. In past times they'd kept men alive for months only to have them die within weeks of being discharged back to their *panbodies*, where nobody had the time or the expertise to care for them, to manage their bowel and bladder movements, to turn them several times a day; no money to buy catheters and equipment. Better let them die sooner than later – the brutal fact of it. He considers how much to tell the family, whether to confine himself to explaining how to care for their father and wait for the inevitable. The bed sores are the worst of it. With luck pneumonia would take him first. Kai glances at his watch. He will have to move if he is to be ready for the start of the operation. If they miss the slot they might have to reschedule.

In the theatre they are ready to begin. Foday has been wheeled down and is already on the table, one arm hooked up to the blood-pressure monitor. He is lying on his back, the massive chest rising above him, both his muscular arms outstretched, the shape of a crucifix. His penis lies flung to one side, shaved balls nestle between strong thighs tapering into underdeveloped calves, one splayed, one now straight, down to the out-turned ankles. On the light box on the wall, X-rays of those same frog legs. Kai bids Foday good morning, earns a smile, silent and serene. Foday's confidence should be heartening. Instead Kai feels a quickening of the stomach muscles. The team is the same as before. Seligmann, the lead surgeon. Kai. The anaesthetist, Salamatu. All except Wilhemina. In her place the nurse who called him to the emergency unit. She is busy layering sterile drapes over Foday's body, returning him to modesty. Her hands are quick, professional, her face unsmiling. She is the sole OR nurse now. From the instrument trolley Kai picks up a kidney bowl of water, iodine and ampicillin and begins to swab Foday's leg. Seligmann is photographing Foday's left leg. He steps forward, shifts the position of the leg and returns to take the photograph. The flash bounces off the white walls causing Foday to raise his head.

'Photograph,' explains Salamatu. She slides a needle into his arm. Reaches up to the IV line and injects a fluid into it.

'Passport photo,' says Kai. 'For your honeymoon.'

Foday rolls his head in Kai's direction and grins at him. He seems about to respond, when his eyes lose focus, the lids flutter closed.

'Good,' says Seligmann, putting down the camera. He peers at Foday.

They are ready to begin. The nurse tightens the tourniquet around Foday's thigh.

'Over or under?' asks Seligmann. 'Under or over?'

They assess the point of entry, agree to go in under the muscle. Seligmann makes the first incision. Blood oozes from the wound. 'Tourniquet,' he says. The nurse tightens the tourniquet further. Kai meanwhile stands by with the diathermy wand. He glances down. The tip of the wand is waving. He takes a quick, deep breath, tries to steady his arm and his hand to stop the involuntary movement of the wand. He looks up to check whether anybody else has noticed. The nurse is finishing off the tourniquet. Seligmann waits to continue the incision. Salamatu is sitting next to Foday's head. None of them are looking in his direction. Kai flexes his arm, at the same time lowering the wand below the level of the table. He counts and breathes. One, two, three. It's worked before. He concentrates all his energy into stilling his hand and arm. The waving is arrested sure enough, but the tip of the wand continues to shiver. He can do nothing to control it. Any moment now, Seligmann will ask him to begin cauterising the ends of blood vessels left by his incision. The nurse has tied off the tourniquet and now resumes her place next to Seligmann. Seligmann bends his head, adjusts his grip on the scalpel and prepares to begin again.

'Sorry,' says Kai. 'Can you excuse me a moment?'

'What?' Seligmann, bent over Foday's leg, looks up at him, incredulous. 'Are you kidding?'

'Yes. I mean, no. Sorry.' He indicates to the nurse to come and take the diathermy wand from him. 'I have to go.'

'Something up?'

Kai rolls his eyes. 'Ate at the Beach Bar last night.'

Seligmann emits a snort of muffled laughter into his mask. 'So even the locals aren't immune. Bad luck. Go! Go! For Christ's sake!' He waves the scalpel in the direction of the door. 'I can manage here for a while.' Chuckles as he returns to work.

'Thanks.' Kai makes his way to the door, stripping off his gloves as he goes, conscious of the nurse's eyes upon him above her mask.

Ten minutes elapse before he returns to the OR; the most delicate part of the procedure is over. Kai had spent the time sitting alone in the changing room, trying to locate the presence of mind required to continue, aware he couldn't stay away too long. He must see this through. Thoughts of Foday. Of the altered technique he and Seligmann were pioneering. In time he rose, changed his robe, scrubbed back in and re-entered the theatre. The nurse helped him with his gloves. He catches a trace of a question in her eyes, wonders how much she noticed.

'Just in time.' Seligmann is wielding a steel hammer and chisel. 'Come and mark off the bone for me, would you?'

At that moment Foday's arm rises from the table of its own accord.

'Anaesthesia, we are moving,' calls Seligmann.

Salamatu pumps more ketamine into Foday's system. Slowly, as if buoyed on invisible currents, Foday's arm drifts back down. Kai marks a groove in the exposed bone. A moment later Seligmann positions the chisel, draws back his arm and with a blow of the hammer drives the chisel through the bone. Behind him the display light box on the wall flickers faintly.

On the operating table Foday sleeps with the angels, while his shin bone is methodically smashed.

★　　★　　★

242

Seven o'clock and he is on his way home. Almost twelve hours since he arrived at the hospital. He has barely rested or eaten. He and Seligmann had sewn up Foday's wound together, the older man talking and telling jokes, full of good spirits on that day. Kai was grateful for it, grateful Seligmann was distracting himself, allowing Kai to concentrate on each suture as though it were the first he had ever performed.

Afterwards Seligmann had accepted Kai's offer to write up the notes and exited the theatre swinging his arms and whistling. Opposites on the surface, the same beneath the skin, both men thrive only in the theatre, a scalpel in their hand, a human body on the table. Seligmann had faced his retirement without equanimity, with the belligerence of a bull. Within six months his marriage had fallen apart. His wife made it a condition of their eventual reunion that he find a way to go back to work. Now here he is, in a country far from home, operating where he is still needed. His wife stays in the house, occupied with their grandchildren, lunches and life-drawing classes. Seligmann calls her every day, never returns home for more than two weeks at a time. In this way they have found contentment.

Exhausted. Still, Kai hadn't wanted to go home where the church meeting would be under way. He'd passed by Adrian's apartment, found the place empty, showered and changed back into his day clothes, rummaged through the fridge. Nothing. Too much effort to send someone out and begin to cook, and in no mood for the canteen, he'd decided at last to go home.

The traffic is slow, the *poda poda* in which he travels inches its way around another of its kind, broken down in the middle of the road. Traffic passes either side like a sluggish river around a rock.

Some time after eight Kai slips through the gate and makes it to the back of the house unobserved. There he takes a beer from the fridge and carries it out to the yard, where he sits in the half-darkness. From the front verandah come the booming words of the preacher, florid and false. He can see the preacher in his mind's eye: the peanut head, myopic gaze, striped suit, leather-soled shoes. His cousin's folly. He takes a gulp of beer. It is warm and gassy. He scratches his scalp, which has now begun to itch, and slaps at a mosquito. He drains the first bottle of beer and goes in search of another one. Within a couple of minutes the second bottle is half empty. From his room he fetches a tape recorder, sits with it under the banana tree buzzing the tape

243

back and then forward, trying and failing to locate a song to suit his mood.

Abass appears before him, dressed in his pyjama bottoms.

'Guess what I saw today,' says the boy.

'Not now, Abass.' He swallows from the bottle. Hunger has been replaced by thirst.

Abass presses on. 'I saw the fifty orange monkeys, they came to my school.'

'I said not now!' The words come fast and harder than Kai intended. He sees the boy blench. Abass freezes, his mouth hangs open, the remainder of a smile upon his lips, eyes liquid bright. He is uncertain whether his uncle is joking. Kai continues to sit, staring at the top of his beer bottle and breathing hard to control a sudden inexpressible anger. 'Go to bed. Go on,' he says in a low voice.

By the time he recovers himself it is too late. The boy has fled. He is into his third bottle of beer when he remembers the man with the spinal injury. The family must have been waiting to speak to him and he had forgotten.

By his fifth bottle of beer he is drunk, and still not ready for sleep.

CHAPTER 29

'Last night I dreamt of Julius,' says Elias Cole. 'We were in some great airy space, like a railway station or a lecture theatre. It was one of those ever-changing spaces that occur in dreams. There among the gathering of people, I was sure it was him. Julius. Yet what was he doing here? I tried to elbow my way towards him, but the more I did so, the more the crowd seemed to thicken. I made to call his name, but my voice emerged as a faint and ludicrous squeak. Suddenly I was in a different place. I was walking down a road. It was dusk, but I had an awareness of space, of something like open fields on either side. Ahead of me I saw Julius. That distinctive walk of his, the way his thighs brushed together. I called, "Julius!" I wanted to ask him what he was doing there. But he continued to walk away, ambling slowly and yet at the same time he seemed to be covering a great distance in a very short time. I ran, but he left me behind.'

'And then what happened?' asks Adrian.

'Then I woke up. Or dreamt I woke up. Later when I woke up my arm was numb. Then I knew I was really awake.'

The old man turns from Adrian to face the window. Outside a second kite is caught on the razor wire. There is no breeze to speak of and yet its wings of black plastic beat like the wings of a bird.

'This urge to order memories arrives with the age. A final sifting and sorting and cataloguing. To leave things in order before we go.' A pause. 'Back then, we were creatures of the air. Julius more than any of us.'

★

2 August 1969

The Dean telephoned me on the Saturday. He asked me to collect Saffia and take her to the place where Johnson worked. I asked no questions but did as I was told. We arrived full of the hope Julius was being released, though Saffia carried a small valise of his clean clothes, insurance against overoptimism. Precisely how long we waited I can't recall exactly. No sign of Johnson, whom I both expected to see and dreaded seeing. We waited on the third floor where the desk clerk refused to accept the valise, which served to graft another layer upon our thin hopes. So we sat, staring at the grey, scuffed walls. The clerk at the desk placed a package wrapped in brown paper upon the desk and called Saffia to sign for it. She wrote her name down. Strange what details you retain from such times. I remember her signature, or rather her lack of one. I'd never seen her handwriting before. Clear, legible, almost schoolgirlish, devoid of flourishes.

Saffia opened the package. It contained Julius's watch. His handkerchief. His wallet. A pair of bolts, a washer and a heavy metal screw: Julius's worry beads. His asthma medication, too. He was supposed to carry it everywhere with him, but often forgot. Too little a thing to fit in the scale of his imagination.

By some blunder we were led into the basement of the building. Three flights of stairs and then another, along a corridor, a grey-walled tunnel. There it was cool, a dampness hung in the air. The clerk opened the door to a room.

With what innocence we entered. Such innocence. We thought it was a waiting room, you see. I was talking, what was I saying? I think I was asking the clerk whether Johnson would be coming down. I stopped when Saffia dropped the package and a screw skittered across the floor. I bent to retrieve it, chasing it with my fingers. When I straightened, Saffia was on the other side of the room. I looked across and saw what she had seen. I walked towards her.

'Don't!' For some reason that was the only thing I could think of to say. 'Don't.' As though we could somehow walk out, close the door of that narrow room and turn our backs on what was inside. And in so doing prevent it from ever becoming real.

She never heard me.

She reached out her hand and pulled back the sheet.

People, when they describe such life-changing moments, often say every action seems suddenly slowed. How true it is. The workings of the brain, I expect, struggling to embrace the enormity of the moment. Afterwards you are left with fragments. The form lying on the trolley. Saffia's hand over her mouth. Julius's face, his eyes half open, the pupils not dull but lucent, so that he appeared to be looking past us at the door, as if waiting for someone else to enter. Saffia's hand on his cheek.

No sound save the banging of my own heart.

What a terrible stillness there is, once the heat and the light have left a body. The death mask, a look of sheer indifference to you, the living. Saffia placed her hand on Julius's cheek, withdrew it and reeled backwards, colliding with me. I tried and failed to hold her. Within the same motion she fell suddenly forward, tore the sheet away from her husband's body and pressed her forehead against his chest. She began to kiss his face. She begged him to wake up. With growing insistence she kissed him and shook him by the shoulders. She straightened, her tears left upon Julius's face. She started to search his body, I could only imagine for some sign of what or who had done this to him.

What the clerk was doing all this time, I have no idea. Did he say anything? Did he try to interfere? I think not. I imagine by then he had realised the scale of his error. At no time did I register him. I wonder, now, if I could even recall his face. Instead I noticed that Julius was wearing the same clothes he had worn the night of the moon landing. And that now Saffia was unbuttoning his shirt, pressing her face into his still-powerful chest, murmuring, 'Don't go there, please, my darling. It's too dark. Too dark. Stay with me.' She ran her fingertips over his naked stomach and chest, his collarbones and down his arms. She held his hands in hers, felt his fingers and held them against her face. She bent over him and searched his sides. But there was nothing, no wound, or bruise, fracture or burn.

All that I remember, bright splinters, silence save for Saffia's keening. Interrupted by a sudden commotion. Footsteps in the corridor. Johnson shouting at the desk clerk. His attempts, futile, to cover Julius's face with the sheet. Saffia's fury as she set herself upon Johnson, beating him with her fists. Johnson's composure gone.

It pleased me, I admit it, to see him finally undone.

There is a quality to grief, I know. Like the first rains after the dry season. At first it fails, slides off the soil, rolling away in the dust of disbelief. But each day brings fresh rain. Saffia did what was expected of her. People came to pay respects, the women to sit with her, the men to offer gifts of money for the funeral and for the Seven and Forty Days ceremonies. I was there, assisting where I could. The Imam called. How that would have infuriated Julius! Saffia sat among the women. She wore a gown of plain black cotton, her hair wrapped in a black headdress. No make-up and not a single bangle, necklace or ring, except her gold wedding band. She was beautiful. She would reward my efforts to help with an otherworldly smile. I say otherworldly, for since the moment in that grey building when Saffia lifted the sheet from Julius's face, she had stepped into a landscape where nobody lived but her.

The students began to return after the vacation, like birds assembling after a long migration, fluttering down in ones and twos, recognising each other from the year before.

That day, the one I am thinking of, the Dean called me into his office. I opened the door to find him at the window, from where he liked to survey his domain, or so it seemed to me. Only this time his attention seemed to be concentrated upon something of particular interest.

'Come,' he said, continuing to gaze from the window.

I did as I was asked.

'What's this?'

I looked down. The courtyard was full of students, hundreds of them. They were all dressed in white, the boys in shirts and slacks, the girls in dresses. Some had covered their hair. It was hard to see what they were doing. If it was a demonstration of some sort, then where were the placards?

'Go down and see what's going on,' said the Dean.

I was due at Saffia's house − Saffia's house, how quickly I came to think of it as that − in a little under an hour, for it was the day of Julius's Forty Day ceremony. I'd helped Saffia with the arrangements and I was reluctant to become involved in anything that might delay me. I allowed my gaze to drift over the heads of the gathered students. More and more of them were arriving all the time. For no reason my eye came to alight on a particular student, a boy. Perhaps because he was sitting more or less alone on the library steps. There was something familiar in his profile, even from this angle. I recognised him as the boy who had been with Julius the day I watched him from my own window, lost so deep in conversation they had stopped to continue their discourse and allowed themselves to be soaked by the rain. Shortly afterwards Julius had bounded up to my office and asked me to lend him the price of a soft drink. I remembered it as if it were yesterday. Like everybody else, the boy was dressed in white, on his feet a pair of white tennis shoes. He wore his hair high in the fashion of the times, a comb pushed into the front. What was that around his arm? I leaned forward and peered at him. It was a black armband. I switched my gaze to the student nearest him. He too wore a black armband. The girl he was talking to, she had a black scarf wrapped around her hair. Over there, the plump girl in the long skirt. A black sash. Another armband. Another. And another.

'Excuse me,' I said to the Dean. He was standing with his arms folded, his eyebrows drawn together, his features arranged into an expression of general and indistinct annoyance. I remembered our telephone conversation that Saturday morning, the day he asked me to fetch Saffia from her home and take her to Johnson's offices. On the phone he had sounded irritated. As though annoyed at being woken at such an hour. And yet by then he must have known what had happened. He must have known Julius was dead.

Down in the courtyard I moved in and out of the throng of students. I saw no other faculty members. One or two of the students greeted me. A nod here, a handshake there. A boy grasped my hand and would not let it go. Instead he hung his head and began to sob.

At two o'clock the library bell sounded and there was a general movement, a shuffling as people began to shape themselves into some sort of order. I allowed myself to be carried along with them; by then I knew exactly where they were going. Despite the atmosphere of mourning, the sombre day and big-bellied clouds that floated above us, the humidity pressing in from all sides, there was something light in the air, and I felt inexplicably uplifted by it. It worried me not that the Dean might be watching, waiting for me to report back to him, all of that I would deal with later. For now I joined the march of students as we turned out of the gate and made our way along the tree-lined avenue towards the town. There was singing, as I recall, but not much. In the main we walked in silence. Forty minutes. A minute for each day that had passed. Finally we arrived.

And those who could not find room in the house filled the garden, and those who could not find room in the garden stood in the street, until the pink house on the hill was all but surrounded.

Julius died of an asthma attack. This is the sum of what we were told. By the time he was discovered it was too late; nothing could be done to save him. His medication, it seemed, had been removed from his possession along with other items of his personal effects. An error, unfortunate. In the room he was being held, in the basement of the building, nobody had heard him dying.

CHAPTER 30

In the corner a woman sits at a table counting piles of battered notes. Her hair is wrapped in a deep-red cloth, wound around her head, twisted and pinned, the ends left rippling and free. The whole arrangement resembles a giant rose. The waitress has a rose pinned into her hair. There is a plastic rose in a vase on the table. At the next-door table are two men; one wears a dog tag, a bracelet and tattoos. His hair is sleek with oil, his accent curious to Adrian's ear. A kind of strangulated American, as though he has learned to speak English from watching *Taxi Driver*. Adrian says this to Mamakay and it amuses her, which in turn pleases him.

'When I was a kid we thought Liberians were so cool. They had ice-cream parlours.'

'You didn't have ice cream?'

She shakes her head. 'We had ice cream. You could buy it in the supermarkets and in the department store. But ice-cream *parlours*. That was something else.'

By Adrian's reckoning they are not far from the old department store where he went looking for Agnes, which now seems so long ago. Adrian must have walked past this restaurant without ever guessing it was here. On the way down the street Mamakay suddenly ducked through a flowering hedge. In that moment Adrian had lost her, before he followed her through.

Here is everything he knows about her. She is a clarinet player. Or, as she would have it said, she plays the clarinet. For it is not a job. Her job is to tutor university students by the hour. The house she shares with two of the other band members. Hers is a small suite of rooms at the back of the house with a view of a yard of moss-streaked concrete and the neighbour's dovecote. Mamakay had sat at one end of a long wicker sofa drinking her coffee, her legs tucked beneath her, while Adrian perched against a railing. The sound of the doves reminded him of home. The woman in the red headdress who greeted Mamakay with a trio of kisses is an old friend, Mary,

251

owner of the Mary Rose. From time to time Mamakay waitresses here to help out.

That is all he knows. Also that she does not wear a watch, for all watches stop on her, as a consequence of which she is frequently either late or early. He would like to know everything about her, but she seems to have begun their friendship at an arbitrary point, dispensing with introductions and preamble. This makes him feel welcome. The place makes him feel welcome. The regulars sit at their tables, sip beer, eat the same plates of rice as Adrian and Mamakay. Nobody stares at him when he is with her. So he behaves as she does and asks no questions. He waits for the layers of her to be uncovered, by whatever wind their conversation is carried upon.

'There's a guy going around with a story about his daughter being bitten by a snake. He says the little girl is in hospital and he needs fifty thousand for the antidote serum or she's going to die.'

A man with an almost identical story had approached Adrian on the beach two days before when Adrian had stopped for a beer. The child had been hit by a car, the man said. Surgeons were standing by to operate but he had no money to buy drugs. Adrian had dug in his pocket for half the amount and the American merchant sailor, newly arrived the week before with whom Adrian had shared a few words of conversation, had given the rest. Afterwards the sailor had shaken his head as they watched the man walk away. Shit!

'Mary says she'd had three customers who have given him money in the last week.'

In the corner Mary holds up four fingers as she continues to count. Adrian is silent.

'I think it's ingenious,' says Mamakay. 'He deserves the money.'

Mary shakes her head. 'Give money to that thief? Better give it to me first.'

'He's not a thief. He's a con man and a good one. All he's doing is trying to survive.'

'We're all trying to survive,' answers Mary, licking her finger and counting off notes. 'Anyway, I heard somebody called the police on that one.' *Wan*, the way she says it.

'I was near the peninsula bridge. I saw a thief caught by a crowd,' says Mamakay. 'His shirt was torn. I think they'd already roughed him up a bit. He was trying to get away, walking. Walking, not running.

252

He knew, you see, that if he started to run it would set them off. They'd go after him like animals. They'd kill him. He crossed the street in front of the taxi I was in. Someone shoved him in the back. It was beginning. The expression in his eyes. He knew he was probably going to die.'

'What happened?' asks Adrian.

'A UN peacekeeper was near by. Though I wouldn't have liked to be in his position. He was armed, at least. Afterwards nobody in the taxi had any sympathy with the thief. They wouldn't have cared if he'd been lynched.'

'Stealing from your own people,' tuts Mary, whose ability to count money at speed and still follow the conversation impresses Adrian. Her fingers flick through the notes faster than the eye.

'Don't you think it's strange?' continues Mamakay. 'The government stole from their own people for decades. They're still at it. Did people say anything? Did they protest? No. Their children dressed in rags and went hungry. Nobody stood up to those men. And yet a poor man would be lynched for stealing tomatoes.'

'So it goes,' says Mary.

'I'm afraid it does,' says Adrian. Displaced anger, one of the most brutal paradoxes of exploited people. The tomato thief paid the price for the Minister's Swiss bank accounts.

'What were you told had happened here? Before you came, that is?' asks Mamakay turning to him. 'Ethnic violence? Tribal divisions? Blacks killing each other, senseless violence! Most of the people who write those things never leave their hotel rooms, they're too afraid. And wouldn't know the difference between a Mendeman and a Fulaman. But still they write the same story over and over. It's easier that way. And who is there to contradict them?'

'What would you say it was?' asks Adrian carefully.

'It was *rage*. It wasn't a war, what happened here, in the end. It was fury. Having nothing left to lose.' She leans back and looks around the room. 'Can we have some coffee, please, Mary?'

Adrian remembers Ileana's words to him the day they first met. Nothing to lose.

When the time comes to pay the bill, Adrian pulls out his wallet, but Mamakay waves the money away. 'Mary owes me.'

He looks at Mamakay, leaning back in her chair, her gaze following Mary as she does the rounds of customers. Mamakay's wide-apart eyes, her softly shaped nose, her hair braided into a knot at the crown, her neck exposed down to the neckline of the cream T-shirt she is wearing. Any moment now she will look round at him and their gaze will meet. And she will know for certain what he is thinking. He must not let that happen. He searches for something to fill the silence, but no words come to him. His brain is too crowded with emotion. At that moment she looks round, straight into his eyes. Her lips are parted, about to speak. But she says nothing. There is the moment of recognition, realisation behind the light reflected in her eyes. Adrian drops his gaze.

They part on the street corner, and he watches her go. She walks swiftly, picking her way along the uneven pavement. He will see her the next morning, maybe, when he delivers water. This small hope is enough to carry him through the afternoon.

Adrian spends more and more time at the mental hospital, helping Ileana restore lost records, those burned or otherwise destroyed during the invasion. In this he is helped by Salia, who keeps the names and history of every patient who has passed through the hospital logged in his memory. Adrian interviews patients one after another. Hours spent listening to delusions, fears, anxieties, dysfunction and dreams, confirming a diagnosis where possible, classifying them accordingly. In this new role Attila seems more inclined to him, less resentful of his presence. They have even conversed once or twice. Adrian finds pleasure in having a structure to his day, pleasure in the respect in the eyes of the attendants, pleasure in Salia's acceptance of his suggestions. So, and for the moment, Adrian is content to occupy himself with this work. Though on his way to and from the hospital he scans the crowds like reels of silent film: people crossing the road, gathered around stalls, waiting for transport, the beggars and madmen, he scans them all for Agnes. He can't help it. He never finds her, never catches a glimpse of the yellow-and-black *lappa*, or the T-shirt with the dolphin, her slender bowed form.

Returning home the day of his lunch with Mamakay, Adrian passes Kai standing by the roundabout in the centre of the town. He sounds his horn, waves and pulls over. Kai climbs in.

'Thanks.'

'Lucky I saw you,' says Adrian. 'What are you doing here?'

'Oh, this and that.' Kai looks away, out of the window. Adrian has learned to recognise these moments, wonders if Kai has any notion at all of how unsettling his abruptness can be. Still, Adrian's mood is good and cannot be easily shaken. He looks across at his friend. Kai's face is drawn, as if all the features had been dragged down. He is resting his head on the windowpane, his forehead bumping against the glass, letting the sights outside slide over his eyes. Adrian has not seen him in days.

'Want to stop off for a beer?'

'Sure. Why not?'

Through Mamakay the landscape of the city has altered for Adrian. For the first time since he arrived, the city bears a past, exists in another dimension other than the present. Places he passes, the Mary Rose, the water pump, already hold memories. Growing in confidence in the city and his place in it, Adrian heads out of town towards the Ocean Club. And because the Ocean Club, like so much else, makes him think of Mamakay and he wants nothing more than to talk about her, he says, 'I tried a new place for lunch today – the Mary Rose. It's good.'

'Oh yeah?' Kai is still facing away from Adrian. 'That old place.'

'You know it, then?' says Adrian, disappointed.

'Sure. Haven't been there for a long time, though.'

Adrian turns his concentration upon the road, tries to hold on to his lightness of mood. At the junction by the petrol station the same traffic policeman he has seen before stands waving his arms. As they approach he holds up the palm of his hand. Adrian comes to a stop and puts on the right-hand indicator.

Next to him Kai sits up. 'Where are you going?'

'To the Ocean Club. Is that all right?'

'You want to keep straight.'

Adrian shakes his head, he knows different now. The city has begun to unravel itself for him, he is becoming privy to its secrets and ways, the geography of its contours. There are two routes to the Ocean Club.

'If we cross the peninsula bridge and take the beach road there'll be much less traffic. It'll be backed up at the other end of this.' He hefts the steering wheel over a few inches, bringing the car into the middle of the road, just enough to shift the vehicle out of the way of a lorry bearing down from behind.

'For Chrissake!'

'It's OK.' Adrian smiles, thinking Kai doubts his driving skills.

'I said stop! I don't want to go that way. Would you just do as I ask and drive on?'

This time Adrian hears the effort at control in Kai's voice and turns briefly to regard him. Kai is sitting forward, kneading his forehead with the tips of his fingers. A vein stands out on his neck, a node visible beneath the skin. He doesn't look at Adrian but stares straight ahead through the windscreen. He looks terrified.

'Of course.' Adrian checks the mirror and swiftly re-enters the traffic. From the tail of his eye he sees Kai lean back, place his hands squarely upon his thighs, his head upon the headrest, eyes half shut.

Inside the club Kai disappears into the toilet. Adrian finds a table, and orders two Star beers. He thinks about what just happened in the car. Kai had genuinely panicked at the thought of taking the bridge road, or it seemed very much like it. Adrian tries to think of whether they have ever taken that route before, and realises they have not. If anyone drives it's usually Kai, or else they take a taxi and Kai is the one who negotiates with the driver. Minutes later Kai joins him, pulls a chair out from the table and turns it around to straddle it. He sits with his elbows on the table, drinking his beer. Adrian watches him for a moment.

'How's Abass?'

'Yeah, he's good. Little man's good.'

'He's a great kid.'

'He is, he is.' Kai shakes his head. He raises his beer bottle to his lips.

It is early yet, and there are no other guests, just a Middle Eastern-looking man at the bar, who may or may not be the owner, and a younger man knocking balls on the snooker table. Outside the tide is on its way in. The crabs are out, high on the dry sand, old men watching the advancing sea. Below them the sandpipers perform their quickstep with the surf, eight steps forward, eight steps back. A young brown-and-white dog appears, dashing across the sand, scattering complaining crabs in every direction. The sandpipers, caught between the sea and the dog, take briefly to the air and regroup a dozen or more yards away. Adrian smiles and looks around at Kai, but Kai is staring at a spot on the floor, drumming his fingertips on the table. A single knee jerks up and down.

'Are you OK?'

'Sure, yeah. Why wouldn't I be?'

'You just seem a bit restless, that's all.'

'Oh, I see.' Kai stops drumming and sits up, then stands and swings the chair around to face the correct way. He sits back down. 'No, I'm OK. Just haven't been sleeping too well, you know how it goes.'

Adrian remembers the first night Kai slept over at his apartment, finding him sitting on the edge of the bed with his eyes wide open, lost inside some dark dream. Since then Adrian has woken in the night more than once, aware of a restlessness in the apartment, of soft footsteps, of objects being moved, the sound of sighs.

'Are you doing anything about it?'

'You mean am I taking anything? No. I've tried once or twice. The pills stopped working a long time ago. No, man. It's one of those things. Just have to see it through.' His gaze shifts away from Adrian again.

'There are other things, relaxation techniques. It might be worth —'

This time Kai interrupts him. 'Thanks, man, but I'm good. Really. One night's sleep and I'll be right back.'

'I was just saying . . .'

'Yeah, got you. I'm fine. Here I am relaxing, see?' He stretches out his legs, takes a deep swallow from his bottle and places it with deliberate care upon the table, but nevertheless misjudges the distance so the bottle knocks against the hard surface.

They sit in silence again. Adrian is used to Kai's silences, his indifference to the kinds of courtesies and pleasantries Adrian was raised to observe. He is even, at some level, faintly awed by the way Kai is, feels himself by comparison to be too eager to please. All the same the mood has shifted.

'Another?' Kai has drained his bottle.

'Sure,' Adrian replies.

Kai holds up his hand for the waiter.

After the man has gone, Kai returns to drumming his fingers on the table, staring moodily at the wooden surface. Behind him two early drinkers stray into view. Dressed in identical grey slacks, white shirts and ties, they wear their hair close-cropped and each carries an attaché case, a name tag on their right breast. Adrian watches as they place their order. The waiter returns with two

Coca-Colas and Adrian silently congratulates himself on his guess. Mormons.

A few more arrivals are drifting in, among them Adrian sees Candy and Elle. They haven't met since the afternoon at Ileana's house. Adrian thinks Candy may have seen him because she looks in his direction, but as she does not acknowledge him he cannot be sure. The two women are accompanied by a short, plump African man, with clownish features and an arm around each of them. Adrian looks at Candy's skinny haunches and broad shoulders, Elle's narrow mouth and small teeth. He thinks of Mamakay, of her hips in the old sunflower dress she wears to fetch water, the outline of her lips, and her nose, the shallow, inward curve of the bridge, the almond-shaped nostrils. The man's hand slides down the arch of Elle's back towards the faint swell above the drop of her buttocks.

Seeing them reminds Adrian of the girl in the purple top the night in the beach bar; he had noticed her as he sat and waited for Kai. The girl had been leaning her body against a Western man. Adrian had watched her and fantasised briefly about what it would be like to have sex with her; she'd turned and caught him staring at her. With the memory his reverie is arrested.

What does Mamakay think of him?

He has no idea.

CHAPTER 31

Three o'clock the previous Friday, Kai arrived at the US Embassy and stated his business to the marine in the glass booth at the front gate. The marine pointed to a long line of men standing in front of a hatch on the outside wall. 'Green-card lottery right there.'

Kai shook his head. 'I'm a doctor, a surgeon,' he said.

'One moment, sir.' The marine leaned forward and pressed the buzzer to allow him through the security gate. 'Office at the end of the hall. Have a good day.'

As he was leaving Kai passed by the queue of men in the street. The line appeared undiminished though he'd been inside the Embassy building for thirty minutes. The men were young, the youngest perhaps seventeen or eighteen. Lean or muscled, dressed in jeans and T-shirts.

From the Embassy he'd strolled up the street to the roundabout. He'd been standing there only a few minutes when Adrian caught sight of him.

That was Friday. Today is Sunday. A Sunday in April. April Fools' Day, no less. He knows this because he has written the date on the top right-hand corner of the aerogramme, but also because he can see Abass sneaking around, up to no good. At this very moment the boy is peeping around the corner, checking Kai's whereabouts and imagining himself invisible.

The trouble with Abass is that he's incapable of keeping a straight face. Kai had already helped a bewildered aunt into her room after she struggled in vain to grasp a doorknob greased with Vaseline. Abass had been stalking the old lady since breakfast.

Kai bends back to the letter. Tejani's last letter mentioned the new girlfriend, what was her name? Kai reaches for the crumpled blue paper and smoothes it out, begins to read it over. Tejani wants Kai to join him in America. Two years after they said goodbye, it looks like Kai is finally coming. Tejani is his best friend, the person he has been closest to most of his life, with the exception only of Nenebah. There

259

had been three of them. Always three. Tejani was the third lover, or was it Nenebah? Sometimes Kai saw himself at the centre, best friend to Tejani, lover to Nenebah. More often he'd seen Nenebah as the centre. They'd both loved her, after all. Tejani left. A year later Nenebah and Kai were no longer a couple. Might it have been different if Tejani had stayed? Kai doesn't know.

Helena. It sounds like Tejani might even marry her. We, he says in his letter. 'We' are going to buy a place. Kai still hasn't congratulated him for his exam pass. He pens a few lines, striving for and falling short of Tejani's cheerful tone.

How Nenebah had envied Kai. He knew, for she had told him. She'd envied him the cleanliness of his work, the moral purity of the task at hand.

They'd been lying in bed, spooned against each other, he was still inside her, savouring the slipperiness of semen and sweat. Once she described for him the sensation that followed his withdrawal from her body if it happened too soon, his *abandonment* of her body. Loss, she said. It felt like loss.

That night was some years after she dropped out of college. What had he done wrong? He never really knew. He had to be up early for surgery. She was broody and angry with him and in a visceral way he knew why. It was for knowing every morning when he awoke, without any shade of doubt, what he was there to do, the certainty she no longer possessed. She'd lost her faith at exactly the same time he'd found his. Neither one of them expected such a thing to happen.

After the lovemaking, she'd pulled away, withdrawing her body from him. Suddenly no longer inside her, he experienced the sensation as a shock. An abandonment. And later, in the middle of the night, he reached for her and failed to find her, saw her standing by the open window. He'd gone over and drawn her back into bed. Lying against her into the early hours, he could feel the rapid beating of her heart. Neither of them spoke. Neither of them slept.

He picks up the pen again and continues to write, congratulating Tejani on the exam pass. In his letter Tejani reminds Kai of the days they'd been forced to revise by torchlight, of the petition the students had raised and presented at the Vice Chancellor's office. The authorities were having none of it and the gathering had grown angry. It is a wonder to him now, to think of it, the students' moral indignation. Where the hell had they even got the idea they had the right to it? The Vice Chancellor's reaction had been one of cold fury. He'd remained in his office while he sent security to deal with them. A security officer had taken the petition, and for a foolish moment a cheer had gone up: the students thought they had a victory.

Instead they had given the authorities a place to begin. A list of dissenters.

Nenebah left soon after. Life on the campus became untenable for her, so she said. Kai thought she'd given in too easily. But he had sensed also the anger in her, the desire to hurt someone for what had happened.

Hey, man, Kai writes, *does the new house come with a pool as well as a couch? Get ready for your new house guest.* When he finishes the letter he seals the edges and puts it in his pocket. He is minded to walk down to the post office, then remembers it is Sunday. The heat has yet to break. Kai can hear the recitatives of the evangelical churches, the exhortations of their pastors, the wild assurances of the congregations. His cousin had gone to church. He has lent her Old Faithful.

'Abass!' he calls.

The boy appears suspiciously quickly.

'Want to go to the beach?'

'Yes!'

'Hurry up then. Fetch your trunks. How about a curry at the Ocean Club?'

Abass races into the house. Kai follows to fetch his own trunks, a paperback and his sunglasses. He finds the glasses on the coffee table in the sitting room. When Abass appears, he puts his arm around the boy's shoulders.

'All ready?'

Abass nods.

Out in the street, away from the shade of the yard, the shadows are sharp, the edges hard, colours brilliant beneath the sun. Kai reaches for his sunglasses and puts them on. Without warning his vision grows blurred, the brightness disappears, the edges of the house grow indistinct and the shadows merge into each other. He stops, uncertain of his steps. He removes his glasses.

'Very funny, Abass,' he says.

The kid is rocking from side to side, clutching his belly, laughing.

Kai makes as though to lunge at him. The child ducks. They walk down the street towards the main road. In the back of the cab Kai peels away the layer of cling film from the inside of his glasses.

Much later, after they have swum together, he watches Abass play on alone in the waves, crashing through the surf over and over. And he feels his love for the boy rise in his chest, pressing against his ribcage, crushing his lungs and his heart, as if it would suffocate him.

Monday morning Kai makes his way to Foday's ward. When he arrives Foday is in the toilet, so Kai sits on the edge of the bed and waits for him. The matron appears and tries to fuss over him, but Kai waves her away. There above the bed is the Polaroid of Foday which moved with him from bed to bed. Foday's talisman – to show him how far he has come. Two operations and so far they'd straightened both tibias, breaking each bone in three places and resetting it. That was the easy part. Next they'd tackle the feet. If Foday had been treated by doctors as a baby it would have been a simple job; now he was an adult the operation was complicated. More so if they had to lengthen the Achilles tendon.

On the night stand are a carafe of water and Foday's few possessions, including the school exercise book which he uses as a diary, keeping careful notes of his treatment and his conversations with Kai. The writing on the cover is as strained and effortful as Foday's walk. Nothing came easily to Foday in life, thinks Kai. But Christ, what a fighter.

At that moment Foday appears pushing himself along in his wheelchair, a male nurse follows behind. Kai stands and raises his right hand in salute and Foday returns the gesture, freewheeling for a few moments. A yard from the bed he manoeuvres the wheelchair skilfully around.

'Looking good,' says Kai.

'Yes thank you, Doctor.' Foday's voice is strong today. The male nurse comes around ready to lift him into bed, but Foday shakes his head. Kai folds his arms and watches Foday. The young man's eyes narrow in concentration. He takes a deep breath and levers himself up. For a moment he is suspended, like a gymnast on a pommel horse, then he eases himself down and rights himself upon the bed, arranging his leg in the cast in front of him. When he is finished, he turns to Kai.

'Great,' says Kai.

Foday grins.

'How's the physiotherapy?' Kai leans forward and squeezes Foday's other calf muscle, slight still from the weeks encased in plaster.

'The lady, Miss Salinas, she says she is pleased with me.'

'Good. You're not overdoing it now, are you? We really don't want you to run before you can walk, I mean it.'

Foday laughs. 'No, Doctor Kai. Don't worry. First I'm walking, then running. After that, maybe cartwheels. Please pass me my book.'

Kai passes him the exercise book. Foday opens it, removes a photograph and hands it to Kai. The picture shows a young woman of around nineteen sitting demurely on a stool in front of a hut, dressed in what appear to be her best clothes and shoes. Her smile is for the camera, for she looks shy, as though she is not used to being photographed.

'Ah,' says Kai. 'Let me guess. Your fiancée?' He studies the photograph for a few seconds more and gives it back to Foday.

'No. She is not my fiancée. I would like her to be, though.'

'Your girlfriend?'

'Her name is Zainab. We were townsmates. She has sent me this picture of herself while I am in hospital. So you see, I think she likes me.'

'It looks that way to me.'

Foday holds the picture up close to his face, then lowers it and smoothes it with his palm before replacing it carefully between the leaves of the exercise book. He passes the book to Kai and pulls himself further up the bed.

'I would like to ask you something, Doctor.'

'Sure,' says Kai, once he has returned the book to its place. 'Ask away, my friend.'

'After my operations maybe I will go to Zainab's family to put cola for her. That's what I am thinking.'

'OK.'

'I will discuss it with Zainab first, of course. But if she has sent me this picture of herself, then I think she will consider me.'

'I have no doubt Zainab will be happy for you to go to her parents.'

'Thank you, Doctor. And you see, what it is I want to ask is whether you will come with me as my elder brother.'

For a moment Kai is quiet, then he says, 'I would be honoured to come as your elder brother. But don't you have any other brothers or uncles you want to ask?'

Foday shakes his head. 'My elder brothers are away in the mines. Besides, if Zainab's family see you, then I know they will want to accept me.'

Kai laughs. He reaches over and pats Foday on the shoulder. 'Sure, my friend. I can do that. But you know the minute they see me they'll double the bride gift, don't you?'

'I know.' Foday shrugs. 'But I have been putting aside little by little. The bride gift will be all right, I think. Besides, if Zainab wants me then she will speak to her parents.'

'Then we have a deal.' Kai offers his hand to Foday, and they shake, snapping fingers and punching each other on the knuckles. A minute or so later Kai prepares to leave, asks Foday if he needs something.

'Maybe you can borrow me a radio?'

'Sure, I'll see what I can do.'

Kai should talk to Foday about his next operation, but he decides to leave it for the day. There's no hurry. Foday's greatest challenges are ahead of him. Kai knows this. Foday knows this. Meanwhile there is Zainab, waiting for him in her Sunday best.

Whatever it takes. Kai says these words to himself, whatever it takes.

Outside the ward he catches sight of Mrs Mara cutting the corner of the courtyard, struggling in her high heels across the uneven grass. He pauses a beat, to give her time to get ahead, then makes his way to Adrian's apartment, where he knocks on the door at the same time as he slips the key into the lock. The apartment is empty. The kitchen is tidy and bare. He puts some water in the kettle and while he is waiting for it to boil searches out the old Philips transistor in the back of one of the cabinets. The radio is bulky and battered but serviceable despite a definable hiss. He drinks his coffee at the kitchen window. A sunbird descends, hovers briefly at the empty feeder, and is gone.

A few minutes later, so is Kai.

CHAPTER 32

In Elias Cole's room, a bustle of activity. Adrian waits in the corridor. In time a doctor emerges followed by a nurse wheeling a trolley of equipment.

'How is he?' Adrian asks of the doctor.

The man, a Swede, possessed of the crisp, antiseptic aloofness Adrian associates with Northern Europeans, looks at Adrian, according him the automatic respect of a fellow white man. 'Not so great. But OK.'

'Can I talk to him?'

'Are you a doctor?'

'I am a counsellor,' he says.

'Oh, I see. Well then, you may as well know he's been treated with corticosteroids. Now it looks as if he's stopped responding. That's not so unusual. Steroids don't work for everybody, and even when they do they don't work for ever. The trouble is there aren't very many other options from here on in. A lung transplant is out of the question.' He bends a little closer to Adrian and lowers his voice. 'I mean, how long have you been here?'

'Since January,' says Adrian.

The other man shakes his head. 'He needs oxygen therapy,' says the Swede, telling Adrian what he already knows. 'He's at risk from hypoxaemia. Oxygen will improve his quality of life and give him some months more to live. Only maybe. I'm going now to talk to the administrator about it.'

Good luck, thinks Adrian. He has spoken to Mrs Mara about an oxygen concentrator for Elias Cole three times. On each occasion she promised to see what she could do. So far she has done nothing. The demands upon her are many. The last few months of Elias Cole's life are lost in the crowd.

'Let me know how you get on,' says Adrian. He watches the Swede walk away, his rubber clogs creaking on the concrete floor.

Inside the room Elias Cole is sitting up in bed. Over the last few weeks he has grown noticeably thinner, his face worn almost to the bone. Around his neck the skin rests in pleats. Standing at the end of the bed Adrian feels like the priest in an old black-and-white movie, the man of God hovering at the deathbed, waiting for his moment. To divest himself of this sensation he goes over to the window and looks out. A kingfisher sits on the telegraph wire. A moment later it is joined by another. Adrian watches them for a few moments, almost forgetting his purpose in being there.

He turns to the old man. 'How are you feeling?'

Elias Cole smiles, a tugging of the corner of the lips. 'That was the last call. I'm in the departure lounge now.'

Adrian laughs. 'There's still some time left.'

'I've been warned I may begin to forget.'

'That's one of the possible effects of hypoxaemia. There's no guarantee it'll happen.'

'There's more I want to tell you.'

★

A year passed. For me, a year of waiting. There was the Forty Day ceremony. Do you know the forty days mark the end of a wife's period of mourning? Among her own people Saffia would be considered ready for remarriage. Life here is too short to mourn for very long.

In November another Apollo mission landed on the moon. Nobody thought of throwing a party. The crew were supposed to send back colour TV images, but something went amiss and the feed failed. Saffia followed the news carefully on the radio, just as she had when the first astronauts came out of quarantine and gave a press conference. I knew she thought constantly of Julius. But as I said, it was a year of waiting.

Then it was 1970. The 1960s were over.

I watched Saffia struggle for survival. Following Julius's death there were practical matters that needed to be considered. The independence which had so struck me at our first meeting had proved to be an illusion, of course. An illusion sustained and perpetuated by Julius, who had spoiled his wife. And also I suppose by the three of us, Kekura, Yansaneh and I, in our own way. For hadn't we revered her? Did we not outdo ourselves to perform for her amusement? See ourselves as her guardians? We had taken Julius's duties as our own. But now Julius was gone. Kekura fled. And Yansaneh broken. I alone was left.

Saffia continued to live in the pink house on the hill with the crone

266

aunt, who came and went between the city and the village. The aunt was a woman, as I think I have indicated, from whom a low-level hostility emanated at all times, who seemed possessed of an infinite capacity for hate. She hated the city people, who were full of themselves. She hated non-believers, but Christians more, because she also distrusted them. She hated the poor, the weak, the sick and the needy. In particular she reviled all members of her own sex. Her attitude to men was somewhat more complicated, for it encompassed both her natural loathing of her fellow man and her sycophancy towards those in possession of some degree of power. That she had disliked me and regarded my visits to the house with suspicion, I knew.

Between Saffia and the aunt there had always been a certain amount of bickering. Her aunt was straight from the rice fields. It was unsurprising, therefore, that Saffia might be easily irritated by an elder full of village superstitions. Balance in matters of social hierarchy, however, is infinitely delicate, accounted for by so many things: family, age, wealth.

The shift in the aunt's manner towards Saffia following Julius's death amounted to relatively little. She was merely, one might say, altogether less careful. Her tone of voice became sharper, her demands more frequent and petty. She seemed to feel Saffia was there to do her bidding. What had wrought it was this: whilst the aunt was the elder, and as such merited a high degree of deference, it was Saffia who had been married to a big man – this in the aunt's view, of course – who lived in a grander house than I am certain the aunt had ever previously set foot in.

Now Julius was gone and Saffia no longer married to a big man.

The woman opposite, a coarse-mouthed fish seller, seemed to have found a new vocation in watching the comings and goings at the pink house, a fact she made no effort to conceal. There were occasions I had waited under her gaze, listened to her remark upon my visit to unseen listeners. I never once saw her husband. Doubtless he was barred from the verandah, for fear he might be drawn to the newly available temptations in the house opposite. Not that the fish mammy's concerns were baseless. A woman alone does indeed attract the attention of men, who scent her vulnerability. It bothered me to think of who might try to take advantage of Saffia's situation. Once I found the dancer fellow up there, ostensibly offering condolences. I sat down opposite and glared at him until he left.

However, it became interesting to observe the shift in the aunt's manner towards me now that she was in the business of encouraging a protector for her niece. As I have indicated, she was the type of woman who adjusted swiftly to any change in the status quo. One evening I encountered her as she returned from the mosque. I raised my hat and greeted her in my most respectful tone. 'Good evening, Auntie.' It stopped her in her tracks and, once she had assured herself I wasn't mocking her in any way, I saw a small smirk of pleasure at being thus addressed. It amused me to think of her as my new-found ally.

It was the aunt who brought it to my attention that the two of them were struggling to pay the rent. Julius had been far too young to leave a pension. Through my efforts and by applying some leverage upon the Dean who sat upon the relevant committee, I managed to secure for Saffia a small grant to cover her work cataloguing the flora that grew in the university grounds. Not so much she could rely upon it indefinitely. The amount of the grant would give her enough to live for exactly a year.

Throughout those months I worked towards a single goal. I threw my energy into research for a paper on the creation of the Native Affairs Department. If I had once been a merely conscientious academic, I was driven now. It is astonishing, the effect of hope. I was working towards a future now, one that included Saffia.

In the morning I dealt with my correspondence and planned my lectures. That lasted until midday. I took lunch in the cafeteria. In the afternoon I went to the library and worked my way through the bound minutes of the Aborigines and Native Affairs Department, pencilling notes in my notebook as I went. Thoughts of Saffia came between me and the letters of the government agent Thomas George Lawson, his fearsome Protestantism and loyalty to the Crown. At about four o'clock I concluded my travels with Lawson on his trips into the interior to settle scores between the chiefs, gathered my papers and deposited them in my office.

The state of nervous anticipation in which I spent my days peaked at about half past four, when I went to see Saffia. Most days I had a reason, for as I think I have told you, I sought to make myself useful to her in as many ways as possible. I dealt with the university bureaucracy, gave her financial advice and moreover attended to many other minor household matters as well. In the months after Julius died I watched as the weight fell away from Saffia's body. Saw how the lines on either side of her mouth refused to fade. Observed from the wandering of her eye her inability to concentrate. From the slight, irrelevant smile with which she thanked me I knew how much pain she suffered. I also knew she would survive. For in the end, people always do.

Stay. Wait. Patience.

An evening we walked in the garden. The idea had been mine. Saffia looked like she was about to decline, but then changed her mind and led the way down the stairs. It was still light, the dense rain clouds had lifted, there was even a little blue in the sky. The garden was looking somewhat neglected. The Harmattan lilies were bent and broken, like soldiers after a battle, many were strewn in tangles upon the ground, their once lovely heads had shrivelled away, the petals darkened and torn. I remember the occasion because it was perhaps the only time she spoke to me of Julius directly, though she often mentioned him in passing.

'I still miss him, Elias,' she said.

'I know,' I replied. 'I miss him, too.' In a way it was true. Julius had left a space in my life. I had not known a great many friendships.

Saffia sighed. 'Perhaps if we'd had a child. But Julius wanted me to finish my studies.'

'There's still time,' I said. 'You're young.' It is the stock response, people say such things to widows all the time. I had spoken without thinking.

But she merely replied, 'Yes.'

One word. Yet so much more. She had said yes. Agreed her life was not over. I looked at her. I was consumed by a feeling of inexpressible joy. Only later did I recognise it for what it was. Hope. For in that instant the beauty and pain of the past, the unbearable present and the possible future all ran together.

In most other respects life had returned to a kind of normality. I saw Yansaneh once on the campus, I think. He seemed to be keeping his head down. No word from Kekura. Nor did I hear from Johnson again. The Dean seemed in reasonable spirits. A lot of universities in our country and elsewhere were closing their humanities departments or else having their grants cut. Liberal arts were the first to be hit in times of economic stress. The government argued certain skills were more in demand than others. Philosophy, literature, drama – such subjects were a luxury, a frivolity even, in times of need. So far the

Dean had proved himself a powerful negotiator in these matters and had somehow managed to save our department the same fate. As the months wore on, Julius, his death, my own arrest – these events seemed to recede into the past.

One unpleasant occurrence. A visit from Vanessa.

It was Saturday when she turned up at the apartment. I could scarcely remember when I had last seen her. At any rate, she hadn't changed, though her look had been updated. I heard later she had a new boyfriend. She wore a large Afro wig and a pair of tight trousers. I have never cared for the look of trousers on a woman. It was hard not to make comparisons with Saffia and I wonder if Vanessa didn't sense my appraisal, for she leant against the kitchen counter and eyed me challengingly.

'You look well, Vanessa,' I said.

'Thank you, Elias. I came by to see how you are.'

'As you see, I am well.'

'Well, I'm pleased about that.' She sounded as though she had heard different. I noticed her glance around the apartment. Then she said, 'Maybe you would like to make me a coffee.'

I'd had no intention of offering her a coffee. Nevertheless, I reached around her and found the Nescafé and evaporated milk. I lit the gas ring and boiled water. I didn't offer her any sugar.

'Is it true you were arrested?' she said.

'No, it isn't,' I lied.

'That's what they say.'

'Well, they are mistaken.' I didn't ask how she knew. It would have been exactly like Vanessa to have contacts among the police, a lover or two.

She watched me coolly. The cup of coffee sat on the counter.

'Your coffee will get cold.'

'It's too bitter,' she said, not taking her eyes off me. 'So maybe it's not such a bad thing for you; what happened to Julius?'

'I don't know what you mean,' I said. 'Julius was my friend. His death is a tragedy.'

She laughed, a short, soft and yet abrupt sound. 'So his wife is a widow now.' Her voice had taken on an insinuating sneer, which I didn't like.

'Yes,' I said. 'Saffia is mourning the loss of her husband.'

That laugh again.

'Vanessa,' I said. 'I'm happy to see you. Come and visit again or I'll come to you. Right now I'm due out.'

For a few moments she said nothing, but continued to regard me. And when she spoke, she enunciated each word, letting them slide suggestively out of her mouth one by one, poison drops. 'Elias Cole. Look at your face.'

I refused to let Vanessa's malicious little call unsettle me; still, it must have done so because later that day I thought I saw Julius. It was a momentary thing. Just a fellow who stepped out of a doorway, something in his profile. He walked on ahead of me and of course it wasn't Julius at all. I could tell by the walk. And of course, Julius was dead. Still, the shock left me suddenly incapacitated; my knees buckled. It took me some minutes before I could recover and continue on my way.

The day I proposed to Saffia I arrived at the house just as she was dealing with a young hustler who was trying to pretend Julius had owed him money. A lie, of course. Julius had been gone nearly a year, but that didn't stop people trying. I saw how tired she was beginning to look, how weary of it all. The grant money was just about to come to an end. I made my offer. A practical, rather than a romantic proposal, a compromise between my position and hers. I alluded to Julius. All the time I spoke I was aware of the aunt listening from the recesses of the house. Saffia asked for time to consider my offer. A month later I reiterated and this time Saffia accepted. As I left the house, I saw the aunt on her way back from the mosque. I told her the news, for I wanted to acquire the official seal of approval as soon as possible. The old woman's face split into an obsequious grin such that I had the impression perhaps she had cared less for Julius than I had imagined.

The Dean, too, offered me his congratulations. He seemed genuinely pleased at the outcome. A few weeks later I was promoted to senior lecturer. And soon after that a house on the campus became available at short notice. The previous occupant had lost his job in the latest round of cuts. It was unfortunate, but these were the facts of life. I kept news of the house from Saffia until I had arranged to have it painted and the roof repaired where the rains had damaged the zinc.

Apropos of all that – Yansaneh, too, was one of the unlucky ones. I went to his leaving party, a sober affair attended by a sprinkling of his colleagues. In his address the Dean thanked Yansaneh for his commitment to the department. Yansaneh rose and said a few words. At one point he seemed overcome by emotion and fell silent, but then regained his voice and thanked several of his colleagues. Only later did it strike me he had made no reference to the Dean, whom convention might have required him to acknowledge. Afterwards people came up and patted him on the shoulder. I shook his hand and offered him my commiserations, but he merely muttered his thanks and kept his eyes fixed on his shoes.

I was sorry for Yansaneh, naturally. But nothing could dent my happiness.

CHAPTER 33

The place name is familiar. This new route to the mental hospital is one Ileana has told Adrian about. It winds up the hill, past the villas of the wealthy, the army barracks and also this familiar name on a hand-painted sign for a hairdressing salon. Because he is in no hurry, Adrian turns the vehicle around the roundabout in the direction the sign points and heads down a track alongside a petrol station, where a number of young men are gathered in the shade of a high wall. They stare through the driver's window as he passes, sullen and silent. The track narrows, the houses press in upon the street. He is driving slowly now, people make way for him. He pulls over for another car, easing his way around the corner of a building that juts into the road. Waiting for the other car to pass he sees the building is a covered market. Near by a woman sits behind a tray of fish, waving intermittently at the flies in the air. A pair of featherless chickens race in front of the car.

Now the road has opened out. In front of him is a dirt football ground, a tall tree and what looks like a school building on the far side. A game is about to begin, people are gathered in the road that borders the ground. A couple of them wave at him, indicating there's no way through. One man in a long tunic approaches the vehicle, taps on the glass and points down another road. Adrian takes it without knowing where it leads. He is beginning to regret turning off the main road. At a crossroads at the end of the street the road to the right leads to a church and a dead end. Straight ahead the road appears too narrow for a vehicle to pass. So Adrian turns left, down the hill. The track is badly rutted now, with deep channels on either side. A pair of schoolchildren stand back to let him pass, their heels at the edge of the ditch. Fifty yards on there is another left turn and Adrian takes it, then changes his mind and decides to turn back. There is just enough space to execute a three-point turn, and he does so badly, tyres spinning on the gravel road, clutch whining. As he prepares to set off again, he notices the house. Small by the standards of the villas he passed on the road up the hill, it sits behind an iron gate. There is a doorway reached by a short flight of stairs. The walls are streaked dark green by water and pale by the sun. An overburdened orange tree grows in the front. It is not exactly as he imagined. For one, it sits higher on the land. But still there is enough for him to recognise it, though it is shrouded by trees, has not been painted in many years. This is the pink house.

Adrian climbs down and leaves the vehicle door open behind him. He walks up to the gates and looks through the railings. There is a side gate which looks like it might lead to a garden. It is hard to tell whether the house is occupied or abandoned, such is the state of neglect of so many buildings in the city. The front gate is closed and Adrian stops short of pushing it open. He turns away and climbs back inside the vehicle. At the end of the street he stops for the same pair of schoolchildren, a boy and a younger girl. They do not cross the road, but sidle down the length of the car, eyeing Adrian as they do so. He smiles at them and they do not smile back. He waves and the boy, who might be six, waves too. Adrian watches as they enter through the gate of the pink house.

Mid-afternoon he is doing the rounds with Ileana.

'How is Mamakay?'

'She's well.'

'I liked her,' said Ileana.

'And she liked you.' Adrian is aware of Ileana's brown eyes watching him. He does not meet her gaze, but pretends to peruse the notes in his hand.

'Be careful, won't you?'

He turns over a leaf, says as casually as he can, 'What's that supposed to mean?' Even he can hear the false note in his own voice.

'You know very well what I mean, my dear. You're a psychologist.'

Just then Salia approaches and nothing more is said. Today several patients are ready for discharge, among them Abdulai, the young man whom Adrian brought to the hospital and who in turn first brought Adrian. He is clean now, drug-free for the duration of his stay. Attila has signed his release. Salia has arranged a final consultation between Abdulai and Adrian. Adrian is touched by the thought, for Abdulai has been under Attila's care. He thanks Salia, who nods formally, before retreating from the ward, his shoes sighing upon the gritty lino floor.

The young man sitting on a chair before Adrian is a different soul to the person Adrian brought to the hospital. He has no memory of that first day when Adrian collected him from the police station and brought him to the hospital.

'The important thing,' says Adrian, 'is how you feel now.'

'I feel well, Doctor. I feel well in my body.' He is sitting with his shoulders bent forward, his hands buried between his thighs. His voice contains a slight tremor, a hesitancy, otherwise he appears perfectly normal, if a little nervous.

'And your head?'

'Yes, I am well in my head. Except sometimes I feel afraid.'

'What is it you are afraid of, can you tell me?'

'Things in my dreams.' He shakes his head hard.

'That should improve. Who are you going to? Do you have family?'

Abdulai nods his head. His family were the ones who had delivered him to the police station. As Adrian recalls the police suggested Abdulai had become violent.

'How will you get home?'

'Mr Salia has given me money for the *poda poda*.'

'Your family can't come and collect you?'

'My mother has passed on. My father is working.'

At the door Adrian gives Abdulai some of his own money and watches the young man walk to the front gate. He possesses not a single item of luggage, nothing but the clothes on his back. He has spent several weeks in chains, received three meals a day. A few sessions with Attila is all the rehabilitation he's undergone. Now he is being discharged.

Later, talking to Ileana, watching her perform her tea-making ceremony, Adrian asks, 'What will happen to him?'

Ileana shrugs and smokes. 'If he manages to stay off drugs he might be all right.'

'There's no follow-up, then?'

'Even if you could get people to attend, who would run the sessions?'

'I could.'

'You'll be gone in a few months.' The cigarette in the corner of Ileana's mouth bobs up and down as she speaks. Adrian watches the length of ash grow, drooping as it increases in length. Just as he is about to push an ashtray towards her, Ileana removes the cigarette and expertly flicks the ash out of the window. 'Come on. Let's drink these in the garden.'

Sitting beside him on the bench, Ileana says, 'There are places he can go. The born-again churches are having a boom time. No surprises there. Same goes for the traditional healers. People believe in them, that's what is important. Though the traditional healers are really quite interesting. Attila has a lot of respect for them. Some of the antipsychotic drugs we use they were on to hundreds of years ago.'

'Really? Like what, for example, I mean what drugs?'

'Reserpine is one I know of.'

'I didn't know that,' says Adrian.

'No, well,' says Ileana in a voice that says she is not surprised. 'We call them witch doctors.'

To Ileana Adrian had made no mention of the fact he was meeting Mamakay later in the day. She is reading now, as she waits for him, her head bent over the open book, an empty bitter-lemon bottle on the table before her, sitting in the clear sunlight at a table with two students. For a moment to Adrian it looks as though she could be anywhere in the world. He slows his pace, to give himself time to look at her. She is unaware of him, lost in the pages of her book. Today she is wearing a fitted print blouse, which exposes her collarbones, and a matching skirt reaching down to her ankles. On her feet a pair of tooled leather sandals. Her hair is tied up high and held back by a scarf. She bites the edge of one thumb, uses the other to follow her progress down the page. She is smiling slightly and he knows, though he cannot see it, that her front teeth overlap very slightly. Her eyebrows are long wings. There is a mole, a concentration of darkness set against dark skin, high on her cheekbone and another below the corner of her mouth. She is not conventionally pretty, the kind of woman Lisa would have called handsome, damning with faint praise a beauty considered to possess too much strength.

Suddenly she snorts, laughs out loud and looks up.

'Good book?'

She raises the volume to show him the cover. *Three Men in a Boat*, Jerome K. Jerome. About the last thing he was expecting.

'Have you read it?' she asks.

'Not since I was fourteen. Which bit were you reading?'

'When they stop for lunch at Kempton Park.'

'And the man tries to move them on?'

276

'That's the part! Harris! He's something, I tell you.' She reads a section aloud and begins to laugh all over again.

Adrian watches her, smiles and laughs too.

She slips the volume into her bag. They walk away from the café, past some of the university buildings. Adrian sees painted signs to various faculties, administration buildings, the amphitheatre. When Mamakay mentioned she would be coming to the university today, Adrian had ventured his interest in seeing it. As they walk she offers him a few items of information, points out a building or two. They wind their way uphill, to where the high-rise buildings give way to older two-storey blocks, and finally to an area dominated by trees and lawns and, set amidst them, a scattering of bungalows.

'This is where the faculty lived. Nice, isn't it?'

'It is.'

'I bet you're surprised.'

'Yes,' he confesses. The grounds are arresting. He isn't sure now what he was expecting. It wasn't the university he'd been thinking about all day.

'Did you study here?'

'Yes.'

They pass a small stream, the water slipping down a bank of rock and pooling at the roadside. Children are playing in it. They stop to watch Adrian pass by.

'Here we are,' Mamakay says.

They have arrived at a curve in the road where the railing has been broken. Adrian looks around, but sees nothing, just the hillside behind them and the trees in front. Mamakay steps through the break in the railing. Adrian follows her along a narrow path. After about twenty yards Mamakay stops. Adrian, concentrating upon his footing, almost bumps into her. He steadies himself, brushing her shoulder; despite her clothing the touch runs through him like a current.

She turns to him and smiles. 'OK?'

He is standing so close to her. For a moment all he can see are the flecks of brown in her irises, her eyes momentarily in shadow as the wind moves a branch above her. He swallows and nods. He is filled with self-consciousness, aware of his own breathing. She turns away and he follows her gaze to the view through the trees: the city reaching out to the edge of the sea, the red-brown tin roofs of houses, the minarets of the mosques, the steepled roofs and spires of the churches, which dwarf the houses and are in turn dwarfed by the massive white warehouses of the port. The sky is striped with cloud, the horizon is lost in haze. The view of the city is one he has never seen before; he is surprised at the scale of it. Here the sounds of the city are muted. It is cooler, a faint breeze touches him like damp fingers.

His heart is thumping, absurdly, within his chest.

Many hours into the night now. They are in her apartment, they sit with the door open despite the mosquitoes. In this place he can hear the night-time sounds of the city, uninterrupted by the thrum of a generator. From far away, floating upon the dense darkness, comes the sound of late-night prayer. So too does the bass beat of a bar lower down the hill. A blue strobe light marking time. Close at hand the sound of people walking through the narrow street behind the house; voices and steps rebound on the concrete walls. Closer still the sounds of the roosting birds in the dovecote.

'He dreams,' says Mamakay of her neighbour, the doves' owner. 'And drinks, too.' She stands up and stretches, her fingertips touch the ceiling, she lets her arms swing back down. She is telling the story of her neighbour. 'Two days ago he came over, banged on the gate and shouted at me.'

'Why?'

'He said I had insulted him. He came around to tell me I was a bad person.' She laughs.

'What had you said?'

'Nothing. He dreamt it all. At first he wouldn't believe it, but the others told him it was true. They'd been in the dream, too, so he had to believe them.'

'That must have been quite confusing for him.'

'Yes. I'm not sure he worked out what was real and what was not. Poor man. Imagine having us hopping in and out of your subconscious.'

'Does it worry you?'

'No.' She shakes her head. 'He was all right before. He will be again. A lot of people here believe in dreams. So do you, don't you? Psychologists?'

'Some branches work to interpret them, yes,' says Adrian. He would not have seen it like that until now, but he cannot say she is wrong. Every day he talks to his patients at the asylum, often asking them about their dreams. What's the difference, really? She is absolutely right.

The wine bottle is empty, and without wine to refill their glasses, Adrian fears the end of the evening. He tells himself he should leave soon anyway, as he has many times in the last few hours, without ever feeling the slightest desire to do so. Coffee. More wine. The excuses, eked out over the hours of darkness, are running out. The electricity failed early in the evening. The two remaining candles burn low, sending shadows shooting up the walls. He watches now as Mamakay goes to fetch another candle, searching around the apartment.

'I swear I bought more. Sometimes the others come in and take them.'

If the candle supply runs out, thinks Adrian, then he will have no option but to leave.

'Ah good. I'd hidden them. I thought so.'

Adrian exhales.

On a side table there is a photograph. He leans to look at it, Mamakay and two other girls. He recognises one of them as Mary, a slimmer, more youthful Mary.

'Our invasion uniform,' says Mamakay. 'That picture was taken right in the middle of things.'

'What's with the jeans?' he says.

'We wore jeans under our dresses. There was a time we dressed like that every day, because nobody knew when they were coming. One day the radio would say the rebels had been pushed back to the border, another day people arrived in the city saying they were at Port Loko. We stopped believing the government. We wore blue jeans.' She pauses and then she gives a short, strange laugh, as if remembering something absurd or possibly painful.

Still he doesn't understand.

Mamakay turns to look at him. 'Have you ever tried to get a pair of tight jeans off in a hurry? It was the only thing we could think of to do. To stop them raping us. Well, to make it harder.'

Adrian wants to ask her all about it, everything that happened. He cannot imagine what it was like. The powerlessness. In that respect war was worse for civilians, for at least the fighters were given the opportunity to act. Civilians were like rats in a barrel.

Mamakay picks up the photograph, looks at it for a moment and sets it back down. 'Sarian's gone now.'

'Where to?'

She makes it sound as though she is dead.

'Holland. They have twenty-four-hour electricity, can you imagine?'

He can, but he doesn't say so. Instead he asks, 'Wouldn't you like to live somewhere else?' He is thinking of England, perhaps.

'No.' She shakes her head.

'You could do so much more, your music.'

'I'm happy here. Believe it or not.'

One hour later and one inch of candle left. Adrian gets up to go. Mamakay walks with him to his car. It is pitch dark. His shoes hit the concrete with what seems to him a remarkable amount of noise. She is barefoot and silent. Curled up in the yard, the dogs raise their heads and watch his progress through opalescent eyes. For a moment the moon shines through the clouds and he sees the outline of his vehicle ahead of him. He is not at all sure of the whereabouts of Mamakay. He aims straight for the car, placing his feet with more confidence than he feels, tries to remember the location of steps and plant tubs. A few seconds later he collides with the car, takes a backward step and turns, disorientated. In that moment Mamakay steps into his arms. At the touch of her his erection, over which he has maintained uncertain control all evening, rises unchecked. He steps backwards, hard into the car, and comes to rest with his back against the door. Now he cannot see Mamakay any more. He opens his mouth to say something, but changes his mind. He reaches into the dark for Mamakay.

Morning. He rolls over and places an arm across Mamakay, who is still sleeping by his side; his hand comes to rest upon her breast. He closes his eyes and inhales. One by one whatever thoughts were in his mind drop out of sight. He begins to move against her, feels the energy change in her body as she crosses from sleep into wakefulness, the faint tension that arises in her muscles. She turns around. He moves down her body, feeling the resistance of the sweat-damp sheet, the heat from her. The night before he had done nothing but hold her at first. Now he lingers over every detail of her as they make love. She is relaxed and unhurried, quite without vanity or false modesty, laughing when her body makes an unforeseen sound, quite unlike any woman he has known.

And later she wanders naked, making fresh coffee, rearranging items, bringing things back to bed: a CD cover, a saved newspaper article. She scarcely stops talking and does not offer Adrian a robe, so that he remains trapped until he finally frees himself from his own self-consciousness and the bed. In the night he'd got up to pee and found the bathroom full of plants. Now Mamakay fetches water and they wash each other standing on a bed of white pebbles in a vine-enclosed shower in the yard. The man next door comes out to feed his birds, rice clatters down on the tin roof, the birds squabble over it. Mamakay fries plantains. They eat with their fingers. Adrian burns his tongue. An orange-headed lizard approaches them, with a mixture of caution and inquisitiveness. Mamakay blows on a scrap of plantain and throws it. The lizard darts forward and collects the trophy on its black tongue.

'Is this where you grew up?' he asks.

She shakes her head.

'Where then?'

'On the campus. Later my father built his own house.'

'On the campus? Where we were yesterday?'

'Yes,' she nods. She is looking at him, frowning lightly, seemingly faintly bemused by his questions. 'My father taught there. He's a professor of history.'

And then Adrian realises he has been slow, stupidly slow. That first day leaving the hospital, he'd been in a hurry. He nodded at her and she looked back at him; the glance had stayed with him the whole of the day. She'd been talking to Babagaleh. Babagaleh was Elias Cole's manservant. At first Adrian had taken Mamakay for another servant. Elias Cole was the reason he had gone to meet her on campus, the reason he'd given himself, background context on a client. He hadn't allowed himself to think. Of course.

Mamakay is Elias Cole's daughter.

For a moment Adrian is quiet. Then he tells Mamakay about Lisa.

'I know,' says Mamakay.

'How do you know?' he asks.

'Not how,' she replies, looking at him. 'Not how, but what. What I know is that you won't be staying.' She shrugs. 'So I suppose the exact reason doesn't really matter.'

CHAPTER 34

Abass is on the balcony surveying the street when Kai arrives home from his visit to the Embassy. He runs to meet him at the gate.

'Mum says you're to make my supper and help me with my homework.'

'And hello to you, too,' says Kai.

'Hello,' says Abass.

'Where are your mum and your aunties?'

'The baby died,' announces Abass. 'It's science homework.'

'Which baby? The one Yeama was looking after?'

'Yes,' confirms Abass. 'A lady had it and then she died. Now the baby's dead, too.'

'That's sad,' says Kai. 'Yeama must be sad. Is her brother back yet?'

Abass stops swinging his arms, he drops his head, his face solemn. 'I don't think he is back, Uncle Kai, because I haven't seen him and I'd know if I did, because he's a soldier and wears a uniform.'

So the man has lost all his young family without knowing it. They'll be buried by the time the news reaches him. No telephones, no post, the far reaches of the country are virtually cut off. Somebody will have to carry the message to him. Every day Kai sees women on the wards lying next to their sick children. The women's listlessness frustrates the foreign doctors, who try to urge them to take better care, to own responsibility for monitoring their child's vital signs. The local nurses, though, show less surprise. And Kai recognises the expression of the mothers. It is submission, submission in the face of the inevitable. People think war is the worst this country has ever seen: they have no idea what peace is like. The courage it takes simply to endure.

'We'll pass by once we've done your homework. Offer our condolences.'

'Offer our condolences,' repeats Abass, testing each word carefully.

'Come on,' says Kai. He catches the child across his chest, holding him tight and resting his chin on the top of his head. He feels bad. Abass was so cheerful a minute ago. 'Food first. Or homework?'

'Umm.'

'Toss for it?'

Kai produces a coin. They toss, and when Abass loses they toss for the best of three. Abass still loses.

'What's the homework?' says Kai.

'It's an experiment. I need iodine and something called an eye dropper. Mum says you'll give me one. Lemons and other things.'

'Let's see what we can do,' says Kai.

In the kitchen Abass stands on a stool at the stove heating cornflour and water in a pan. While they wait for the mixture to boil Kai's thoughts are occupied with the events of his day.

First thing he had gone into town to the Embassy for an appointment with an immigration liaison officer, who told him his application was being processed and gave him a further set of forms. From there Kai had gone to the telecom offices to call Tejani, but realised he'd forgotten the five-hour time difference. Tejani would be asleep. So he bought a prepaid telephone card and then stopped by the Mary Rose for lunch, the first time he'd seen Mary in many months. As he ate he watched her moving around her restaurant, exchanging good-humoured jibes with her clientele. Mary seemed to have let go of the past. In between serving customers she came to sit with Kai; they talked about the hospital, Mary's plans for a takeaway and home-delivery service. Kai did not mention his appointment at the Embassy. When he made to leave she'd taken both his hands, her eyes locked on to his, and holding him prisoner thus forced a promise out of him to come again.

After lunch he'd found a quiet place in the park and called Tejani on his mobile. Tejani yelled when Kai gave him the news, then seemed at a loss for words.

'My man, my man, my man,' he repeated. Kai heard him call to someone in a back room; Helena, he presumed. And finally, 'So you're really going to do it. I'm so pleased.'

'Good.' Kai could imagine Tejani standing in his new house in a pair of shorts, silhouetted against the summer sun coming through the sliding doors to the yard, shaking his head in the way he had. Then Kai remembered it was cold still in Maryland and they'd not moved to their new house, or even found the financing yet.

'You're going for the H1-B visa, right?'

'Is that what it's called?' said Kai.

'Yes. Highly skilled migrants. Doctors are top of the league. It'll be easier if you have a sponsor here, but it isn't necessary. You'll have to take the professional exams for your licence. We should get an application in for those right now, you can always defer. Man, I can't believe this!'

Kai listened to his friend's voice; there was a faint echo on the line. Believe this. Believe this. He noticed the American inflection that had entered Tejani's voice, remembered how they'd affected American accents at school, adopted American slang at university. Converse sneakers. Rap.

A sense of having turned a corner into the inevitable entered Kai, bringing with it a chill. 'It's not definite yet,' he said.

A pause. Tejani spoke again. 'I want you here, man. What can I say? I miss you, man.' Miss you, man. A static-flecked silence.

In a fresh voice Kai said, 'You're right. What am I saying? I'm coming.'

They talked for a quarter-hour more. Tejani made plans, offered advice. Kai told him of the trip back to the waterfall.

'Did you go through Port Loko?'

'Yes.'

'I wonder how that guy is doing?'

Kai knew immediately who Tejani was talking about. He'd wondered the same himself. Dr Bangura, the Lassa fever specialist.

Tejani continued, 'Man, I'd love to know what happened to him.'

When the beeps on the line warned Kai's credit was about to run out, Tejani offered to call back, but Kai said he needed to get back to the hospital. He put the phone in his pocket and for a quarter-hour more remained sitting on the bench, watching the children on their way home from school.

'I think it's ready now.' Abass is staring into the recesses of the saucepan.

'OK. How much iodine do we need?' Kai consults Abass's exercise book, where the instructions for the experiment are written out in spiky, child's handwriting. 'It says here we have to add some of your solution to a jug of water first.' He finds the eye dropper.

'Let me, let me!' Abass climbs down from the chair.

'Where are your fruit and vegetables? Shouldn't you have them ready?'

'Oh!' Distracted now, Abass begins to search randomly around the kitchen.

In time he's ready. They carry out the experiment to test vitamin C levels in different foods. Abass is mesmerised by his power to alter the colour of the purple liquid by dropping pieces of fruit and vegetables into it. He is still testing as Kai prepares to fry the chicken. He confines the child to one side of the kitchen, allows him a piece of raw chicken skin to drop into his test tube of iodine solution, and later describes for him the symptoms of scurvy, which the child copies down slowly amid much rubbing out and revision. Kai repeats phrases patiently as he coats each piece of chicken and places them into the pan of hot oil.

At eight o'clock his cousin is still not back. 'Come on,' he says to Abass. 'Let's take something to Yeama.'

He places several pieces of chicken in a plastic container. From his bedroom Kai collects a wad of notes from the store in his chest of drawers. They make their way up the lane and arrive at Yeama's to find the women sitting in a loose circle, in the middle of which a pair of lamps burn low. Kai gives Abass the chicken to give to Yeama, and presses the money into her hand himself. From the gathered women comes a muttering of approval. Abass stands shyly in front of Yeama.

'He's growing up fine, this one.' She reaches out her hand to stroke Abass's arm.

Abass doesn't move, but stands, arms at his sides, his belly sticking out, while he continues to regard her.

'No father.' Yeama nods as she says this, as if to confirm the wisdom of her own observation. 'But he has a good mother.'

There is a general murmuring of consent; Kai hears his cousin's voice thanking Yeama for the compliment.

Yeama continues, 'And he has you, too.' She nods at Kai then gives Abass's arm a final pat and pushes him gently in Kai's direction.

Nobody expects them to sit long with the women, and so after a few minutes Kai makes his excuses and leaves. He and Abass walk down the hill towards the house. The boy is silent, keeping pace with Kai in the darkness.

It is coming, Kai knows, one day soon. Every time somebody like Yeama makes a remark it brings the day a little closer. Inside Abass's head he can sense the child's brain working, trying to form thoughts out of feeling, thoughts which will in turn give rise to the questions, questions that have yet to crystallise.

One day.

Three o'clock in the morning. Kai listens to Abass's adenoidal breathing. The child asked to sleep in his bed again. Now he is lying, leg bent, flung out across the middle of the bed. Kai stares into the darkness, then slips out of bed and goes into the yard.

Kai wasn't woken by dreams about the bridge, or even a dream at all. But a memory, a sudden intrusion of conscious thought upon his world of sleep. The last time he saw Abass's father, sitting on the tailgate of a pickup, on his way to his station in the east. He made the journey home twice a month. Just as the vehicle had been about to move off he'd jumped down to shake hands with Kai and climbed back in. He was always particular about his beret; Kai watched him adjusting it and readjusting it against the wind as the pickup gathered speed, wearing his habitual expression of peaceable wonder. In another world he would have been happy as a postman or a farmer.

Rebels invaded the town where he was stationed two weeks later. For days his blackened corpse, fused flesh and rubber, lay on a traffic island from where no person dared to retrieve it.

Perhaps, thinks Kai, he should talk to his cousin. Suggest it was time they thought about telling Abass the circumstances behind his father's death. He ponders the question a few moments. His thoughts move to his cousin, to the Pentecostalists to whom she has given space in the house, the slight distance she keeps even from her own son. Abass craves her, turns to Kai in her absence. It is not Abass she is protecting. But who is Kai to judge her? For he'd never told Nenebah about the bridge. Or of what happened with the young nurse, Balia. He'd hidden those things from Nenebah.

One night, lying beside her in bed, sleepless, knowing she too was awake. He heard her draw a breath as she half turned towards him and placed her hand on his chest. She moved her hand down across his chest, her fingertips brushed his nipples, which tightened instinctively in response. Then her fingers were on his belly, the muscles of which contracted almost painfully beneath her touch. Kai held his breath. He shivered, held on to the tightness of his stomach muscles, diverted all his mental energy towards her hand and felt himself respond supremely to her advance, so that by the time her fingers snagged softly in his pubic hair he was fully erect. Her fingers found his cock and closed around it. He exhaled. For a moment he relaxed. And was lost. He tried to regain control, to re-engage his mind with his body, with her hand. But it was impossible, the images crowded into his mind, jostling for control, squeezing out the present. Even when she replaced her hand with her mouth, all he felt was her tongue working around his limp state. The entirety of him rested curled inside her mouth, an entirely new sensation. It was she who eventually came up, leant over and kissed him on the mouth. Neither of them spoke. She'd tucked herself under his arm and gone to sleep. It was still good enough between them for that.

A month later came Tejani's announcement of his departure. They'd discussed it many times before, Tejani the determined one from the start. Kai had seen his friend off, punched fists with him and promised to follow. But he had never followed.

Close at hand a dog adds its voice to those of the others. Kai thinks of the day and the journey he now has before him. He does not lack the courage for it. No.

Rather it was the courage to stay that had failed him.

CHAPTER 35

'How have you been sleeping? Any more dreams?'

Elias Cole laughs, a phlegm-filled rasp. 'This is not the place for a good night's sleep.'

'You're being woken?'

'There's always something, somebody dying or trying to. The doctors and nurses make it their business to interfere.'

'Do you manage to sleep again?'

'I wonder who's next, afraid this sleep will be the final one. On the other hand, if the dream is good . . .' The laugh again.

Adrian smiles. 'I can ask the doctor to prescribe something, if you like.'

'What would be the point?'

'Let me know if you change your mind.'

'Of course.' He pulls himself up, in the slow, deliberate way of a man whose every movement is laced with pain. He coughs and the coughing takes over his whole body.

Adrian waits.

Elias Cole wipes his mouth with a cloth. 'I'm not a superstitious man. I was born in the city. I don't hold with Babagaleh's country beliefs. For him there's no such thing as a natural death, we'd all live for ever, but for the curses heaped upon us by our enemies.' He looks up at Adrian. 'In the dark all manner of thoughts come to mind. You begin to imagine.'

'Imagine what?'

'It's something of a coincidence, is it not? The way I'm dying, so similar to Julius's own end . . .'

'And you think perhaps your pulmonary fibrosis is the result of a curse?' Adrian shifts in his chair, interested. The old man turns, their eyes meet. Elias Cole smiles and in that moment looks suddenly quite different: keen, cold, alert. Adrian catches the glint in his eye. The side he sees of Cole is not his public face. Elias Cole had been quite a different animal on the outside, ten, twenty years ago. It occurs to Adrian he would not have liked to come up against him.

Adrian leans back.

'Let's just call it dramatic irony, shall we?' says the old man.

Our first night together we dined at the Ocean Club. I felt people were staring at us. At a time when talk could have undesirable consequences, gossip filled the void. After we had eaten Saffia and I returned to the house on the campus.

The work on the house was finished and, on the whole, well executed. I guided Saffia from room to room. Some things still needed work. The stock of furniture that came with the property was underwhelming and looked as if it might have been chosen by a blind man. Curtains in a toxic shade of yellow. A wooden-framed sofa covered in red print. A chair covered in yet another brightly patterned fabric; it was a rocking chair, which we later discovered had a habit of overreaching its tipping point and depositing the occupant on the floor.

I was never a man of taste; the decor in my own apartment had never risen far above the merely functional. But Saffia had an eye for detail. And so in my imaginings I'd show her the house, newly roofed and painted. And then we would laugh together at the furnishings, and in the weeks that followed Saffia would make redecorating the house her first project. Or so I hoped.

She surveyed the room from the edge. Impossible not to notice how her gaze never alighted upon an object, but hovered restlessly. I made some quip or other, asking her opinion. A little game I had planned in which I pretended momentarily to admire the decor. Foolish, as it turned out. Saffia turned to me and smiled, held me in the same unseeing gaze with which she had contemplated the room, and said, 'It's a very fine house indeed, Elias. Thank you.'

Did she love me? I don't think so. Did it matter? Not at the beginning. I thought by then Saffia had moved beyond ideas of love.

But I am a jealous man. I'd been jealous of my younger brother. Not so much for the fact of my mother's love for him. It was his joy I envied, I suppose, the very quality that made people respond to him as they did. He was an absurdly *happy* child, and I could never fathom why. I'd been jealous of Julius, for possessing Saffia. I'd even grown jealous of Kekura and Yansaneh. Of the dancer. Of any man who came near her.

Imagine then, how it feels to find yourself in a love triangle with a ghost. Your rival, complacent in death, can never misstep or disappoint. Julius had left Saffia, yet in dying he had at the same time atoned for all his sins, for his colossal selfishness and grandiose stupidity. And if I sound like I am contradicting myself, I am not. I merely describe the contortions of which the human heart is so eminently capable.

A memory.

Making love to Saffia.

I touch her back. For a few seconds, until she turns to me, she is utterly immobile. I kiss her. I caress her. She places her arms around me. But there is something held back. Her touch on my skin is altogether too light, as if she hesitates to make contact. In the moonlight that slips into the room from behind the blind, I see her eyes are open.

I remember Vanessa, her whispered encouragement and breathy endearments. With Vanessa I could succeed in losing myself. Vanessa had mastered the tricks of coquetry and seduction and she applied them to my pleasure. Vanessa could be a generous lover to those lovers who were generous to her. I remember the simulated passion of the girl from the bar. At least she showed me some gratitude. She admired me. A man needs some encouragement. I even feel a little tenderness towards her.

It is not true. I feel no tenderness towards the girl. A girl whose livelihood depended upon feigned pleasure. The same is true of Vanessa. Vanessa merely occupies a higher league, her ambitions greater and hence her abilities all the more finely tuned.

The truth, if you want it, was that it had never bothered me. I did not expect a woman to enjoy the act in the same way as a man. There was a time when these women were good enough for me. The act of lovemaking as performed with them was good enough. But no longer.

I am not comparing what I had with them to what I have with Saffia. It is all a lie.

Instead I am remembering a day. A day when I drove from the university campus to a pink house on the hill with a truckload of chairs for a party that evening. I cannot halt the memory. It enters my brain like a thief, slipping like the moonlight behind the blind.

I am remembering entering through the open door into the darkened recesses of the house. I am remembering standing alone in that wide, open space listening to a sound. A sound coming from somewhere behind a closed bedroom door. I am remembering the coarse humour and laugh of the truck driver. And I am remembering the heat rising in my face.

And this, the truth now, is what I was thinking. That, until the truck driver laughed his filthy laugh, I had been unable to place the sounds we both heard. They were unfamiliar to me because I had no idea what a woman's pleasure sounded like. And when I heard it for the first time that day it sounded nothing like Vanessa. And I knew. I knew what Vanessa had been doing to me and I was angry. I heard the visceral reality, wild, abandoned, unheeding and unmistakable.

That is what I remember as I lie with Saffia.

Despite myself, the memory arouses me. But Saffia does not feign her pleasure. The anger returns, it rises and keeps me going. I become frenzied.

And suddenly I am spent.

There came a time when I became jealous even of Saffia, what she kept inside and would not share. My jealousy – frustrated and unappeased – transformed into anger, a low, unworthy rage. I wished to break her. At mealtimes I would sit watching as she chewed her food, observing the working of her jaw, the way she swallowed. For a while it became a minor obsession. I watched her surreptitiously as she moved around the house, as she read a book, sewed or made a shopping list. If ever she happened to turn in my direction and see me looking, she would smile at me, that skin-deep smile with which I had become so familiar. And I would smile back. I watched her at other times, too. In the old days I might have contrived to bump into her in this place or that place, discover her plans and make sure they coincided with mine. Now I tried and failed to catch her out in small lies and evasions. I read meaning into even the most open statement. I looked through her papers and belongings. I didn't know what I was looking for. I suspected her of nothing at all, except of not caring for me. Meanwhile she ran the house, planned my meals, attended to every domestic duty; she listened and replied to my conversation. That was what made it so terrible.

A Tuesday. I'd been working in my office all morning. The short walk to work was one of the conveniences of living on campus. Sometimes on my way between the library and the office I would walk the hundred yards up the hill. I could tell if Saffia was home by whether or not the car was parked outside. I might wander up there two or three times a day. Thanks to my recent promotion I was less and less often to be found among the archives. I still lectured and I still researched and wrote, but more of my work was now made up of administrative duties. I didn't complain. It suited me, to be honest. Simple, measurable and on the whole achievable goals. I kept in touch with developments in the academic world; over the years I published several papers. One of them, on early monetary systems, achieved significant critical praise and contributed to my eventual professorship. Though all that was yet to come.

The car was in the drive. I was about to turn away when I saw Saffia leaving the house, her head wrapped in her distinctive orange scarf. She didn't get into the car and drive off, as might be expected. Instead she set off in the opposite direction, across the campus. After a moment's hesitation I followed her. I followed her all the way to the eastern gate of the campus. The entrance was little used for the simple reason it was a long walk from the main campus buildings. However, it enjoyed the advantage of leading straight into a parade of houses and shops, one of the old Creole villages. It was an alternative place to pick up transport. Saffia hailed a taxi, slipped inside and drove off.

At dinner that night I asked her about her day. I noticed she said nothing about her trip outside the campus.

The next day I called Babagaleh. He was with us by then. Sent from the village by the aunt, though altogether a much more amenable personality. Much easier for Babagaleh to go unnoticed. There was a risk involved in my request. He was one of Saffia's people, his loyalty to me was untested. I forget how, but I made it sound as though it was all being done for Saffia's sake. A hint that I was concerned for her health.

Babagaleh acquitted himself well. The first two days she did nothing more than pursue her regular errands. Babagaleh was, rather I should say *is*, a man of minimal speech. One of his better qualities is his ability to resist the urge towards embroidery and irrelevance people of his class so often possess and which they seem unshakeably to believe will be read as empiric evidence of their efforts. Babagaleh knew what was required of him. He watched, he waited, and when he had the information he delivered it to me plainly. In his own words, she had been to the house where she had once lived with Mr Julius.

Interesting he knew the detail, because as far as I knew he had never visited the house before.

The dry season was at its height. The view of the hills from the town had virtually disappeared and the sun looked more like the moon, pale behind the veil of dust. I remember it was January because that was also the month of the faculty wives' dinner.

That year, the one I am talking about, it was a cool evening; gusts of desert wind blew through the gathering. The Dean, naturally, was there and we spoke for a few minutes until he left us to go and work the room, as was his way. His efforts would pay off when ten years later he was appointed Vice Chancellor.

One thing of note occurred: Saffia was unwell later in the evening. She'd been drinking, brandy and ginger ale. I put it down to her inexperience with alcohol.

This had all been in the days before I noticed Saffia leave the house with her orange scarf wrapped around her hair. I wondered why she didn't take her car. Now the decision made some sort of sense. She still drove the Volkswagen Variant. It wouldn't do to draw attention to herself on her old street.

I considered my alternatives. I decided to pursue my own line of enquiry.

One afternoon I made my way to the pink house. It had been two years since I'd last visited, three since Julius had died. Not much had changed. The neighbour, the fish mammy as I thought of her, was still in residence. At least her chair occupied the same place upon the verandah and I thought I heard her voice coming from behind the house. The orange tree in the yard was overgrown, the branches bowed. The door of the house was solidly locked. New tenants had arrived after Saffia and her aunt left. I supposed they must have moved on and the landlord had his own plans for the place.

The whole place had an air of neglect. What was it that made it so? The darkness at the windows? The absence of tread upon the stone stairs, now covered in dust? Or just the inexplicable lack of a life force. The pink house was utterly still.

I walked down the side of the house, where I knew there could be found a small gate. It had been rarely used, except by Saffia when she was delivering the potted plants and hanging baskets she sold for weddings and other events. The gate opened easily. Somehow this was exactly as I knew it would be. The garden was ordered and neat. Somebody had been here recently. The thought entered my mind that the landlord had employed a gardener while the house was empty. As I walked on I knew the idea carried no weight. No doubt at all, this was Saffia's doing. I made my way down the path to the end of the garden and back into the past. The place I had stood drunkenly under the tree and stared at the stars on the night of the moon landing. Where I had stood with Saffia before the Harmattan lilies in the first weeks of our meeting. And again two years ago, when she had briefly alluded to the possibility of a future and my heart had crowded with hope.

The lilies were splendid. Dozens of them, deepest crimson, their great funnel-shaped heads turned towards me. Can a flower adopt an expression? I ask because I know you will think me fanciful if I say so, or thought so then. Standing there, it was as though I had opened a door upon a roomful of silent children: watchful, listening, waiting. I knew I had found what I'd been looking for. I turned to go.

The fish mammy was there on her verandah when I left. I felt her eyes upon my back as I walked down the street. For once she was silent.

And in her silence she was more eloquent than in anything her barbed tongue could produce.

In the final weeks of 1972, our daughter was born. I told myself I had given Saffia the one thing Julius had not. It made no difference. Saffia remained as remote as ever. A stillness came over her. It was as if she had realised her error in marrying me, but now it was too late. So, as many women do, she swallowed the bitterness of her regret and submitted. The stillness was what was left.

The aunt came back from the village and Saffia relinquished most of the responsibility of the child to her. In our gratitude we named the child for the old lady. Not the little girl's real name, for that had already been chosen, but her house name, the name we called her by.

As for me, I loved the child from the start. And she loved me in return. I have no doubt this is the experience of all men, or at the very least a great many. Perhaps even to talk of an infant's love is a foolishness, for doesn't a child love selfishly, like a puppy, whoever will take care of them? But for once in my life I never had to ask what somebody saw in me, or question why she might wish to spend her time with me, wonder at her motives. She was my daughter. I, her father. The first love I had ever been able to take for granted.

Even Babagaleh came under the child's spell. She taught him his letters, you know. I would find him sitting among her dolls and teddy bears in front of a toy blackboard. She liked to play teacher. Later he sat with her while she did her homework. He'd copy out the same sums and sentences alongside her. In this way he learned to read, and he reads perfectly well, though he is careful to maintain otherwise. He would take her to the mosque with him on Fridays and show her off . . . pretend . . . his own daughter . . .

Wheezing. A flailing arm. A shaking hand. The old man's body convulses upon the bed. His mouth opens and closes. Adrian jumps up, puts his arms under the old man's armpits and pulls him up. He runs to the door and calls a nurse. He waits in the corridor while the nurse attends to her patient.

All around him is silence, save for the hollow scrape of a bucket being pushed along the floor of the corridor, the slosh of water. The sound of the hospital gates opening and a vehicle entering.

Adrian thinks about the last part of Elias Cole's story. The child, of course, was Mamakay.

CHAPTER 36

In a bar, Pedro's, where Adrian has been with Kai. Adrian has left Mamakay at the table while he goes to fetch drinks.

'One beer, one rum and Coke,' he says to the barman, holding up a finger against the din. The bar area is crowded. With difficulty Adrian turns himself around and leans against the bar so he can see Mamakay.

'Great place!' says the man next to him.

Adrian turns and nods. The other man is young, younger than Adrian at any rate, dressed in chinos and a polo shirt, the modern uniform of the European in the tropics; his skin is sweating and yellowish. He sits with his back to the bar, his thumbs hooked into his pockets, fingers framing his crotch. On the other side of him a sullen-faced woman leans curled into his body. Her left hand slips up and down the inside of the man's thigh. Adrian nods at her and as he does so recognises her as the girl in the purple top he'd seen here once before.

The man is still speaking. 'My base is upcountry. I'm in town for a meeting with our funders. Have to take them round a few of our projects, reassure them we're putting their money to excellent use, let them have their picture taken with a disabled kid, or better still a former child-soldier. That's the sort of thing makes them cream.'

'Is that right?' says Adrian. He looks around for the barman.

'Well, keep your fingers crossed for me. Because I like this place and I plan to stay.' The man next to him is still talking. 'The women,' and here he whistles, leans over and whispers, 'buy them a couple of Cokes and they'll let you fuck them all night.'

At that moment the barman arrives with the drinks. Relieved, Adrian prepares to move on. As he makes to leave the man says, 'I'm Robert. Hey, bring your girl over. Make an evening of it.'

'No thanks,' says Adrian.

At the table Mamakay watches him as he sets down the drinks. 'Do you know that man?'

'No,' says Adrian quickly. 'God, no.'

'What were you talking about?'

Though Adrian does not particularly wish to repeat Robert's remark he does.

Mamakay sits in silence, not looking at him or apparently listening any longer, but staring at Robert, who in turn appears oblivious, his attention occupied by the girl who has now moved to stand in front of him, her legs straddling his knee, rotating her hips in time to the music. Mamakay jumps up and heads to the bathroom. Adrian sits and waits, drinks his beer, wonders how to bring back her mood. He spots her coming back from the bathroom. She smiles softly at him as she takes her seat. He is about to ask her if she is all right, when a disturbance at the bar draws his attention away. It is Robert, he appears to be involved in an argument. Adrian sees the girl who'd been stroking his thigh snatch up her handbag and stalk away. Mamakay is watching, too. When it is quiet again, she picks up her drink and takes a sip.

'What was all that about?' says Adrian.

'While we were in the Ladies I told her what he'd said to you.'

It takes a moment for Adrian to absorb this. He looks sideways at Robert, but the aid worker has his back turned to them.

'I see,' says Adrian eventually.

Mamakay speaks again, more quietly this time.

'I beg your pardon.' Adrian bends in to hear her.

'She was my classmate. We were at school together. Her name is Josephine.'

A residual memory of his thoughts when he first saw the girl in the purple top flushes Adrian with shame. When he looks at the bar, Robert is gone.

He did not come here expecting to find happiness.

In the evenings they go out, sometimes to old places, sometimes to new ones. He wants to know this city of hers, he wants to share her world. They eat together, at Mary's or else buy food from the women who sell to working men from roadside stalls. Less often she cooks. She eats with her hands and laughs at his jokes; she can sometimes be outrageous and flamboyant in his company, as he, Adrian, is in hers. He barely recognises this part of himself, though it is not new, just forgotten. They make love often. Adrian does not know how he is capable, but he is, and still achieves new pleasure. It amazes him that she feels cold at night. She falls asleep, once during an embrace, her thighs either side of him, her upper body curled on his chest. He lies there for an hour, scarcely breathing, to allow her to sleep on. He looks at her, from this awkward angle, too close. Yet manages to memorise the configuration of every hair on her head. Once he dares to lift his hand and touch her hair. There are questions he wants to ask. How many lovers has she known? Who are they and what are their names? Who was the first and who the latest? Did she love any of them? He wants to ask, but he does not dare because he is afraid of what would happen once he began, because he knows he would never be able to stop.

An evening they are sitting up on the balcony upstairs. The occupant of the flat is away for a few days. They carry their beers up the outside stairs. 'For a change of scenery,' she says. 'I'm tired of looking at concrete.' There is a view of the roof of the house in front, of clusters of huts, *panbodies* as Adrian now knows them to be called.

A group of ragged children march across an open space, pushing one of their number ahead of them like a prisoner. One of them smacks the boy in front in the back and he staggers.

'Hey!' Mamakay is on her feet and shouting at the children, who stop and look up. One by one they drop their gaze and shuffle off.

'You couldn't do that in Britain.'

She sits down opposite him. 'Is that so?' She seems amused.

'Yes,' says Adrian. And then, 'Did you have brothers and sisters?'

'No,' says Mamakay.

'That's unusual, isn't it?'

She nods. 'I don't know why. I wanted a little brother, you know, like little girls do. I used to ask my mother. She never said no, and she never said yes. After a while I stopped. I must have changed my mind. So, no. No brothers or sisters.'

Adrian has yet to tell Mamakay about his relationship with her father. There is no genuine conflict of interest, he tells himself. Elias Cole is his patient, not Mamakay. And Elias Cole is not really a patient, not as such. It requires handling, though. In Britain his relationship with her would undoubtedly be viewed as problematic from a professional standpoint. This, though, is not Britain.

Something flies out of the darkness and drops into a pawpaw tree, the sound of its wings like a mainsheet loosed against the wind. The tree is the height of the balcony, the leaves almost within reach. Mamakay shines a torch into its recesses and they see a fruit bat. Adrian can hear the sucking sound as it eats the fruit, apparently undisturbed by their proximity. A second bat arrives and nestles into the same crevice. Adrian is unprepared for how black they are, an unreal blackness: wings, snouts, claws, as though all the darkness had gathered in this one living creature. He would like to draw them, but they only come after dark, says Mamakay. She fetches an oil lamp and sets it on the table between them. She sits with her heels resting on the lip of her chair, her arms across her knees, one hand holding her beer bottle. The light illuminates the planes of her face, the edges of her lips, the reflection of her eyes. He discovers she studied history at university, like her father.

'Did you ever think about getting a position at the university?'

She replies, 'I never finished my studies.'

'Because of the war?'

'In a manner of speaking.' She stands up, changing the subject. 'Are you hungry? I'm hungry. I need to eat. Let's go out.' Suddenly she is no longer relaxed but restless.

'Sure,' says Adrian, who has yet to deny her anything.

When he is away from her, he tries to conjure up her face. He closes his eyes, but the magic eludes him. When they are together he watches, learning her features, her gestures. Still, afterwards, he cannot make it happen. It is as though when she goes she takes everything of herself with her.

He realises too that she asks him almost nothing about himself, not even when they will next meet. In those moments they are together, she gives him her attention entirely; by the same token he draws none of her curiosity. It bothers him. As he watches her lying with her back to him, a memory of the night at the bar: the girl with the purple top arrives, skewed and bent out of shape, moulded into something else. The paranoia of a man newly in love. She senses something because she rolls over to look at him, frowns slightly. 'What is it?'

'Have you done this many times before?' he asks.

She raises herself up on one elbow and traces his Adam's apple lightly with her forefinger. He is afraid to ask. She removes her finger and says, 'What are you asking me?'

He can barely breathe: 'Have you done this before?'

She is gazing at the ceiling, an arm extended, drawing circles with her index finger in the air. To Adrian there is something mesmeric about that finger, as it passes in and out of the shadows cast by the moon.

'No,' she replies.

The relief is so immense his bowels turn to water.

Still tracing patterns on the ceiling, she continues, 'Have you?'

'No,' replies Adrian.

She says, 'Fine, then.' And rolls over with her back to him once more. His relief disappears.

'You make me happy,' he says to her back.

'Good,' she replies to the wall.

'And it frightens me.'

She turns to face him. 'You shouldn't be frightened,' she says, not whispering like him, but speaking in a normal voice.

'Why not?'

'Because it is pointless. Whatever happens will happen.'

Now he rolls over on to his back and watches the moon shadows on the ceiling. There is thunder in the distance. He rolls back to her, misjudges the distance between them and knocks his head hard against her face. The violence of the blow jars his teeth. He finds her mouth, kisses her and tastes blood, fetches a box of matches and strikes one against the dark.

'I've hurt you,' he says, peering at her lip. The match dies. He lies back down and places his arms around her. He can feel her shaking; a giggle escapes from the place between them. Suddenly they are both laughing.

In the morning, because he has already said things he did not intend to say and now is reckless, he asks, 'Who have you loved the most?'

'A man, you mean?'

'Yes.'

'Not a dog?'

'No.'

'Or a bat?'

'Not a bat, either.' He is happy to banter, but also insistent.

She is cleaning the kitchen, rubbing Vim on the surfaces. He likes that he is privy to her small domestic routines. She turns around to face him, her hands white with powder, a scouring sponge in one hand; milky water runs down her arm, drips off her elbow. Her face is smiling and yet serious. 'You really want to know?'

'Yes. Have you been in love before?' He wants to know whether what is happening has happened before. As lovers always do. He feels like a cliché, it does not stop him.

'Once.' She holds up a whitened index finger. 'Just once. We practically grew up together. We were together for ever, at least it felt like it.'

'Would you have married him?'

'Yes,' she replies. There is no hesitation and it hurts him, a tiny thorn, though he had asked her to be honest. He is silent. She turns away to put the sponge in the sink and he comes up behind her, places his arms around her waist and rests his chin in the dip of her shoulder blade.

'What happened?'

'What usually happens. We grew in different directions. He was more ambitious than me. Eventually we'd grown so far apart we couldn't touch each other any more. He changed, too.' She shrugs.

Adrian stands still. She continues to rub at a stain on the counter. This game is too dangerous. He doesn't want to ask any more questions. He stops speaking.

And Mamakay naturally asks him nothing at all.

CHAPTER 37

Given the extra shifts he'd worked Kai was owed any number of days off. He let Seligmann know he'd be away for a day, preferring to avoid Mrs Mara. Abass was on holiday, bored at home, so Kai had invited him to come along. They left the city by way of the hospital, where Kai checked briefly on Foday. A doctor was a farmer, he told Abass; patients were crops that had to be watered or cows that needed milking. Together they passed by Adrian's flat and found it empty. Kai noted the reordering of items, the books taken down from their shelves, the pair of coffee mugs.

They encounter little traffic and no accidents and thus make good time. There are vehicle tracks on the road to the falls. A couple of British military observers, a woman and a man picnicking on the rocks, provide theatre for a group of children. Kai raises a hand in greeting, but the couple do not return it and their gaze travels through him. And so, though Kai could free them from the bondage of the children's stares, he chooses not to do so.

Abass goes to fish in the crevices between the rocks. Kai strips down to his shorts and dives into the cool water. The swim does little, though, to ease his restlessness. Like the British couple, he would have preferred to be alone. Once, on a trip here with Nenebah, they'd been invaded by a group of foreign engineers on a sightseeing trip from the dam. Tejani had driven away to explore the town, the two of them been on the point of making love interrupted by the arrival of the delegation in khaki shorts and open sandals. By the time Tejani came back, the men were gone. He'd thought they were fooling.

Did Nenebah ever come back here?

He climbs out and lies upon the rocks. Abass's shadow looms over him, holding a sand skipper in his cupped hands. The Europeans get up and leave. One more swim, Kai tells Abass, and then it is time to go.

Past the petrol station and the queue of vehicles, they enter the town. In the square Kai parks the old Mercedes by a row of stalls and climbs down. Abass is hungry now and hovers in front of the food stalls. They buy chicken and wait while the stallholder griddles it over hot coals. Kai buys some bread from a neighbouring stall and they eat leaning against the car. Afterwards he gets behind the wheel and they move forward at a crawl, driving the route he walked just once, in the middle of a night six years ago.

'Where are we going?' asks Abass.

'I'm looking for somebody I met here a long time ago.'

'Will they still be here?'

'I don't know,' answers Kai.

Abass winds down his window and hums. Kai is trying to feel the route, pacing his driving against the distantly remembered conversation of that night, the lefts and rights. The layout of the streets could have changed. Back then they'd been accompanied by soldiers, who'd led them, to their surprise, straight to the door. He swings the car around to the right, descends a steep section of track. Outside a low, bunker-shaped building he halts, orders Abass to wait, pulls his shirt over his mouth and nose and pushes at the door. Inside are the old refectory tables, broken glass and a burned mattress. Otherwise no sign of the laboratory that once stood there.

Somewhere in this town Kai has a cousin. In the marketplace he stops again at the food sellers to ask where he might find the street where the family live. Minutes later they arrive at the house. Somebody is sent to fetch Ishmail and he arrives smiling and buttoning his shirt, punches fists with Kai and then with Abass. They settle with their backs against the wall. Last time they met was some years before the war, before the city where Kai lived became an island within the rest of the country.

'Long time, my friend,' says Ishmail. 'What brings you here?'

Kai tells him he is looking for Dr Bangura, the Lassa fever specialist. His cousin nods first, then shakes his head and tuts. The doctor is gone. Not the war, a pinprick to his finger. He was infected by the disease he'd been researching.

Kai is quiet, remembering the doctor working diligently over his samples late into the night, the household rubber gloves, the snorkel and mask in place of proper safety equipment. He would have died in agony.

Through the streets of the town, a slow, late-afternoon stroll. From time to time Ishmail raises a hand to people sitting on the steps of houses, shakes another's hand, introduces Kai as his brother. Once they pass a house upon whose balcony six or so young men lounge. Unlike outside the other houses here there are no women, no children. Ishmail nods. One or two nod in return. There are no smiles and Ishmail does not introduce Kai as he has before. Down a road enclosed by houses on both sides, Abass, ahead of them, turns and, with a child's expert memory, declares, 'This is where we found Uncle Adrian after the bicycle hit him.'

Ishmail laughs. 'Who is this that was hit by a bicycle?'

'Uncle Adrian. We found him here and took him home.'

Ishmail turns questioningly to Kai.

Kai lets Abass get ahead once more, before he tells Ishmail. Afterwards they continue in silence until they reach a motel, partly rebuilt and painted, bristling with bamboo scaffolding. In the courtyard a nanny goat and her kid are tethered. The goat is bleating, a melancholy, repetitive sound. Abass is given a Fanta, which he carries outside to sit and watch the goat. Two men are following the football at the bar, dressed in the typical attire of government utility workers. Ishmail leads Kai to a table in the back of the room.

'I heard something about this man,' he says presently, 'the one you say was hit by a bicycle. I heard a stranger was hurt.'

'Who told you that?'

Ishmail shrugs. 'People talk.' He is sitting hunched over the table, facing Kai, one arm curled around his beer. He speaks in a low voice. 'Some bad business.'

'He was attacked,' says Kai. He tells Ishmail all he knows about Agnes, Adrian's imprudent visit to her house. The son-in-law.

Ishmail nods as if somehow it all makes sense to him.

'Do you know what it was about?' asks Kai.

Ishmail shakes his head. 'There are some bad people here. You were not here during the fighting, you didn't see. I was not here much of the time, but I was here before. I came back after and saw how things were different. Now they say it's over, but it is not over. You see those men we passed?'

'Who?' Kai looks at the men at the bar.

'No, not these ones. Them that we passed in that house. They arrived at that time and they are still here. People want them to go, but they don't go. The government told the fighters to return to their own homes, but many stayed.'

'Why?'

'Maybe because they found a better life. Maybe because they have nowhere else to go.' Ishmail shakes his head, positions his beer bottle on the damp cardboard mat, turns the label carefully round to face him and studies it. 'So they stay. Why not?'

'Was it one of them who attacked my friend?'

This time Ishmail shakes his head emphatically. 'No, I don't think so.' He takes a drink of his beer. On the television a player misses a penalty. One of the men slams his bottle down on the table and exclaims. Ishmail picks at the label on his beer bottle and says no more. Kai decides to confide in Ishmail about his plans to go to America. His cousin grins and congratulates him, raises his beer bottle. They both drink.

'When you get there send something small for me.'

They finish drinking and Ishmail stands. 'Let's go,' he says. Outside they collect Abass, who has collected some grass and leaves and laid them in front of the goat, though his offerings have gone untouched.

'Maybe she's thirsty,' suggests Kai. As Abass goes to ask the kitchen for a bowl of water, Ishmail says, 'This is a good friend of yours, this man who was beaten?'

'Yes,' answers Kai. 'A good friend. Though he's a visitor here, we have become close through the hospital. I stay at his place often. He wants to help.'

Ishmail nods. 'We should all have friends. Look at Abass. He can create friends across the species.'

The goat is down on her front knees drinking from the bowl. Abass stands by happily, arms dangling at his sides. They walk out into the darkening streets, back the way they came, until at one point Ishmail turns away from their route saying, 'Let us use this road. Perhaps I know somebody you can talk to.' Kai follows, saying nothing. Presently they reach a house. A curtain hangs in front of the open door, glimmers of light behind. Ishmail knocks on the door frame, pushing the curtain gently aside. Kai waits. He hears Ishmail speaking to somebody. He is beckoned inside. A woman is sitting on a stool shelling groundnuts. She wipes her hands on her dress.

'I have told her what it is you want to know,' says Ishmail. 'She is my wife's aunt. She agrees to help you.'

The woman offers him the back of her wrist. Kai touches it with the back of his own.

'Agnes was not always this way,' she says. 'Before she was like you and me. And then she became crossed.' She removes the stool from beneath her, brushes the seat and sets it down. 'Please.'

Kai sits.

She offers him some of the groundnuts and leaves the room with Ishmail. Kai prepares to wait.

How many hours he sat there he would not later recall. At some point the boy, sleepy and tired of waiting outside, crept in to be with him and Kai allowed him to stay, sheltered beneath the wing of his arm. People were sent for. A neighbour. A young woman without a smile. An older woman with a creased face and white hair. Kai waited and listened without interrupting or speaking except to greet each new arrival, watch while they took a seat and were told what was required of them. He didn't speak even when they faltered; he offered no solace but left it to others. Each person told a part of the same story. And in telling another's story, they told their own. Kai took what they had given him and placed it together with what he already knew and those things Adrian had told him.

This was Agnes's story, the story of Agnes and Naasu. In hushed voices, told behind a curtain in a quiet room and in the eye of the night, from the lips of many. By the time the last speaker had finished the moon was well past its zenith and Kai understood the storytellers' courage.

Mohammed remembered Naasu. How every Monday she walked the same route to the bus stop wearing a pair of high-heeled shoes and a suit made of shiny fabric. Every Friday the bus carried her back, and this time she wore a simple cotton dress. On Monday when she walked to the bus stop, Mohammed and the other young motorbike-taxi riders would watch her pass from their place by the roundabout. Mohammed would sometimes offer her a lift and sometimes, too, she accepted. She would sit with her legs to one side and be carried down to the bus stop. A lot of young men had an idea they might put cola for Naasu, who was one of the finest girls in the town and from a good family. You could see it in the way she held herself. She had the job in the city department store. Some of the young men teased her. When are you coming to take me to the big city with you, Naasu?

And she smiled and teased them back. She was bold, but in such a way as you understood there was nothing in it. For they had all known each other for a long time, they were her classmates. Everybody knew Naasu. Sometimes she stopped by her father at the nursery with fried doughnuts for his sweet tooth. They would sit on the frame of an old tractor. If Naasu was sitting with her father outside the nursery that meant it was a Friday, the day she returned from the city. During the curfew months she used to arrive home a little earlier, when the buses became cautious about travelling the roads at night. Naasu's father and she ate sugared doughnuts sitting on the rusting frame of the old John Deere tractor the last Friday Naasu was home.

Naasu was away in the city the day the thin men came to the town.

This is what Mohammed remembers about Naasu.

On market day, at six o'clock in the morning, Binta rose and dressed, washing from the bucket in the corner of the yard. By six-thirty she was ready to walk the half-mile to the town with her small basket of cucumbers and tomatoes. This was the part of the day she liked the best, the moments of quiet on the walk to the town past the sugar-cane fields. Within the hour the sun would be strong enough to dry the dew, drawing spirals of mist from the earth. As Binta passed the avenues of sugar cane she saw shadows moving between the rows. Somebody's goats must have broken free.

On the outskirts of the town she passed Agnes working in her vegetable garden. They called to one another. '*Ng' dirai?*' Agnes's husband was there in the background; the rising sun lent a dark edge to the shape of his body. He was too far away for Binta to greet him, so she walked swiftly on, hoping to beat Agnes, whose tomatoes were always so plump and shiny, to the first of the customers.

By eight o'clock Binta had set up her stall and the first buyers had already appeared. Agnes was there, two stalls away from Binta. A customer dropped a tomato and Binta bent to retrieve it, annoyed to see it had bruised and the skin was split. While she had her head below the level of the stall, she heard the sound of gunfire. She had heard it before, only never so close. All around her people started at the sound and began to move, some in one direction and some in another, like a herd of sheep on a road, uncertain in which direction safety lay. In the end they stood still.

A group of men entered the square; one was talking into a

megaphone, calling people to gather in the marketplace. This man was wearing fatigues and looked like a soldier. But the men with him were not like soldiers. Soldiers were given more rice than anybody else in the country and they carried the weight of it upon their bodies. These men were narrow and angular, curiously dressed. Jewellery and amulets around their necks, rows of bullets like necklaces, dark sunglasses. Others went barefoot and dressed in rags. Strange, thin men. They reminded Binta of the puppets from the shows she was taken to as a child. They had frightened her even then. The thin men ran around the houses, beating upon the doors and ordering the people outside. There were more sounds of gunfire, of splintering wood, the smell of smoke.

The man with the megaphone ordered everybody to sit down. As new people arrived in the square they were pushed down to the ground. By the end only the man with the megaphone and his men remained standing. He announced his name: Colonel JaJa, and began to speak. Binta listened. At first the talk sounded to her like a political speech, with words like 'government' and 'elections'. He told them the government had betrayed the people, and he spoke a name that before she had only read in the newspapers.

And she realised who these people were and guessed everybody else did too.

Binta's mouth went dry.

Colonel JaJa shouted an instruction and four of his men came forward bearing a pair of bamboo cages strung between poles. In these boxes were men, tightly huddled into the small space. One of the boxes was opened and the man brought out, an army soldier, Binta guessed, by what remained of his uniform. He struggled to stand and held his side where his uniform was darkly stained. A rope around his waist led to one of JaJa's men, who pulled at it. The man on the end of the rope offered no resistance and only stumbled after him, his head lowered like a child playing bull. The commander lowered the megaphone from his lips and his words were lost to Binta. She couldn't take her eyes off the soldier. She missed the motion of the hand to the belt, the drawing of the weapon, the way JaJa took lazy aim before he shot the army soldier in the head. She heard the sound of cheers and claps from JaJa's men. Somebody near by said, 'O Kuru.' My God. The body lay in the dust; the legs thrashed and were still.

A second cage was opened, another man brought forward. He held his bound hands up and Binta could tell he was begging for his life. Seconds later he too crumpled to the ground. Fear surged through the crowd, people began to panic. The commander spoke into the megaphone and warned them to remain still. Men were brought forward and ordered to move the bodies. Binta recognised them as the workers from the nursery, Agnes's husband among them. She heard Agnes's gasp.

The report of the gun. JaJa's voice. Agnes's gasp. Other than these sounds it seemed to Binta everything she was watching happened in silence. Dark smoke drifted beyond the roofs of the houses and the dusty smell of burning brick reached the square, carrying with it the magnitude of what was happening that day.

In the middle of the square Agnes's husband, the eldest of the men, was struggling under the weight of one of the corpses. He was recently out of hospital, where he'd had a hernia operation. Agnes had talked to Binta about it. He stumbled, was hit by one of the thin men, and fell to the ground. The other nursery workers stood still. Binta saw them turn open-handed to JaJa, remonstrating, the way people do when they are afraid. From where she stood she could sense the anger in JaJa, for Binta had known men like him in her life. Men who yearned to inspire fear in others, and yet were angered when they saw it for it reminded them of themselves. The nursery men, though, seemed not to understand and kept coming, their palms turned upwards. Agnes's husband clambered to his knees, holding his stomach, and reached out his free hand to touch JaJa. No, thought Binta. Don't touch him. The old man's fingers grasped at the Colonel's clothing. The young commander stepped out of reach, then turned and walked away. For several seconds he stood motionless with his back to them all. Binta stopped breathing. Suddenly JaJa swung around and returned to the old man with a swift, unbroken stride, raised his weapon and shot him in the chest. There were screams. The sound of more shots, this time into the air. Somebody held on to Agnes, but there was nobody to hold her younger daughter Yalie, who ran to her father where he lay. The thin men gathered around laughing until one of them pulled her away. JaJa snatched a mattock from one of his men. Binta saw again the certainty in his movements. The thin men stood back while he hacked at the nursery worker's neck with the blade, picked up the head and tossed it to Yalie, who instinctively reached out to catch it. The thin men cheered again.

Agnes's husband's death was the first of many. Afterwards the thin men were unleashed upon the town. This was the advance party. Now the war is over she knows their name. G5. She has heard it broadcast on the radio. Responsible for 'coordinating relations between the civilian population and the rebel movement', according to the spokesman for the rebels. Some called it the Sensitisation Unit.

There Binta stops speaking. Her hands have remained in her lap, still and quiet, her palms flat on her thighs, long, tapered fingers.

The nursery was on the way into town, somebody explains to Kai. They took the men from there as they entered the town over the bridge.

Yes, Kai nods.

Eleven o'clock. In the chair is a woman in her fifties, cropped grey hair and a thin scar enfolded by the soft flesh of her cheeks. Isatta was in the refugee camps in Guinea with Agnes and with her two years later when they made the long journey by foot back to the town.

In the camp it seemed they faced more dangers than on the outward journey. In the forest the dangers were from snakes, buffalo and rebel soldiers. In the camps there was hunger, typhoid and cold. But the greatest threat of all came from their own kind, gangs of men who searched the weak out from among the rest: those without family, women without menfolk. The first day they arrived Isatta and Agnes saw a row of girls lying at the edge of the camp, blood leaking from between their open legs. And on many mornings to come the bodies of young women were found dumped behind the tents, their *lappas* bunched around their waists. During the day families came to collect the bodies of their daughters. Those girls without family remained where they lay. Agnes and her two daughters were alone without men. So Isatta invited Agnes, Yalie and Marian to share a tent with her and her son. Just fifteen, Hassan had run out of time to become a man.

They survived by clinging to order: queuing for food, washing their clothes in the river, fetching water, hunting for firewood and edible plants in pairs. Scrubbing down the sides of the tent became a daily routine. In the evenings they slept together and Isatta's son lay across the entrance. Outside lean shadows stalked between the tents. They prayed nobody would notice they were four women, protected only by a young boy. The refugees lived in fear of rebel raids, but those never came. Instead two cholera epidemics arrived within the first year. The third took Yalie. Marian died six months later, poisoned by a cut on her foot.

The day after Marian's death Agnes disappeared. Isatta and her son searched the camp until dusk drove them to their tent. All night Isatta lay awake, fearing for Agnes. For if age was a woman's protection at home, it was no protection here. The next day she found Agnes sitting on the other side of the stream, unharmed. She guided her back to the tent. For days Agnes neither spoke, nor moved, nor ate. Isatta was not disturbed by Agnes, for many were the women who mourned in such a way.

Order. Isatta never lost her belief in it. After a few days she urged Agnes on through a rigid routine of her own devising. Every morning after bathing they went to the Red Cross tent to check the list of new arrivals. In nearly two years Agnes had had no news of Naasu. But they'd both heard of the sacking of the city where they thought Naasu must be living – living without a father, a mother or a husband.

The Red Cross tent was where people exchanged news of home. New arrivals were especially sought after, for the information they might bring with them. In this way they learned of the turn in events, the troops who had come from overseas, the regaining, mile by mile, of rebel-held territory. Now, after eighteen months of fighting, the government had almost reached the border and the camps. More and more of the new arrivals were people travelling from one refugee camp to another searching for loved ones. One day a Red Cross worker approached Agnes and asked her name. 'Follow me,' she said. 'We are holding a message for you.'

The message had been there for a month. It was from Naasu, searching for her father, her mother and sisters.

Naasu travelled to the halfway point of their journey home to meet them. Agnes, Isatta and Hassan had walked the distance. Now there were vehicles on the roads and with Naasu's money they were able to obtain transport the rest of the way.

In the back of the *poda poda* Naasu told her story. She had stayed in the city for almost a year, sheltering in the house of a workmate. After the arrival of the foreign troops she waited until she heard it was safe to return to her home town, fourteen months after the Friday when she had sat with her father and eaten doughnuts on the John

Deere tractor. Agnes embraced Naasu and said her father and sisters were dead and in her choice of words let Naasu believe they had all died in the camps together. Naasu wept. Isatta stared at Naasu. So beautiful and healthy: there was flesh on her arms, her hair was black where theirs had turned dry and red. Such elegant clothes. Naasu explained that she had met a man who offered to take care of her and she had married him. She begged her mother's forgiveness for marrying without her permission and Agnes gave it easily, for a good man was what she had prayed Naasu might find. That at least was God's true work.

Then Naasu reached across, took her mother's hand and placed it on her belly. Agnes felt the roundness of her daughter's stomach and for the first time Isatta saw her friend cry.

In this way they made the journey home.

The marketplace was empty, they saw nobody. Many houses were abandoned, others destroyed. They reached Agnes's home first and what she saw silenced Isatta. The house was neat and the plaster was new. Chairs stood on the verandah much as they had two years before. It was all her husband's doing, Naasu told them as she ran up the stairs. It was nearly dark and she invited Isatta and her son to eat with them and to stay the night. Since the food they had brought with them was finished, Isatta accepted. The three waited while Naasu went to find her husband. Isatta thought of her own house and wondered what she would find the next morning. She was happy for Agnes and envied her, too. Soon Naasu returned, her new husband following behind. Naasu was smiling, a sheen of excitement upon her skin as she brought him forward to greet her mother. The man stepped out from under the eaves of the house and into what remained of the light.

The old woman stops speaking. She is no longer looking at Kai, but down at her own lap. He can hear her breathing. There is silence. Somebody in the room urges her to continue. It is Ishmail's aunt. The old woman looks to her and then back down at her hands.

'What did you see?' asks Kai, speaking for the first time.

She swallows and her voice drops almost to a whisper. 'I saw JaJa.'

They are driving through the dark. Abass wide awake in the passenger seat, buckled in by his seat belt. Kai drives at some speed, propelled by what lies behind him, slowing for the bright lights that come at him out of the darkness.

Ishmail had accompanied him as they made their way slowly down darkened streets back to Old Faithful. Kai unlocked the car and Abass climbed inside. He turned to Ishmail and put out his hand. Automatically, they clasped hands and clicked thumbs and fingers. Kai thanked him. Ishmail inclined his head. They stood awhile in silence until, as though in completion of some shared observation, Ishmail sighed and said, 'So now you see us here. This is God's wish.'

'Is that what you believe?'

'You ask me one day, I would answer no, I don't believe it. You ask me the next day, after these things have occurred, I would not know how to answer you. Such things happened everywhere, for what reason I cannot tell you.'

'No.' Kai sighed and shook his head. 'Nobody can.'

'So what is there to do but pray?'

Kai hadn't answered. Instead he embraced his cousin, slipped behind the wheel of the vehicle and drove out of the town.

He remembers now that they've eaten nothing since the chicken they bought in the marketplace. He pulls over at the next junction and buys four ears of roast corn. They drive on.

'Better?' he says to Abass.

The boy nods. He has been silent since they left the town. Instead he has been sitting, watchful and still, gazing at the darkness ahead of them, unblinking even in the face of the oncoming headlights.

'So the man killed the lady's husband and then he married her daughter,' Abass says.

Kai doesn't spare the child, but replies, 'Yes.'

'And now she has to live with him and keep quiet because her daughter doesn't know what he did.'

He had been listening to every word spoken in the house.

'That's right,' says Kai.

'And everybody else keeps quiet, too.'

'Yes.'

'What about us?'

Kai turns briefly to look at Abass, who does not return his look but stares straight ahead. The darkness seems to hurtle at them, breaking apart on the windscreen and closing up again in their wake. Abass says, 'Do we have to keep quiet?'

'No,' says Kai. 'No, we don't.'

'What if we lived in that town? Would we have to be quiet then?'

In the silence all Kai can hear is the rush of air. 'I don't know,' he says.

The hospital is in darkness, save for the glow of security lights. Kai and Abass pass the wards. A door stands ajar; through the gap he can see a nurse at her station. Hushed footsteps, whispers, the slow squeak of wheels and of rubber on lino.

Kai unlocks the door of Adrian's apartment and switches on the main lights. There are the books, the pair of mugs on the table undisturbed since morning. He turns and leaves.

CHAPTER 38

Adrian reaches Elias Cole's room at a quarter past four. Fifteen minutes late. A downpour and an overflowed gutter halted traffic in the streets. He'd stopped by his apartment for a change of clothing. On the door of the old man's room hangs a laminated sign: *No Visitors*. He stops short with his hand upon the doorknob, hesitates and withdraws it. Then he turns and walks away.

CHAPTER 39

The young man shifts in his chair and surveys his feet. His voice is almost inaudible. The others seated in the circle of chairs watch him, as if from a distance.

'Here.' He taps the side of his head. 'They put it inside your head. Afterwards you are powerful. You do battle.' On the cheekbone below his temple is a series of short, thick keloid scars. His name is Soulay.

Ileana had given Adrian Soulay's records before the start of the session. A government soldier turned rebel, he'd then been recruited back into the army as part of a new deal. It hadn't worked. In a second shake-up, Soulay had been discharged. He'd worked as a security guard, but failed to hold on to any of his jobs. Soulay had a prolonged history of violence and erratic behaviour and also suffered agonising headaches, which he claimed were due to the drugs he'd been given. Adrian doubted the two were connected, though that fact made the migraines no less real.

'What was the last dream you had?'

The young man shakes his head. It is slow going. A shuffling and a snorted laugh from somebody in the room. Adecali.

'Yes?' says Adrian, turning to look at Adecali.

He is becoming used to the laughter now. Strange and surreal, it permeates so many moments, not just in the hospital but outside. A memory of Mamakay comes to him, as one seems to every few minutes, of her translating for him a phrase he'd heard and not understood. 'It means, "I fall down, I get up again." When somebody asks how you are, perhaps you can't honestly answer that you are fine. That's what it is saying.' Grim humour. Adrian pulls himself back to the present.

'What is it, Adecali? What do you want to say?'

'He hollers for his mama. He jumps out of his bed.' Adecali suffers nightmares, too. Also incontinence. He has a terror of fire, of the wicks of oil lamps, matches, lighters. Nobody knew precisely from where this stemmed and Adrian wonders what memories fire brings

316

back to Adecali, who also suffers from a complex combination of twitches and a stammer. 'M-m-m-mama'. Of the four patients in the room, he appears the most outwardly deranged.

'Would you like to talk about any of *your* dreams?' Adrian finds the sessions demanding. By the end he is exhausted. He is also exhilarated. It is what he has longed for.

Adecali drops his gaze and shuts his mouth.

'We are here to listen and to help each other.'

They are nothing if not compliant. Boys, still. Their commanders had taken the place of their parents and now they look to Adrian. None had questioned the purpose of the sessions, or considered their right to attend or not. They did as they were told, as they always had. Now the effort of attempting to obey causes Adecali to knead his brow.

'I dream. It is such that I am afraid to sleep. But it m-m-m-makes no sense. Sometimes in the day they come, sometimes by night.' His fingers work upon his forehead. 'Sometimes I smell something that is not there.'

'Take your time.' Adrian urges Adecali on, careful not to push the pace too much. 'What is it you smell?'

'I smell roast meats. I hear screaming and banging. And then I smell roasted meat.'

In the afternoon Adrian has a meeting with Attila. He makes his way to the man's office, forces himself to drop his shoulders, to take deep breaths of the sea-dampened air and walks on past the ornamental palms, the edges of whose great leaves move in the wind, creating a rattling sound which reminds him, as it did the first time, of the spinnakers of yachts at the quay in Norwich. High in the sky a pair of vultures wheel on the rising currents.

Five minutes later he is in the seat opposite Attila. Attila leans far back into his chair, elbows on the table, fingers laced, considering Adrian from beneath hooded lids. He loves a game of cat and mouse, thinks Adrian. Still, it was true to say that though the chief psychiatrist had more or less ignored Adrian he'd also given him the free run of the hospital, had not hampered his efforts. Adrian clears his throat and begins to speak, describing the sessions, their nature, the patients he selected to attend and the reasons for those choices. His choice was heavily determined by whether or not they spoke English, something he does not mention now. Attila listens in silence.

317

When Adrian has finished he waits for Attila's response, noticing for the first time the glossy darkness beneath the other man's eyes. Despite the robustness of his physique, he looks exhausted. Attila leans across and moves a pen a few inches across his desk, shifts a paper or two. It is all an act, thinks Adrian, this ponderousness. Attila is sly and quick and clever. He is dedicated to what he does. Nobody else would do this job.

Adrian likes him, he wishes he could tell him so.

'What do you aim to achieve with these sessions?'

The cat pawing the mouse.

'To return the men to normality, to some degree of normality. So they can live their lives. Achieve everything anyone else could expect to achieve.'

'And what is that?'

'Sorry?'

'What is it they can expect to achieve?'

'To hold down a job. To enjoy a relationship. To marry and have children.'

Atilla nods his head briskly. Suddenly he places his palms flat on the table and pushes himself up. 'I have to attend a meeting at the Health Ministry. Why don't you ride along with me?'

Adrian, who has things he could do, though nothing that could in any way be called urgent, senses this is a moment to comply. It is in the interests of his relationship with this awkward, heavy man.

'Of course.'

Adrian follows Attila out, waits while he selects a key from a large bunch and locks his office door, then follows him to the front entrance of the hospital. Attila eases his bulk behind the wheel of his car, Adrian slides into the passenger seat. They pass through the centre of town, past the turning to the old department store. It is hot and Attila's car does not have air conditioning. Adrian feels the sweat on his shirt and the back of his thighs.

Now they are away from the grid of roads, the traffic moves more freely here; a light breeze enters the vehicle. Adrian might have been relieved, except the breeze carries with it a foul odour of rotted fish and the high, sweet smell of sewage. The road leads sharply downhill. Tin huts reach out in either direction, an endless landscape of rusted tin. On the right is the sea. Not the green-blue sea visible from the campus, but water the colour of shit. Attila slows the car. Neither of them had spoken during the drive. Now Attila says in a conversational tone, 'A few years back a medical team came here. They were here to survey the population.'

He pulls over, applies the handbrake and looks out of Adrian's window, like a tourist pausing to appreciate the view. Ahead of them two shirtless men labour to push a cart loaded with scrap metal up the hill. Their bodies are lean and muscled, glowing with sweat and sun. A filthy dog, with perhaps the worst case of mange Adrian has ever seen, trots across the road. There are people moving in, out and around the huts. The rush of air as a car passes brings a fresh gust of the terrible smell.

'Do you know what they concluded?'

Adrian shakes his head. Attila has said neither who the researchers were nor indicated the purpose of the study.

'They were here for six weeks. They sent me a copy of the paper. The conclusion they reached was that ninety-nine per cent of the population was suffering from post-traumatic stress disorder.' He laughs cheerlessly. 'Post-traumatic stress disorder! What do you think of that?'

Adrian, who is entirely unsure what is expected of him, answers, 'The figure seems high but strikes me as entirely possible. From everything I've heard.'

'When I ask you what you expect to achieve for these men, you say you want to return them to normality. So then I must ask you, whose normality? Yours? Mine? So they can put on a suit and sit in an air-conditioned office? You think that will ever happen?'

'No,' says Adrian, feeling under attack. 'But therapy can help them to cope with their experiences of war.'

'This is their reality. And who is going to come and give the people who live *here* therapy to cope with this?' asks Attila and waves a hand at the view. 'You call it a disorder, my friend. We call it *life*.' He shifts the car into first gear and begins to move forward. 'And do you know what these visitors recommended at the end of their report? Another one hundred and fifty thousand dollars to engage in even more research.' He utters the same bitter chuckle. 'What do you need to know that you cannot tell just by looking, eh? But you know, these hotels are really quite expensive. Western rates. Television. Minibar.' He looks across at Adrian. 'Anyway,' he continues, 'you carry on with your work. Just remember what it is you are returning them to.'

It is as close as he has ever come to praise.

Attila drops Adrian off outside the government building and walks away, leaving Adrian standing in the car park. As he makes his way to the main road to hail a taxi he considers Attila's words. He recalls the conversation with Kai, two months ago now, after the attack by Agnes's son-in-law. *This is our country*. He was rejecting Adrian's offer of help. It was this that had stung so much, the idea he was neither wanted nor needed. It had simply never occurred to him.

Attila. The man is right, of course. People here don't need therapy so much as hope. But the hope has to be real – Attila's warning to Adrian. I fall down, I get up. Westerners Adrian has met despise the fatalism. But perhaps it is the way people have found to survive.

Saturday. The air is so still the woodsmoke from cooking fires lifts vertically into the air. The clouds are unmoving in the sky. Everything is quiet. No traffic on the roads. Even the birds are silent. Adrian is sipping coffee on the verandah of Mamakay's upstairs neighbour.

'I should be going,' he says, meaning the opposite. He wants to know whether she is available for the rest of the day.

'You can't.'

He smiles. 'Can't I?' he asks teasingly. 'Why not?'

And she answers, 'No, I mean you really can't go. It's Cleaning Saturday.'

'What does that mean?'

'It means you have to stay in until midday, to clean your yard. Nobody is allowed on the streets except to clean them.'

He has never heard of it before. Mamakay explains. One of the juntas introduced the cleaning days. Their first act in power. By making everyone clean their neighbourhood on the last Saturday of the month they transformed the city. The optimism was short-lived. In the years that followed the capital was sacked twice. Still, Cleaning Saturdays survived and that was something.

'What can I do?'

'I was out this morning. Before you woke up.'

The quiet, the absence of traffic on the roads is explained. Now that they are trapped here for two hours Adrian fetches his sketchbook and pencils; he plans to sketch a view of the dovecote, but instead he begins to sketch Mamakay's profile as she sits with her back to the morning light. He hasn't attempted a human figure since his days at school. But Mamakay is unselfconscious, does not stiffen or attempt to arrange herself into a more formal or flattering pose, indeed she is not bothered to pose at all and moves as she pleases. Adrian draws freely: a series of small, rough sketches, attempting to capture the curve of her spine, the swell of muscle at the back of her thigh, the line of a heel.

'Babagaleh tells me you spend time with my father.' She is sitting on the armrest of the sofa, watching him.

Adrian draws the line from Mamakay's chin to her collarbone. 'That's right.'

'What does he want?'

'To talk.'

She nods, rests her chin upon her arm and switches her gaze out over the balcony.

There had always been uncertainty in Adrian's mind about the exact nature of his relationship with Elias Cole. Elias had never identified a specific problem or asked for help. He certainly didn't seem to suffer any neuroses. A long time ago, almost from the start, Adrian had given up treating Elias as a case or even a possible case. He kept clinical notes because he felt it was the least that was required of him. Elias seemed to him to be a lonely man in search of a peaceful death. Adrian might have been priest, imam, counsellor or layman.

'What did Babagaleh say?' he asks.

'Nothing.'

'Really?'

'He's a secretive soul. He has learned to hold his counsel. Like everyone else.'

'What do you mean?'

'Have you never noticed? How nobody ever talks about anything? What happened here. The war. Before the war. It's like a secret.'

Adrian remembers his early patients, or would-be patients, their reluctance to talk about anything that had happened to them. He put it down to trauma. Since then he has grown to understand it was also part of a way of being that existed here. He had realised it gradually, perhaps fully only at this moment. It was almost as though they were afraid of becoming implicated in the circumstance of their own lives. The same is true of most of the men at the mental hospital. Questions discomfit them. Remembering, talking. Mamakay is right, it's as though the entire nation are sworn to some terrible secret. So they elect muteness, the only way of complying and resisting at the same time.

All except Elias Cole. The thought strikes him for the first time. On the paper the line of pencil lead loses its way and tapers off. All except Elias Cole. Adrian frowns, his head still bent to the paper.

Mamakay is speaking. He looks up. 'Sorry, what?'

'I asked how your drawings are.'

'Oh fine. I think. Yes, I'm quite pleased. You're easy to draw. Does that sound foolish? Perhaps it does.'

'No,' says Mamakay. 'It doesn't. Though I can't draw. My mother could draw. Plants. She was a botanist.'

'What was your home life like?'

'My parents weren't especially close, I was the go-between. I remember outings with my mother and outings with my father. I don't remember any outings with my mother *and* my father. My mother kept to herself a lot, though she would sometimes take me to collect specimens. I used to dry my own flowers, I had a little press and everything. But I didn't like the way the pressed flowers looked, the colour and life all gone from them. My father, he took me to Sunday school and told me stories, he talked to me about history.'

'Is that why you chose history?'

'Yes. When I was older I was allowed to help with his research, fetching books from the library and marking the relevant pages. It made me feel very important. He took me to the archives at the university. We would discuss subjects, whatever he was writing about. I guess I wanted to please him. As little girls do.'

'But you never finished your degree.'

'No.'

Adrian waits for Mamakay to continue, but she does not. For the second time Adrian has a sense of something unspoken. Mamakay breaks her pose and stands up to lean over the balcony. It occurs to him that he has barely ever seen her at the hospital. Only that once, talking with Babagaleh. He's never seen her visit her father, though imagines she must do. She turns to face him, her back to the light. He cannot read her expression.

'It's midday,' she says. 'We're free.'

CHAPTER 40

In the sack carried over his shoulder he had a loaf of stale bread, some onions, a piece of meat wrapped in paper. A man stopped and asked him for food, Kai shook his head, but the man persisted, and reached out to touch Kai. The touch made Kai angry. He knocked the man's hand away. But the man would not be deterred and touched him again. Kai turned around to confront him and saw it was the soldier from the hospital, unmistakable from the nature of his injury. Part of the man's face was missing, most of the lower jaw had been blasted away, leaving the roof of his mouth and teeth exposed. He was in the country serving with the foreign task force. Kai had found him sitting on the floor of the hospital corridor, next to a three-hour-old corpse and a pool of oily, blackened blood, lucid still and in remarkably good spirits, believing himself saved. Kai knew he was going to die.

But something was wrong. What was he doing here? Kai could see the huge tongue flapping obscenely as the man tried to talk to him. Kai understood he was hungry and asking for food. Kai didn't want to give him any, but the ruined face loomed in front of him. He swung the sack from his shoulder and bent to open it, but when he looked up the man was sauntering away down the road, whistling an Elvis song.

Kai began to run. Suddenly the man was behind him, following him, gaining on him in great bounds. In a moment he would catch him. Kai needed to reach Nenebah's house. But he did not want to lead the freakish man there, so he switched direction. Running was becoming hard work: to make his legs move required every fibre of his being. Despite himself he was slowing. He felt the man gaining on him. And there ahead of them both, the bridge road, long and empty. The man had overtaken him and was running straight for it. Stop! Kai wanted to shout. The man kept on going, Kai behind him. They were on the bridge now. Kai could not see to the end, only the soldier ahead of him. The bridge began to break up, he couldn't keep his footing. He felt himself falling. He opened his mouth to scream, but the force of the wind knocked the air out of his lungs.

He wakes with a start. He is sitting on a chair in the staff room. Around the coffee table three doctors and a nurse are talking between themselves. At the computer Seligmann works and whistles 'Love me Tender'. Kai sits still. His breathing is heavy, his armpits damp. Sweat trickles down his neck. He looks to see if he has been observed, but his other colleagues continue talking between themselves. He waits another minute, then goes to the bathroom and splashes water on his face. Cupping his hand under the tap he drinks. He looks at his face in the mirror and thinks of Nenebah.

Throughout the second invasion he had acted as a lifeline to the household. As a doctor he was given transport and protection. He used his influence to acquire small amounts of food. The city was split into two, one side under rebel control, the other side under the control of the government troops and task force. A bridge divided the city, though not the one from his dream. This one spanned the east of the city to the west. The besieged residents of the west were trapped by the rebel army on one side, the sea and mountains on the other side.

Kai leaves the staff room and crosses the quad towards Adrian's apartment. A light rain is falling, dampening the heat. He has set aside this afternoon to advance his application to work in the US. Despite Tejani's assurances the quantity of paperwork is daunting. References, certified copies of his degree and other medical qualifications, his birth certificate. The records offices in town had been looted and burned, adding to the challenge. He is also required to undergo a full medical. This should be easy enough to arrange, except that Kai hasn't yet told anyone at the hospital of his plans. The same goes for references. Who should he ask? Seligmann? To do so would seem like a betrayal.

He ponders matters as he walks down the corridor towards the flat.

At home two evenings ago, Kai had been sitting studying some of the forms. Abass had come in, tired from playing, and lain, legs and arms draped across the back of the sofa, his chin resting on Kai's shoulder. From there he'd read the paper in Kai's hand and asked in a loud, enquiring voice, 'What's the Department of Immigration?'

Kai felt his cousin's quick glance as she looked up from her book.

'Do you know how rude it is to read over another person's shoulder?' he said to Abass. Placing the papers face down on the coffee table, he hauled the child off the back of the sofa and began to tickle him, felt his cousin's covert gaze upon them both.

Inside the empty apartment Kai sits on the cane sofa and places the envelope of papers before him. He fetches himself a glass of water from the kitchen, sorts the papers into a single pile and begins to read through them. For ten minutes he works in this way, before getting up to turn on the fan. The rain, as it does so often, has brought only temporary relief, clearing the clouds away only for the sun's rays to shine through more strongly. Kai hasn't seen Adrian in weeks now. Work at the mental hospital must be keeping him busy. Kai hasn't even managed to tell him of his return trip to Agnes's home town. He must do so.

In the days following the visit Kai had thought a lot about the woman's story. He didn't dwell on the more gruesome facts, for atrocities such as these were the facts of war. He'd administered to the consequences of them often enough. In Agnes's case it was the unbearable aftermath, the knowledge, and nothing to be done but to endure it. For a while Kai had dreamt even more than was usual. And though they were *his* dreams, *his* own experiences, to him they were in some way connected to Agnes.

On the table, a reference book belonging to Adrian. Kai picks it up and it falls open in the place where the spine is broken. Idly, he turns the book over to read the title. *A History of Mental Illness.* Kai returns to the text and reads, guided by Adrian's markings and annotations, at first casually and then with greater intensity:

Fugue. Characterised by sudden, unexpected travel away from home. Irresistible wandering, often coupled with subsequent amnesia. A rarely diagnosed dissociative condition in which the mind creates an alternative state. This state may be considered a place of safety, a refuge.

During his life as a surgeon Kai has seen people arrive at the hospital with terrible injuries, wounds that would seem to defy their ability to retain consciousness, let alone walk or talk.

Once during the war, he and the other hospital staff had been called outside to attend the passengers of a truck that had arrived from the provinces. The first person Kai helped down from the tailgate was a woman, both of whose hands were almost entirely severed, they flapped from her wrists like broken wings. He'd seen a man, hopping, clutching his own amputated foot in both hands. There were dozens of them, men, women, children. Some had survived for days in the

325

bush. In the theatre Kai worked harder, faster and more furiously than he had ever done in his life.

And afterwards, if you had asked any of the survivors how they had managed it, they would not have been able to tell you. It was as if those days in the forest, the escape to the city, had passed in a trance. *The mind creates an alternative state.*

Kai thinks of the conversation with Adrian here in the kitchen the evening after Adrian had been attacked by JaJa. Kai had presumed JaJa to be a common hoodlum, a drug smuggler. He'd understood little about Agnes's sickness, except what Adrian had told him. Adrian said Agnes's journeys, the kind of journeys described in the book, were made because she was looking for something.

But Agnes isn't searching for anything.

She is fleeing something. She is running away from intolerable circumstances. Escaping the house, her daughter, most of all escaping JaJa. The difference between Agnes and the injured people who arrive at the hospital is that for Agnes there is no possibility of sanctuary.

Kai replaces the book on the table. He must talk to Adrian. Adrian deserves to know. Whatever comes next, if anything, is for the future. He will wait here for Adrian.

He looks at his watch. Two-thirty. Suddenly he is exhausted. He stretches out on the sofa and within minutes is asleep. Images pass in front of his eyelids, a waste of burned buildings, of flailing limbs, sometimes Foday walking and smiling, other times people – those from the truck, without hands and feet. Balia the young nurse smiling shyly at him. In his ears the chatter of the man with his jaw missing.

There is no coherence, nothing that amounts to a nightmare. Just a record of images that float before him.

Thus he sleeps.

CHAPTER 41

Adrian makes his way to Elias Cole's room direct from his meeting with Mrs Mara. The meeting had not gone especially well. The new oxygen concentrators were held up in customs.

'He could die,' said Adrian.

'He's dying anyway,' she'd replied. 'We're talking extra weeks or months.'

Perhaps he shouldn't have pressed it but he did. Suddenly Mrs Mara stopped talking, sat down heavily and rubbed her eyelids. Adrian felt like a bully.

Now memories of his last conversation with Mamakay reverberate as he crosses the courtyard. Here in the land of the mute, Elias Cole has elected to talk. It has never occurred to Adrian to ask why, just as he never questions the presence of a patient in his office, only asks how he might be able to help them. The difference between Elias Cole and the men at the mental hospital, as well as those early patients Adrian saw, is that Cole is educated. The more education a person has received, the more capable of articulating their experiences they are. Also of intellectualising them, of course. Those with less education tend to express their conflicts physically through violence or psychosomatically: deafness, blindness, muteness, paralysis, hallucinations – visual and olfactory. Adecali's roasting meat.

It isn't considered acceptable to talk about these differences outside psychiatric circles, but this is the fact of the matter. In Adrian's opinion the second category of patients are much more straightforward to treat; the first hold the interesting challenges. He steps into Elias Cole's room.

'How are you?'

'I am exactly as you see me,' says Elias Cole. 'Surviving.' He coughs and spits into a handkerchief. 'I apologise about last week. The doctors feel I have been straining myself. They tell me I should try not to talk.' He gives a colourless laugh. 'I sent Babagaleh with a message, but he was unable to find you.' He looks at Adrian, who feels a spasm of guilt. He wonders what Elias Cole knows, whether there is anything contained in his look.

'I'm sorry,' he replies. 'When I'm not here I'm generally at the mental hospital.'

'Ah! And how are the inmates? I hope you are bringing them peace.'

'It's interesting you should say that. Is peace what you'd like for yourself?'

That look again. What does it hold, exactly? Mamakay has inherited it, though in her it appears more amused, less calculated. Adrian doesn't entirely expect Cole to answer, but then the old man says, 'I told you once there were two endings to this story: we are but waiting for the third.'

★

My promotion to the position of Dean coincided with our move away from the campus. There was no doubt things had changed. The campus was not the place it had once been. There were troublemakers among the student fraternity. As it happened I had done well enough over the years to build a house, an ambition I had nurtured for some time.

The new house was in the west of the city. I had the good fortune to be able to buy several town lots together and the house boasted a sizeable garden. After years on campus where the grounds were taken care of by a team of workers, Saffia had her own garden again. She set to work terracing the land, planting an orchard towards the rear, lawns and formal beds at the front.

As for me, my work at the university kept me occupied. The Dean had been promoted to the position of Vice Chancellor. There were shortages and frequent power cuts. There were strikes and petitions – the young by then so different from my day. They seemed to think we could magic light out of the darkness and were convinced they must find somebody to blame.

We had been married for twenty-one years and lived in our new house for four.

It doesn't make me proud to tell you I was elsewhere that day. So it happened that Babagaleh was first to hear the news.

This is your first rainy season, so you see now how the rains behave in this part of the world. And what you see now is only the beginning. They drive across the Atlantic, and here on the edge of the continent we catch the full force of them.

Saffia had maintained her business delivering flowers to weddings and suchlike. Not many people marry during the rains, most people prefer the end of Ramadan, depending on when it falls, or Christmas. Sometimes, though, it happens. A couple may have their own reasons.

Even now I can see Saffia standing in the driveway in the mornings while Babagaleh loaded pots into the back of the car. She had never sold the Variant, which she retained for her own use. That day she had a delivery, a wedding party up in Hill Station. I can't remember whether I knew this or not. It is as likely I didn't.

The road from our house up to Hill Station is one most new visitors generally find unnerving to drive. A railway line was cut into the hillside once. It had a narrow gauge with a single carriage hauled up the steep track by the engine. When the road to replace the railway was laid the dimensions were retained, though the traffic now moved in two directions. Nobody ever thought to put a guard rail in place. During the rains the water pours off the hillside, carrying mud and rocks on to the road.

She had delivered the flowers successfully, as far as I later understood, and was on her way home, driving a twenty-year-old car. No other vehicle was involved, according to the police. Nobody else was hurt. The sole witness, the driver of the car following, said she had edged over to make way for an army truck coming in the other direction. It seems she misjudged the depth of the curve. Doubtless the rain reduced visibility, made the road all the harder to navigate, for Saffia was an excellent driver. The car rolled thirty yards down the hill. No seat belt, I don't believe the Variant was even fitted with them. She suffered little in the way of injuries; her neck, though, was snapped.

The police would not come out during the rains. One of the occupants of the huts nearby recognised the car. He sent his son to our house and found Babagaleh. She was gone already by then. Impossible to move the body during the downpour. Babagaleh hurried up to the campus. I was not there. Instead he happened upon my daughter. She knew, just by his appearance on campus, something dreadful must have occurred.

Later Babagaleh brought the news to me. Somehow he knew where to find me. I have no idea how.

★   ★   ★

He stops speaking, turns his head on the pillow.

'Pass me that, please.' He stretches out a hand.

Adrian rises and picks up a framed photograph. He is about to hand it to Elias Cole.

'No, I meant for you.'

Adrian looks at the photograph expecting to see a picture of Saffia. Instead he finds himself looking at a photograph of Mamakay, taken when she must have been about sixteen. She is looking at the camera slightly askance; behind the look of youthful defiance in her eyes, the same look of detached appraisal she still wears on occasion. She leans into the back of her chair, her body is turned away from the photographer, though her gaze is directed towards him. Her elbow rests on the edge of the seat, the stiff cloth of her gown rises unevenly at one shoulder and slips from the other. A narrow necklace follows the contours of her collarbone and disappears behind the neckline of her dress. Her hair is caught in a heavy and elaborately knotted headdress in a print that matches her dress. She doesn't smile and evident between her eyebrows is the faint smudge of a frown. Yet Adrian sees nothing stern in her expression. Rather she seems to be assessing the situation, contemplating the camera, and through its lens those who might observe her in the future. Her expression suggests compliance more than participation with the act of being photographed. Seeing her thus, so unexpectedly, leaves Adrian momentarily disorientated. He pulls himself up short and replaces the photograph.

'She had wanted to be a historian. After that day she lost faith in me. At first I thought she was mourning her mother, but a distance opened up between us and was never again bridged. She was of that age, no longer a child, yet still a child. Somehow she found out. People gossip, impossible to stop them.' He closes his eyes. 'Impossible. I had my enemies, they must have delighted in it.'

Outside the sun has almost set. The rains have cleared and the colours of the earth have suffused the sky with a deep red. The skeletons of the two kites flutter on the razor wire. Outside somebody is walking down the corridor; the sound of their footsteps mounts and then recedes down the hall.

Adrian says, 'I'm not sure I understand.'

The old man sighs. 'Babagaleh knew where to find me. Don't you see? I expect he must have known all along. Perhaps Saffia knew too, who knows?'

'Where were you?'

'I was with my mistress.'

Adrian covers his surprise.

'Yes, my mistress. From the fourth year of my marriage to Saffia I had kept a mistress. Always the same one, in that respect I was loyal. You must understand . . . no, I would *like* you to understand, she gave me something Saffia never did. With her I did not feel wanting, second-best. All very banal, I'm sure. Believe me, I was aware of it at the time. It made no difference.'

'And you were at her home at the time of Saffia's car accident?'

'With Vanessa, yes.'

CHAPTER 42

The heavy air holds the last note of the clarinet as she crosses the patio. Adrian has half risen from his seat when she drops into the chair next to him, picks up the bottle of beer and raises it to her lips. Her dress is damp, her face and neck wet. He kisses her cheek, a taste of salt and sweet.

She puts the bottle down and gasps, like a child. 'How was it? Could you hear properly?'

'Absolutely. It was great.'

She nods and adds, 'Except the duff note halfway through.'

'It was fine,' says Adrian, who wouldn't know.

'It was so-so.'

People pass by the table. Mamakay high fives with one of the other band members and the man slips into the seat next to her. They converse for a few moments about music, in language opaque to Adrian.

During the course of the day Adrian has thought of little else except his conversation with Elias Cole, until Mamakay stepped out on to the stage and began to play. He takes a sip of his beer. Mamakay has almost finished hers. He holds up a hand for two more.

Elias Cole had been asking him to help. He didn't know, at least Adrian was fairly certain he didn't know, about Adrian and Mamakay. So in that sense it was not a direct request and Adrian could yet ignore it. Nor is it in any way his professional responsibility. At the same time it is not in his nature to shirk what ought to be done, for he was raised otherwise and now it is embedded in his character. And there is Mamakay. Elias Cole is her father. Elias Cole is dying. Adrian takes a swallow of beer. He watches the people in the club, the people still standing on the dance floor in the wake of the performance, a waiter in oversize shoes crossing the floor with a large tray of drinks, the bare-shouldered hookers at the bar, Mamakay talking to her friend. He watches the way her hands and fingers fly and flutter, the same way she plays the clarinet. He remarked upon it once and she told him it was a mark of poor technique. She is never detained by fantasy, only the escape provided by her music.

Last night, when the moon was less full than it is now, he watched her sleeping. He watched the movement behind her eyelids and knew she was dreaming. He wanted to wake her up, just to ask her if she was dreaming of him.

He loves her. Last night he would have told her so. He would tell her now, but he mustn't. It is too difficult, too complicated. There is home. There is Lisa. There is Kate. Oh, God. Kate. He mustn't think it. He looks away from Mamakay towards the sea, out into the blackness. Behind the noise and music comes the sound of the waves on the shore, like shattering crystals.

And because he wants to talk about her, about the two of them, but most of all about love, instead Adrian talks to Mamakay about her father.

Walking down the darkened beach. Behind them the Ocean Club is slowly emptying of people. Adrian relates the conversation of earlier in the day, while he sat at the old man's bed, does so as accurately as he can, careful to choose the right words. Not everything, just that which concerns her. When he is finished they walk on. Silence, softly punctuated by the sound of their steps, the faint squeak of wet sand. He turns to see her profile traced in moonlight.

'He'd like to talk to you, I'm sure.'

Mamakay doesn't reply. Adrian waits through her silence. No sound save the sound of the surf, the occasional sweep of a car on the beach road. Ahead of them a sparse constellation of lights marks the peninsula. Presently they reach a beach bar, closed and empty. There are cement tables set into the sand. She sits on one of them, tucking her legs under her.

'You don't understand about my father,' she says.

'I don't know him as well as you, no.'

She shakes her head and looks past him to the sea.

'Try me,' says Adrian. 'Tell me what I don't know.'

'OK. I'll tell you a story. I'll tell you a story about my mother and my father. Something that happened. That made me begin to understand what was going on between them. I told you I always acted as the go-between, remember? We never did anything as a family,' says Mamakay.

'I remember.'

'Well, once when I was ten or maybe eleven, my mother took me out for a treat. We went to the Red Rooster, a chicken restaurant in town. It wasn't anywhere near my birthday and I remember I asked her why we were going. She told me it was because I was such a good daughter. I didn't really believe her, a child can always tell when a parent is palming them off. Still, I didn't care. I was happy to have a treat. So we went to the Red Rooster and we ordered chicken wings and soft drinks. My mother was in a good mood, making jokes. I liked it when she was like that; it didn't happen often. Around my father she was, well, she was much more reserved.'

Mamakay stops, takes a breath and tilts her chin up at the sky. 'We'd been there half an hour or so when a friend of hers came in. It's a small city. It was even smaller then, everybody knew everybody else. You've seen how it is. And yet I'd never met this man before. I didn't recognise him from my parents' circle of friends. The Red Rooster was in the centre of town and a lot of people from the offices around used to eat there, so I thought this man worked near by. He was wearing a suit, I remember, but his hair was quite untidy and his beard untrimmed. He had a nice way about him: he spoke to me directly and treated me like a person instead of just a kid. My mother became very animated in his company; I remember I felt jealous because *I* had been enjoying his attention. They started to talk to each other and more or less forgot about me. I sulked for a bit and then it was time to go home.'

Mamakay swings her feet down from the table and walks towards the sea. Adrian follows.

'In the car on the way home my mother told me not to mention we'd been to the Red Rooster to my father. She said he'd told her not to spend money on treats, so we should make it our secret.' She shrugs. 'I said OK. I didn't really think about it again. Later, when I was older and all the girls started talking about boys, I wondered if my mother was having an affair with the man at the Red Rooster. In my head I sort of settled on that as a suitably dramatic explanation.' She laughs. 'But in time I forgot about that as well. God, I feel like a cigarette. Do you have one?'

Adrian, who doesn't smoke and didn't know she did, says, 'No. Shall we buy some?'

'Don't worry. Let's go.'

334

On the walk back along the sand Mamakay removes her sandals and allows the water to run over her feet. 'Some years went by. I must have been about fifteen. I was rummaging around my mother's sewing box. I found an old newspaper cutting. I remember it because it had been cut with pinking shears and the edges of the paper were jagged. There was a photograph and a story. I recognised the picture. It was the man we had met at the Red Rooster that day. It said he had tried to blow up the bridge over to the peninsula.'

Adrian stops walking. 'Jesus!'

'Exactly.'

'Did you ask your mother about it?'

'I did. He was an old friend from a long time ago, she said. Claimed not to remember the day at the Red Rooster. She said she hadn't seen him in years. But I knew I hadn't misremembered. The next time I went into her sewing kit, I noticed the cutting wasn't there any more.'

'What was his name? The man? Do you remember?'

'It was Conteh. Kekura Conteh.'

For a few moments Adrian is quiet. They are approaching the Ocean Club again. He says, 'Kekura was an activist. Could your mother have been involved in something?'

Mamakay laughs lightly. 'No. At least I don't imagine so. I'd guess the attack on the bridge was before we met him in the restaurant. Even though there was no date on the cutting, it looked really old. The paper had started to colour and the ends roll over. Maybe they really were just friends. The point is that when we came home from the Red Rooster she told me not to tell my father. I thought, or at least I fancied, it was because she thought my father would be jealous. But that wasn't the reason at all.'

'What was it?'

She turns to Adrian. 'She wanted to keep it a secret because she didn't trust him. Don't you see? My mother didn't trust my father.'

They are back at the Ocean Club. Mamakay sits at a table, her chin in her hand, fingers covering her mouth. The place is empty. The owner brings over two bottles of beer and waves at them to take their time.

Adrian says, 'Are you sure you're reading that right? As you say, children can place different interpretations on things. There could be another explanation.'

'OK. Something else happened,' she says. 'Years later, some months after my mother died. There'd been protests on campus. The students were growing tired of the authorities. It was happening everywhere, but the campus was the centre of it all. There were constant power cuts at one time, we were all trying to revise for exams. A group of students got a petition together to demand the Vice Chancellor's resignation. I signed the petition along with everybody else. I had an exam the day they marched to his office and handed it in, otherwise I would have been there.'

She's not looking at Adrian. Her gaze, unfocused, rests somewhere upon the table amid the beer mats and cigarette burns.

'After the exams the students celebrated. There were parties on campus every night, it was the end of the academic year. All my friends were living in hall, except me. I stayed at home to keep my father company that term. The last evening my father called me and told me I was not to go up to the campus that night. He didn't say why. Instead he said a lot of things. I was out too much. I was out with the wrong crowd. There was talk about me. I was angry and shouted at him. There was talk about him too, I said. About him and a woman called Vanessa.'

Adrian glances at Mamakay.

She catches his look. 'Oh yes. I knew about Vanessa. I'd known for a long time. I went up to my room and stayed there. I told myself my father was being unreasonable. The strange thing was that if anything he had a tendency to spoil me. After a while I went back downstairs and found him in his study. He wasn't doing anything, just sitting there behind his desk. I felt sorry for him. I thought perhaps he was thinking about my mother, as I was. I sat on the floor and put my head on his lap. He just laid his hand on my hair.'

Silence again. She does not lift her gaze from the table, but presses her fingers against her bottom lip. When she speaks her voice is low with controlled emotion.

'That was the night security forces raided the campus. They attacked the students. A lot of people were hurt. They went through the halls of residence. Twelve students were arrested. Most of them were the ones who had organised the petition. They were expelled and we never saw them again. All of them had been at the party I'd been invited to in one of the fraternity houses. They said it was the first place the police went. Afterwards they forced their way into the dorms. By then the students knew what was happening; some of the male students tried to barricade the doors and to fight back. You can imagine what they did to them . . .'

There she stops, except for one last sentence. 'They were my friends.'

'You dropped out after that.'

'Yes. I dropped out. I was ashamed.'

She calls the owner and asks for a cigarette. He offers her one from his own pack. She takes it and lights it inexpertly, inhales two or three times. Neither of them speak. As she stubs the cigarette out half smoked, she lifts her eyes to him. 'So you see there are things about him you don't know.'

CHAPTER 43

Seligmann has gone for the afternoon, an appointment at the Ministry. Little chance he'll be back before the day is through, which leaves Kai working alone in the operating theatre with an anaesthetist. Next door Mrs Goma is performing an amputation with quiet efficiency and power tools. The theatre nurse divides her time between the two surgeons.

Kai sits on a stool, bent to his task, music playing on the theatre CD player. When next he looks up at the clock he realises an hour has passed.

Today he feels good. Today he feels in control. Last night, alone in Adrian's apartment, he'd slept for four hours, worked six, and miraculously slept another six. No sign of Adrian, Kai had breakfasted in the staff canteen before going to emergency to deal with the first of the day's cases. Together he and Seligmann took care of the usual cooking-fire burns and hernias, more interestingly a newborn with an imperforate anus. After that, not much. Seligmann headed into town, Mrs Goma came in to perform the removal of a gangrenous limb scheduled from early morning. Kai had offered his help, but she waved him away. It was a routine operation and she, like him, seemed to enjoy moments of solitude in the theatre. So Kai fetched himself a coffee and carried it down to the surgeons' room, where he sat writing up notes. He'd only just begun when the call came for a surgeon to report to emergency.

The woman, partially anaesthetised, was sitting on one of the beds. Her eyes rolled back into her skull, she'd looked on the point of passing out. An odour of ammonia and sweat rose from her. Kai removed the swaddling from her right hand to find her wrist slit so deeply as to sever all the tendons of her fingers, with the possible exception of her thumb. With Mrs Goma busy and Seligmann away Kai had begun the procedure to reattach the tendons on his own. It is a job for a microsurgeon, but there are no microsurgeons on the staff or in any other hospital in the country. Today Kai is this woman's

338

best chance. It's proving tricky – locating the ends of the tendons from where they have receded into the wrist, pulling them down, maintaining sufficient tension until he can connect the two ends. He is patient. Still, if Seligmann were to come back from the Ministry early, thinks Kai, it would be to the good.

He looks up at the anaesthetist, sitting bolt upright and wide-eyed on her stool, the telltale look of a person fighting the urge to sleep.

'What happened to her? Do we know?'

At the sound of his voice she jerks slightly and shakes her head. Kai swivels around to read her admission notes, moving the paper with his elbow. *Possible suicide attempt.* He recognises the handwriting as belonging to one of the Swedish doctors, or is he Dutch? He turns back and searches for the end of another tendon amid the flesh of the woman's wrist. There it is, narrow and pale. Not once in Kai's career has he treated a would-be suicide, or even heard of one. He'll refer her to Adrian. These last few weeks, Kai has barely caught a glimpse of him.

From Adrian his mind wanders to thoughts of Tejani. A matter of months now before he would see his old friend again. Rather than anticipation, the thought arrives with a flush of trepidation. Kai feels his heart deliver one extra, uneasy beat. Only a few weeks ago he'd felt the weight of the yoke every time he stepped down from the *poda poda*, walked past the line of people waiting to be seen and into the hospital building. Now he feels anxiety at the thought of leaving it behind. He tries to imagine the journey, the arrival, Tejani and Helena's home. He lets his mind move forward, in a way he does not usually let himself do, to some unnamed future in an unnamed hospital. He imagines wide, white floors, shining lights, hushed movement. The faces of the people remain featureless.

With the forceps he pulls at the end of a tendon. The forefinger of the woman unconscious upon the table moves as though beckoning to him.

'Hold this,' he says to the anaesthetist.

He wonders if Tejani has ever attempted such an operation. He goes to the door and looks through the glass panel. The lower half of a human leg sits in a bucket on the floor. Mrs Goma is bent over, stitching a flap of folded skin over the remaining stump, neat as a hospital corner, watched by Jestina, the theatre nurse brought in to replace Mary. Kai knocks on the door and pokes his head inside.

'Mrs Goma, may I borrow Jestina?'

Two hours later and Kai has done his best. The woman will never play the piano, but she might wash and dress herself. Kai leaves the theatre through the swing doors. Up in emergency all is quiet. He passes Mrs Mara's office. He should speak to her, tell her his plans, put things in motion. Outside the door he hesitates. He can hear her speaking on the telephone, calling for her assistant. A moment later Mrs Mara opens the door. How much older she looks, he thinks. She smiles. Kai is one of her favourites, he knows.

'Hello. What are you doing there? Did you want to speak to me?'

'No worries. It can wait.'

'No, come on in.'

'It might take a bit of time. I'll come back later.'

Mrs Mara smiles again. 'OK. By the way, if you see Alex, tell him I'm looking for him.'

'Will do.' He smiles back at her, feeling like a hypocrite.

After lunch in the staff room a game of boules is under way. As Kai opens the door a silver ball rolls across the black-and-white tiles towards him. Kai steps backwards. The ball comes to a full stop. One of the medics, a short man with a bald head, darts forward and measures the distance between two balls using his thumb and forefinger, and whoops. Kai never joins in these games, played mostly between the overseas staff. Today he thinks how pleasant it might be. He feels energised by the morning's work. For a few minutes he sits, watches the silver balls rolling across the floor, gently knocking each other. There are things he could be doing: notes, correspondence. But Kai is in no mood for paperwork. He decides to take a turn around the hospital. Check in with emergency to see if there's anything new. Maybe he'll call in on Foday, purely for a social visit.

Outside the sun shines between silvered black clouds. The air is hot, vibrating with the electricity of distant storms. Beneath the corrugated-iron shelter that passes as a waiting area, a dozen pairs of eyes follow his approach. Kai can sense the anticipation grow with his every pace, the collective deflation as he moves beyond them without calling a name or pointing at a patient to follow him. He heads up the ramp to the building when a man runs up behind him.

'Yes, sir, Doctor!'

Kai turns.

'You are Dr Mansaray, yes?'

Kai nods. 'How can I help you?'

The man, a slim, well-spoken Fula, says, 'They told me you attended to my wife this morning. She had injured her hand.'

'Yes,' says Kai. 'She'll be on the ward now. It went well. In fact' – he looks briefly at his watch, then at the doors to the emergency department – 'we can go along now and see how she's doing. Come with me.'

Together they make their way along the covered walkways. Kai explains how the operation went, the best that could be expected. Possessed of no expectations of his own, the husband nods and thanks him again. Remembering the note on the woman's history, Kai asks, 'What happened?'

'It was my fault, Doctor. My wife was very angry with her niece. She wanted to slap her. But I held on to her. Then my wife's niece took this opportunity to say some bad things. My wife tried to break free from me and I let her go. This was my mistake. She went forward too fast and her hand broke the window.'

It figures. An injury on such a scale would be hard to self-inflict. And Kai has never once treated a would-be suicide. War had the effect of encouraging people to try to stay alive. Poverty, too. Survival was simply too hard-won to be given up lightly. Perhaps the Swedish doctor imagines himself trying to end it all if he lived here. No need therefore to refer her to Adrian, which in some ways is a shame.

But Kai still needs to talk to Adrian. As soon as he's finished with the woman and her husband, he'll go to the apartment and, if Adrian isn't there, this time he'll leave a note. A drop of rain touches his arm. He quickens his pace.

Several hours pass before Kai reaches Adrian's apartment. The sky is reflected in discs of water across the courtyard. The waiting patients have gone home, to return another day. The building is quiet, even the children's ward, where it is time for the afternoon nap. Kai passes it, deep in thought. He could take the opportunity to go and see Mrs Mara, though it can wait until another day. If Adrian is there perhaps Kai will suggest a beer someplace. It's a long time since he relaxed. He'd like to talk to someone about his plans and there's no one else to talk to. Not Seligmann or Mrs Mara. Not his cousin. He is about to take a step that will change his life, something he has never done before. Though in the past years his life had indeed changed immeasurably, none of it had been of his own doing. He'd imagined his life differently, both of them had, he and Tejani. War had frustrated all his hopes, shut out the light. Everything had ceased. The foreigners fled, the embassies shut down, no flights landed or took off from the airport for years. The country was a plague ship set adrift.

Once, standing in an open space, he'd seen a commercial airliner pass overhead, on its way from one country to another, the sun golden upon its wings. It seemed incredible to him that there were people inside, drinking wine and eating from plastic trays, pressing a button for the hostess. Did they have any idea what was going on directly below them, a nation devouring itself? He felt like a drowning man watching a ship sail by.

And afterwards, when it was finally over, he and Tejani caught up on three years of missed movies, watched Mel Gibson in *Lethal Weapon 4*, Keanu Reeves become freed from a virtual world only to return, people discover a lost island where the dinosaurs still roamed.

How desperate they'd been to get out, they could hardly articulate it. It was never so much a feeling as a frenzy. As each one of his friends, family and classmates made it over the fence, Kai had felt pleased and bereft in equal measure. He had stayed. Nenebah had stayed. The difference between the two of them was that Nenebah, alone among their friends, family and acquaintances, never experienced the desire to leave. The more people left, the more fiercely she clung. She loved the country the way a parent loves the child who wounds them most. What happens if everyone leaves? She demanded he answer her question. She'd made him feel guilty.

So now his turn has arrived and he has never felt more conflicted. For here in this building where he barely has a moment to himself, he has never been so sure of who he is. He can walk the corridors, courtyards and wards blindfolded. Out on the streets he is recognised by his patients and he in turn recognises them. The change had occurred outside of his awareness. In this place of terrifying dreams and long nights, he knows who he is.

His rubber flip-flops suck at the wet concrete. A momentary breeze sends a shower of heavy raindrops from the branches of a tree down upon him. Kai lifts his head to the sky and feels the wind trail across his face. In his pocket he finds a mint, unwraps it and places it in his mouth.

For a moment he is as he once was, before the war, during his university years. He is back there and whole again. The hospital buildings shrink, spread and grow into different buildings with different dimensions. The trees transform into flamboyant trees, like those on the campus, with white-painted trunks. The quadrangle becomes a lawn.

He looks up, and sees her. There is Nenebah, she is walking towards him. For a moment he holds her in his gaze, her long-tailed scarf, books held to her chest. Then the present reasserts itself, the buildings resume their former shape, the concrete hardens. The woman who looks like Nenebah is still there.

The woman does not look like Nenebah. It is Nenebah.

He opens his mouth to call her name, but his voice fails him. For in the next instant he sees that the door of Adrian's apartment is open and there is Adrian, coming out after her. He sees Adrian's hand at her back, and the answer of her slight smile, he sees that they are together. He does not know how, but he knows this beyond doubt. He stands in the courtyard while the rain falls lightly on his shoulders. And he is drowning.

CHAPTER 44

'Yes please. Mr Adrian?'

Adrian turns his gaze towards Salia, suddenly aware he hasn't heard a word the man has been saying. 'Sorry. Can you repeat that?'

Salia regards Adrian for a moment, then repeats, with no hint of hurry or exasperation, what he has just said. From his other side Adrian is aware of Ileana watching him. He closes his eyes and takes a breath. With an effort of will he focuses upon the sound of Salia's voice.

An hour later the morning meeting is over. Adrian collects his papers for the group therapy session from the desk he keeps in Ileana's office. Ileana follows him, stands in the middle of the room watching him.

'Carry on ignoring me and I might throw something.'

He turns to her. 'Sorry, I'm a bit distracted.'

'Tell me about it.'

'It's nothing.'

'No,' she says. 'I don't mean you to actually tell me about it. What I said was *tell* me about it. I can see you're distracted. You OK?'

'Yes,' nods Adrian. He bends his head back to his desk, hears Ileana grunt and move away. He looks up. 'Are you free for an early lunch?'

'Sorry,' she says. 'I need to go and see my landlord about renewing the lease. Another time?'

'Sure.'

Minutes later Adrian makes his way over to the meeting room. He unlocks the door and leaves it standing ajar, moves around opening windows, lifting chairs from the stacks at the end of the room and arranging them into a circle. In his mind he returns to the events of the night a week before. Mamakay's silence in the car. His own effort not to let himself be disturbed by it, though he was for some reason, and profoundly.

In the end he'd said, 'He called you Nenebah.' The only way he could think of to get inside.

'Yes,' she'd replied, her face turned away from him.

'Is that your name then?' He sounded irritable, he knew, already the jealous lover. An image of Kai, of his bare arm and shoulder as he shrugged on a shirt.

'Yes,' she said.

'Sorry, but I don't understand.' The emotion moved so fast. He felt ridiculous. He strove for a normal tone. 'I thought your name was Mamakay.'

'Mamakay is my house name. I told you I was named after my aunt. Nenebah is my real name.' She shrugged. He hated the gesture, the indifference it projected.

'I see.' And he'd thought he knew so much about her.

It turned out he didn't even know her name.

A sound makes Adrian look up. Adecali has entered the room, wordlessly, and is helping with the chairs. Adecali is making progress, though he continues to be haunted by smells, most notably of cooked meat. Two weeks ago a trader set up outside the front gate of the hospital selling skewers of beef roasted over a charcoal fire. Ileana and Adrian had bought some for lunch, so had a few of the men who were not confined to their wards. One of them carried his portion back to a bed near Adecali. Ten minutes later Adrian was called to the ward, to find Adecali straining at his chains, blowing snot and saliva. Since that day Adrian has held several private sessions with Adecali, trying to encourage him to talk, which sometimes the young man did at an insistent babble and sometimes not at all. He was punctilious, though. Never missed a session. Small steps, steps in the sand. But in the right direction.

'Thank you, Adecali,' says Adrian.

The other patients are beginning to appear, shuffling in to take their seats one by one. Whatever scepticism there had been among the staff at the hospital about his sessions – and Adrian had overheard one or two remarks from among the attendants – the men seemed to want them. Adrian found it had soon become unnecessary to go round the wards, for like Adecali they came of their own accord. Once, held up by the traffic, he arrived late to find them all waiting for him in silence outside the locked door.

'OK,' says Adrian, when they are all seated. 'Who is going to begin today? Anyone?'

The night before Adrian had slept fitfully and woken with the sun on his face. Mamakay was already up, preparing breakfast. They sat

345

and ate in the yard. Adrian wished it was a Saturday so he didn't have to go anywhere. He wanted to talk to her. There had been no lovemaking the night before and now they ate in silence. Adrian put down his plate.

'You were close then?' he asked her. They both knew exactly what he was talking about.

'Yes, we were together when I was at university. I haven't seen him for a long time. He wanted to go abroad. It's what he always talked about.'

'He's a surgeon.' Then when she didn't say anything more, he asked, 'He was the one you told me about. The one you said you loved.'

And she'd chosen not to spare him at all, looked away and simply nodded.

Five o'clock. Something is burning outside the walls of the hospital. A smell of woodsmoke, scented like cedar, the smell that woke Adrian a night soon after his arrival, the night he'd met Kai. He'd looked out into the corridor and seen a woman give birth to a dead baby. Kai was the first person Adrian had talked to properly since his arrival; they'd become friends. That was six months ago. How much has he learned since then? Sometimes it feels like a great deal, other times not much at all. Adrian lifts his eyes to the sky for a brief moment, enters the darkened corridor and makes his way to Elias Cole's room.

In his work Adrian has met many kinds of liar: pathological liars, compulsive liars, patients with different kinds of personality disorders. Broadly speaking though, when it comes down to it, there are just two types of liar: the fantasist and the purist. The fantasists are the embroiderers. Simplest to spot because they have a tendency to contradict. A liar should have a good memory, said Quintilian. The trouble with the fantasists is that, in their eagerness to impress, they become careless about the details. The purists, as Adrian thinks of them, are of distinctly cooler temperament. Intellectually-minded, they understand the fallibility of memory, prefer to lie by omission. The silent lie that can neither be proved nor disproved. The fantasists and the purists have one thing in common, and this they share with all liars – the pathological, the compulsive, the delusional, the ones who suppress and repress unbearable memories. They all lie to protect

346

themselves, to shield their egos from the raw pain of truth. And one thing Adrian's two decades of study and practice have taught him is to discover the purpose served by the lie.

Adrian raises his fist and knocks on the door of Elias Cole's room. He cannot decide if he is in the mood for this or not. As he steps over the threshold the scent of woodsmoke disappears, to be replaced by another smell: clinical, like powdered aspirin. There is a new sound, too, a whirring. The oxygen concentrator.

'So it came at last,' he says.

Elias Cole removes the mask from his face. 'I take it as a sign of how bad things must be. People like to leave it to the end before they salve their consciences.'

How true, thinks Adrian. He sits down, crosses his legs and laces his fingers, copybook pose of the clinical psychologist. 'What did you want to talk about today? Was there anything in particular?'

The last time they had been talking about Mamakay, but Adrian would rather speak of anything now than her. To his relief Elias Cole shakes his head slowly.

'I've told you what there is to tell. Now all I want is to die in peace.'

For the first time Adrian feels a faint, cold gust of hostility towards Elias Cole. He says, 'Something that interests me.'

'Yes?'

'Why did Johnson agree to release you? After your arrest?'

Adrian sees Elias Cole shift slightly, and turn to look at him. His surprise is small but evident. 'The Dean knew Johnson. He had some way to him. That was how he was able to come and see me when I was in custody. But for him I would probably still be there to this day.' He laughs softly, abruptly.

Adrian doesn't laugh. He continues, 'The Dean asked you to cooperate . . .'

The old man interrupts. 'I told Johnson what I knew, which anyway was nothing of consequence.'

'But you said you'd already told him everything. You held nothing back.'

'I had tried. Johnson was a stubborn man. He wouldn't believe me until the Dean's intervention.'

Adrian continues, gently insistent. He has never spoken to Elias Cole this way, has taken him at his word. 'When we spoke about those events, or rather when you told me what had happened, you used a very specific word. You used the word "arrangement". The Dean said all you needed to do was come to an arrangement with Johnson.'

'Yes.'

'Repeating what you had already told Johnson doesn't quite fit the description, somehow. Surely he would have wanted something more. As you say he was a proud man. Some sign of victory would have been important.'

Elias Cole is silent. He purses his lips, turns his head away from Adrian. He lifts the plastic mask, places it over his mouth and nose and inhales. Finally he speaks. 'The Dean asked me to give Johnson my notebooks. I used to write down much of what happened. That's something I told you. They were not diaries as such, more notes to myself, aides memoires. There were times, dates, places, people's names. I kept a note of Julius's movements and Saffia's. It was something I did. There was a note of the first time I had seen him, addressing the students – although, of course, on that occasion I was sent along by the Dean. Also of the first dinner I attended at their house. The conversation when Julius proposed a toast to the first black man on the moon. The same phrase that appeared in the newspaper editorial. I think I even made a note of the music that was played. It was all there. Johnson pounced on it, of course.'

'And that was the reason they released you?'

'Yes. It was the reason they released me. And the reason they held Julius, too. They thought they had something to go on. But for those notebooks he would not have been kept there for those extra days.'

'You told me you were angry with Julius – for the position you found yourself in.'

'It was a very distressing experience. You've never been in such a situation: what would you know?'

Adrian is silent, his fingers on his lips, regarding Elias Cole.

Elias Cole averts his gaze, looks to the blank wall. He says with bitterness, 'Julius acted as though he was my friend. All the times he would stop by my office, take me for a drive. We went gambling together. They borrowed my office, my typewriter. And he never trusted me enough to tell me.'

'He betrayed you?'

'Exactly.'

'But you were betraying him.'

So fast it comes straight off the back of Adrian's words, the old man snaps, 'Julius's betrayal of me was far greater.'

Mamakay stands up and moves several paces across the verandah. Barefoot, soundless. She picks up the clarinet, places her fingers across the keys. Moonlight reflects upon the polished surface of the silver. She is wearing a sarong twisted and tied around her neck. She replaces the clarinet and comes back to where Adrian is sitting. Her face is drawn and thoughtful, she pulls gently at her lower lip contemplating all that he has told her. A moment later she stands up again. Adrian waits.

He has taken the risk of repeating the afternoon's conversation with Elias Cole, the admission which he sees as a small breakthrough. Whether he cares to admit it to himself or not, he wants to stir her. He wants to find a way under her skin. He wants to make her think about him and nobody else, to show her what he can do. He wants to matter.

She disappears downstairs and comes back with two beers, hands him one.

'That man, Johnson.' She is silent, resting the bottle against her forehead, her eyes closed. For a minute she remains that way, then she looks up, directly into Adrian's eyes, wags a finger twice in the air. 'My mother.' She stands up and walks to the railing, turns around to face him. 'How can I describe my mother to you? She was an extremely composed woman to the point it seemed she was holding something back. It upset me when I was older, after I found out about Vanessa, she had never once confronted him.

'One day, when I was quite young, we were in town. It was a Saturday. My mother would go to the supermarket, the dressmaker, the covered market for vegetables and meat. She'd take me along to help carry things and keep her company. This one time we had just come out of the supermarket in town – down where all the money changers are nowadays, that was where the supermarket used to be. We were leaving when a man came in. He spoke to my mother, said hello to her, he even used her name. And she cut him dead. It was the first time I had ever seen my mother be so rude. I was astonished. I felt sorry for him. We walked straight past him. I turned back and saw him standing there, his wire basket in his hand. Thin as a bird, in his black suit.'

She sits down and picks up a leaf of paper lying on the small table, begins to fold it, an occasional habit of hers. Adrian has seen it before. He watches her now. She is folding and refolding the paper, fashioning something which she pulls apart before it is completed.

'Eight or nine years later, just after my mother died, the same man came to our house. My father asked me to bring a bottle of whisky to the study. You know how I knew he was somebody important? Because I carried through the Red Label and my father made a big show of sending me back to fetch the Black Label. It was him, I'm sure. This man's name was Johnson. He was there a few days before the trouble on the campus, and he was there again a few days afterwards.' She continues slowly, 'Johnson must have been a part of it. I told my father who was going to the party. My father told Johnson. My father used me to betray my friends.'

Adrian is looking at the piece of paper, half folded, discarded. What is it meant to be? A house? A bird? Where did she learn to do origami? It could only be from Kai. 'You can't be sure.' He is distracted. It's the wrong thing to say.

Mamakay turns to face him fully. Her voice is harsh. 'Do you know what it took to survive in a place like this, where everyone was watched all the time, when you never had any idea who your friends were? Waiting to see who would be next.'

Adrian stands up and moves towards her; he wants to take her in his arms. 'I imagine it took great courage,' he says.

She moves away, as though his touch would burn her. From the other side of the verandah she looks at him and laughs humourlessly. 'Oh of course, the new orthodoxy. Everyone's a victim now. It's official. But you see, that's where you're wrong, Adrian. Courage is not what it took to survive. Quite the opposite! You had to be a coward to survive. To make sure you never raised your head above the parapet, never questioned, never said anything that might get you into trouble.'

'I see what you're saying. But still, they could have got the information from somewhere else.'

She turns to look at him, a pitiless look he has never seen before. 'Everyone talks about they. Them. But who is *they*? Who are *they*? People like Johnson? Paid to do the things they do? Or the people who help them along, who keep their mouths shut and look the other way? My father survived. No, he didn't just survive, he thrived! And there came a point' – she takes a deep breath, wraps her arms around herself and half turns away – 'there came a point I had to ask myself, how could that be?'

With the tips of his fingers Adrian kneads his brow and sighs. This is not what he wanted, to argue. Mamakay continues. 'Sometimes I think this country is like a garden. Only it is a garden where somebody has pulled out all the flowers and trees and the birds and insects have all left, everything of beauty. Instead the weeds and poisonous plants have taken over.'

Adrian is silent for a moment and so is Mamakay. Then he says tiredly, 'I'm a psychologist. It's not my place to make moral judgements. I heal sick minds, or at least I try to. What I don't do is judge them.' He intends his words to calm her, to signal a retreat.

'Who was it who said "History will be kind to me, for I intend to write it"?'

'Churchill,' says Adrian. 'Winston Churchill.'

'He's using you to write his own version of history, don't you see? And it's happening all over the country. People are blotting out what happened, fiddling with the truth, creating their own version of events to fill in the blanks. A version of the truth which puts them in a good light, that wipes out whatever they did or failed to do and makes certain none of them will be blamed. My father has you to help him. You're just a mirror he can hold up to reflect a version of himself and events. The same lie he's telling himself and everyone else. And they're all doing it. Whatever you say, you will go away from here, you will publish your papers and give talks, and every time you do you will make their version of events the more real, until it becomes indelible.'

And in Mamakay's words Adrian hears the echo of his own thoughts of earlier in the day, only differently stated. The silent lie.

Past midnight Adrian lies with Mamakay in his arms. They have made love not once but twice. He is grateful. Her anger is finally gone. It is too hot to be so close to another human body and yet he will not let go. Only when it becomes unbearable does she finally break free, roll on to her back and say, 'There is something I need to tell you.' She never whispers, not even in the dark. 'I am going to have a child.'

CHAPTER 45

'Worked for Byron,' says Seligmann. 'Nothing women love more than a limp. Brings out their maternal side. What do you say we just fix the one? Leave the other. He'll thank us. Find a wife faster than he can run.'

With his leave due, Seligmann is uplifted. A whole month at home by the end of which Kai knows he will be bored and fractious as a toddler. Seligmann's contract with the hospital has just been extended, too. Kai knows the reason why, even though Seligmann still does not.

'What do you say, Jestina?' Seligmann wiggles his eyebrows and winks at the new nurse over the top of his mask.

Jestina giggles through her mask and stares at her toes.

'A club foot, it's a high road to fame and fortune,' continues Seligmann. 'Emperor Claudius, Dudley Moore.'

'Goebbels,' says Kai.

Foday lies between them on the operating table, his entire body swaddled in green surgical cloth, his left calf and foot exposed. Seligmann flexes the foot this way and that, gives each toe an experimental pull. He turns around to gaze at the X-rays on the board and then bends down to peer closely at Foday's foot.

'This could take a little time. We'll fix that knee now, as we agreed. And get the big tendon done. That should be straightforward enough. Then go inside the foot and loosen off some of those ligaments. If we need to play around any more we can do that when we begin on the other one. That's a few months away, at any rate.' He tickles the underside of Foday's foot. 'No giggles? Good. Dreaming of angels. Houston, we have lift-off!' And he slips his scalpel through Foday's skin.

Mrs Mara took the news of Kai's leaving better than Kai dared to imagine. She wished Kai luck with his future career and told him she never expected to hold on to him, only hoped that she would, and finally promised to help in any way she could with his application. It had been that bad.

Her short-term solution was to approach Seligmann and ask him to stay for another six months, in which way she'd averted an immediate staffing disaster. But Seligmann is in his seventies, long retired, working for the love of orthopaedic surgery. He can't stay on for ever.

Two and a half hours later they have completed work on the knee and the Achilles tendon. The real work would begin in physiotherapy, of which Foday has months ahead of him. Seligmann whistles Elvis's 'Love Me Tender' as he leans forward and inspects the inside of Foday's foot. 'Hello,' he says. 'What do you say we try switching these two tendons around?'

Kai nods. The day is coming soon when he will have to tell Seligmann that he plans to leave. Seligmann, who loves his work here almost as much as he loves his own wife.

Late in the afternoon Kai climbs the hill in the garden of the old house. He needs to call his parents, see what they want to do, whether rent it out or board it up. So far there have been no thieves, not counting the looters during the first invasion when his parents still lived there. This time he notices a broken window at the back of the house. And it looks like people have been climbing the wall of the garden – to collect firewood and fruit from the trees, very likely. The garden is overrun. The grass has grown so high as to obscure the fact of the terraces. It reaches halfway up the trunks of the candelabra trees. Kai pushes his way towards the verandah, swings himself up and over the low railings. Coming straight from the hospital he has no key. He wanders around the side of the house. At the corner he stops. There are scorch marks on the marble floor. An empty Peak Milk tin rolls in and out of a corner. The big metal kitchen door stands ajar. Silently he moves forward and enters the kitchen. There is the cooker. The fridge is gone. Old newspapers and plastic bags fill the sink. Kai tries a tap, nothing. Idly he tries a light switch, and is amazed when the bulb flickers on.

The house smells of mildew and dust. The door of the master bedroom is missing. Inside the bedroom a mattress lies on the floor, a great scorch mark like a black petalled flower at its centre. Kai tries the drawers of the dresser. For the most part they are empty; inside one he finds an old prescription and in another a single gold earring in the shape of a swallow. He recognises it as belonging to his mother and puts it in his pocket. He checks the bathroom and then the other rooms one by one.

For several months after his parents' departure Kai had stayed on in the empty house, alone with a three-piece suite and a television, the only items of furniture he hadn't given away. He passes the room where his sister used to sleep. The room at the end of the corridor is where he spent most of his growing years. He'd left behind a full set of *Encyclopaedia Britannica*, purchased by his father by mail order and appropriated by Kai, moved from the family room into his bedroom. What innocence, he thinks, in the idea that the sum of human knowledge could be held in twenty bound volumes.

When Kai had spoken to his sister by telephone, they'd agreed to keep the news of his leaving from their parents until it was confirmed. She'd sounded serious rather than elated, had asked him if he was sure. Yes, Kai had said. Yes, he was sure. Almost telepathically she'd asked him whether he had news of Nenebah. No, Kai lied.

Nenebah. She'd looked just the same, and for a moment − the moment before she saw him − it seemed to him she looked happy. Then she had turned towards where he stood in the middle of the quadrangle, exposed, body and soul. He watched her smile vanish. They'd greeted each other with the formality of lovers whose wound is not yet healed. So unlike Nenebah, the careful solicitous voice, asking after his mother, his father and even his sister with whom she had rarely seen eye to eye.

For so long he had done everything in his power to avoid thinking about her. Gradually, without realising it, he'd let her slip back into his thoughts.

There was Adrian, standing behind her, a hand on her shoulder, looking from Kai to Nenebah and back again, the smile slowly setting on his face. What would have happened, Kai wonders, if Adrian had not been there, if they'd been alone?

He pushes at the door to the room. The first thing he notices is the smell, of sweat and stale cigarette smoke. The windows are closed, upon the bed is a nest of sheets and in the corner of the room a pair of shoes, old-fashioned men's lace-ups that once belonged to his father, cracked and polished, stuffed with newspaper. Books have been removed from the shelves and stacked upon the floor. An empty can serves as an ashtray. From a piece of wire strung from a window bar to a nail on the wall, a pair of trousers hangs. The mystery of the missing fridge is solved. Kai crosses the room and pulls hard at the door. The suction yields suddenly and audibly. The fridge is empty, the stench from inside appalling. He follows the lead to the plug lying on the floor. Then he crosses to a window and pushes it open. A sound makes him turn quickly. The bathroom door is open, where before it was closed. Somebody is watching him from the darkness.

'Who's that?' says Kai. 'Hey, you.'

He moves towards the bathroom. The face disappears. Kai reaches out for the door, but before his hand touches it a person dashes past him, knocking his arm aside. A boy. Kai snatches at his shirt, but the boy wrenches himself free and races for the door. Kai goes after him and grabs his arm.

'Hey,' he says, softly this time. 'Stop.'

For a moment the boy looks him full in the face and Kai sees something familiar in him. He relaxes his grip. The boy is motionless, his eyes never leave Kai's face. Suddenly he pulls away and makes for the door. This time Kai abandons the effort of following. He notices the boy's fingernails, his hand upon the door – fingernails painted pink. And then he is gone. Kai stands still and exhales. Now he's forgotten what he'd been doing here in the first place. Yes. He thought he might take the encyclopaedias home for Abass. But there is nothing here for Abass, or for him. As he leaves he closes the door behind him, makes his way through the house, leaving the doors open as he found them, and descends the hill to where he parked Old Faithful in the shade of an avocado tree.

On the drive back down the hill towards home Kai places the boy. The son of one of their old cooks. Kai's parents had paid his school fees for a few years, until Kai's mother sacked the father for pilfering. He stops the car and sits for several seconds with his hands on the steering wheel, then reverses up the hill. He walks into the house, to his old bedroom, plugs the fridge into the socket and switches it on. And this time when he leaves, he doesn't look back.

Kai enters his cousin's house to find himself surrounded by noise. In the middle of the room two of his aunts appear to be pleading or possibly remonstrating with his cousin. His cousin meanwhile is shaking her head, holds her hands up in front of her as though fending them off. Everybody is talking at once. Of Abass there is no sign. It takes Kai ten minutes to discover what has happened.

Abass had sworn at his mother. Now he has locked himself in his bedroom.

The word, the exact word he'd used, was sufficiently bad for his mother to propose a beating. The aunts were begging for mercy on Abass's behalf. Neither spoke English and so could have no idea of the meaning of the word, for otherwise they would most certainly have joined in the call for a beating. As it is, neither Kai nor his cousin is inclined to be the one to explain to them, and so a compromise is reached.

Kai knocks on the bedroom door and softly calls Abass's name. No answer. Kai turns the handle but the door doesn't yield. Abass has drawn the bolt on the other side.

'Abass,' he calls. 'Come and open the door.'

Silence.

'Will you let me in? Your mother wants me to talk to you.'

The sound of footsteps. Abass opens the door. He looks small and serious, worried but with an overtone of defiance. Kai slips inside the room and Abass closes the door after him and slides the bolt. They sit side by side on the bed.

'That was bad, what you called your mother.'

Abass shrugs.

'Well, wasn't it?'

Abass doesn't reply and Kai senses he has no idea of the meaning of the word for which he is now in so much trouble.

'At least you must know why you did it. Your mother asked you to help her with the church chairs and you disappeared instead. That's not good either, is it?'

Abass shrugs again. Kai exhales lightly with frustration. 'What's up, my friend?'

'All she does is go to church.'

'Who, your mother? Your mother is a Christian: that's a good thing, isn't it?'

Abass shrugs again.

Kai says, 'You don't want her to go to church?'

'I don't like them coming here. All they do is pray and pray and then take all our money. They used to come once a week. Now they come nearly every day. And I don't like them.'

Kai couldn't agree more, but it would not do to say so. Instead he asks, 'What would you like to happen instead?'

Abass shakes his head and shoves his hands between his knees.

'Well?'

The boy mumbles something, so low Kai hardly hears it. 'I want her to play with me.'

'I see.' He puts an arm around Abass. 'Well, you're getting a bit old to play, aren't you?'

'I mean stay with me . . .' He tails off.

'You want to spend more time with your mother, is that it?'

Abass nods.

'I see.' Kai looks across the top of the boy's head, across the room. There on the windowsill, the row of origami animals he has made for Abass over the years, faintly red with dust. He says, 'I think it gives your mum comfort to pray. And I think that's something we should respect, whatever we think ourselves. We must just be patient and polite, even to the preacher.' He nudges Abass lightly and the boy giggles and then grows serious.

'What does she need comfort for?'

There it is again. Soon there will be no avoiding it. Abass believes his father died a natural death and a peaceful one, which is as much as he has been told. Kai needs to talk to his cousin, to make her listen. For now he says, 'We'll talk about that another time. Meanwhile you apologise to your mother and then you and I can do something.'

Abass turns, looks at him and says, 'But you're going away, too. You're going to live in America.'

'Well, I'm not going any time soon,' replies Kai. Until now he hadn't realised quite how much Abass has been quietly working out for himself.

And only several hours later, by which time the church congregation had departed and Abass was fast asleep, does Kai realise exactly what Abass had said.

'Going away, too', without even knowing it. Abass had said 'going away, *too*'.

CHAPTER 46

In her room Ileana performs her own particular tea ceremony: silvered pot, Lipton tags, canned milk. To Adrian the teapot makes her look like a Roma.

'How far gone?' she says.

'Three months,' answers Adrian. A week has passed, a week since Mamakay told him she was pregnant with his child. He feels the responding tension in his stomach. His emotions are in the wind.

Ileana crosses the room and places the tea on the desk in front of him.

'In my professional capacity I would have to say physician, heal thyself. These things don't just happen.' She pats him lightly on the shoulder like a dog, the first time that Adrian can ever remember her touching him, evidence of the magnitude of her sympathy. 'Jesus, you've crossed the line so many times, I don't know which side of it you're on any more.'

'I know,' says Adrian, shaking his head.

Later he walks alone in the Patients' Garden. Ileana's bluntness came with wisdom. Not how but why, more importantly what would happen now. He is a man with a wife, a child, a job to go back to, a home. Beneath his feet the ground is damp with recent rain, the Patients' Garden smells of earth and moss. Rain drips from the leaves high up on to those below, musical notes. Under the heavy cloud, the garden is almost in darkness. After the months of heat and dust, Adrian still enjoys the rain, can soak it up. At night, hearing it upon the roof and during the day as he watches from his window, he marvels at its power. The rain hurls itself down with such force it seems to rage at the earth, like an angry woman throwing herself upon her lover.

He thinks of Mamakay, the equanimity with which she seems to accept the fact of her condition. From the moment they met she had appeared to expect nothing from Adrian and now it is as though what is happening to her is taking place on another plane, a higher one, from where she can see years into the future beyond the details of their liaison, towards a different horizon. She has made the greatest decision by far and by which all the others are measured, and she has made it alone. She intends to create a life. Adrian might feel grateful that she would make it so easy for him. He might, but he doesn't. Her self-possession draws him to her; there is the desire, the compulsion almost, to breach it.

He hears rather than feels the rain begin again, striking the ground around him, hitting the upper leaves of the tree. Eventually it finds its way to him. For a few minutes longer he remains seated, letting the rain soak into his cotton shirt and touch his skin.

A cigarette stub left burning in the ashtray marks Ileana's departure. Adrian crushes it out, and as he does so looks up to the board behind Ileana's desk. The coloured pins and Ileana's earring are there still, stuck into the map, tracing the journeys made by Agnes. Though Adrian regularly checks the admissions records both here and at the medical hospital, Agnes has never come back. Once Salia had gone of his own accord to the old department store to find the former doorman and obtain his promise to be informed if anything was heard or if Agnes reappeared. Since then, nothing.

Adrian takes Agnes's file and opens it, leafing through the pages to remind himself what is written there. In the short weeks he had known her he'd used his time well. The incident with the gold chain had seemed like a blessing, empirical evidence of her dissociative state. What is he to do with all this information, now rendered useless? For he lacks the crucial element, that which would bind it all together – whatever it is that impels her journeys. The thing that makes Agnes do what she does.

Babagaleh is outside Elias Cole's room; he tells Adrian the man inside is sleeping. At other times Babagaleh will enter and gently wake his master, but today he says Cole had passed a bad night. Babagaleh has placed himself in charge now, a sure sign Elias Cole is dying.

Leaving the old man's room Adrian catches sight of Kai ahead of him, recognising him even in the poor light of the corridor by his habitual flip-flops, theatre greens and T-shirt, wonders in that moment whether to call out, opens his mouth, hesitates and in his hesitation the moment is lost. Kai turns the corner and disappears.

359

From the apartment Adrian dials his home telephone number and listens to the distant ringing. He's about to replace the receiver when Lisa comes on the line, breathless. 'Hello?'

'Hello.'

'Hello, it's me.'

'Hello? Sorry, who is it?'

'It's me. Adrian.'

'Oh, hi. Sorry, I could hardly hear you. Some of the girls are round for lunch.'

'Do you want me to call back?'

'No, it's OK. They're fine. They've just opened another bottle. How is it going? When are you coming back?'

They never speak without her asking the question. Today, he can hardly bear it. Instead of answering he describes for her the new sessions. In the last he achieved something, in getting the men to remember and write down or draw – for several were illiterate – their experiences. A small triumph, but significant. He remembers back to when he first arrived, how high his expectations had been, how broad his assumptions. He'd been all wrong. So much ground needed to be laid before he could even begin to build their trust. Only now does he feel he is making progress.

'Lisa?'

A pause. 'In the cutlery drawer, Anne. Sorry. Well, that sounds all very good. They're certainly lucky to have you. I hope they realise it.'

'Thanks.'

Another small silence. He can hear her draw breath. 'Darling, I'm pleased for you, I really am. But what can you expect to achieve with these people? How many problems can one man solve in a place like that?'

He has to admire her gift for putting her finger right on top of it. He tries for flippancy and fails. 'Someone has to do it.' His words are followed by a burst of background laughter, the scrape of chairs, someone calling for Lisa.

'Well, someone doesn't have to be you,' and then, with her customary restraint, 'Let's not argue. I just hope you haven't forgotten your priorities.'

'Of course not,' Adrian replies.

When they have said goodbye he goes to the kitchen and, though it is early, pours himself a tumbler of whisky, carries it back to sit on the cane sofa. He thinks of Lisa and her girlfriends in London. Summer there now. They'd be in the conservatory. No husbands, of course. If Adrian was ever at home, he'd remove himself to his study or to sit at the bottom of the garden or else go out on some imaginary errand. He sips his whisky, presses the cool glass against his forehead. He is aware of something absent in his emotions and it takes him a moment to realise it. He does not miss home, at all.

Later he calls his mother. He pictures her in what he still thinks of as her new home: a triple-glazed bungalow by the sea, a model of architectural efficiency, free of any kind of charm and easy for her to manage on her own. A fortnight before his departure Adrian made a farewell visit. He'd arrived early and stood waiting for her at the gate, looking at the sculptures made out of jetsam and driftwood that decorated the lawn. In the distance he saw her coming towards him, a seventy-year-old beachcomber, in a corduroy jacket, her windswept hair a silver flame around her head. More masculine in manner and dress than before, as though she had shifted ground to fill the space left by his father. That day she'd been as happy as he'd seen her.

'We had such a storm here last night,' she tells him over the telephone. 'She was furious about something, my goodness.' To his mother the sea is always female, prone to womanly moods. 'Thought she would sweep us all away. What a noise! But the light this morning was quite marvellous. I counted at least six dead birds. Gulls. Two avocet. Looked like they'd been washed out of the sky. Rather picturesque in their own way; I went back and fetched my camera.'

He listens to her and for the first time realises from where his love of birds most likely comes. He'd never given it much thought. Probably she used to take him for walks and talk to him about these things. It had all stopped with his father's illness. But the memories, doubtless, had lodged in his subconscious. Suddenly he feels immensely grateful to her.

'So how are you doing out there? How's the work going?'

They talk for a while longer. She listens. At the end she says, 'Well, you keep at it. We're all very proud of you.'

And Adrian says without thinking, 'Why don't you come out and visit? It's not as crazy as it sounds. Come on. I think you'll like it. At any rate, it'll be interesting.'

'Oh, darling, what a wonderful idea. Don't you think I'm a bit old?'

'No, I don't. There are old people here, I see them every day.'

She laughs.

'Don't say no,' he tells her. 'Say you'll think about it.'

'All right, dear. I'll think about it.'

He hangs up. He realises they have never spoken about his reasons for coming here. He had taken it for granted she would understand that his connection to the place came through her. He has no idea how she actually feels about it, if she feels anything at all.

How does a man like him believe in love? A man trained to analyse the component parts of emotion. Measures of neurochemicals, of serotonin, hormones, oxytocin and vasopressin. He who would name, classify and diagnose every nuance of the human soul into attachments, complexes, conditions and disorders. There exists, somewhere, a scale for love invented by one of his profession. Others have identified the neurological reward pathways of the brain, the tripwires that mark the way to love. And there are others still who say love is but a beautiful form of madness.

Adrian does not know.

Above a moss-strewn yard, the night sky, so many, many stars. Next to him a woman lies sleeping, her head upon his thigh. The second when she passed from wakefulness to sleep he recorded as a momentary heaviness in her body, to which his own body responded with minute adjustments.

He didn't come here looking for happiness. He came here to change who he was. And in her he has found his escape, this sleeping woman, for she offers him a way out of himself, away from the person he might have become. She wandered by accident through a portal into the hollow of his heart and led him out into the light.

How does a man whose task in life is to map the emotions, their origins and their end, how does such a man believe in love?

Adrian does not know. But he believes. There it is. He believes.

Again.

CHAPTER 47

'Why do you wish to work in the United States?'

The woman at the US Embassy visa section had not looked at Kai since he entered the room, concentrating instead upon studying, at some considerable length, the letter advising him of this appointment, which he'd brought with him as instructed by the letter itself. A woman with a smoker's tired hair and skin, she peers down at the signature at the end of the letter. The signature he assumes belongs to her, Andrea Fernandez Mount.

'Well?' she says. 'What is your reason for wishing to work in the United States?'

What is the right answer?

To live the American dream.

Because it is there, like Everest. Was it Everest?

'To advance my career,' he says.

Andrea Fernandez Mount's right eyebrow lifts.

'My medical career,' he adds. 'I wish to gain clinical experience and to sit additional professional exams.'

So now she looks at him.

'Are you looking for permanent residency?'

'No.' He shakes his head. Kai has no plans ever to return, but he does not intend to say so, it isn't as if there is anything honest about this process. The Embassy official's job is to make Kai jump through certain hoops, to persuade herself that this man wants to come to her country, to live in a house like the one upon which she has just taken out a mortgage, shop in the stores where she shops and send his kids to school alongside her own. He exists to validate her dreams. Doctors are given special dispensation. Because the truth, again – only if it matters – is that they want him. But Andrea is careful not to reveal any eagerness. There are only a limited number of places each year, even for medics; this gives her a little leverage, restores a little of her authority.

Kai looks at his feet. He realises he has forgotten to change his shoes and is still wearing flip-flops. There is a smear of blood on his cuff. In the street outside the Embassy a queue of men wait for the green-card lottery. Kai had been five minutes late for the interview. They'd kept him waiting nearly forty.

'Have you brought your preliminary documentation with you?'

Kai pushes the envelope across the table. Andrea Fernandez Mount opens it and removes the contents, placing each one on the table in a row, like a detective perusing evidence. Copies of his birth certificate, passport, school certificates, medical degree, medical licence.

After a while she says, 'Fine. Somebody here will need to interview you, but there's a wait list of three months now. In the meantime you can take your medical exam and a language proficiency test. I can give you a list of Embassy-approved clinics.'

'May I undergo the medical at my own hospital?'

She glances at him briefly. 'If it's on the list. Do you know yet which state you're going to be working in?'

'I'm not sure. Maryland, I think.'

'Once you have an offer of work you'll need a state medical licence. Your employer should help you out with that. Sometimes the application can be held up waiting for the visa to come through. We can't give you a visa until you have the licence.' She shrugs. 'Catch 22, but that's the way it goes till some person fixes it. Let them know your visa is being processed. After your formal interview I'll be able to tell you more.' She pushes her chair back. 'I think we're about done here.' Quite unexpectedly she looks up and smiles warmly at him. 'You can pick these up in a week.'

Kai stands up. 'Thank you,' he says. He's been inside her office no more than five minutes.

'Let me see you out.' The meeting over, her manner seems to have changed entirely. As she walks with him to the door she says, 'Well, who knows, I might see you around. It's a small town, after all.' She extends her hand. 'Maybe you could tell me which your favourite restaurant is. It's always good to have a local recommendation when you're new to a place.'

Kai takes her hand, feels the slight pressure of her thumb on his. 'I'm sorry, I don't get to eat out much,' he replies, smiles briefly and turns away.

Out in the street, he walks past the line of men. They look at him, with the same silent yearning as the patients waiting to be seen outside the hospital, working out who he is, whether he might be in a position to help them. He sees them notice his flip-flops and turn away. Never will any of them meet Andrea Fernandez Mount.

Kai goes to Mary's for lunch, the second time they have seen each other in a month. It is early yet, the place is quiet. She spots him the moment he enters and advances towards him, manoeuvring her stomach between the tables. She reaches up to kiss him, her belly pressing against him. It feels warm, soft and at the same time resistant. He experiences a sudden urge to press his face against it.

'You look good, Mary,' he says.

'Thank you.' She is standing looking at him, her head on one side; the smile on her face is tinged with tenderness.

She knows, he thinks. She knows about Nenebah. And because he cannot bear the expression on her face, with all its pity, he says it first.

'Ah, so you already know. Well, it will be good for her.'

There is firmness to her nod. She pulls a chair out, indicates for Kai to sit opposite her and claps her hands for the girl. 'What will you have?'

'Soda water,' says Kai.

'Nothing more?'

'I'm in surgery later.'

'Bring a soda water and a Guinness. Cold.'

They are silent while the girl opens the drinks, pours them, then places the bottles on the table and leaves.

'Well,' says Mary. 'There's no such thing as going back.' She raises her glass to Kai, who clinks his against it.

'No,' says Kai. 'Keep moving, isn't that right?' He takes a deep breath.

There is to be no hiding from Mary.

'So anyway,' she says. 'Tell me your news. How come I'm getting to see so much of you?'

Perhaps he would not have told her if they hadn't spoken of Nenebah, but now he feels differently. He tells her about his decision to leave, his appointment with Andrea Fernandez Mount.

When he's finished speaking she says, 'Well, you and Tejani never stopped talking about it. Remember me to him, won't you? And since you've told me your big news, let me tell you mine.' A pause. 'I'm bringing my son back. I told my parents it is time. Enough. I want my two kids to live with me. Together. This one and that

365

one.' She pats her stomach and gives him a turned-down smile. 'So it's decided.'

Kai shakes his head. 'I'm really pleased for you. How old is he now?'

'A year the month after next. I want him back for his birthday.'

Half an hour later they say goodbye. People are beginning to arrive for lunch, Mary's distraction grows and Kai stands up to leave. Her big belly bumps him again as she moves forward to embrace him. This time he cradles it in his hand, bends his head and presses his forehead against it, straightens and kisses Mary on the cheek. 'You two take care of yourselves. I mean, you *three*.' At the door he raises his hand and drops it. She has already turned away.

October 1999. So many children born in a single month. In Kai's view Mary's capacity to forgive seems, quite simply, immeasurable. Mary's parents had taken her son away to raise in the village. Who knows how many children born in the same month in the same year are being raised all over the country like that? Children like Mary's son who have one thing in common. They were all born nine months after the rebel army invaded the city.

Friday prayers and the streets are emptied of people. No *poda podas*, no taxis. A boy passes Kai pushing a load of jelly coconuts in a child's pushchair. Kai stops him, buys one and waits while the boy hacks off the top then fashions a spoon for him out of the broken fragment. He stands scraping out pieces of coconut flesh and scooping them into his mouth, watching the people pass him on their way to the mosque. Three Fula money traders in long, pale djellebas and embroidered round hats. An elderly *haja*, white cloth wrapped around her head. A small group of office workers, heavy black shoes beneath their gowns. The boy stands watching Kai as intently as Kai watches the passers-by, as though he is watching a sideshow. The sun is beating down and Kai can feel the blood throb in the veins on his scalp.

He turns to his companion. 'You want one?'

The boy's eyes widen slightly, he nods sharply, neither speaking nor smiling, waiting to see what kind of joker Kai turns out to be. Kai hands him a coin. The boy takes it and serves himself one of his own coconuts, with all the care and delicacy he would a customer.

Somewhere, thinks Kai, there are towns and cities in a place called America. New York, Washington, San Francisco, Atlanta, Maryland.

He tries to imagine it, but this time he succeeds only in summoning images from films and advertisements. He cannot think how it will be, only that it is far away from all this.

In the final days of the invasion the rebels retreated from these streets. In their anger the residents discovered their courage and finally turned upon their oppressors. The doctors would sometimes leave the hospital to tour the city collecting corpses, issuing death certificates and stuffing the dead into the hospital mortuary. A vain effort at record-keeping, imposing order on the unruliness of war. On this street Kai had seen a young girl, lying upon the road, angled in death. Fourteen, sixteen at most. Someone had tried to remove her clothing. She lay in the street in a scarlet bra and panties, doubtless at one time looted from an upmarket boutique. The people who lived there refused Kai and his team leave to touch the body. She'd been the commanding officer in charge of the attack. They would deny her the dignity of burial. The teenage commander, in stolen, silken underwear.

Kai stares at the spot where the girl had lain. Ripples of hot air rise from the tarmac. In the mirage he sees her, the brilliance of the underwear against the dark skin. He looks away. When he looks back the road is empty. The boy is watching him. Kai hands him the unfinished coconut and walks away.

The thing to remember, he tells himself, the thing to hold on to is this: that since he decided to leave he has been sleeping at night.

'There will be a storm tonight, yes. I think so.'

Foday is the kind of patient the Western doctors complain no longer exists and for whom they yearn. He asks no questions and accepts whatever Kai tells him. Foday makes the foreign doctors nostalgic for the days before patient charters obliged them to shroud their work in secrecy and pronounce as little as possible. They like Africa. Africa is full of believers. Foday is a believer. Kai wishes Foday had a little less faith. He shifts Foday's supper tray and leans his buttocks on the window ledge.

'I know Mr Seligmann has already spoken to you, but I'm just reiterating what he said, so you're clear. We'll know more in a few weeks once the cast is off for good. You'll have it changed in the meantime, we'll shift the position of the foot so we can stretch that tendon. We'll get an idea then, and of course, an even clearer picture once you begin physiotherapy. How does the foot feel now?'

'It feels very well, thank you.'

It has something to do with gratitude, in Kai's opinion, as though admitting to pain was somehow to demonstrate ungratefulness, and that in turn might jeopardise the doctors' goodwill. The nurses seem equally to subscribe to the view that patients are undeserving, and are consequently reluctant to hand out as much as a single codeine tablet. Also because for years they'd had to guard precious supplies.

'Ask the nurse for something if you feel any discomfort.'

'I will do that, thank you.'

'Good.'

'Sometimes my leg itches,' offers Foday, as though he has alighted upon a titbit to satisfy.

'That's normal. Try not to scratch it.' Kai smiles. 'How's Zainab?'

'Oh.' Foday smiles in return. 'Zainab has written to me again. My cousin brought the letter here yesterday. Now I feel sure she likes me.'

'I'm certain she does,' says Kai.

'She says she's travelling to the city, she would like to come and visit me.'

'That's good.'

'Perhaps you would like to meet her? I'm sure she would like to meet you.'

'I can't think of anything I'd like more,' says Kai.

'Good. I am happy. And, Doctor?'

'Yes?'

'May I thank you for the radio. I'm enjoying it.'

Kai had completely forgotten about the radio.

'Yesterday I was listening to people talking about an army of soldiers made of clay in China and buried underground. They were placed there to guard an emperor in the afterlife. This is something extraordinary. Please pass me my book.' Foday points to the window ledge.

Kai swivels around, finds the exercise book and hands it to Foday, who opens it and begins to read. 'For the First Emperor. Eight thousand soldiers. Five hundred horses. More than one hundred chariots. And you know what else they say?' He looks at Kai, who shakes his head compliantly. 'Not one of the warriors has the same face. Every one wears a different expression. This is something the craftsmen ensured, in the way they carved them and then painted them. And then these very craftsmen, after all their labours, were buried inside. I found this story very interesting.'

'It certainly is,' says Kai.

Foday grins. 'They said this emperor wanted to wage war in the afterlife, to found a new empire with another emperor who was already deceased. Either that or these soldiers were for his protection.' Foday laughs out loud. 'I think this man was either very ambitious or very much afraid.'

'Yes,' agrees Kai, laughing too.

'Or maybe both.'

Kai is silent.

'I would like to see it for myself,' says Foday.

'Maybe you will one day,' lies Kai.

But Foday shakes his head. 'No. But if you find a picture for me, I would like that. Do you wish me to return the radio?'

'No,' says Kai. 'You hold on to it.' He'd taken it from Adrian's room several weeks previously. Difficult to return now. He has not seen Adrian, much less spoken to him. He directs every ounce of his energy to not thinking about him. Not thinking about Adrian and Nenebah.

Kai says goodbye to Foday and as he walks away down the ward the thought occurs to him for the first time: he may not be here for Foday's final operation.

Eight hours later and Kai lies on his back watching a silver spear of moonlight trace across the ceiling from the gap between the curtains.

He is wide awake.

CHAPTER 48

A handful of the men are playing football, not enough to make a five-a-side team, but enough for a kick-about. The pitch is a scraggy patch of tough grass and dirt. Discarded chains serve as goal markers. The men play barefoot, shirtless and with intent. Attila had given permission for the football games on the proviso Adrian came in to supervise them. Ileana and Attila were too busy and none of the nurses were considered sufficiently qualified to be left in charge of the unshackled men. Nobody, though, doubted the benefit of exercise to the men. Now Adrian watches the game, alert to any change in mood. So far, so good. Their concentration is upon the ball. On the opposite path he sees Attila followed by Salia. The psychiatrist stops and watches the game, nods at Adrian, who nods back. On the pitch the men play on.

After the game, Adrian has a session scheduled with Adecali. The young man arrives looking exhausted and underweight and does not sit down until Adrian invites him to do so. For a few moments Adrian watches Adecali's left knee jerking up and down. From time to time his neck, head and shoulders convulse in a massive shudder. He has not looked directly at Adrian once since entering the room. At first Adrian had been troubled by the consistent failure of most of the men to make eye contact. It was Ileana who told him that to look an elder in the eye is regarded as an act of defiance. Still, Adecali's gaze, darting about the floor as though in pursuit of an erratically moving insect, is anything but normal.

'Do you remember in class we talked about having a special place, somewhere you can go when you're finding things getting on top of you?'

Adecali nods.

'Have you been going there?'

There have been a number of disturbances involving Adecali recently, one in the canteen just yesterday. His progress in the group sessions, initially so promising, has taken a turn for the worse.

Adecali nods and then shakes his head.

'What does that mean, yes or no? Speak to me.'

'I cannot always remember what you told us.'

'Well, shall we practise it now? Whenever you have a frightening memory, something that upsets you, you can make yourself feel better. What about the relaxation techniques, the breathing?' Though the men come willingly enough to the sessions, hardest of all is to get them to carry out the exercises on their own. The question is one of trust. The men are beginning to have confidence in Adrian, but his methods are still beyond them. They are uninitiated in the ideas of psychotherapy. And to find the required peace and stillness on the wards can't be easy.

Adecali shakes his head.

'All these things will help you to feel less stressed and less frightened. They will help you cope. Shall we try it here together?'

Adecali nods.

Adrian stands and crosses to the window, where he looks out at the ruffled surface of the sea. A fishing canoe is returning to shore, dipping in and out of sight. Adecali's knee has stopped jerking. Adrian says, 'Now I want you to take a deep breath . . . hold it . . . exhale.'

One by one he takes Adecali through the exercises, has him clench and release his fists and then his forearms, his shoulders, roll his head around his neck, tense and relax the muscles of his face, where most of Adecali's tics occur. Finally his chest, legs and feet. Adecali is entirely biddable, as are all the men. Adrian never fails to find it remarkable, even accounting for the sedative effect of the drugs.

'How do you feel?'

'Yes, sir. I feel better.'

Adrian takes a breath. He says, 'OK. Close your eyes. Now think about your special place. You can tell me about it if you want.'

'The place I chose is a tree outside my village where I grew up.'

'Is it somewhere you used to go as a child?'

'Yes, if my mother beat me. Sometimes I sat underneath it. Other times I climbed up.'

'OK, I want you to sit there and remember how it felt. What could you see from up high? What could you hear?' Adrian is silent for a minute, watching Adecali. Then he says, 'What I want you to do now is to talk about one of those times when you remember something from the past, something bad. You are going to describe it to me and we are going to talk about it. And then I'm going to teach you something that will help you stop these memories from coming at unexpected times and making you upset. Do you understand?'

'Yes, sir.'

Adrian knows now, from their previous sessions, from whence Adecali's horror of fire derives, so too his dread of the smell of roasting meat. Adecali had belonged to the rebel Sensitisation Unit. The Unit's task was to enter a town marked for invasion ahead of the fighting contingent of the rebel army and by their methods to ensure the villagers' future capitulation. As a strategy it worked. It saved on casualties – among the rebel forces, that is. It saved on ammunition. The Unit's planning was meticulous, the process merciless, the outcome effective. Adecali's job, his particular job, was to burn families alive in their houses.

'Shall we begin? Would you like to describe one of those moments to me?'

Adecali is silent. Words seem to fail him. This happens often. Without Adrian's prompting, the men seem incapable of acting. Perhaps this is how it worked in the battlefield. Adecali's spirit, broken in much the same way as he set about breaking villagers' wills. Now, without the gang, the drugs and the drink, the spur of violence, out beyond the triumph of survival, the desolation steals up and surrounds them.

Adecali begins to rub his forehead with the palm of his hand.

Adrian says, 'Some time ago I was called to the ward. You were very upset. Do you remember why?'

Adecali nods.

'What happened?'

Another silence, shorter this time. When Adecali begins to speak his words come in between rapid, shallow breaths. 'They came with meat.'

'Who did?'

'Them that are on my ward.'

'And why did that upset you?'

'It made me feel sick in my stomach.'

'Go on. What else did you feel?'

'I felt fearful.' He is quiet. His eyes are open now, staring at the floor. 'I heard noises in my ears. I saw visions.'

372

'What were those visions? Tell me exactly what you saw, from the beginning.'

'I saw thatch burning, the thatch of a house. The smoke is in my nose and my mouth. I hear people shouting and screaming. There is a lot of noise. Singing. The people gathered around to watch, we make them come to see what we are doing and to chant and sing. It was my job. That is what I remember. A welcome song. *Sene-o*. I feel drumming in my ears. We pass around palm wine. I am the conductor, I have a baton. I conduct them. A woman refuses to sing. She makes me very angry. She has a baby on her back. I tell myself it is time to teach this woman a lesson. What will other people think of me if she does not sing?' His leg has begun to jerk again. Bubbles of sweat pop out on his forehead. Adrian is aware of a rank odour rising in the room.

'Keep going.'

'I need to teach this woman a lesson. For refusing to sing. I take her baby and I throw it on the roof. The woman sings then, she sings. I make her sing.' He is babbling now, rocking back and forth in his chair. 'But now she is coming after me. She is in my dreams. She appears even when I am awake.'

'What does it mean to you to see her?'

'Her spirit sees me and is coming after me, for causing the death of her child.'

Adrian leans forward and touches Adecali on the shoulder. 'OK, stop there.'

Adecali blinks.

Adrian comes to sit down opposite him.

'Would you like a glass of water?' Adrian fills a glass from the carafe on the table in front of him and pushes it across the table. Adecali drinks noisily.

'What you're experiencing,' says Adrian, 'are called flashbacks. A flashback is a memory of a bad thing that has happened, but sometimes these memories are so strong it makes it feel as though the thing is happening all over again, as though you are back in the same place. Sometimes you forget where you really are. The day in the ward, for example, when I came to help you, at first you didn't recognise me, you had forgotten where you really were. Could I be right?'

Adecali nods. He is gripping the glass, resting it on his knee.

'You can put the glass on the table now. What I want to do is to teach you some ways of coping with these flashbacks when they come, OK? We're going to replay parts of that memory until you get used to it and it stops frightening you so much. You can learn to control it, just as though we had taped it and were playing it on a video player and you had charge of the remote.'

Adecali is looking at him with what appears to be intense concentration, biting his bottom lip.

'You know what a video recorder is, don't you?'

Adecali nods slowly once.

Thank goodness for that. 'And so you know how to use one?'

Adecali shakes his head.

After Adecali is gone Adrian, halfway through writing up his notes of the session, puts down his pen, stands up and goes to the window. The fishing canoe is gone. A freight liner is moving, almost imperceptibly, across the horizon. If only it were so easy to rewind the past, he thinks. To where might he return? How far back would he go? What, if anything, would he change?

For nearly six months now Adrian has been listening to Elias Cole's story; Cole has been using him as a confessor. The question is why. In Adrian's experience it isn't unknown for a patient endeavouring to conceal an uncomfortable truth – from themselves as much as anyone else – to confess to something lesser. The therapist is handed the role of judge and juror. If he accepts the version of events presented, the patient sees himself as absolved.

So what is Elias Cole's real story?

Inside his room Elias Cole is being given a bath. He lies naked to the waist while Babagaleh holds up an arm, sponging the underside with water from a large basin on the side table. The older man's thinness is pitiful, the shadow of his ribs visible either side of the sternum. The slack skin falls away from the bone, a cloth slung over a heap of sticks.

'Stay, stay,' as Adrian prepares to withdraw. 'Babagaleh is finished here, anyway.' He indicates to Adrian to sit. And to Babagaleh, 'Go away now. Come back later.'

Babagaleh dries the old man off, pulls the bedclothes up over his chest and folds them over neatly. Unhurriedly he gathers up the basin, soap and towel and leaves the room.

'How are you?' says Adrian. No sign of the oxygen concentrator today. Mrs Mara must have had it repossessed.

'As you see. I have been unwell, but now I am a little improved, though my trajectory remains in the same general direction.' He smiles thinly. 'How are you?'

'I am well, thank you.'

'You look a little different, somehow. Let me look at you.' Cole cocks his head and regards Adrian. 'You are looking rather solemn, if you don't mind my saying so. I hope everything is all right.'

'It is,' says Adrian, summoning a smile. He draws his chair closer to the bed, decides to get straight to the point. 'Have you heard of the Prisoner's Dilemma?'

'The Prisoner's Dilemma? Yes, I am loosely familiar with the theory. Though it has been some time now.'

'What do you understand from it?'

'Two men are being held in jail for the same offence. The police don't have enough evidence to make a charge, so instead they make a deal with each man to inform on the other. It is the same deal, the broad result of which is that, if each stays silent, then each is convicted of a lesser charge. If one gives information about the other, he will get off, but the other man will suffer an even greater penalty.'

'That's right,' says Adrian. 'And if they both confess, they will get a sentence longer than if they remain silent, but shorter than if one has been informed on by the other.'

'You are talking about me and Julius.'

'Game theory. That particular form of the game was devised by a mathematician in 1950 or thereabouts. It's been in play ever since.'

The old man inhales and then exhales slowly. 'I see.'

'It's a non-zero-sum game as opposed to a zero-sum game. It allows for the possibility of cooperation. There's a move that benefits both players.' He watches Elias Cole's face carefully.

'Yes, as I said, I'm familiar with the theory. I'm not sure how it relates to me and Julius, except that we were, quite literally, prisoners. The point you're missing, of course, is that I could not confess to anything as I was not involved in anything. So that option was not open to me. I followed the only recourse there was.'

'Of course,' says Adrian. 'I understand that perfectly. Let's stick with the game for the time being. You see, it really concerns questions of self-interest and betrayal. If Prisoner A decides to act in his own self-interest he wins.'

'But only if the other prisoner doesn't do the same thing.'

'Precisely, if the other prisoner does then they both lose. Unless of course Prisoner A knows Prisoner B is unlikely to betray him. It puts Prisoner A in a strong position. It's really quite fascinating. It isn't just mathematicians and philosophers who are interested in the outcomes. Economists, too. Rival companies manufacturing, oh, I don't know, soft drinks, dog food. They have to decide whether it's better to price fix or compete.'

Elias Cole grunts. His gaze flicks over Adrian and settles on the end of the bed.

Adrian stands up and moves into his eye line. 'There are variants of the game. In the most popular the two people play the game repeatedly. That way they can learn each other's responses, you see.'

'Indeed I do, though I'm still not at all sure where you are headed with all of this. I did nothing wrong except to give Johnson what he asked for, which was a small amount of information. I did not lie, or manufacture evidence. Johnson was a police officer.'

'Though you knew what kind of man he was.'

'He was a police officer, for heaven's sake!'

'As I was saying, in this variant of the game, the same people play each other any number of times. They get to know how the other one is likely to respond, but also they get the opportunity to punish each other for past betrayals. So suddenly the game shifts quite dramatically.'

Cole does not respond, he is watching Adrian. Adrian looks directly into the void of his stare.

'So let's say that now we *are* talking about you and Julius. Could it be you were punishing him for a betrayal, one already committed?'

'And what betrayal is that?'

'The one you told me about the last time we spoke. For not including you in what was going on.'

Elias Cole gives a short, harsh and derisive laugh. 'What? For not involving me in producing some rag of an underground newspaper?'

'You seemed upset enough about it last time.'

'I was angry with him precisely for *getting* me involved. For using my room and my typewriter. For letting me be arrested.'

Adrian is quiet for a moment. 'For not trusting you enough to tell you what was really going on. You thought you were closer to him than you really were. But it turned out not to be true. Yansaneh, Kekura — they were Julius's real, trusted friends and not you.' He's heckling the old man now. He ought, perhaps, to stop but he doesn't want to. He throws in one final sentence. 'So you gave Johnson your notebooks.'

'Yes, I gave Johnson my notebooks. But not for the reason you suggest. Because Johnson had harassed and humiliated me.'

'Did you feel better when you had done it?'

'Of course not!'

Half an hour later Adrian walks down the corridor towards his apartment, thinking about Adecali and Elias Cole, two very different conversations. He hardly dares admit it to himself, but he'd rather enjoyed sparring with Elias Cole. The old man maintained that giving Johnson his notebooks did not amount to an act of betrayal and certainly he could tell himself that, he might even partly believe it. Johnson, after all, represented the law, the arm of authority. But Cole was holding back. He had cooperated with Johnson, but something that occurred around that time had created a bond which had lasted years after the event, of this Adrian felt reasonably certain.

As for the Prisoner's Dilemma, the game theory had once comprised a seminar when Adrian was at university. In the present circumstances, as an analogy, it is remarkably apt. But what is most interesting about it is that, although at first glance self-interest and betrayal seem to be the winning choice, what happens when the game is played repeatedly among large numbers of people, or even by computers, is that altruism becomes the sensible recourse.

Adrian recalls the lecture theatre, the strip lighting and 1960s concrete flooring. His professor, what was the guy's name? Quinnell. Proving, Quinnell had told them, rocking forwards on the lectern, that in any society good moral thinking and self-interest are one and the same.

There comes a time when the knowing makes itself known.

When they make love he finds he cannot bury himself deeply enough inside her. He pushes his face into her neck and tastes skin, salt and sweat. A leg is pressed against his cheek. Hands grip his arms. His chin fits in the dip above her collarbone. He reaches up and finds her calf, her ankle. Her hand slides between their two bodies and gathers his balls. He, who has ceased to breathe, exhales his soul.

Afterwards she plays with parts of him. Licks a nipple. Curls a hair around a forefinger. Inspects an insect bite and gives it an experimental squeeze. Grooming him, he teases her. Once she even scratched the back of his knee. Later, when he thought about it, he shook his head and swore to himself he had said nothing of the itch he felt there.

In these idle moments, to him anything but mundane, the physical separation between them ceases to exist.

And this is where he is when the knowing makes itself known. He is lying on his front across her bed, trapped by her leg cast across the back of his thighs. Outside the night-time rain has started, weighted drops tumbling out of the sky subduing all other sounds. When she rises to fetch a glass of water, he feels a moment of loss and he knows he never wants to be without her again and he says so. But she, standing with her back to him, fails to hear above the rain and the sound of pouring water and so gives no answer.

She turns around. 'What's the matter?'

He sees his mistake, struggles out of the terror the thought of rejection brought with it and repeats his words. 'I want you to come with me when I leave.'

She sits and places a hand on his back. She is silent and he hates it, starts to slide towards the fear once more. 'I don't want that,' she says.

He drops his gaze.

'This is my home. This is where I want to live. I want to raise our children *in this place*.' The last three words pronounced emphatically.

He is overtaken by relief. Aware of his breathing, of the wild thumping of his heart, he makes an effort to bring both under control. He pulls her to him. For now he doesn't want to think about the rest. Nothing is simple, except this one thing, this feeling he has for her.

Children, she said. *Our children.* He has already forgotten the rest.

Outside the rain crashes down, dulling the senses. Next comes the thunder. Adrian closes his mind to everything but her touch.

For now everything else can wait.

CHAPTER 49

An inventory of his clothes: T-shirts in various stages of wear, thirteen. Acceptable, five. Pairs of jeans, three. Good shirts, two. Kai slips on one of the shirts he last wore to the party after his high-school graduation and can scarcely button it across his chest. He places it on the pile of clothes by the door.

On his way to the British Council, he stops by Government Wharf, where bales of second-hand clothes are unloaded from ships. From a trader he selects two shirts, nearly new. Also a pair of trousers, creased but serviceable. He pulls his T-shirt over his head and changes into one of the shirts there on the street. The trousers he folds over his arm, pays the vendor and heads up the hill to the Council building. In the men's toilets he changes into his new trousers and then doubles back to reception, where he explains to the girl behind the desk he has come to take the English language aptitude test. There are twelve other candidates in the room, though nobody he knows. The receptionist hands out the papers and leaves. The first three pages of questions are multiple choice. *Select the correct verb-ending from the list below. Select the correct noun from the list below.* A man in a grey three-piece suit chews his pencil, applies slow strokes of pencil to paper. Kai flips through pages. The last question requires a short account of a recent news item. Kai, who has not listened to the news in months, writes of the terracotta armies in China. He does not review his work but collects up his papers and leaves, handing them to the girl at reception as he goes.

Less than fifteen minutes have elapsed since he entered the examination room.

So now he is free until midday. He's about to leave the building, when he changes his mind and ascends the stairs to the library. The whole place has been remodelled since he was here last, though the smell of clean air and paper remains. As a child he passed hours in here looking at the medical books, not to thumb through to explicit images like the other kids, but to stare at the diagrams, repeat to himself the Latin names of bones, muscle, tissue, organs.

To the librarian he mouths, 'History,' and is pointed to the back of the room. Africa. Europe. Oceania. India. China. He finds what he is looking for among the outsize books: *The Terracotta Army of Emperor Qin Shi Huang*. The book is more than fifteen years old, does not contain the most recent findings; still, the images are various and in colour.

At the front desk Kai waits while the librarian searches among the index cards for his old membership number, hunts and pecks the letters of his name on the computer keyboard. He moves away to browse the periodicals.

There, standing in the narrow aisle, he sees her. She is working at one of the desks facing the wall, her back to him, head bent over a book. Several other volumes sit upon the floor by her foot, two more next to her elbow. Her chin is cradled in the palm of her hand. With her free hand she flicks the end of her scarf over her shoulder, with a gesture so utterly familiar it nearly winds him.

For a year nothing, now twice in a matter of weeks.

For all of those months he had lived inside the cold, bright tunnel of medicine. Once he'd passed her standing at the roadside, her arms full of books. He did not wave or call to the driver to stop. Instead he sped past, away to a future without her.

Now Kai stands and watches Nenebah. It would be so easy to speak to her. He should tell her, perhaps, that he is leaving. After all those arguments. Now none of it matters. And yet what of consequence can he tell her in just a few minutes, here in a public library? What can he say that would make any difference? He should tell her about that night on the bridge, the days before and after. At the time he had closed in upon himself, denying her a place of entry. She was tenacious, aggressive as a lover, had tried to prise the pieces of him apart. Only when she failed had she finally let go; by then months had passed. She loved like she was going to war, but she was also not the kind of woman to wait for a man. Valiant in battle, noble in defeat. She walked away and never looked back.

As with all the most traumatic injuries, the pain followed later. He'd tried to find her, to go back to her. By then she'd left her father's house and was moving around the city. He went to find Mary, but Mary had gone too. In the scale of what had happened in the city, the echoes of which were still ringing through the streets, Kai had felt shamed. He went back to work. And had never stopped working since.

Now he couldn't stop thinking about her.

But what of Adrian? Kai might have told himself the relationship with Adrian was meaningless, had he not known that with Nenebah nothing was meaningless. She brought an intensity to everything she did. Whereas for Kai, only one thing really mattered and that was medicine. And Nenebah. Two things mattered, nothing else.

She shifts in her chair and the movement brings him back to himself. He is about to go to her, but still he hesitates and remains standing in the aisle, holding on aware in some distant, unconscious way, of balancing upon an axial moment in his life. With the first step he will put into motion a sequence of events that will play out into the future. The ramifications are enormous. He made a mistake in letting her go. Now he wants to go back. It is not too late.

Somebody comes down the aisle, and Kai steps aside to let them pass. As he does, his view of Nenebah alters. For the first time he can see the pages of the book open on the desk in front of her. The person who passed him has stopped further down the aisle. Kai waits for them to move on. He angles his head so he can see what Nenebah is reading. From this distance he can just about make out a diagram, the figure of a woman, a pregnant woman. Kai looks down to the books on the floor. The volume on the top of the pile shows a picture of a child held in its mother's arms. Something for Mary, perhaps? Mary was probably too busy to visit the library, she might have asked Nenebah to look something up for her. Even as Kai tells himself this, he knows it isn't true. In front of him Nenebah stretches and flexes her spine, before relaxing back into position. More telling than the visible swell of her stomach is the way she touches it with her right hand, a slow, circular caress, before she turns another leaf of the book.

The library, the shelves, the strip lighting have all disappeared. Kai cannot hear, he is in a deafening tunnel of wind. He reaches out and holds on to a shelf. Inside his mind he is rushing backwards, away from the place in his mind he was only moments before, the place from where he had seen the possibility of a future with Nenebah. The man in the aisle is looking at him. Kai concentrates on closing the thoughts off, one by one. Realigning his whole being. His command of himself is almost total; it is an effort of will.

And when control has been resumed he turns and walks back to the front desk, where he picks up the book for Foday.

For an hour Kai walked the streets, carrying with him the great book on the model armies of China. Now he understands the reason for Mary's look. It wasn't the fact of Nenebah having another man, for in Mary's mind such matters were always reversible. But a child, a child was something different.

He hails an empty taxi. He is in no mood now to return to the hospital. He directs the driver out towards the west of the city, to the bars along the beach, promises him sufficient fare not to take other passengers.

Sitting at a bar, one he has never been to before, Kai orders a beer and sits with the book upon his lap, staring at the horizon. After a few sallies the barman has abandoned his attempts at banter. Now the man sits on the opposite side of the bar, staring as moodily as Kai at some unknown point.

A white woman is walking up the beach, dressed in tight black shorts and trainers, a ponytail pushed through the back of her baseball cap, arms bent like a jogger, her chin pointed forward and her backside pushed out behind her. Kai watches as she heads up the beach, the ponytail swinging from side to side like a metronome. About a hundred yards further on he sees her turn back on herself. He is still watching her as she heads up the beach towards the bar. She sits on a stool and orders from the barman. She is not, Kai thinks, especially pretty, though she behaves otherwise, flicking her blonde ponytail and wriggling on the bar stool. Any minute now she will start to talk to him, begin to ask him questions and demand that he reveal himself to her. Before such a thing can happen he places the book on the bar, swings himself off his stool and heads out across the sand towards the water. At first his intention is to do no more than walk along the line of the surf. But the sand is hot underfoot. He feels constrained by his shirt and undoes a few buttons at his throat and then a few more, before he removes it altogether. Trousers and flip-flops follow. In his shorts he walks down to the water and through the crashing surf. A wave breaks against his thighs, forcing him to brace. When the wave recedes he continues his assault upon the ocean for several more paces, before he puts his arms above his head and dives into the next wave.

Silence.

Water warm as blood; he feels himself being pulled out to sea by the strength of the undertow, stretches out his arms and allows himself to drift. He opens his eyes. The water is hazy. Angled reflections of sun upon the sand. A piece of seaweed hovers horizontally in the water in front of him, like a curious passer-by. Muted sounds of pounding surf upon sand. Above him the glassy surface of the sea, through which he sees, as if through a stained-glass window, a wavering, distant sun. He crashes through the surface, and turns on his back, sucking air into his lungs, and kicks out.

How long he lies there, feeling the sun dry the salt on his face, the cradling motion of the waves, he does not know. By the time he walks back up the beach to retrieve his clothes, the barman is gone, his book has been placed on a shelf behind the counter. Kai reaches over and takes it, places a note on the bar where the book had been, and covers it with a glass. Eyes stinging, he pulls his clothes on over his wet skin and heads for the road. Back to the only real sanctuary he knows.

Eight o'clock. Kai had eaten his evening meal in the canteen, pretending to read papers as an excuse for sitting alone.

Now he carries the book about the Emperor Qin Shi Huang under his arm as he crosses the courtyard. A wind rustles around the hospital buildings and high in the trees. The coppery scent of rain is in the air. Too early yet for a moon, the night is in its darkest phase.

Inside the ward the smells are of iodine and dust. All is quiet. A nurse sits at her post bent over a book of puzzles, as though in prayer to the plaster statue of the Virgin on the desk before her. She smiles and would have risen, but he waves at her to stay seated. He walks down the ward, his progress marked by a head lifted here, a hand raised there, small stirrings, a breeze through a cornfield.

A ward light shines over Foday's bed. Ordinarily he is awake at this hour, radio pressed close to his ear. Not so this evening. The radio sits on the windowsill, alongside Foday's neatly stacked belongings. Foday is lying on his back, asleep. An arm has fallen free from the bedclothes. Kai places the book on the windowsill and goes to fold the stray arm away. Beneath his fingers Foday's skin burns. Kai bends to look at Foday. He is shivering, his brow coated in sweat, his breaths shallow and noisy. Foday's eyes are open, unblinking, gazing at Kai.

'Jesus!' Kai reaches for the bell cord. From her post across the room the nurse rises from her desk and comes, first walking, then running towards them. 'Call the OR. Tell them to get ready. Get me a porter!'

She looks at him and blinks, momentarily frozen, snapped back into being by the sound of Kai's voice. 'Move!'

He waves a hand in front of Foday's face and is pleased to see him respond. There is even the shadow of a smile. 'What are you trying to do here, my friend?' Kai says. 'Undo all my good work?'

In the operating theatre Kai takes a circular saw and cuts through the cast on Foday's leg, pulling apart the two sides with a sound like splitting wood. A fine layer of plaster of Paris dust coats the floor and his feet. Bending the overhead light down over the foot he checks carefully each of the surgical incisions. They appear to have healed well a month on from the operation. The cast has been changed once already. 'Get me a torch,' he tells the nurse. 'And ask someone to find out if Seligmann is around.'

Kai moves the light of the torch inch by inch, over the sole of Foday's foot, where the skin is dry and flaking from the weeks in plaster.

'Hold his leg up for me, please.'

Now he inspects the long tendon scar. There. He missed it the first time. A sinus tract over the healing scar tissue. He takes a scalpel and makes a small incision close to the wound, presses with his fingertips. A thick stream of pus jets out. Seligmann enters through the double doors, gives a long, low whistle and a shake of the head.

'This country of yours. Everything rots. You must make very good compost.' He bends to gaze at Foday's leg. 'Explore. Debride. Remove any necrotic tissue.' He blows out under his face mask. 'Textbook stuff. Still, looks like this is going to set us back a bit.'

What time is it? Midnight? One o'clock. He doesn't know and, now he thinks about it, doesn't care. He is lying on his back, staring at the stars. Now, which is the Plough? He has never, for the life of him, been able to see why it should be so called. People in the past had tried to show him, to point out the shape, but he couldn't see it. He couldn't see it at all. He hiccups and then burps, wetly. He is drunk.

Nenebah. He would have liked to touch her. Just to hold her hand in his. To feel her skin. He used to like to grip her lightly with one hand at the side of her neck. She would tilt her head and trap his fingers.

How easily they spoke of love. And yet, when she'd needed the certainty of his feeling for her, he'd let her slip away, never able to bring himself to tell her about the ways in which he'd been changed. He'd been incapable, and in being incapable he'd let Nenebah believe the problem lay with her.

Something bumps the side of his head, a piece of wood, something covered in tar, a lump of old polystyrene. He sits up slightly and flounders in the water, is hit by a passing wavelet and momentarily submerged. He wipes his face and looks at the distant shore. There are still people at the beach bar to which he had returned late in the evening and where the barman had unctuously welcomed him. Spurred by a memory of the peace he had found in his mid-afternoon swim, Kai had taken to the water for the second time in a day. Drifting along like an abandoned boat, one whose occupants have drowned. A pitch black, perfect peace.

He lays his head back in the water and searches for the Plough. He ought to be getting home. He lifts his head again, tracks the cones of a car's headlights down the long beach road.

Ah, he thinks, and lays his head back upon his pillow of water.

CHAPTER 50

A silver sea, smooth and still, the reflection of a gull moves across the surface, a few clouds in the sky, elliptically shaped, like a school of porpoises. Here and there other gulls float undisturbed on the water. On the shoreline, a mother and her toddler. The child, wearing red wellington boots, is running through the surf away from his mother, looking over his shoulder at every turn to make sure she is following. Adrian can hear, dully through the glass, the sound of the mother's voice. She is smiling and at the same time calling warnings. A perfect autumn day, thinks Adrian. Busy looking over his shoulder the child loses direction and veers into the sea; water splashes over the top of his boots. Now the mother is pulling them off and pouring the water out of each one. She is holding the child tight to her in one arm; his feet dangle several inches above the sand. But the child struggles to be free and so the mother sets him down. He runs away. The mother follows behind carrying the boots. The child runs away, away: shrieking, giddy with freedom. His blond hair blown about in a wind of his own making.

'No biscuits. Sorry, darling. I should have got some in, but I only drive into town once in a while and I don't eat them any more myself. When you called I'd no idea you'd be here quite so quickly.'

'It's fine,' says Adrian. He turns away from the window and the boy, moves to take the tea tray from his mother and set it down upon the low table. He says, 'You must spend a lot of time just looking at all of this.'

His mother nods. 'It's never the same from one hour to the next. It's the sky, you know. People complain Norfolk is flat, but they're looking in the wrong place. You need to lift your head. It's the sky that matters. Of course, you know that. I forget sometimes.'

He'd arrived the evening before in a tepid light, feeling drained by the long drive from London. During supper, eaten on their knees opposite each other in the sitting room, he'd been more aware of the reflections on the glass, of his mother entering and leaving the room than of what lay beyond the darkness. The meal they ate was sparing, his mother's once lush cooking sacrificed to the austerity of cholesterol and blood-sugar levels. They had not spoken of his reason for being there. Adrian had volunteered nothing and his mother had not asked, her forbearance itself a clue as to how serious she must imagine it to be. She had opened a bottle of rather good wine, a gesture he felt was replete with solace as much as celebration.

Ileana had driven him to the ferry which would take him across to the airport. The plane flew into darkness across the Sahara and this time Adrian did not see the dunes or the dust rising up to the aircraft's wings. When he woke up they were over mountains, the Alps, perhaps. The plane touched down in the early morning, the airport brightly lit, cold and empty. Passports were checked at frequent intervals. From the airport Adrian had rented a car and driven straight to Norfolk. The pace of cars on the road shocked him.

'Milk?'

'Yes, please.' Fresh milk. And yet he finds himself so used to the faint metallic flavour of the tinned variety, he misses it.

The previous evening both Adrian and his mother had retired early. Adrian pleaded exhaustion, feeling at the same time alive with nervous energy. After his mother had gone to bed, he left his bedroom and returned to the sitting room to read the paper and then to watch the news on the twenty-four-hour television news channel, the flickering television images reflected on the obsidian wall. So much seemed to have happened while he had been away. By the time he watched the bulletin on its third loop, the stories had all become familiar. Once in the night he'd woken to a strange noise, like the call of a night bird. He laid his head down, listened to the sound of the sea, a giant's slow breathing. After a few minutes he dropped into a deep sleep lasting seven hours.

He woke to a pale amber early-autumn day. The sea was still, the tide far out. Miles of glowing wet sand.

He watches his mother pour the tea, with her free hand smooth back a single lock of silver hair that dips into her eyes. The number of sculptures on the lawn had grown since last he was here. Something that looked like a horizontal Stonehenge. A man and a woman, he composed of jagged rocks, she of smooth, round pebbles, a cleft stone at the meeting of her thighs. After breakfast they'd taken a walk down the beach, during which Adrian told his mother the reason for his return and his mother listened in between picking up pieces of jetsam and occasional pebbles, ramming them into her trouser pockets, until she bulged like a child with pockets full of tuck and conkers. Once she had stopped and looked at him, shading her eyes from the sun, her expression thoughtful and serious. But in the end she'd said nothing more than, 'Hmm.' And then, 'See, looks like amber. Of course, it's not.' Tossed the pebble back among the others. Finally, 'You seem to have given it a great deal of thought.'

They walked in silence for half an hour more and climbed a dune at the far end of the beach. Once or twice Adrian stopped to extend a hand to his mother, but she waved him away, a somewhat terse gesture, made, as it was, in silence. At the top they sat and looked out over the sea. His mother plucked a blade of grass, put the end in her mouth, lay back on the rough grass and closed her eyes. She remained still so long he began to think she'd fallen asleep.

Finally she said, 'Does Lisa know you're here?'

'Not yet.'

'Have you thought about Kate?'

'Of course I have. I think about her constantly.'

'Nowadays, I suppose, you follow your dreams.' Her tone, lacking the true spirit of accusation, so very matter-of-fact, made him feel whimsical and foolish. Without waiting for an answer she stood up, not bothering to shake the grass seeds from her hair or brush the sand from her trousers. He followed her down.

They'd lunched in the sun next to the open window: ham, boiled eggs and salad. Hard to imagine this as the same sun that bore pitilessly down upon the Equator. This water, the same body of water reached from here to there, at some point changing colour from grey to blue, silver to green. Adrian thought of Mamakay and imagined her practising her clarinet. The thought occurred to him he had never heard her practise. Only once he arrived unexpectedly to a yard full of music. Mamakay playing below, her neighbour and fellow band member on his trombone above, an improvised serenade. He wonders what Mamakay is doing at this moment. Only an hour's time difference; the sun would be at its height.

After lunch his mother lit a cigarette, something he had never seen her do.

'I know, I know.' She caught his look and shrugged. 'What, frankly, does it matter?' She set the lighter on the table: a heavy ivory table-lighter he recognised as once having belonged to his grandparents.

After lunch she put him to work on a small series of jobs. Her television aerial, loosened by the wind, swung back and forth issuing a mournful plea every time the wind blew. He'd fetched a ladder and climbed up to the roof, discovered it to be the source of the sound he had heard in the night. A piece of tarpaper had come loose and Adrian called to his mother to bring roofing nails and a hammer, was surprised when her head appeared over the horizon of the roof.

'How long are you staying?' she asked as she handed the hammer to him.

'I'm not sure yet, a day or two? Maybe longer.' He wasn't as sure of his place here as he'd been while she remained in the old house.

'Good. Then perhaps you can help me with something. A small deck at the front. Can't possibly do it on my own. I was going to hire somebody, one of those Eastern European fellows, but now you're here. Shouldn't take too long with two of us at it.' And she'd disappeared again, taking his assent for granted. 'I'll make tea,' she called.

A low sun strikes the room, dust mites spin slowly in the air, are sent rushing in one direction and then another by the occasional movement or draught. The hum and tap of a dying bluebottle. A lone dog searches the waterline, no sign of an owner. On the edge of the frame a boat with a blue sail disappears behind a curve of rock.

'Now a boat *would* be a fine thing,' says his mother, as though apropos of a continuing conversation.

'What kind of boat?'

'A sailing boat. Something reassuringly solid and wooden. The sort of thing the owl and the pussycat would have owned.' She laughed lightly. 'Held together by layers of varnish.'

'Sail away for a year and a day,' says Adrian. And then, so suddenly he is surprised by himself: 'Did you ever think of leaving Dad?'

A pause. His mother pours milk into her tea and sets the jug down carefully upon the tray. 'Your father was ill. He needed me. I would never have left.'

'But, I mean, didn't you . . .?'

She interrupts, as though this is something she is sure of. 'Never.'

They drink their tea more or less in silence. Adrian tries to apologise, but she brushes him off. He notices a stillness has come over her and he regrets his incaution; he'd been enjoying the new ease they had found in each other's company.

While his mother is clearing the kitchen (for she will hear nothing of him helping) Adrian stands outside in a new breeze. Beneath his feet the grass is springy, growing in tufts upon the sandy earth. He notices one of his mother's sculptures, a great abstract snail, its shell a curl of seashells of decreasing size. There is another, a feather, the vanes of which are composed of dozens of real feathers. A piece of driftwood several feet long, from a particular angle it resembles an animal. Balanced upon its back a second piece of wood, dark twisted limbs, a boy perhaps, straddling the back of a great bear. Adrian looks out to the horizon. Upon the sea white horses have begun to form. Watching them, Adrian feels on the brink of something momentous, like a sailor embarking upon a voyage hundreds of years ago. He does not feel afraid and nor does he feel courageous; the only emotion he is aware of, in addition to the surge of feeling he experiences when he thinks of Mamakay, is shame: hot and heavy as tar.

His mother joins him outside. 'What would you like for supper?'

'We've only just had lunch.'

'I know. Still, these things have to be planned, always did.' She smiles.

Children took so much for granted. Children took happiness for granted.

'Why don't I take you out?' says Adrian.

'Oh, no. It would be a waste.'

'Come on. Let's do it. Where would you like to go? Where's good around here?'

'Well, if you insist. We could drive up the coast. There's a pub I've been to a few times.'

'Fine.'

'I'll book it, then.' And she turns back into the house.

At five o'clock they return from the garden centre. For the remainder of the afternoon and into the early evening Adrian works on the new deck, laying a network of joists on the old concrete patio, checking each joist with a spirit level as he goes. He works stripped to the waist. The sun is warm on his back, an occasional tear of sweat runs into his eyes. He has reached an age, he realises, when he considers manual labour to be somehow rewarding. Today in particular he welcomes the refuge it offers; concentrating upon his hands forces him beyond the vortex of his own thoughts.

A goal. He will have the frame ready before they go out to eat. He straightens to review his work, feels the ache and release, almost pleasurable, in his vertebrae and the muscles of his back, standing amid the cross-hatch of wooden beams as if upon a raft, the sharp scent of fresh timber mingled with the sting of salt.

Elias Cole had not sent Babagaleh to Adrian in the weeks leading up to Adrian's departure. Adrian passed by the old man's room several times, to be told he was indisposed. He wondered whether he'd pushed him too far at their last meeting. Adrian said goodbye to Mrs Mara and the other members of staff, though he'd not seen Kai once. Kai was avoiding him, Adrian felt certain, and knew that he, too, was guilty of the same. He wasn't entirely sure of the reason for his behaviour, which he had declined to examine too closely. Adrian is not, he tells himself, a jealous man. But then there was the sense, the constant sense he had had, of something lingering. How alike they were in many ways, Kai and Mamakay, like siblings really. In the way they both resolutely occupied only the present, kept doors closed, showing only what they chose to reveal. Both Kai and Mamakay had places from which all others were excluded, from which Adrian was excluded. Even now the fear coiling around his heart is that in those closed-off places is something the two of them share from their past, some arc of emotion, incomplete, requiring an ending.

Is he doing the right thing? Sometimes he feels he is losing his mind.

'Damn!' A splinter of wood slides under the nail of his forefinger. The pain is pinpoint and exquisite. Adrian presses down on the bed of the fingernail and then sucks the end of his finger. The sky has a sulphurous cast; dark clouds boil on the horizon. Adrian's mouth tastes of blood and iron. A drop of rain touches his skin and then another. Within moments the sand is turned dull and the pebbles sleek. Adrian collects the tools he has been working with and goes back inside the house.

In the shower before dinner, hot water powering down upon his shoulders. He thinks of her at times like this. In the heat of the bathroom he could be in her apartment. He feels his body's response, turns his face up to the shower-head, holds his breath. In his mind he watches her coming towards him. What does she do? A short time later he lets his hand fall back to his side, watches the semen swirl and slide away with the water. The outward tension, briefly, is dissipated, the yearning inside remains.

The place is more of a restaurant than a pub, interconnecting dining rooms, tiled floor and green-painted dado rail. On the wall opposite Adrian is a portrait of a woman cast in a shadowy garden-room light, who might be Virginia Woolf. He watches his mother as she reads the menu through her spectacles. She has dressed for the occasion, exchanged her corduroys for a pair of velvet trousers and a velvet shirt. At the door a man, the restaurant's owner, had greeted her with some familiarity, so Adrian thought. Adrian struggles to imagine his mother coming here. With whom? Who are her friends here? he wonders. He catches himself. The same challenge for every one of us, he thinks, to release our parents from the bondage of our own imagination. He lowers his head to the menu.

His mother orders with confidence, Adrian less so, unsettled by so many choices. In the end he duplicates her choice, then changes his mind and orders local crab followed by duck. Several times he lifts his wine glass to his lips. He feels, if he is honest, a little detached from reality. Mamakay, Ileana, the wards of chained men, all there where he left them. He wonders about Adecali and whether his nightmares are troubling him, whether he is remembering to practise going to his special place. Practise, practise, Adrian told him before he left. Keep control of your own mind. The group sessions were planned to continue without him, the football games, though, had to be cancelled.

What he appreciates about his mother, now he thinks about it, is that to her he can, if he chooses, talk about such things. Never does she make him feel as though his work, his dealings with the darker side of human lives, is something he must keep to himself, as if such talk was somehow embarrassing for polite company, did not go alongside goat's cheese and Gressingham duck.

He realises too that all this means nothing to him. Places like this restaurant, fine wines, he could enjoy it all but somewhere in the last year it had ceased to matter.

An elderly couple make their way across the span of the dining room, telltale trembling in his limbs. Adrian feels his heart constrict. He glances at his mother and finds her looking at him.

They take dessert and coffee in the bar, sitting side by side on a cushioned bench.

'It made him so angry,' his mother says, stirring crystals of brown sugar into her coffee.

'What made who angry?'

'Your father. His illness made him angry. It frustrated him. He took it out on you sometimes.'

'He took it out on you as well.'

'Oh.' His mother picked up her coffee cup in both hands. 'That didn't bother me. I understood. There were so many reasons he was angry. The disease, the way it crippled him and took the years away. But I always felt he was angry *for* me, not angry with me.'

'What does that mean?'

'He was angry with himself, on my behalf. At the beginning he would disappear into these long, dark days. He felt I never should have married him. We came here a couple of times before we married. Of course, it was very different then. Your father had a motorbike when I met him; he bought a sidecar for it. I couldn't squeeze into it once I was pregnant, but we kept it until the year after you were born. We took you out in it once or twice. We got stuck in the sand. Right here.' She points with her spoon in the direction of the beach. 'What a hoot! We came in here afterwards to dry off. They had rooms back then.'

Adrian sits quietly for a moment. He cannot remember his father as anything other than brooding and intense. He has no memory of the sidecar, not unsurprisingly. He does, though, have a memory of a photograph of it, a man astride the motorbike and the empty sidecar. It was a black-and-white photograph with crenellated edges; they printed them smaller in those days. Odd he remembers it so clearly. It must have been taken with a camera that was already old. Adrian had always thought the image was of his grandfather. So it was his father. His mother, presumably, had been behind the camera.

'And how did you feel?'

'Me? I thought it was hilarious.'

'I don't mean about the sidecar. I mean, were you angry that he became ill?'

'Only at God and the angels. We *knew*, you see. Even though the doctors misdiagnosed it at first. They thought it was thyroid-related. But your father had had an uncle with the disease and he reckoned he knew better and that the doctors were wrong. It turned out he was right. He never hid it from me. I was the one who insisted on the wedding. He was angry because the miracle we assumed would happen when we were young and in love never materialised.' She smiles and stares into her cup, before setting it down on the saucer. She draws a finger across her dessert plate to collect the last of the cream, puts it in her mouth. 'He couldn't stop himself envying you, but he was so proud of you. If there's one thing he would have wanted, it would be to see you become the person you were meant to become.'

Three days later Adrian stands in front of the long window. The last of the moon is reflected in the silver of the sea. The darkness is giving way to dawn. A fine mist slips in and out of the faraway dunes. He slides open the door and steps barefoot outside on to the new deck. The scent of wood resin hangs heavy in the cool air. He walks down to the grass and then to the shoreline. He picks up a flat stone and sends it skimming across the surface of the water. One, two, three, the stone sinks out of sight.

Six hours later he turns the wheel of his rental car, heads off the motorway on to the slip road and into the London-bound traffic.

CHAPTER 51

On a plastic seat in a row of others, Kai reads his most recent letters from Tejani:

My brother,

Today is the first day I have a chance to write to you. It's been crazy busy. This is the first time in weeks I've even had half an hour to myself. I keep thinking I could email you and it would be so much quicker. But then I forget you have to go and wait who knows how long at an Internet café. Man, I don't know how you put up with it. I can't believe you still have to write all the records at the hospital by hand. So I guess then we stay with what we know. When you come over here we're going to take some time to teach you how to use a computer properly. But truth is, friend, I don't mind so much, even though there is only one place in the whole town that sells airmail paper. It gives me time to breathe.

So I'm sitting at a table in the kitchen. It's fall (as they call it here) and the weather is cold already. Man, once it starts, it eats into you. I need to get myself an attending position or maybe a fellowship somewhere warm. Atlanta, where it feels more like home. I hear there are a lot of our people in that part of the country. Not sure Helena is so keen on the idea, though. She's working two jobs at two different care homes. She's a hard worker and she's making good money. We're working towards that down payment. Helena says she wants to study, which I'm not saying I'm against, only we're going to have to make a choice: the duplex or the college fees. So, anyways, we need to talk about that. Hey, you know what I'm thinking – I see an opportunity to exercise a little leverage here, persuade her to move south where the real estate is cheaper.

So you saw big, beautiful Mary, who's even bigger now. I take it Mamoud's the lucky man. Tell them both congratulations. Hell, I love that woman. Tell her that for me. I don't care if Mamoud gets jealous. Tell him he only has her because I allowed him and I might come back and take her away from him, so he better watch himself. Better treat her fine, because she's one fine lady . . .

A nurse, sullen and avoidant, steps out of the doctor's surgery and resumes her place at her desk at the far end of the room without a glance at those waiting. Kai has been sitting there an hour already. The line moves at an interminable pace. A patient emerges from the doctor's office, followed by the doctor himself, who calls the next patient's name from his clipboard. A man with a large sore on his neck covered in a clot of strong-smelling herbs rises. Everybody shuffles along the bench. Kai waits. He'd chosen this clinic because of its distance from work, having decided not to do his medical at the hospital. So far only Mrs Mara knows he is leaving. Coming here seems like the simpler thing to do.

He returns to the last lines of Tejani's letter:

When do you think you will get here? It seems to be taking a long time. You have to keep at them, man. Next thing you know they've lost all your paperwork. I would have expected you to be about ready to book your flight any time now.

Another letter, dated some three weeks later:

Hey, bro,

No point asking when you're coming. I guess it takes as long as it takes. No worries. The sofa is still here waiting for you.

So maybe you heard about what happened here in one of the primary schools? It was all over the news for two days. Some crazy guy with a machete went into a kids' playground at recess, Monday. Hacked a whole bunch of them, and the teacher too. Bad, bad stuff. Happens a lot here, so actually maybe the foreign press didn't bother to report it. Anyway, the point of my mentioning it is this – guess where they brought the wounded kids? Right here. There were four of them. I had been on duty for about an hour when the call came in. Man, you should have seen me. I was flying. Nobody else round here could work out where I learned the stuff, how a junior like me gained so much experience working wounds like that. I didn't say a word. Who would have believed me, if I said I learned it all during a war in Africa in a country you never even heard about? One of the kids was DOA, but the other three made it through. The chief of surgery asked for me to come see her and offered her congratulations. How about that?

The real bad news is Helena and I split. Guess it had been coming a long time. So there you have it. No big drama, no arguments. She's looking for a place to move into. In the meantime I'm sleeping most nights at the hospital. Though I can stay here if I want, I guess it's easier not to. We had some good times together. I'm going to miss her.

That's it for now.

Cheers, man,

T.

PS. If there's anything you need me to do at this end, let me know.

And the last letter:

Dear Kai,

I feel like I should start the letters 'Dear diary' or something, because it feels like you're the only person I talk to. I don't mean literally, because I talk to people all day. And I don't mean I don't have any friends. It's just, there's talking. And there's talking. You know what I'm saying, right? No, of course you don't. You were always the quiet one who drove the women crazy. I was the one used to think I had the gift of the gab, but the girls always went for you in the end.

I've been forgetting to ask after Abass. Your kid cousin. How's he doing? He must be coming up for about eight now. Shit! Can't believe it. Tell him hi from me. Remember me to his mother.

When you come here we should head up to Canada and pay your sister and your parents a visit. I should have gone before, only working for those exams kept me occupied. We could hire a car and drive. I've been wanting to do that. See the Niagara Falls. Hey, how do you think it compares with our very own falls back home? We had some good times there. Apparently there are people who go over the side of the Niagara Falls inside a wooden barrel. It's true, man, I promise you. I'm not kidding. And do you know those falls freeze in the winter? I started to plan our trip and I saw a picture, a photograph from 1911. Frozen from top to bottom, the whole thing. There were people walking on the ice. Maybe we should go in the summer. Makes me laugh to think how excited I was the first time it snowed. I kept a jar of it in the freezer.

Actually I haven't done too much travelling. Money was short at the beginning. Also, my travel was restricted because of the way I entered the US. But it will be different for you. So now I guess I'm waiting, my friend. There's a lot to see just around here. My first few months, man, I went around with my eyes popping. I don't go out so much these days, but we can hit the town a few nights.

Am sitting here wondering why I haven't heard from you. Flash me and I can call you back. Or tell me when is a good time to call. It's expensive, I know. Don't worry about the money, let me call you. As soon as you get this letter. It would be good to hear your voice.

Take care, man,

Tejani

Three times now Andrea Fernandez Mount had written to remind Kai he needed a medical, proof of his good health being the only remaining bar to his deliverance to the United States. She'd also written to tell him of his successful pass at the English proficiency test. So, he'd thought to himself, he could speak English after all. Well, that was always good to know. Kai turned the letters into a boat, an aeroplane and a pineapple and placed them upon the windowsill in his bedroom.

'Mansaray.'

Kai folds Tejani's letters across the same dirt-lined creases, returns them to his back pocket and follows the doctor into the room. The doctor is a man in his fifties, grey-haired, dignified and tired. He reads the letter Kai had given to the nurse. If he is surprised by the contents, it does not show.

'Take a seat.'

Kai sits.

'How do you feel?' he asks. 'Everything OK?'

'Yes.'

'No complaints?'

'None.'

The doctor signs the bottom of a typed form and hands it to Kai.

'Is that it?' asks Kai.

'What more do you want?' The doctor shrugs.

Kai stands. The doctor follows him to the door and calls the next patient.

In the street Kai hails a taxi. Time is short. A cab pulls over and he checks the driver's route, squeezes in next to the other passengers. At the US Embassy he drops down, enters the building, says to the marine, 'Miss Fernandez Mount, please.'

CHAPTER 52

The rains are over, seemingly fled the skies. Adrian feels the relief. The tide of red silt has cleared from the sea. The traffic speeds, the people slow. Today the patients are out in the sun raking the newly cut grass, a line of eight men bent at the waist. From his office Adrian watches Salia watching them, arms crossed, legs apart, white uniform spotless. At that moment Salia looks up, sees Adrian and raises a hand in salute. Adrian waves back. He turns away from the window.

Somewhere out there in this city is Mamakay. What is she doing? He imagines her in the crowds at the market, searching out bargains among the stalls. In the mornings he encourages her to spend the money he has given her to furnish the house. But she moves slowly and reluctantly, and Adrian waits for her the way he has learned, like a horse whisperer, with his back half turned.

He is happy. The new house, modest, white-painted but with good floors and a small garden, became theirs for a modest rent three weeks ago. The balcony at the back faces the mouth of a small river. Adrian worried about mosquitoes, but Mamakay assured him there would be none, and in this matter she has proved correct.

He is happy. Each morning he wakes up to absorb the fact of his new life. A week last Wednesday, outside a supermarket, he saw the deaf boy again, the boy he had first seen at the police station, arrested for who knew what reason. The boy had recognised him. Adrian gave the boy a coin. The boy pressed the fingers of both hands against his lips, gestured towards Adrian and smiled. He watched the boy run back to his friends. When they'd first met, he and the boy, Adrian had been a different person. He feels this so strongly he wonders how the boy had even recognised him.

He is happy. Except in those moments when he thinks of Kate and Lisa; a jolt from his conscience surges through his body hot like electricity. He looks in the mirror and sees the traces of grey which his hair has held for years, the two vertical lines between his eyebrows. He wonders how he can be doing what he is doing. At those times he hides himself from Mamakay, for fear of allowing her to see what he sees, that he is undeserving.

At night he and Mamakay read together, out of necessity making their own simple entertainment. They talk and play cards. Once Mamakay brought out a Ludo board, at once a reminder of Kai. Adrian pictured Kai, his erratic beard, too youthful to grow into a full beard. Jealousy like a snakebite to Adrian's heart. For some reason he found himself pretending he knew nothing of the rules of Ludo. He used it as an excuse not to play.

Last evening she lay on her back listening while he read aloud from a book and rubbed scented oil into the skin of her stomach with slow circular movements. From outside came the sounds of the mosque, of the football match playing at the video centre. Like a child she can hear the same story time and time again, though unlike a child she might snatch the paperback from his hand and read a section for herself, improving upon his inflection. She has a gift for it. Like a child she knows sections of the narrative by heart. ' "They say when trouble comes close ranks," ' she says in an accent incorrectly, yet somehow appropriately, of the Deep South. She has read *Wide Sargasso Sea* four times, though never *Jane Eyre*. He makes a promise to himself that he will find her a copy, it will be a gift, though he has no idea where he might find a Victorian novel in this city. He stores them up, these future gifts, in his mind, moments to be spun out into the future. He leans across and places the palm of his hand flat on her stomach. He thinks he feels the child inside, though it is but the shadow of her heartbeat.

Once she gave him a gift of her own. A miniature bottle of indigo pigment she'd found in a market a long time ago. The bottle had attracted her, tiny, sealed with lead, never opened. He wears it on a leather cord around his neck, tucked inside the breast pocket of his shirt. He tells himself that if he falls the glass will pierce his heart.

Most often the fear comes at night. He leaves the bed and wanders through the empty house. The electricity supply is erratic and means he must light a candle or else rely upon the moon. In those dark moments he thinks of the scale of what has been sacrificed, of Kate and Lisa, of the worst that could yet happen, that happiness such as this cannot last. He moves through the rooms and returns to bed, counting steps, counting seconds. When he slips back into bed alongside her, the fear lies low, below the surface.

One night he dreams he has lost her and wakes full of anguish. Her side of the bed is empty. When he finds her at the back of the house talking to a neighbour, absurdly anger comes as strongly as relief, that she should abandon him during his nightmare.

He watches her to see if he can catch a glimpse of what she is feeling. He sees her pleasure at his arrival, at his embrace, his small gifts and compliments. He sees no fear at all. And he asks himself, can this be so? Perhaps she does not love him. For she has never said she does and still does not talk about the future.

On Monday, three days from now, he has an appointment with Elias Cole. He has seen the old man twice since he arrived back in the country, though on neither occasion had much of consequence been said. Cole is dying. In the time Adrian had been away his condition had deteriorated again, the oxygen concentrator brought back to his room for the final road. There has been no reconciliation with Mamakay, for which Adrian considers himself responsible. It had been a disappointment when Cole declined to call for him. Adrian has become genuinely interested in the outcome, in getting to the point of Elias Cole.

That night, for the first time in many weeks, Adrian takes out his drawing pad and pencil and begins to sketch. He draws the fruit bats in the tree in the yard of the new house. For half an hour he struggles with a soft pencil to capture a likeness: the intense darkness of their faces, the brilliance of their eyes and small teeth, the elegance and fragility of their wings. He uses a flashlight to get close to them and they seem unperturbed. One of the bats is carrying a baby upon her body. Gradually he discerns differences between them, of character and features. After a while he reviews his work. There are several sketches. The first a study of the head of a bat. The second an image of the mother and her baby. A third of a spread wing: sheer matt skin, taut edges and graceful points. It seems to him unimaginable he ever found these creatures ugly. Quite simply, they are beautiful.

'I like that.' Mamakay, who has stolen up behind him, places her hands on his shoulders. 'Can I see?'

He holds up the sketchbook for her.

'May I keep it?' she asks.

'Of course.' He takes the sketchbook and tears out the page. Mamakay disappears and comes back with an empty frame. Adrian turns the pages of the pad, back to the earliest sketches of the sunbird outside the apartment at the hospital. He thinks of Kai and wonders if he still sleeps there. Or if Mamakay still thinks of him.

'There!' Mamakay holds up the drawing of the bats inside the frame. He smiles at her. Yes, it is one of his best. The best he has done since he came here.

Late in the evening, long after they have eaten and made love, he picks up his sketchbook again. Mamakay is lying on the wicker sofa; a *lappa* is wrapped around her body, twined around to the back of her neck, where it is caught in a heavy knot.

The rain is gone and the evening air is light. The heat, for once, has slipped back into the earth. A breeze toys with the hem of Mamakay's garment. The city seems very far away. He watches her for a long time, the sketchbook lying in his lap. It is hard to resist the urge to touch her. She is reading in the yellow lamplight, lying on her back and holding the book inches from her nose, her other arm thrown behind her. She lays the book upon her chest but otherwise remains as she is. Adrian picks up his pencil.

This night he draws her, eschewing studies and sketches, endeavouring to capture every line of her body. One by one, the lines fall upon the paper, each in its place. He works with intense concentration, can feel the tightness in his stomach. He is alive in the moment, nervous of making the next stroke, but knowing at the same time he cannot stop or whatever rhythm, whatever alchemy of brain and eyes and fingers that currently propels him will be lost. Once on paper, the moment will be held for ever, he can never forget it. He wills Mamakay not to move. On he draws until the precise moment comes when he is finished. Perhaps for the first time, he recognises the moment as it arrives. Not a single stroke erased or redrawn. The picture of Mamakay is a series of lines, curved and tapering. A curl of hair, the soft swell of her stomach. It is unlike anything he has ever drawn before.

'If you like bats so much, I can take you somewhere.'

He'd thought her asleep, she'd lain so still.

Where are they? Adrian has no idea. He turns to see the canoe, steered by the old fisherman with his single, narrow paddle, head back into the waves. A cannon lies half submerged. A small jetty reaches to the sea. A fort, ruined stone, thickly veined with creepers, stands above them. Mamakay's stride is shorter now than before, her breathing labours slightly. It is already late, perhaps six o'clock.

A path leads away from the small, gritty beach towards the interior of the island, past a graveyard in which stand half a dozen headstones. Adrian stops to read the names upon them and wonders what it took, all those years ago, to have words carved upon Scottish granite and brought back to be laid upon the tomb of a sailor whose own life-span upon this island had lasted only a matter of months. A row of undulating mounds stands almost as tall as Adrian. Hills of oyster shells, thousands upon thousands, marking long-ago years, when the men who lived here dined on oysters and rum; the bottles lie upon the beach, are wedged between the boulders, rock back and forth upon the sea bed.

They are walking downhill now, away from the oyster hills, a narrow path around the edge of a disintegrating wall.

'Here.' Mamakay turns and stops. They are in front of a doorway, or perhaps it is the mouth of a cave. Adrian leans into the narrow portal. A colossal, crowded darkness, seething with life, the sound of a billion beating hearts. To Adrian it feels as if the island itself is a living creature, whose centre the two of them have penetrated.

Outside, in front of the cave opening, they wait for night. As the darkness outside deepens, they hear inside the cave a stirring, awakenings. The first bat emerges, noiselessly, and is gone. It is followed by other bats, singly and then in twos and threes, leaving slipstreams of wind, treacle-soft and warm. Now in tens and twenties, finally in their hundreds, bats fly past them. Adrian stands unmoving, holds his breath for the minutes it takes for the bats to leave the cave. The air is turbulent with wings, dense with bodies. Threads of wind trail across his face and arms, seem to cling to him. The wind brings the tears to his eyes and he closes them. They are everywhere, above him, around him, though they never touch him. Their numbers seem unending, until suddenly everything comes to a halt. Adrian finds himself standing holding Mamakay in his arms. The breath comes fast and hard from their lips, their bodies tremble. They are holding each other, laughing.

Adrian opens his eyes and is instantly awake. The sun is strong and the sky a deep blue. It is the morning of his meeting with Elias Cole. Twenty minutes later looking into Elias Cole's face, Adrian finds himself searching for traces of Mamakay. There, in the line of the lips, the contour of the eyes, the slight prominence of the upper teeth. And when Cole smiles, as he did when Adrian entered, the likeness was there in the bottom lip, where it caught on and was pushed forward by the edge of the front teeth. How strange it is to see the face of a young and beautiful woman hidden within the folded curtains of an elderly man's skin. It occurs to Adrian he and Elias Cole are practically kin.

Cole removes the breathing apparatus from his face.

'Good morning,' says Adrian. Somehow seeing Cole like that makes him draw several deep breaths, like a thirsty man drinking water.

'Good morning.' The voice as dry as paper.

'How are you getting on?'

Cole shrugs. 'I have nothing to complain of.'

The air in the room is cooler than outside. Grateful for this, Adrian sits in his customary seat. Over the last two days he has reread his clinical notes in their entirety. Even after he had done so Elias Cole still retained a certain opacity. As a man he was possessive, controlling and ambitious, though none of those to a degree that was by any means pathological. His was a case of mediocrity rising. If he'd been possessed of any real talent he would have been seen as a threat by the Dean and eliminated like so many others. He had allied himself with the Dean and ridden on the back of the Dean's ambition. When the Dean became Vice Chancellor he promoted Cole to his old position. In England Adrian met people like Elias Cole every day; some of them were his colleagues. Cole was jealous of his younger brother, whom he also loved. Parallels there between the brother and Julius. Cole had alluded to them himself. In some ways he appeared to know himself well, which made whatever he was concealing all the more cleverly hidden. Unless of course the occlusion was taking place on the level of the subconscious. Adrian doubted this. He suspected Cole had been manipulating him.

'There's something I wanted to ask you.'

'By all means.'

'Did you ever see Johnson again?'

Silence.

Will Cole take the easy way out and lie? Adrian half expects him to. Instead he replies, 'So someone has been talking to you. That is always a danger in this place. Full of gossips and whisperers.'

Now it is Adrian's turn to be silent as he considers his reply, at what point to mention Mamakay, when Cole continues, 'But then again, Babagaleh tells me you and my daughter have become acquainted.'

'Yes,' says Adrian.

'Did you think perhaps I didn't know? Or were you worried I would disapprove? Well, I don't. Get her out of this place. There's nothing for her here.'

'She wants to stay.'

'I don't doubt it. She was always contrary in that way.' A pause. 'And it was from my daughter you learned I kept occasional company with Johnson?'

'Yes,' says Adrian.

'Hmmph.' Cole gives a soft snort. 'And who told her?'

'She recognised him when he visited your house. She'd seen him before.'

Cole nods slowly. All the time he is thinking, moving the fingers of his right hand, flexing them one after the other, so they ripple like a fan. Adrian can almost hear his brain tick. He looks away.

'It was a social relationship,' says Cole presently. 'We drank whisky. He had a taste for Black Label, as I recall. It cost me a fortune. We discussed the state of the country. I was Dean by then. It was important to have a sense of what was going on.'

'Can you see how that would seem strange to someone on the outside? Given what you told me about him, your feelings for him?'

Cole flicks his fingers and then closes them into his palm. His tone is subtly changed. Adrian listens carefully, trying to define the shift, but fails to pinpoint it.

'As you so rightly put it, you are an outsider. This is a small country. You've never lived in a place like this. Here enemies are a luxury only the poor can afford. The rest of us have to move on – to use your terminology. I made my peace with power. I had no other choice.' He smiles thinly at Adrian.

'You were friends.'

'Acquaintances would be my preferred term.'

'How did it happen? I mean, how did it happen that you found your way into his company again?'

'I forget now. I believe he came by the house. I don't really recall.'

'Sometimes people can find themselves thrown together by events. Something that binds them in an unlikely way.' Johnson was ambitious and clever, but lacked a truly first-rate mind, the fact of which he concealed with belligerence and obtuseness. If Cole couldn't see the similarities between himself and Johnson, Adrian could. It was remarkable, in fact. Projection? Perhaps. Though it didn't do to be too clever about these things. Johnson might just as easily be exactly as Cole described. On many occasions Adrian had asked himself whether the connection with Johnson went deeper than Cole allowed.

Cole frowns. 'He was an acquaintance. Nothing more.'

'Who gave Johnson the list of students? Was it you?'

Cole's face remains impassive, though Adrian sees the light change in his eyes, a muscle flinch in his cheek. He regards Adrian with an expression emptied of meaning.

'What is it you think you know of these matters?'

'I only know what you and your daughter have told me. In her view you betrayed her friends the night the campus was attacked. You delivered them to Johnson.'

The silence this time is longer. Cole shakes his head. He seems to have regained control of his composure so fast Adrian is momentarily unsure now whether he even lost it. He says, 'It is what she believes.'

Cole continues to shake his head until he provokes a minor coughing fit. He pulls himself up, his elbows angled sharply outwards, raises his head, breathes deeply and exhales, closing his eyes.

'Could you call Babagaleh for me, please?'

Adrian does as he is asked. He doesn't follow Babagaleh back into the room, but waits in the corridor, his back against the warm grit of the bare concrete wall. Through the door he can hear the sounds of movement, the murmur of the oxygen concentrator, the whisper of voices. He cannot make out what is being said. Fifteen minutes elapse. Adrian waits. His conversation with Elias Cole needs to be finished, taken to its conclusion, whatever that might be. Cole is tiring. The change Adrian heard in his voice when he first entered the room, behind the rattle of the stiffened lungs, the vocal cords taut and dry: Cole is wearing out.

The door opens and Babagaleh steps into the corridor, nods at Adrian, who pushes open the door to the room. Cole is lying on his pillow much as Adrian left him, his eyes closed.

'We all live with the consequences of our pasts, don't we? One might ask what brought you here? Compassion? Career? The failure of marriage symbolised by the ring you no longer wear? And why here?

'Babagaleh tells me your grandfather's name was Silk. That he was posted here before the war. I mean *your* war, of course. Naturally I find that interesting, as a historian. Fortunately our recorded history here is short enough for me to be able to remember most of it. Our last Governor was Beresford Stuke. Silk served under his predecessor. An undistinguished career, if you'll forgive my saying so. Apart from the minor fiasco of the chief's rebellion, I dare say he would have gone on to something quite good.

'Babagaleh's brother – I use the term loosely, he claims so many – is a barman at the Ocean Club. Did I ever tell you that? The chap must be about due for retirement now. He was even there in my day.'

Adrian is silent. Cole, who is not looking at him but out of the window, continues. 'There are some things that may have happened in the past that carried less weight then than they do now. Or vice versa. That seemed important then, and now are all but forgotten. Time presses hard on me, lying here. It's hard not to think of these things.

'Where were we? Oh, yes. We were talking about Johnson. What a fellow! I disliked him. In fact it wouldn't be going too far to say I hated him. But, you see, you don't make an enemy of a man like Johnson. Not if you have any sense. Keep your friends close and your enemies closer, isn't that what they say? Whatever I did, I did for Mamakay. She was too close to where the trouble was. She risked being caught up in it. Johnson was on to them. With or without me, the net was closing. I had to take care of my own. Any father would have done the same. If I gave Johnson a list of names, it was because I had no choice. Was I to know what he would do with them?

'Julius was a fool. He refused to see the change coming even though it was in the sky. Perhaps he imagined he could alter the weather. He riled Johnson, just as he riled the university authorities.

'Sometimes I wonder, if he had lived, who would he have become? Would he be Dean of his faculty? Not likely. He was a dreamer. He dreamt of building cities, bridges, raising towers up to the sky, flying to the moon, for God's sake!

'That night, the first night I was in Johnson's power, was the worst of my life. I told you what happened. He stole my cake, duped me into believing he was coming back, left me there and never returned. I banged on the door and nobody came.

407

'Nobody came for one, two, I don't recall how many hours. I was left alone. But in the end somebody did come. Not Johnson, for he had gone home, one of his guards. I was taken from that place and led downstairs to another room. It was much cooler there, I was grateful for it at first. But gradually it turned cold, and the cold bored through me. I tried to sleep. At some point in the night I had that image of myself, a dark, untidy shape. A shape devoid of detail and yet unmistakably mine, the shadow of me. I slept again and was woken, I think, by a cry somewhere in the building. I sat and listened. Silence. The cry, if that was what I had heard, did not come again. Instead I heard something else, a sound like a tiny spinning top, a whirr and a clatter. It came regularly, at intervals. The same sound, but with enough variance to suggest human agency rather than the sound of a machine. In time I thought I recognised it. You remember I told you Julius almost always carried something in his pocket, something to fiddle with. A screw, a bolt and washer. Julius's worry beads. The sound was coming from the other side of the wall. I heard coughing. Julius. I listened. I knocked. The coughing stopped. The knock came back to me. I was sure, then, it was Julius. I did not dare speak, for fear of attracting the guards. But Julius had no such fear. "Hello," he said. "Hello? Who's there?" He had no way of knowing it was me. I'm not certain he even knew I'd been arrested, unless Johnson had told him. I hesitated. I opened my mouth to reply and then I heard someone coming. A sharp rap on Julius's door. The rest of the night passed in silence. Silence, save for the sound of Julius's worry beads, the spinning top wearing itself out over and over again. At some point even that stopped.

'The next night, after a day of enduring Johnson's torment, I was returned to the same cell. I lay with my face pressed into the grit of the floor. I did not hear Julius's worry beads. It occurred to me he'd been moved, possibly even released, though I doubted that. He was, after all, the main object of Johnson's interest. I was afraid for myself. Johnson had succeeded in constructing such a case against me I was almost convinced of my own involvement. I did not see how I was going to get out of this. And even if I did, my career, my reputation, these things were sullied for ever. It was Saturday night and nobody in the world knew where I was. I feared the night and I feared the next day.

'At some point I slept and woke. An insect crawled over my face.

Too dark to see the hands of my watch. I guessed it was somewhere between two and four o'clock in the morning. I stared into the darkness. I listened, desperate for a sound to assure me I was alive. In the room upstairs I'd at least been able to hear something of the outside world. Down here there was no window, nothing. As I listened I became aware of a sound. I crawled over to the wall on the side next to where I thought Julius was being held. I pressed my ear against the wall. Yes, I could hear it clearly now. A wheezing. No, it was somehow a more desperate sound than mere wheezing. A gulping noise, is how I would describe it. I tapped. Once, twice. But this time nobody tapped back. In my heart I had no doubt it was Julius.

'What should I do? If I called for a guard, I doubted very much anybody would come, and if they did they were equally likely to become heavy-handed with me. We were in an unforgiving place. I could end up making more trouble for myself, for Julius. I pressed my ear against the wall. I leant back and considered matters. Surely Julius had his medication. I struggled to decide what was best. I told myself he didn't sound so bad. That he was surely capable of calling for aid himself if he was indeed in trouble. At other times I worried how long he had been in this condition. I reasoned the guards must have been in and out of his cell in the course of the day. In this way my thoughts moved back and forth. At one point I heard a cough. I read that as a good sign. Somehow I fell asleep. When I woke it was dawn and I was still living in the nightmare.

'That morning the Dean came to see me. A deal with Johnson was suggested. I gave him my notebooks in return for my freedom. I never returned to the cell in the basement. In those first few minutes I was so relieved to be free I forgot all about Julius. The Dean accompanied me to my office in the faculty building to collect the notebooks. He was irritable, angry at being called out to attend to me when he should have been in church. I could tell my odour offended him, for I had spent two days under duress without washing.

'If Johnson was in any way pleased to receive my notebooks he chose not to show it. Why was I not surprised? Because by then I knew the man had all sorts of tricks and power games of his own making. He merely thanked me and asked one of his men to take us to the entrance of the building. It was then I remembered Julius. I stopped and turned at the door. The Dean saw me hesitate. I looked at Johnson, who looked straight back at me. The Dean looked at us both. "For heaven's sake, what is it now?" Johnson was silent, but continued to look at me with a calm regard. And I saw in that moment that Johnson knew. I could tell it from his eyes. Johnson knew everything. I was within seconds of walking out of that building for ever. I had everything to lose. I closed my mouth. We turned to leave. And that was the last view I had of Johnson: standing behind his desk, the books held to his chest, a black-suited figure, a devilish pastor.

'So you see what happened? I did nothing. Johnson was the one who let Julius die. But the truth, the truth if you want to know – and I have thought about this for many years. The truth is Julius brought it upon himself. He never knew what was good for him. He presumed too much.'

So this is how the entire course of a life, of history, is changed.

A day later Adrian stands at the window and watches the men rake the grass. They are nearly finished now and the work has done much to raise their spirits.

A life, a history, whole patterns of existence altered, simply by doing nothing. The silent lie. The act of omission. Whatever you like to call it. Adrian collects his briefcase from its place by the door, steps out and locks the door behind him. Elias Cole would never take responsibility for his hand in Julius's fate. The fragmentation of the conscience. Cole absolved himself the moment he handed responsibility for Julius to Johnson, in the same way he handed the list of students to Johnson knowing and yet refusing to acknowledge the likely outcome. He absolved himself of responsibility for the greater crime and yet it could not have occurred without him. There are millions of Elias Coles the world over. Suddenly Adrian is tired.

One or two of the men nod to Adrian as he passes by. They do not smile or speak, but he knows that now he is held high in their regard. Salia is there and raises a hand. The fragmentation of the conscience. Adecali, tortured by those acts he had committed. Elias Cole unperturbed by the many he had not. Adecali was made to feel shame, was held culpable. Cole was venerated. Yet where does the greater evil lie, if evil is what you call it? Somewhere in the place he calls a soul, Elias Cole knows. Adrian has been his last attempt at absolution, his last attempt to convince himself of his own cleanliness.

Adrian drives slowly home. Though the roads are heavy with

cars and minibuses, the traffic keeps moving. At a junction he stops and watches a man with matted dreadlocks feed crumbs of cake to a skinny dog lying curled against him. Both dog and man look entirely content. He crosses each of three bridges. The first, which divides the west of the city from the east. He reaches the junction where the traffic policeman with the wheeling arms stands. There he turns right over the peninsula bridge, where Julius as a boy was once lowered over the side by the men who built it, in order that he might write all their initials in the wet cement on the side. The boy had watched them every day for months as they built the bridge. Julius's bridge. The final and smallest bridge is the one over the river next to his new home. Adrian turns down the track.

He is early. He knows Mamakay likes to sleep in the heat of the afternoon those days she is able, for the baby keeps her awake at night. There are times he has returned home to find her asleep on the cane sofa on the verandah. For some reason it embarrasses her to be caught sleeping. The thought makes him smile. He will surprise her. There she is. His footsteps must sound in her dreams for she begins to stir as he mounts the last few steps. He walks towards her, she opens her eyes.

He smiles.

She blinks, looks up at him, her eyes wide, frowning slightly.

'What is it?' he says.

She half rises. Her hand is feeling among her skirts, patting the cushions of the old sofa as though searching for a lost ring. Adrian follows the movements of her hand, until he sees the wide, dark stain spread out upon her skirt and the covers of the chair.

CHAPTER 53

In front of Kai, Zainab behaved demurely, just as she appeared to be in her photograph, a girl possessed of the manners of the village. She regarded his footwear when she spoke to him, giggled behind her hand and smiled with her lips held together. In Kai's opinion she nevertheless succeeded in giving the impression of being in possession of some impertinent secret, some item of unwholesome knowledge about him. Foday gazed at her with open admiration. And Kai too had taken a liking to Zainab, despite scarcely succeeding in pressing a word out of her. It was in the clarity of her gaze that Kai saw a young woman who knew exactly who she was in this world.

Later, passing by the window next to Foday's bed, Kai hears Zainab's giggle transformed into laughter: full-throated and rebellious.

Kai retires to update Foday's records. The main consequence of the infection is to delay what comes next: removal of the cast, physiotherapy, the final operation on the right foot. He closes his eyes, leans back in the chair and immediately is drawn towards sleep, sliding backwards only to be jerked forward. There are times the desire for sleep became so urgent it is the very thing that keeps him awake. Somewhere a door slams. Kai opens his eyes and sits up straight, shakes his head and opens his eyes wide. The light in the room seems to fracture and fragment, particles of bright light appear and disappear. He rubs his eyelids. The long nights of sleeplessness always return in the end. As a child he'd been afraid of the creatures that lived under his bed, though somehow the fear never prevented him sleeping. Well, now he'd take back the monsters any time.

Yesterday he had gone into town to an Internet café and sent an email to Tejani, then sat and waited for the email to go. Everything was done, he told Tejani, the process complete. Andrea Fernandez Mount had called with the news herself. Kai's application had been accepted. His visa had come through. Afterwards he'd walked the whole way home, moving through the heat, traffic, dust and crowds as though contained inside his own invisible tunnel.

He rises and makes a tour of the hospital: emergency, the wards, intensive care, the labs.

Eight o'clock. He is in the laboratory checking on the results of a blood sample when he sees Seligmann pass by, propelled forwards by the speed of his gait, a half-doughnut in one hand. Kai hands the slide he is holding back to the lab assistant and follows Seligmann to the operating theatre. By the first door he sees Adrian, wonders briefly at his presence there. Kai does not nod or call or wave. It is dark. Most likely Adrian, who is standing under the light, cannot see Kai crossing the quadrangle, for he does not wave or call either. It is months since they last spoke. Adrian is not looking his way, but talking to Mrs Mara. Kai is in a hurry. He walks past them, hears Mrs Mara call his name. He doesn't want to stop now. Because of Adrian, because of Seligmann. He'll deal with whatever she wants later. He looks around for Seligmann.

Afterwards he will remember the faces. Not Seligmann's, for Seligmann was the only one who didn't realise what was happening, but the faces of the others. The eyes. Some following him. Others downcast. The silence. None of the banter of the OR. At the time he had thought nothing of it. He was tired, relieved not to be forced into a jocularity he didn't feel. A memory of Mrs Mara reaching out for him as he went by, as if to touch him on the shoulder. He had walked quickly past them all. All except Seligmann, whom he went to assist.

At first he does not recognise her. Seligmann is talking to him. Kai is listening to the older man. But Kai is the kind of doctor who looks into the faces of his patients and surely, soon enough, he looks.

She is conscious, still. She smiles to see him. There is no sign of fear in her eyes. She tells him she is glad he is here, because she had asked for him. Before she can say any more the pain comes. He can see the power in it as it builds, a mighty surge. It is awesome. Her fingernails press into his forearm. He feels the pressure in his arm turn to pain, wishes he could transfer all that she is feeling from her body to his own. He watches the pain take her, like a dam bursting.

'Go on,' he tells her. For God's sake, go on. Shout. Scream. It doesn't matter to me. But she does not hear him and no longer sees him. The breath leaves her in a long shuddering groan.

'Somebody you know?' asks Seligmann.

Kai nods.

Seligmann's eyes are upon Kai's face. For once the older man is not whistling. 'We have to get the child out of there. She may have ruptured. Are you up for this? I can bring someone else in.'

'I'm fine.'

'Then let's get going.'

Kai doesn't want her awake for this. He doesn't want her asleep either. He wants her conscious, so he can talk to her, comfort her. Now that he has her again, he does not want to let her go. He goes to her and takes her hand.

'I'm here. I love you,' he whispers. He wants to reach her.

She smiles. 'I know. Didn't you say you'd deliver all my babies? Or did you refuse? I can't remember.' She opens her mouth: 'Alph . . .'

Then she is in pain again.

Kai nods to the anaesthetist, who depresses the syringe, releasing the fluid into the plastic line. He holds Nenebah's hand and watches her face. Feels her fingers tighten in his, and then relax. Sees his reflection in her eyes, the theatre lights above him, watches the light shimmer and still, the eyelids close.

On a hillside. When? Five, six, a thousand years ago, before a war came along and blew them all in different directions. They were students sitting in their favourite place in the hills above the university. He proposed to her and she accepted him in return for a ring of plaited grass. See here. She shows her finger off to Tejani. Kai sets about weaving her a necklace and a crown of grass, entwined with flowers. Ants, drunk on nectar, crawl from the blossoms. An ant crawls across her bare stomach, merging briefly with the two moles below her navel. Kai blows the ant away. Hey. She slaps him softly. That was our firstborn. You blew away our son. He buries his face in her stomach, bites the flesh. There'll be more. Millions more, you'll see. She hits him with her crown of flowers, showering him with ants and petals.

For a month they made up names for the ant babies, until they had a list of twenty names memorised by heart. Then, because it was altogether more practical, they decided to use those twenty names in alphabetical order for the millions of ant babies to come. Alpha, Brima, Chernor . . .

For some reason they were all boys.

★   ★   ★

Kai watches the blade of Seligmann's scalpel slip between the two moles.

Behind him, through the double doors, a nurse enters with a message. Adrian is outside in the corridor wanting to speak to him. But Kai cannot speak to Adrian now.

'Tell me what I should say?' asks the young nurse.

'Tell him to stand by to give blood.' He glances at her, notices how her eyes do not meet his.

CHAPTER 54

As a boy, Adrian loved many things. He loved the freedom of cycling the roads around his house. He loved the water, swimming, the icy pull of the North Sea. He loved to lie on the lawn and feel the sun upon his eyelids. He loved birds in all their varieties. For days one summer he watched as a wren built her nest in the vines which grew against his bedroom window, watched her as if on a screen, warming her eggs and feeding her young, unaware of Adrian on the other side of the glass. Another summer, spent by the sea, he had sat up all night listening out for the bittern's echoing call. When it came his companions were all asleep and Adrian hadn't woken them, but instead stayed awake alone through the long night waiting to hear it again. During those hours, as he sat hugging his knees in the cold clear night, surrounded by sleeping bodies, the flat land and immense bowl of the sky, the dark water slipping through the reeds, listening for the call of a bird so rare as to be all but extinct, he had for the first time in his life become deeply aware of his own mortality. It was, he thought later, the first time he had seen himself as a finite being, with a beginning, a middle and an end. Up until then he'd never imagined death could touch him. He had no idea why it should happen on that night, whether it was connected to the disappearing bittern, or prompted by some change in the circumstances of his life, his father's illness, perhaps, or whether he had simply come to an age when he could remember there being a past, and when the future seemed for the first time visible instead of hazy, consisting of more than just the afternoon or the day ahead. He was sixteen.

In the months and years that followed he left behind the lives of birds and immersed himself in the world of humans, qualifying one decade later as a psychologist. Several years afterwards, in a street in Norwich, he had bumped into one of his companions from the camping trip, now a father of three running a dry-cleaning business. The other man had been unable to recall any of the trip. Pressed by Adrian, he shook his head and shrugged. Adrian had spoken of the bittern's cry. Not me, said the fellow. I've lived here all my life and never heard a bittern. And Adrian remembered that nobody had heard the bird but him, and so he had no way of knowing whether it had ever truly occurred. There were days, some, when he imagined the night was nothing but a dream.

Now, standing in the corridor, in the sickly shadows of the fluorescent light, he returns to that place. The night of the bittern, the place of solitude and mortality. He knows nothing about how this will all end, except that it will surely end. He tries to imagine himself into a future, somewhere past this point, but he cannot. There is nothing to do but to keep on existing, in this exact time and place. This is what hell must be like. Waiting without knowing. Not hell, but purgatory. Worse than hell.

A nurse comes to him and asks him his blood group. Adrian doesn't know. She pricks his finger, swabs the blood on to a glass slide and departs. Adrian sucks hard at his finger, forcing out the drops, is reminded momentarily of standing outside his mother's house on the half-finished deck with a splinter in his finger. It feels more like a dream than a memory.

People pass him, going in and out of the operating theatre. At some point he is asked to move, by whom he cannot remember, told he is standing in what is strictly speaking a sterile area. He is shown into a small room, given a cup of coffee. He has made few friends at the hospital, did not think his relationship with Mamakay was well known. He is considerably older than most of them. And yet here they are, showing him kindness. At some point in those hours Mrs Mara comes by and tries to coax him to wait in her office. Adrian shakes his head. He can barely focus on her words. His body is numb, his brain a vortex of half-formed thoughts. At moments he paces the room unable to sit, at others he slumps, suddenly inert, as though the bones have been sucked out of his body. Everybody around him seems to walk with speed and purpose. There is no one to talk to, no one to ask what is happening. He wants to catch one of them by the arm, but he is afraid of becoming a distraction, aware of how irrelevant he is to all of this, how purposeless his presence.

It is so quiet. None of the whisper and murmur of other hospitals he has been inside: the cushioned floors and draped curtains, the breathing of air conditioning and electronic heartbeat of monitors. Only the slap of rubber shoes on cement, the banging of doors. Hard, comfortless sounds. Even the light is hard, shines so bright it hurts the eyes and yet barely illuminates.

Another time he steps out of the waiting room. He realises he has no idea how much time has passed. An hour? A minute? He thinks it must be past midnight. He sees the nurse who swabbed blood from his finger. 'What about the blood?' he asks. 'Shouldn't I go somewhere to give blood?' But she shakes her head and tells him he is not a match, not the right blood group. She smiles at him, and he tries to read her smile for whatever information it might contain. He returns to the room and sits down on the bench upon which has been placed a thin mattress, leans his back against the wall, feels the palpitations of his heart.

Sounds in the hallway. A commotion. Adrian stands and then sits back down, stands again and opens the door. The corridor is empty, the hard light reflecting on the painted floor. Suddenly sound and movement burst upon the emptiness. A gurney appears wheeled by a pair of orderlies. A man, awake and moaning in pain, lies upon it. The man's leg is exposed, his trousers have been cut away. There is a bloodstained dressing. Nurses appear. The door to the operating theatre opens, to the theatre where Mamakay is. A surgeon comes out – what's his name, Seligmann? Yes, Seligmann. Now he is looking at the man on the gurney, giving a rapid series of instructions to a nurse as he inspects the man's wounds. The nurse is fitting a strap to the man's arm. Adrian feels the tension rising in his chest. He has stopped breathing. Who is the man upon the gurney? He wishes the man away, wishes he would vanish or die, he just wants Seligmann to go back inside the theatre. This man, this new patient, is an unwanted diversion.

He made a mistake in staying here, in letting her stay here. He sees it now. Too wrapped in love, seduced by the beauty of this broken country, this was his failure. This is not a place to live one's life. It is his fault, not Mamakay's, for she knows no other life. He should have known better, he let things go to his head, let the place seep through his pores and into his soul. When this is over he will take her away. They will go together to Britain. He will take care of her. She will be fine with the idea, because it is for the best. There will be none of this. There will be order. There will be quiet. There will be people to explain. There will be understanding. Everything will be clear. She has waved away suggestions of leaving, but she will see it now. Here there is nothing, they are both at the mercy of this place, like everybody else. At home, his home, it will be different. She will be happy, for what is there not to be happy about living beyond the shadow of disaster. Her anger will be calmed, her restlessness stilled, once she is far from the events of her past.

Please God, let it not be too late.

It could be that simple. It is that simple.

It is never that simple.

He knows what he is doing. He's already bartering with God, making offerings. It is for just such times humankind invented gods, while hope still exists. When hope disappears, men don't call for God, they call for their mothers.

Adrian sits down on the bench, his elbows on his knees, his face covered by his hands, feels his breath hot in his cupped hands. He is aware of a scent of her upon his fingers. He inhales deeply and holds his breath for as long as he can. The longer they are in there, the more serious it becomes. He stares into the darkness he has created. He prays.

Once, twice, he hears the sound of footsteps, the sound of the OR doors swinging back upon themselves. Each time he rises and goes to the door, but by the time he looks out whoever it was has passed by and disappeared.

He wishes he could sleep simply in order to wake up and find all this had never happened. The moment of his arrival home, the bloodstains on Mamakay's skirts, watching her face collapse in pain, her fear for the child, the drive to the hospital, the hideous traffic.

He tries to smell her again upon his fingers, but the scent eludes him. Perhaps he imagined it.

Two o'clock. A moth is banging itself against the ceiling and the bare, bright bulb. Silvery, dark smudges upon the white paint. Adrian's body aches, the sweat in his armpits has dried and grown damp several times over. He needs air. He rises and exits the room and then the building. He stands in the courtyard. People are sitting huddled on a mat spread in the corridor – the family of the man they brought in, presumably, one of them a woman nursing a baby. Adrian turns away from them, stands and stares at the sky. He feels tears well and subside. He takes a deep breath of the warm air. He closes his eyes. A sound rises in his throat, a long low sigh, of which he is entirely unaware. He is desolate.

After a few moments he turns and walks back into the building, down towards the room where he has waited out half the night. As he approaches the last of the doors, he sees, through the square pane of glass, that the doors of the operating theatre are open. They are coming out. He starts to run, sees the first person appear. It is Kai. Kai!

But Kai doesn't hear him, doesn't turn or look up, is pulling his mask from his face, and as he walks his feet barely clear the floor. He does not hear Adrian because the sound of Adrian's call, before it began, died in his throat. Something in the set of Kai's shoulders. Why is he walking like that? It is all wrong. Adrian pushes through the door, begins to run down the corridor.

'Kai!'

At the sound of him Kai lifts his head. Suddenly he no longer looks defeated but very alert. He turns square to Adrian, begins to move towards him down the corridor. He walks fast, very fast indeed. It crosses Adrian's mind how strange it is: Kai walking towards him, his head lowered, arms by his sides, fists clenched, at such a pace. Now he is lifting his arms. Adrian stops and waits, puzzled, unmoving. Standing thus, he takes the full force of the push, feels the heels of Kai's hands hard against his chest. Out of his mouth is expelled all the air in his lungs. Winded, he doubles over, sees Seligmann hurrying towards them. A nurse, eyes round above her mask. Kai's face above his, Kai's voice ringing in the empty corridor, calling Adrian a bastard. Now Seligmann is there. A hand on each man, on Kai's arm and Adrian's shoulder. Seligmann is pushing Adrian back against the wall, peering into Adrian's face.

Adrian wants to speak, to ask Seligmann about Mamakay, for Seligmann surely knows and will tell him. He tries to take a breath, to form the words, but he cannot.

Four o'clock. Adrian places the glass back on the table. He watches the movement of his hand, listens to the knock of the glass against the table surface. Opposite him sits Kai. They are in the old apartment, now returned to its former use as a place for on-duty staff to rest. Salt has dried on Adrian's cheek, his skin is dry and tight. He feels the contractions in his empty stomach, but they come without the accompanying desire for food and he mutes the pangs with shots of whisky. They sit in silence. Seligmann is long gone, knowing he was neither needed nor wanted. The whisky is courtesy of him. They are, neither of them, drunk. Though Adrian longs to be.

A sigh from Kai, who sits with his fist clenched, shakes his head as he stares at the floor. For the last three hours his mood has swung the short distance between grief and rage. Adrian has wept, but so far Kai has remained dry-eyed. 'Sometimes I kid myself into believing it might be over, finally,' he says.

'That what might be over?'

'The dying, the killing. That perhaps the bloodthirsty bastard up there might have had enough for the day. Or might pick on someone else for a change.'

Adrian is silent.

'Why? Why the fuck?'

'I don't know,' says Adrian.

'She survived everything else, survived the war. She was never afraid, you know. I never saw her afraid in all that time. There were times I was afraid, Jesus, yes – but not her. Even when they brought her here tonight. Fear equals defeat in her vocabulary. Fear of what, it doesn't matter. The trick is – you didn't give in.' He changes tense as he speaks of Mamakay, from present to past, to present. 'Like death was a big dog or something. You should never show it you are afraid. I told her that once. She liked it. Death the dog. Or perhaps it was fate. Yes, fate – you must never show fate you're afraid.'

'I believe that,' says Adrian.

'What?'

'That she treated fate like a big dog.'

Kai laughs, as if remembering something else. A moment later the smile drops off his face and he clenches his fist again. They sit in silence for several minutes more.

'I wish I knew what to do,' says Adrian.

'Go home.'

Adrian blinks and looks up at Kai.

'Go home,' repeats Kai. 'What in the hell did you ever come here for, anyway?' He speaks tiredly and does not raise his voice.

Adrian looks down.

'Well?' Louder this time.

Still Adrian doesn't answer.

Kai continues, 'I'm serious. It's a genuine question. Why did you come here and have you found whatever it was you were looking for?' He is slipping back towards anger of which Adrian has seen plenty that night.

To Adrian a memory of their first meeting, here in this room. Kai had called Adrian a tourist, had always questioned his right to be here, even once they'd become friends. 'What makes you think I was looking for something?'

Kai shrugs, continues to stare at the floor. 'Everybody who comes here wants something, my friend. You came here because you wanted to be a hero is my guess. So do you feel like one now?'

To Adrian, Kai's anger is understandable. If Adrian had never come here, these events would never have taken place. Mamakay would be alive. It is the logic of grief. Equally, thinks Adrian, if he had taken her away from here, back to England – she would be alive, too. He replies levelly, 'You know already why I came here. I was sent as part of a medical team. I came back to help. That's the sum of it.'

Now Adrian looks back on the past it seems disordered, a tangle of days, weeks and months. Looking forward, he sees nothing, only the narrow walls of the tunnel of his existence and the thought that he will never see Mamakay again. The thought is too enormous for his mind to hold on to. He lets it go. He should go home, but he doesn't want to. He doesn't want to be alone. Being with Kai is as close as he can get to Mamakay, even though Kai is angry.

'And have you?'

Adrian has forgotten what they were talking about. He looks up. 'Have I what?'

'Helped? Have you helped?'

Now Adrian feels a small starburst of anger. 'Yes,' he says, to put an end to it. He looks directly at Kai at the same time as Kai looks up. Their eyes meet. In Kai's face there is cold rage. Adrian opens his mouth. He could give Kai the names of men at the hospital, talk about the group meetings, the sessions with Adecali. Attila's smiling scepticism. He drops his eyes, rubs his eyelids. He offers none of this. It is not the point. And anyway, everything he has done here is worthless. He says, 'You have nightmares.'

Another shrug. 'Who doesn't?'

'Plenty of people. The occasional bad dream, perhaps. But not recurrent nightmares. Not nightmares that stop you sleeping for nights on end. Not nightmares that result in insomnia – chronic insomnia, that is – so that your functions are impaired the next day.'

'I see,' says Kai. He is leaning back now, regarding Adrian through hooded lids. 'And you're sure of this?'

'What? That other people don't suffer recurrent nightmares? Yes. I am sure. Though I am also sure there are a lot of people in this country who do, people who have survived a trauma. It would be extraordinary if it was otherwise.'

'No, I mean about me.'

'I know you suffer nightmares. The rest is an educated guess. I know you're afraid to cross the bridge. The one over to the peninsula. You always drive the long way around.'

'Yup, you're right. I dream. I dream about the same thing. I dream about something that happened. I could tell you, but it wouldn't make any difference. You can't undo it. And how could you ever understand? Unless you were here how could you ever understand? The truth is none of you wanted to know then, so why do you care now?' Kai is not looking at Adrian but staring into his glass, swirling the liquid around and around. He stops, raises the glass to his lips and drinks, recommences the same circular movement.

On the table lies a small red paper fan. Adrian recognises it as Mamakay's. Left behind during one of her visits when he still lived here, maybe even the same day they saw Kai. Adrian reaches for it. 'You loved her, I know,' he says.

'Yes,' Kai replies. 'I loved her. I love her.' He snorts softly again and shakes his head. Silence. Then, 'There was never anyone else.'

Adrian rises and goes to the window. A cat moves in and out of the moon shadows, its mouth closed around a small animal, a mouse. Death everywhere. Death so ordinary. Still with his back to Kai, he says, 'I don't think she ever lost her feelings for you.'

'It doesn't matter now.'

'It matters. Not for me. You hate me right now, I understand that. But for her, it matters. And for you.'

'I don't hate you.'

'I think she still loved you,' says Adrian. There, he has said it now, the one thing he never let himself think, which had nevertheless tormented him. Kai and Mamakay were so much the same in so many ways; perhaps that is why Adrian had cared for both of them. He remembers his jealousy of Kai. He is jealous no longer. The feeling is gone, obliterated by everything that has happened.

A hospital porter, arriving for work, moves like a shadow along the far wall. Adrian watches him until he rounds the corner. Life going on as normal. Isn't that what the bereaved always say? How everything seemed so normal, the day their lives were changed. The blue sky, the falling leaves, the song on the car radio, the car crash.

Nothing to do but pour more whisky.

'She wanted the baby raised here,' Adrian says, still with his face to the window.

'I know,' says Kai. I know.

'She was happy here.'

'We all were happy here once.'

Adrian stands at the window and does not move or say anything more. Behind him he can hear the swirl of liquid in Kai's glass. After perhaps ten minutes he goes and sits down again. 'There are ways, you know, of controlling the nightmares,' he says.

Kai shrugs. The gesture sits oddly on him.

'One day. Whenever you're ready,' offers Adrian. 'There's no hurry.'

Silence again. Suddenly Kai straightens and places his glass hard on the table.

'Now.'

'What?'

'Let's do it now. Come on.'

'Are you serious?'

That awful shrug again. 'Sure, I'm serious.'

Adrian takes a deep breath. 'If you want, we'll do it some other time.'

'Ah,' says Kai. 'Come back when it's more convenient.'

Adrian feels the inaudible snapping of one strand of his self-control. He stands and goes into the kitchen, where he leans against the worktop breathing deeply. He helps himself to a drink of water. Outside the dark has turned to grey, shifting in shades towards dawn. Adrian stands and lifts the edge of the curtain to look out of the window. An orderly is sweeping the walkways. He can hear the swish of the brush, oddly disconnected from the movements of the man, like a badly dubbed film. Kai is right. For years nobody wanted to know about the killings, the rapes. The outside world

424

shifted its gaze, by a fraction, it was sufficient. The fragmentation of the conscience. What indeed did Adrian think he was doing here? The truth – he had never known for sure. Times he had come close to touching a kind of conviction, only to lose it again. He'd found something, finally, in Mamakay. Something else, something better. He wants to sob and scream, to ram his fist through the glass of the window. Attila is right, Kai is right. What people want is hope and last night Adrian learned what it is like to lose it. He presses his forehead against the glass.

He wants something he can never have again.

He wants to go home.

In the chair Kai sits with his eyes closed, his forearm along the armrest, fingers loosely grasping the whisky glass. For the first time Adrian notices an intravenous needle taped to the inside of his arm. There is a bloodstain on the front of his T-shirt. Adrian moves to take the glass. Kai starts, opens his eyes.

'Go ahead. Sleep,' says Adrian.

Kai gives a soft laugh. 'I thought you knew, man. Sleep isn't something I do.' He closes his eyes again. After a while he says, 'I was serious, you know.'

Daylight. Noise. Adrian wakes from a dream. Riding in a rickshaw on a rutted road. He noticed he was not wearing shoes. He called to the rickshaw driver to stop and climbed down to search among the market stalls for a pair of shoes. He could not find any, he began to panic. He was going to be late. Late for what, though, he did not know, couldn't remember. Mamakay appeared and pointed to a pair of black flip-flops. 'These will do,' she said. 'Are you sure?' Adrian replied. He felt better now she was with him. She smiled. 'Yes,' she said. 'It really doesn't matter.' Arrows of sunlight. Around him the images disperse. Reality displaces the dream: the apartment, the events of the night before. He is stiff and weary as if he had been beaten. From outside, the sound of a cockerel calling. The juddering is still there. Adrian looks up to see Kai shaking in his sleep. He rises and touches Kai on the shoulder. 'You're dreaming,' he says.

Kai opens his eyes, blinks and wipes his mouth. 'Sorry.' He stands and goes into the bathroom. When he emerges his face and neck, the front of his T-shirt are damp. Standing in the kitchen, Adrian feels the presence of the other man as Kai comes in to stand silently behind him. He watches the coffee granules as they dissolve into the hot water.

'I'd be prepared to try, if you want, that is. There's one thing we could do,' says Adrian.

'What's that?'

'It would involve returning you to the scene of whatever happened.'

'Hypnosis.'

'Not hypnosis. I won't put you in a trance as such, though I will ask you to focus your concentration on what happened. It's a way of reprocessing past events and desensitising you to the impact of them, I mean the way you think about them, if we know what those events were. In this case we do, at least *you* do. It can reduce the symptoms you experience, the dreams.'

'Does it work?'

'I believe so. But it's only fair I warn you . . .'

Kai interrupts. 'Will it make it worse?'

Adrian exhales. 'No,' he says.

'Then what do I have to lose?'

CHAPTER 55

Kai follows Adrian's index finger as it switches back and forth. He can hear his eyes click in their sockets. He concentrates on keeping track of the finger. Sometimes he seems a millisecond ahead of it, sometimes a fraction of a beat behind. He is sitting on a chair, not the soft wicker armchair, but upon an upright hard chair, his feet square to the floor. Adrian sits opposite, about two feet to Kai's right. He is holding up his index finger.

'Keep your eyes on my finger.'

Kai follows the movement of Adrian's finger, left to right, right to left. He feels, gradually, acutely aware of his own body, of the interlocking bones, the muscles and sinews stretched between the joints, the blood coursing throughout. He feels the hardness of the floor, the weight of his body pressing down on the soles of his feet, the physical effort it requires to sit upright, to keep his body taut and balanced.

'Think about what you are feeling when you think about the bridge and what happened. What do you think about?' Adrian's voice is calm and level.

'There was a girl. Her name was Balia.'

'What about Balia?'

'I couldn't . . .' Kai stops and swallows. 'She didn't . . .' He shakes his head.

'Keep following my finger.'

Kai concentrates on the movement of Adrian's finger. He breathes deeply. He forces his mind to return to the past.

He is walking down the corridor of the hospital, stepping over the bodies of men, the chemical scent of blood in the air. The background noise is of shouted orders, gurney wheels, the whimpered groans of the wounded. Behind the sound of human voices comes the drum roll of machine gunfire, the bass note of mortars exploding in the hills and in the east of the city.

Day Eighteen. 24 January 1999. Every nurse and doctor who could be located had reported for work. The wards were in ceaseless turmoil. All non-emergency patients had been discharged to make way for the new intake, even the paediatric ward had been emptied. It was as though plague had struck, a plague which tore open men's chests, blew off limbs, ripped through muscle and bone, unleashed arrowheads of shrapnel into soft flesh. Nights on end Kai did not sleep, or slept standing up, for he had no memory of sleeping and could not later imagine where such an event might have taken place, there was not a spare bed, chair, or inch of floor space. He made his way down the corridor, the first time he'd left the theatre in many hours. Last time he walked down this corridor it had been daylight, and now it was day again.

A smell of coffee. In the staff room he found the new nurse making mugs of weak coffee, heaped teaspoons of sugar and powdered milk. The new nurse was very young and very pretty; he found it hard not to be aware of her evident attraction to him. What was her name? Balia. Balia offered him a cup of coffee, blinked and smiled with embarrassment. He smiled back at her, said thank you and used her name as he did so, left the room bearing the mug, sipped the coffee and felt the heat hit his stomach and moments later the sugar enter his bloodstream. The arrival of the injured showed no signs of slowing. Apart from coffee Kai had fed on nothing but adrenalin for days. All things considered, the hospital was about the safest place to be. Evidence of the fight that was taking place out in the streets of the city was strewn all over their floor.

Kai picked his way through the dying and injured, looking for his next patient, someone likely to survive. The medical staff had to ration their resources, their skills, their energy. Kai's eyes travelled the lines of slumped, bleeding men, assessing injuries, life chances, rejecting those who looked too far gone. A soldier whose jaw had been blown away wore the uniform of the foreign fighting forces. Kai's eyes passed over him and returned, drawn by the nature of the injury. The man was sitting up with his back to the wall, nodding and gesturing, making the effort towards speech with the local reporter who stood above him. As Kai watched he reached into his pocket and withdrew a document, an ID card or a photo, and handed it over. Astonishingly, absurdly, above the hole that had been his face – and this you could tell from his eyes – the man appeared to be smiling.

428

Kai was there, coffee in hand, making his way down the corridor, momentarily arrested by the sight of the injured man, when he heard the sound of gunfire close at hand. He was too exhausted, too focused on the task at hand to feel anything approaching fear. He turned to see the intruders enter the building. The reporter, who had, a moment before, been standing just a yard away from Kai, was suddenly gone. For the first time in days, there was silence, a brief moment of silence.

Then, a single word.

'You!'

The man holding the gun pointed it at Kai's chest. Balia, coming out of the staff room, straight upon the scene, was seized by one of the gunmen. Kai was still carrying his coffee as they walked towards the car. He didn't feel afraid. But someone kept pushing him from behind, making him angry. He turned and shoved the barrel of the gun away, slopping coffee down his front. He glanced at Balia, her face stiff with fear, walking with small, reluctant steps.

Nobody bothered to blindfold them. Nobody wore a mask. That meant something, surely, Kai thought, as they drove through the stillness of the city. He wondered if he should feel afraid.

They arrived at an old, partly burned government building. The patients were all fighters. Young, adolescent, their arms, legs and guts full of metal. The rebels spoke to each other in many different languages of which Kai recognised some and not others. The commander, to whom Kai was taken, was perhaps seventeen. Kai heard those around call him Amos. Kai told Amos he could be of no help without supplies. While Amos consulted his aides, Kai waited and looked around him. There was little furniture left in the room, the President's portrait bore the scars of a bayonet, someone had drawn hopscotch squares on the carpet. Kai was put into the back of the same car and driven through the town to a pharmacy, where his captors looted the shelves of morphine, sterile dressings, rubber gloves, saline solution and IV equipment under his instruction.

A heavy wooden door served as the operating table. For hours Kai worked with Balia at his side. They worked well together, efficiently, though Balia's hands never stopped shaking. Amazingly, Kai succeeded in losing himself in his work, in forgetting his surroundings and the circumstances, seeing only wounds, what could be debrided, sutured, what was a viable limb and what was not. All of the injuries were fresh. A young combatant, having lost the affections of a girlfriend and unable to endure the teasing of his colleagues, had torn the pin from a grenade and tossed it into the back of the lorry that contained his tormentors.

At the end of eight hours there was insufficient light to continue working. Kai called for Captain Amos and asked for his permission to leave. The young commander looked at him with eyes that were darkly opaque and seemed to absorb the remaining light. He told Kai he might yet be needed, they were both to stay. In the morning they would be released.

They lay on the floor by the wall. Kai stayed awake, to guard over Balia. He listened to the sounds from outside, far away and close at hand, terrifying comings and goings. He tried to reassure Balia, but his words rang hollow in the darkness. The scent of ganja. Laughter, hard and humourless. Shouts. Music. Swearing and singing. Screams. Swells of cheering. More than once he thought he heard a helicopter. There were other, unexplained sounds. Then footsteps. Somebody passing by rapped upon the door, causing Balia to whimper and huddle closer to him. Kai listened carefully, trying to make sense of what was happening.

Several hours into the night, the door opened. Somebody held a kerosene lamp close to Kai's face. There were seven of them, Kai counted carefully. It seemed they had come to stare, as though they had known there was something unexpected to be found in the room. There were some changes of places, people entered and left, called others. Kai felt his heart contract. He got to his feet to be on the same level as the newcomers.

'What do you want?' he said.

'You're the doctor?' From his voice he was young. Kai had the sense they were all young, all smaller than him at any rate. He could hear a bottle being passed in the darkness behind.

'Yes,' said Kai, hoping perhaps he was needed.

'Who is this? Is this your girlfriend?'

'She's not my girlfriend, she's a nurse.'

'She's your girlfriend. Look how fine she is. Why don't you share your girlfriend with us? You tink say because you na big doctor, you deserve better than we.'

Kai asked for Captain Amos, but got no reply. It was hard to make out who he was speaking to: he could smell better than see them.

430

Somebody reached around him, seized Balia's arm and pulled her away from him.

'We want to fuck your girlfriend, Mister Doctor.' The speaker raised his eyebrows and smiled broadly, confidently. Kai could see the gleam of his teeth as he waited for Kai's reaction. Kai didn't speak. His brain worked cold and fast. Whatever came next was critical. Then from Balia a sob. She began to plead, a low, wavering, ululating sound. Laughter. Balia twisted and strained.

'She is a nurse,' said Kai. 'Please let her go.'

Somebody sucked his teeth.

Somebody else said, 'These two came from the hospital. I saw them there. Let us leave them.'

Kai was quiet, praying for whoever had just spoken to speak again. He might yet be able to talk his way out of this.

Then Balia screamed. Hysteria convulsed her. Kai was hit in the face and fell backwards against the wall. For a few moments he lost all sense of what was happening. The next he knew an argument had broken out between the boys and Balia was crouched on the floor by their feet, her arms crossed in front of her breasts. He pulled himself upright. He could feel blood trickling down the back of his throat. Something had changed since the morning when Kai and Balia had been taken from the hospital, in the eight hours during which they worked in their makeshift theatre. Kai knew there was only one thing it could be. The rebels had staked everything on the battle for the city. Now they were losing. The prize was slipping through their fingers. It was unthinkable that they would go back to the bush. This recklessness was the result of knowing it was all over for them. Nothing awaited them save death. They had nothing to lose and they would take Balia and Kai down with them.

Even so, Kai tried to reason. Again he asked for Amos. They laughed. Somewhere close by a shell exploded. Somebody threw a bottle, which smashed in the corner of the room. One of the boys pulled Balia up by the arm and began to yank at her clothing, push his hands between her legs. Kai sprang at the youth. The larger of the two, Kai pulled him away easily enough. Then they were on the floor. The boy jerked and wriggled, grabbed at Kai's face, clawing at his nose and lips. There was the sound of jeering. Someone sloshed liquid over them. Kai freed himself from the boy's fingers, pulling them back one by one. The others had formed themselves into a circle around the fighting pair, were watching, waiting for what came next. Kai stood up. A moment of silence, all eyes were upon him. He made to step out of the circle, to find Balia. In his mind he had the idea that he had only to start walking and not stop; if he did so with sufficient boldness they might not challenge him. He managed two more steps. Blocking his way was the self-appointed leader, he of the cocky grin.

'Please step aside,' said Kai.

The boy grinned at him.

'Get out of my way.' Kai reached out his left hand, made to shift the boy to one side with the back of his hand. The boy held his ground. His eyes were locked on to Kai's. He looked unearthly: a strange, beautiful creature, intelligent and possessed of lethal instincts. That's what Kai was thinking when the rifle butt smashed into the back of his skull. He felt his teeth jar in his skull, a burst of pain. Then he was down on his knees again, and suddenly they were all upon him. He tried to crawl forward. Blows and kicks fell down upon him. Somebody jumped on his back and rode him, hands around his neck, cutting off his air supply. He held out briefly, then collapsed under the weight of bodies. He felt the bodies lifting away from him. Air. He was distantly aware of hands plucking at his clothing. Fingers at his belt, hands at his ankles. They were stealing his clothes.

Naked now, he lay in the ring of children. The leader walked around him, aiming lazy kicks at him. Every now and again one of the others would dart in to deliver a blow of their own. Kai tried to raise his head. His thoughts were of Balia, but he couldn't see her. Somebody spat at him, and he felt the dribble of phlegm on his cheek.

'Where's your girlfriend?' The now familiar voice. 'Maybe they already fucking her. Or maybe you go fuck her first? Not so? Because you bigger than us. Not so? How our parents raised us. Elders first. Hey?'

Kai didn't answer. Somebody fell into him. It was Balia. She struggled to right herself and sat, hugging her knees, keening from side to side.

'Show us how you fuck, big man, Mister Doctor. We just small boys. Teach us how to fuck this fine woman. So we can learn from you.'

Somebody struck him on the buttocks with a stick. He heard a click and the barrel of a pistol was placed at his head. 'Fuck her or I kill you.'

Kai pulled himself up to his knees. He did not know what to do. Could see no way out. They would kill him and Balia, too. Of that he was certain. He made to move towards her. She did not shrink back, but hugged herself and sobbed. All around him they were baying now. The person with the stick hit him at intervals. He stopped still. He felt the gun at his temple.

'Fuck her or I fuck you.' First spoken and then screamed into his ear, combining with the ringing in his head to make him dizzy. 'Fuck her or I fuck you.'

The gun was removed from his temple. Kai tried to force himself to think. He was helpless. He felt something – the gun barrel – being pushed between his buttocks, heard the laughter, felt the end of it being rammed into him. The pain was acute and rippled through his body. Clapping. Cawing laughter. The gun barrel was thrust further into him. He flopped forward and was forced up, back on to his hands and knees. He was aware of Balia only peripherally, as she lunged, the sharp report of the gun, the shallow arc described by her body in the air as she fell backwards.

She was dying, not yet dead when he carried her to the vehicle. He was ordered into the back and struggled to lift her over the tailgate. Nobody helped him; they watched him and screamed at him. He was terrified of failing, of being made to leave her behind. The city was burning. He felt the heat of the fires on his naked skin, the broken glass in the soles of his feet. The rebels were in retreat. He climbed up into the back and cradled Balia in his arms.

They drove west, towards the hills. Dawn was coming, a glow upon the sky. A cock crowed, a sound so ordinary it seemed to come from another world. The noise of the battle receded. They turned at a junction, heading for the peninsula bridge and the beach. He tried to concentrate on the moment, on what he should do, to force himself to think, make a plan, but he could not. He held on to Balia.

They reached the bridge and stopped. Someone with a gun ordered Kai down. He stumbled, dragging Balia with him. They ordered him to stand by the metal railing. He felt it cold against the small of his back, remembered his nakedness. Absurdly it occurred to him that if they let him go he would have no clothes. The driver was climbing back into the vehicle. Kai felt a moment of hope. The driver's companion was making his way around the other side of the vehicle, opening the door, preparing to climb inside. Kai stood holding Balia. He watched. He waited. He saw the man stop and retrace his steps, much as though he'd forgotten something. He came back around the vehicle, approaching Kai with sudden determination. Kai knew what was coming. He saw the man pull the gun out of his belt, raise his arm and take aim. Kai closed his eyes. He leaned his body backwards, holding tight on to Balia, backwards over the railing, until he felt himself topple under the weight of their combined bodies. He kicked out. Something thudded into them. A bullet. He could not tell whether he had taken it or Balia. He was falling.

A rush of air. He feels his cheeks distort, his body cartwheel through space, his guts and stomach trailing behind. Impossible to breathe. He has lost his hold on Balia, feels her body tumble past him. He is falling. Then comes the sting of the water. Only that.

The sting of the water to tell him he is alive.

TWO YEARS LATER

CHAPTER 56

October 2003

He has friends in Norfolk. A small group of people he has met since he started coming regularly. They are, on the whole, retired folk. Still vigorous and, as his mother did, choosing to live out their lives close to the elements. In the mornings, tracing his mother's footsteps along the beach, Adrian passes people he recognises. The old boy in tweeds who walks back along the beach in the mornings from the shop with his newspaper under his arm, accompanied by an arthritic Labrador. Adrian does not yet count him as a friend. They have only ever exchanged greetings at a distance. The older man will raise his hat in a friendly enough way, though something in his demeanour, the pace of his walk and the way he retains the direct line of his route, makes Adrian feel that conversation is not desired.

The couple in the next bungalow but one had known his mother when she was alive. They tell Adrian that the man in tweeds is a widower these five years. They welcomed Adrian's appearance with a card on the doorstep and an invitation to sherry. He had been a lecturer at the university. She is a former dance teacher and had given him a photograph of his mother, wearing a fluid grey jersey dress, posed in the style of Pina Bausch. In the evenings, to ease the possibility of an incipient loneliness rather than an actual mood of loneliness, Adrian will occasionally stop by for sherry, which is taken each day at five o'clock. The bungalow next to Adrian's had been bought by weekenders, who rarely, if ever, made the journey from London.

Adrian is neither a weekender nor a resident, rather something in between. Following his mother's death he'd chosen to retain the bungalow. It comes in useful for writing and sometimes for weekends with Kate. His other friends are an assortment of ages, some from his past, his school and student years who still live near by, others are attached to the university, one or two – like the sherry couple – had been friends or acquaintances of Adrian's mother. Interesting, when

437

he thinks about it, to find oneself of an age where it becomes possible to have friendships in common with one's parents.

He is not unhappy.

In the evenings he often dines at the Lamb and Anchor, where the owners have done a reasonable job of creating an ambience of simulated authenticity and where the local drinkers, with their dogs and habitual places at the bar, render an equally convincing imitation of a hearty welcome. Adrian is fine with it. He will drink a Guinness, because this is what he ordered the first time and is now presumed to be his 'usual'. He will say his hellos, take a seat by the fire, whose embers gleam even in the summer, read his newspaper and order the day's special. With his meal he will drink a glass or two of the perfectly decent house red, or else order a half-bottle of claret. When he visits with Kate, the regulars, mostly men, will tease her in a gruff fashion to which she will respond politely and in perfect seriousness.

It amuses him, Kate's unsettling of these men, of which she is entirely unaware. He admires the way she can brilliantly deadpan a joke, her ability to sum up a person's nature in the moment of meeting. Over dinner he watches her careful rearrangement of her cutlery. At other times he has seen her dancing alone, believing herself unobserved, and he is reminded of Ileana. Adrian has come to look forward to the time they spend alone in each other's company and in which he has found a new and entirely unexpected love for her – a gift from the end of his marriage. After the main meal the publican will insist upon a free dessert for Kate, who expresses a preference for cheese.

In the city he is busy. During the day he is occupied with his clients, his evenings – and he makes sure of this – are filled with obligations, departmental meetings, board meetings for the various organisations he is involved in running, papers to write, dinner parties.

It is here, in Norfolk, he most often thinks about her. Sometimes he will make the journey to the coast for no other reason than to do so. Something to do with the water, the sea. Today he is alone. Kate is in town with her mother and he is not in the mood for company or sherry, so he lets his thoughts go to her. He watches the sea and imagines, as he has so often, the waves joining up, turning from grey to blue to green, drawing him into the past. At those times he experiences a surge of yearning as powerful as the movement of the ocean.

The moment has long since passed when the loss had outlasted the duration of the affair itself, though the love Adrian feels is as strong as ever. Unlike those earlier occasions – mourning a lost affection of his youth – this time there is to be no imagining her altered features, her new occupations, no unknown rival or replacement upon whom to project a wild jealousy. For death takes everything, leaves behind no possibilities, save one – which is to remember. Adrian cannot believe with what intensity one can continue to love a person who is dead. Only fools, he believes, think that love is for the living alone. So he sits and watches the sea and thinks of Mamakay.

During his last days in the country Adrian stayed in the apartment with Kai. Kai came and went in between his shifts and cooked meals for them both, took charge of day-to-day matters. Adrian never returned to the home he had shared with Mamakay. Each evening Adrian and Kai spent in each other's company. When Adrian heard the sound of Kai's key in the lock he was glad. It allowed him an excuse to stop the pretence of work, of trying to keep himself on track. Kai's company offered distraction and comfort at the same time, the comfort of feeling close to Mamakay.

Adrian never saw Elias Cole again. From Babagaleh, who cleared the house where Adrian and Mamakay had lived, Adrian learned the fate of the remaining actors from Cole's story. Yansaneh, who was removed from his lecturer position in the humanities department and assigned to the northern campus: killed when the campus was overrun early in the war. Vanessa, Cole's mistress, living with a foreign speculator who arrived in the wake of war. One day, idly searching the Internet, Adrian came across a lecturer in international media studies at a university in one of the southern states of America. His name: Kekura Conteh.

It was Babagaleh, too, who had undertaken many of the practical arrangements for Mamakay's funeral. The wake was held at the Mary Rose. Adrian found he did not know very many people, which was perhaps unsurprising, for his relationship with Mamakay had barely left the tight confines of the world they had created with each other and for themselves alone. Ileana came, naturally. And Attila, for which Adrian had felt a gust of gratitude. Some of the guests, assuming he had been brought along by somebody else, made polite conversation with Adrian, asking him how long he had been in the country and with which agency he had come to work, how he found living there. And Adrian answered them in kind, could not bring himself to tell them he had been Mamakay's lover, could not help but notice it was Kai to whom they displayed the deference reserved for the most greatly bereaved, to whom they offered consolation. Adrian watched and found that he did not mind. He stood with his back against the wall and observed the mourners. Once his eyes alighted upon Babagaleh moving through the room, in between the people, continuing unnoticed with his tasks. Babagaleh would survive them all, thought Adrian. He wanted to ask Mamakay a question about Babagaleh, remembered where he was and considered how the question would for ever remain unanswered. A hundred times a day it happened: he turned to her with a thought upon his lips.

Elias Cole had been too unwell to attend his daughter's funeral.

The morning of the next day Adrian, awaking to the conviction that he wanted to return to England, walked through to the sitting room where Kai was asleep on the settee and woke him to inform him of his plans. The yearning for the familiar overwhelmed him. Kai nodded slowly, but said nothing. An hour later Kai left for work, returned in the late afternoon and sat opposite Adrian.

The decision they had arrived at they arrived at together and early in the evening. Afterwards Adrian could not remember to whom the suggestion belonged. Whether it was merely the inevitability of it, the impossibility – practical or otherwise – of anything else. Or simply as Mamakay would have wished it. They spoke of her late into the night, for the first time since the night of her death.

The last Saturday they spent at the beach at Ileana's house, arriving to a viridescent light. Lightning slipped across the sky. Thunder unrolled a dark shadow. Afterwards the three friends walked in a new brightness, breaking the rain-soaked membrane of sand to leave warm, dry footprints. Nobody else was around, the beach was deserted. They passed the empty hotel, with its bar and snooker table still awaiting the return of guests called suddenly away. The fishing villages were quiet, canoes upturned upon their stands, nets abandoned where they lay. Curious, remarked Ileana, that fishermen should so dislike getting wet. The remark left them incapable with laughter. Some things seemed to make no sense at all. Ileana raised her head and a hand, said look. Ahead of them, on a distant sand spit, a black heron unfurled a single wing.

One day perhaps he will return. He sees himself stooped under the sun, the prospect of his own death upon the horizon, searching for those places and people among whom he lived for those months and whom he had loved.

At other times he looks at Kate and he thinks of what he has left behind.

This is the time of year Adrian loves most on the coast. The birds have begun to arrive. A small flock of sandpipers, strutting along the waterline. He keeps a pair of binoculars on the table by the window and now raises them to his eyes. Almost daily there are redstarts, shrikes and yesterday a glimpse of a pied flycatcher. They will be headed south soon, to the coast of West Africa.

And yesterday, too, a letter from Kai, who writes erratically but with reasonable frequency and no longer avoids using the computer. This time, though, he returned to his preferred form. Enfolded into the letter was a document composed of eight handwritten sides of paper. Adrian opened it and began to read, carried it out on to the deck, into the early-morning sun. It was the story of Agnes, her husband and daughters, of Naasu and JaJa. Everything Adrian had known must be true but had never been able to discover, never been able to prove.

Everything he needed was there.

And there was something more, on the bottom of Kai's letter, in the same blue Biro, as though for a few moments Kai had been called from the room and left his letter unattended on the table. Something Adrian saw only on his third reading. On the bottom right of the page.

A child's careless scribble.

★

The child stops and stands to stare at her feet, as though seeing them for the first time. She grips sand between her toes and lifts one foot and then the other. One foot and then the other. She raises her shoulders and rocks her head between them, stamps her feet and laughs. The boy Abass goes to her, stretches out his arms to pick her up, but she evades him and runs away along the waterline. In three strides he has her; hands under her arms, he swings her up. Presently he sets her down and they walk away along the edge of the shoreline. Something left on the sand by the sea's withdrawal catches their attention.

From high up on the beach Kai watches them as they begin to dig, applying themselves silently to the task. Abass, dark-skinned and angular. By contrast the girl is chubby and bronze, her hair a mass of black ringlets. Of the hair Kai's aunts are delighted and despairing in equal measure, for it will not be bound, springs free of braids and defies their hair oils and combs. The child squirms beneath their hands and pulls out the bands and ribbons. Kai can see the salt crystals sparkling among the curls as the girl moves under the sun. This evening Kai's aunts will tut at him as they begin work to undo the effects of sun, sea and salt upon the child's hair. They will chide each other and vie for ownership of the comb, just as earlier that morning Kai's aunts gently competed with one another to dress the child in her swimsuit, rub lotion upon her back and send her in search of her sandals. The whole expedition was alien to them, for they were village women from the arid interior, whose lives had been spent swathed in cloth against the heat and dust. But they enacted their roles and officiated over the preparation of the child with such conviction that Kai's cousin, passing through the living room on her way to church, stopped to watch, twisted her mouth into a wry shape and exchanged with Kai a look as long as either of them dared.

They left in Old Faithful, bellies of fried plantains, smoked fish and pepper, pawpaw and lime. To Ileana's. It has become a regular event, every fortnight or so, the trip to Malaika beach and to Ileana. The adults sit on chairs in the shade at the front of the house and watch Abass lead the little girl on to the rocks to search among the rock pools for aquatic life to capture and place in a makeshift aquarium on the steps of Ileana's house until it is time to go and those creatures that are still swimming, crawling or hovering, by virtue of having survived, will have won their freedom. Kai watches. At the end of the rocks stands a lone black heron and Kai is returned to a time two years ago, a week after he had handed the curled newborn to a wet nurse. In those days he came and went between Adrian's apartment and the neonatal ward, tending to both man and child.

He remembers standing inside the women's ward observing how the wet nurse lifted the child from his arms and returned her to her own body, strapping the infant in the place between her breasts; he saw in the meticulousness of the woman's movements the first evidence that she believed the child would survive. It would take time, but everything in the way the woman tucked and folded a cloth around the infant said time was something she had.

The day is coming to a close. They should be going if they are going to make it to the ferry port. Still, Kai prefers, for a few more moments, to watch the children play. The little girl dances on the tide line, Abass scoops up fistfuls of wet sand. And then whatever it is they have been seeking has been found, and the little girl laughs.

The laugh comes back to him, time and time again. It comes in the night, and at other unexpected moments, in his dreams – an echo of its pitch and timbre. But from the little girl it comes whole, pure and absolute. It is Nenebah. And in an instant the sound of that laugh can return Kai to a hillside overlooking the city eight years ago, to the moment following a lost joke, the playful bite during a morning's embrace.

During his days at the hospital he pauses at occasional moments to think of her. One day last week a lizard dropped from a door lintel on to his shoulder and then on to the floor. The creature backed itself into a corner of the room, watched Kai out of one rotating eyeball, before hastening past him through the open door. The sort of occurrence that would have made Nenebah smile and search for hidden meanings. Kai walks from theatre to ward to staff room, crossing the courtyard under the glare of the sun. He arrives early in the day when the south wall of the building is purple with the morning glory that now grows there. By the time he leaves in the evening, the flowers are twisted sweet-papers. Yesterday he altered his route out of the building for no particular reason except that he felt like it, so it took him through the children's ward, where he walked the length of the room while a paper plane circled in the air above him, carried on the eddying wind of the fan.

On other days Kai passes the room where Elias Cole died, one day before dawn two years ago. Nobody else had been present, so there was no saying in what manner he had faced his end. A preacher was called. The man administered a belated blessing, requested from Kai his taxi fare home and a donation to the church. Babagaleh cleared the room of Cole's belongings. To Kai, Babagaleh gave the photograph of Nenebah, in which she appeared both to turn from and to confront the camera. Kai kept it alongside her other possessions and her clarinet. He passes the old house from time to time. It is closed up now. Babagaleh has returned home to the north and the love of his estranged wife.

Last night, the first time in many months, Kai woke during the night. He had been dreaming and, though the images of the dream were lost to him, he was left nevertheless with a sensation of well-being, of possibility. He left his bed and walked out into the yard. There was a breeze, unusual for the time of year, it was still early for the harmattan. It carried with it a hint of moisture, of night blooms and wet fruit. In the darkness the city dogs sang to each other. Somewhere in the long grass a frog called for an unknown mate. Kai breathed deeply. He sat down upon the step, his back to the house, and settled down to wait. And finally, above the houses, he saw rising slowly the muted, insistent radiance of dawn.

Today Tejani comes home.

The little girl's laugh lingers in the air, is swept away by the tide. Kai stands up and calls the children. They make a race of returning to him. He meets them halfway down the beach. The little girl opens her hand to show him a five-petalled sand dollar lying upon her palm. They have arrived rolled in sand, like a sugar coating, and Kai leads them back down to the water. The little girl likes to ride into the waves upon his shoulders, rides him like a bull through the white horses.

From the front of her house, where she stands surrounded by sleeping dogs, Ileana waves goodbye. And then they are in Old Faithful, driving along the beach road. People have polished their vehicles and brought them out for the Sunday cruise, a motorised promenade. A blind man, a yellow bag slung over his shoulder, uses a broken crutch to tap his way along the road. The sound of the metal tip sings through the noise of the traffic and the crowds. They stop in front of a young girl sitting by a basket heaped with silver fishes and the line of traffic is overtaken by the blind man. In the back of the car the children play with an old stethoscope given by Kai to Abass. They take turns pressing the metal disc on to each other's chests, the car window, the sand dollar, the space between Kai's shoulder blades.

Ten minutes and they are on the move again, turning around the roundabout, leaving the other cars behind. Now they are driving with their backs to the sea. Ahead of them the peninsula bridge unfurls, straight and true. Kai rolls down the window on the opposite side of the car and briny marsh air flows through the car. There are people out in the marshes, searching for shellfish; the sound of their voices resounds across the emptiness. Kai pushes the cassette into the player and leans back, one hand on the steering wheel. The sudden sound of the drum beat causes the children to stop playing with the stethoscope.

They stand and squeeze themselves into the space between the front seats. *Well they tell me of a pie up in the sky.*

They all see the kingfisher flash from a street lamp down to the water right in front of the car. The bird rises, a fish glints on the end of its beak. The little girl screams with pleasure. They do not see, for they cannot, as they cross the peninsula bridge, the letters traced by a boy's forefinger into cement on the far side of the bridge wall half a century ago, beneath the initials of the men who once worked the bridge. *J.K.*

ACKNOWLEDGEMENTS

The Memory of Love is a work of fiction. There are those, however, upon whom I have relied to research certain aspects of the background, setting and factual detail of the story and to whom I would like to offer my thanks. The patients and staff of Kissy Mental Hospital, Freetown, and in particular Dr Edward Nahim, who helped me towards a greater understanding of mental illness and of PTSD. For opening up the world and work of the orthopaedic surgeon, my thanks to the staff and patients of the Emergency Medical Hospital, Goderich. And for general medical advice and the practical challenges of running a hospital in Africa, the late Dr Mambu Alphan Kawa. I would also like to take this opportunity to remember the late Dr Aniru Conteh, a specialist in lassa fever who in 2004 died of the virus he had spent his life combating, as does Dr Bangura in *The Memory of Love*, the sole character in the novel some details of whom I have based upon a real person.

My thanks also to the following who read and commented upon the manuscript: psychotherapist Polly Bagnall, the psychologist and psychoanalyst Louise Lyon, Michael May and Blake Morrison. I would also like to thank David Godwin, a master of positive thought who always sees the big picture. To the team at Bloomsbury, in particular Michael Fishwick, a great friend and discerning editor, to whom I can hand the reins with confidence, and have done three times now. And to Simon Westcott who walked every step of the long crossing with me.

Adrian's reference to 'the fragmentation of conscience' is drawn from the work of M. Scott Peck, *People of the Lie*. 'The plain fact of the matter is that any group will remain potentially conscienceless and evil until such a time as each and every individual holds himself or herself directly responsible for the behaviour of the whole group – the organism – of which he or she is part. We have not yet begun to arrive at that point.'